CW00551460

RED STAR GOLD

RED STAR GOLD

Frederick D J Thomas

UPFRONT PUBLISHING
LEICESTERSHIRE

RED STAR GOLD
Copyright © Frederick D J Thomas 2003

All Rights Reserved

ISBN 1-84426-237-5

First published 2003 by
UPFRONT PUBLISHING
Leicestershire

Printed by Lightning Source

*In memory of my late wife Diane,
a lovely Somerset girl who graced this
green and pleasant land with her
wonderful presence from 1945 until 1998,
when she lost her battle with cancer
and sadly passed away.*

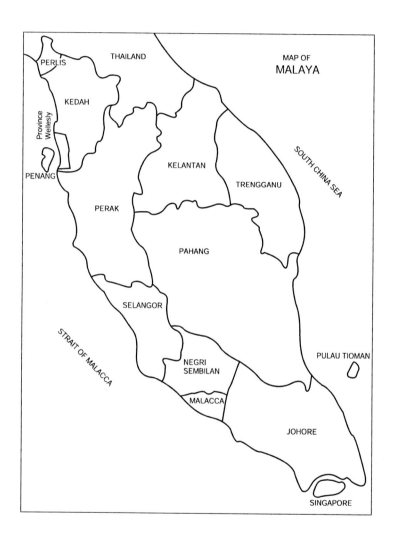

PERLIS

THAILAND

MAP OF
MALAYA

KEDAH

Province
Wellesly

PENANG

KELANTAN

TRENGGANU

SOUTH CHINA SEA

PERAK

PAHANG

SELANGOR

STRAIT OF MALACCA

NEGRI
SEMBILAN

PULAU TIOMAN

MALACCA

JOHORE

SINGAPORE

Introduction

This story is set in the Far Eastern land of Malaysia during the year of 1957. In those far off days the land mass which housed the seat of government in the capital city of Kuala Lumpur was known as Malaya and consisted of a Federation of Malay states, and throughout this novel will be referred to as Malaya.

Malaya is a country situated in South East Asia. The Malay Peninsular juts out south-eastwards from the southernmost border of Thailand. At its southern tip lies the island of Singapore that is linked to Malaya by a railway and road causeway. The waters of the Strait of Malacca lap the west coast of Malaya and the South China Sea, the Eastern Shores. The Malay Peninsular, including Singapore, has an area of 53,240 square miles, it is about the same size as England and is 200 miles across at its widest point and stretches 400 miles south from the Thailand border.

About four-fifths of Malaya is covered by rainforests that thrive along the central mountainous spine, the peaks of which rise up to heights of 7,000 feet. The forest occupies the valleys between the high ground, it grows thickest in the places that have been cleared and then allowed to grow back to its natural state. These areas and other parts of the forest that are thick with undergrowth can loosely be termed as jungle. The rainforest is evergreen and vegetation growth is rapid. In parts of the highlands some of the trees tend to be stunted and along the coastal regions grow the tangled mass of the mangrove swamps, but otherwise, the forest consists of healthy trees that grow to two distinct heights.

Above 2,000 feet the trees grow up to a height of 100 feet and the terrain is fairly free of undergrowth, there are lichens, ferns, mosses, liverworts and orchids. The tree roots are enormous and stand buttress-like being up to six feet high and ten feet wide, giant water vines hang from the lofty branches.

Below 2,000 feet is another type of growth that is more

characteristic of the country. Trees force their way upwards to 200 feet, the undergrowth is dense, consisting of palms, tree ferns and herbaceous plants; the most common of the palms being the attap.

Both kinds of terrain are known as primary forests, or to the British soldier, as virgin jungle. The tree canopy blocks out the sunlight, stunting the growth of vegetation at ground level. Although the undergrowth is still thick, troops can move along in single file without having to cut their way through it. In the lowlands where the smaller trees are to be found and sunlight has penetrated the canopy, the thick undergrowth really flourishes and produces what is known as secondary jungle. Here are to be found dense thickets of saplings and attap palms, festoons of creepers and thick clumps of bamboo.

Through these vast tracts of forests and jungles flow the great rivers of the peninsular. For a country as small as Malaya, the rivers are really huge and constitute the main highways of the hinterland, many of the Malay states are named after them.

To give you some idea of the variety of vegetation, the species of trees to be found growing in Malaya exceed in number all those of India and Burma; and there are 9,000 different types of flowering plants and ferns.

The rivers teem with fish and the jungle abounds with wildlife including elephants, tigers, wild boar and buffalo. Reptiles such as crocodiles, alligators and iguanas lurk in wait for the unwary whilst snakes slither and slide in search of prey. Primates crash around in the treetops, and together with the many species of birds, keep up an incessant and deafening cacophony of sound. The insect world is well represented too; there are scorpions, hornets, centipedes, millipedes, ants, leeches and mosquitoes, to name but a few.

The remaining fifth part of Malaya is made up of hundreds of coastal settlements mainly situated around the river estuaries. But only the western areas were opened up for development: rice, tin and rubber being the most important industries. During the period covered by this book, Malaya had 700 tin mines, 3.3 million acres of rubber plantations and great areas of rice paddy fields had been cut out of the wide northern plains in the states of Perlis, Kedah, Kelantan, Malacca and Negri Sembilan.

This Federation of Malay states sitting between two and seven degrees north of the equator and so rich in natural resources (rich too in history, class and culture from the many races that had inhabited it), was ruled over by the British. During the fifties, the loggers had yet to make great inroads into the rainforests and Malaya enjoyed a stable and predictable climate, daily temperatures reached 94°F all the year round and you could set your watch by the rain that fell every afternoon at four thirty. To those old British colonial empire building romantics Malaya was indeed a green and pleasant land, but they were in for a rude awakening as communism reared its ugly head and the hopes of thousands of hardworking people were threatened by armed conflict.

In 1948 an army of twelve hundred Communist guerrillas, nearly all of them Chinese, went to war against the British rule in Malaya. The Chinese guerrillas, known as CTs, returned to their wartime jungle camps from which they had once helped the British fight the Japanese during the Second World War. They recovered weapons from long-hidden arms caches and launched their offensive, first targeting the native workers of the west coast rubber plantations. The CTs forced rubber-tappers (a title given to rubber plantation workers, whose job is to collect small containers of rubber that has been sapped from the trees) to watch as they murdered foremen and other minor officials. The message was clear; this is what happens if you work for the British. On 16 June 1948, following the execution of three European planters, a state of emergency was declared; it was to last until 1960. It was a bloody and protracted war with little quarter being given by either side, it was fought by the British and Commonwealth troops; and together with the Federation of Malaya Police Force, they won it outright.

War brings out the best in most people but unfortunately more than a few hangers-on take advantage of the misery and confusion to line their pockets from the proceeds of the black market and plain racketeering. War produces bent policemen and government officials too. Add to all this the inevitable involvement of the Chinese Tongs (Triads) and you have a hotbed of greed, corruption, blackmail and intimidation; in a word, terrorism equal to that being meted out by the CTs from their jungle lairs. In 1957 Malaya gained its independence and the war was all but over, but a great deal of mopping up had still to be done.

The Guerrilla Army High Command stubbornly hoped that they could save the situation by pulling something out of the bag. Their troops were on the run with most of them hiding out over the Thailand border, lines of communication and supply were in disarray and the British hearts and minds campaign was robbing them of their main weapon, terrorism. They did, however, have an ace up their sleeves; a secret track that ran the whole length of the country from north to south following the central mountain spine through some of the toughest terrain in the world. The CTs planned to use this hidden courier route to man-pack orders, arms, equipment, paper money and gold. Whilst pretending to negotiate a ceasefire and possible surrender terms with the British and Malay governments, they ordered the movement of a consignment of smuggled gold bullion to the main jungle headquarters so that they could begin to completely reorganise their scattered forces. But luck was running out for the terrorist organisation.

The plan to move the gold into Malaya from Macau was uncovered by the Colonial Police in Hong Kong, and MI6 in Macau. A trap was set and as a result of subsequent police and military action the destination of the gold shipment was discovered. Unfortunately the information fell into other hands too, the wrong hands of the all-powerful Tongs and their gangland lackeys from the Malacca riverside area.

A vital piece of information was taken from a wounded and captured CT; he wore the khaki cap of the guerrilla army with the CT cap badge, a red star. The information triggered off a dangerous game of cat and mouse intrigue, the race was on. A race between the Communist Terrorist Guerrillas and the British Army in support of the Malay Police, and the gangland bosses of Malacca; a race against time for the Red Star Gold.

Prologue

For the sake of argument let's say that you believe in the gods of Greek and Roman mythology. Imagine that you have just performed an act of outstanding bravery on the field of battle. Your heroism has not gone unnoticed, indeed, Mars the god of war is smiling benevolently down on you.

Mars summons Minerva the goddess of warlike wisdom and protector of heroes, for deeds such as yours deserve just rewards. They consult – you cannot eavesdrop because there is no need for words between gods – soon Minerva nods in approval and favours you with a glance of admiration; she raises her hands to the stars and beckons forth the winged horse Pegasus. As the beast descends from the heavens, Minerva points a commanding finger towards you and in the twinkling of an eye you find yourself astride the magnificent white charger. Pegasus takes you on a triumphal tour of the battlefield where friend and foe alike hail you a hero. Then to the echoing cries of adulation he speeds you off to scenes of bygone wars in order that you may identify with many more of your brothers in arms.

The horse's godlike magical powers transcend such things as speech, speed and time; he soon brings you to the Black Sea and the Crimea of the mid-1850s. As you look down on the south-western tip of that Russian land a gap appears in the smoke-laden area around Sevastopol and Balaklava, it is the acrid smoke of the Crimean War. A montage of events is unveiled and a war that took over a year to fight flashes before your eyes in a matter of seconds. The individual battles unfold, first the British and French attack on the Russian artillery emplacements, these were heavily fortified positions on top of some cliffs known as the Heights of Alma. The Royal Fusiliers and the Rifle Brigade led the British assault, they scaled the cliffs and after hours of bitter fighting and much bloodshed they won the day, the actual guns being taken by the Fusiliers. Next it was the turn of the British cavalry, in this instance, the Heavy Brigade. The Russians had sent in an army of 30,000 men with orders to stop the British Army attacking Sevastopol from the direction of Balaklava. Despite being hopelessly outnumbered, the Heavy Brigade charged at the Russians, then cutting and thrusting with an intense ferocity that belied their numerical inferiority, they sent the enemy reeling before them in disarray. As the Russians fled the field they turned their attention towards a solitary British infantry regiment that was positioned in their path. The full might of the Russian cavalry bore down on the extended line of exposed infantrymen who stood facing them with fixed bayonets, it was a furious fight but when the turmoil had ended and the dust had cleared, it was the British infantry who held the field. For their heroic action that day the proud 93rd Sutherland Highlanders were immortalised as The Thin Red Line. The Russian Army now began a full-scale retreat, dragging some captured Turkish guns with them. The British cavalry were sent forward to intercept them but their orders were confusing; the charge of the Light Brigade was magnificent and glorious, it ended in tragedy and inspired those famous words to be written, 'Into the valley of death rode the six hundred'. Sevastopol finally fell to the allies on 8 September 1855; the Russians fought to the last man.

Pegasus speaks to you from within, 'There was much bravery here on both sides, do you see those cannons down there?'

'I do indeed,' you reply.

'Well the bronze from those guns is used to make your country's highest military award, the Victoria Cross. Hold on my friend, I must make haste if we are to accomplish all.' Leaving the Crimea behind, you are whisked away north-westwards to the Russian town of Kirsk. There in the summer of 1943 the German Army launched its last major offensive on the Eastern Front. Marshall Georgi Zhukov's Red Army tanks, infantry and Cossack warriors fought with fanatical ferocity and inflicted such a crushing defeat on the German Panzer divisions that they never fully recovered and 'retreat' became the order of the day for this once invincible fighting machine. The Russian soil passes beneath you as does the battle scenes in the fast forward mode; Pegasus hums the *1812* overture as you soar past the French retreat from Moscow. You watch as the citizens of Stalingrad emerge from the rubble of their ruined city after the German siege. They rose triumphant, these tough people who had not been troubled by diseases from rats because they had devoured the vermin as fast as they could breed. The rape of Poland under the Germans. The bombing of Dresden, Hamburg and Bremen by the British and Americans. The list is endless. You visit the German town of Minden where six regiments of British infantry and a battery of the Royal Artillery completely routed a far stronger force of French cavalry. On this occasion, the British troops were fighting on the side of the House of Hanover. High above Holland, the great white horse goes into a dive giving you a rendering of *Ride of the Valkyries* as he does so, finishing his musical masterpiece as he levels out over a bridge that spans the mighty River Rhine. 'I have a soft spot for these troops,' states Pegasus as you witness the British First Airborne division fight the battle for Arnhem. On you fly to Belgium and Flanders Fields, the battle of Waterloo and the huge tank action in the Ardennes known as the Battle of the Bulge. The carnage of the First World War now opens up as you wing your way over France; Arras, Marne, Cambrai, Ypres, Meziers and Mons, to name but a few places which helped deplete the population of Britain by a complete generation of men. Down below is the French coast and another world war. British riflemen are fighting a rearguard action to give precious time to the beleaguered British Army on the beaches of nearby Dunkirk. They got their time and as a result the most famous evacuation in the annuls of military history was made possible. To this day those riflemen are remembered on the cap badges of the Royal Green Jackets in the form of the battle honour, 'Calais'. From the rifle green berets of the 60th and 95th Rifles we turn to a lighter shade as you watch the commandos storm ashore at the French port of Dieppe; an epic raid in which so many brave Canadians sacrificed their lives alongside their British comrades. A flashback in time reveals the Battle of Crecy that was fought in 1346, the epic action at Poitiers ten years later and the historical English victory on the field of Agincourt in 1414. Three examples demonstrating that well-sited troops, marksmanship and expertly directed supporting fire can overcome vastly superior numbers with devastating effect; at Crecy the Welsh longbow men of the English Army killed 10,000 of the enemy with a loss of only 200 to themselves.

Now it is dark and Pegasus picks up the trail of three World War II gliders as they descend over the fields of Normandy in 1944, the pilots steer their cumbersome craft towards a bridge over the Caen Canal and eventually they land near to the bridge defences. Soon a company of troops from the British 6th Airborne Division clamber out of the Horsa gliders, and after a brisk but bitter struggle, they take the bridge from the German defenders. The paratroops then hold the objective against fierce opposition until Lord Lovet's Commandos relieve them many hours later. The winged horse takes you down to the bridge. 'Look,' he says pointing at a memorial sign proclaiming Pegasus Bridge, 'the Paras have named the bridge after me because I am their adopted idol and I go everywhere with them on the divisional signs that they wear on their arms.' He snorts proudly and then you are on your way again pausing briefly to salute the commandos as they blow up the lock gates at St Nazaire. Around Spain you roar taking in the battlefields of the Peninsular War. Although Britain won many of the battles such as Salamanca, Talavera and Madrid; and the deployment of Sir John Moore's light infantry regiments together with the chosen men of the 60th and 95th Rifles as skirmishers proved advantageous and their marksmanship became legendary, they lost the war. France again and the spectacle of Hannibal's elephants crossing the River Rhone on rafts, you follow his army of 30,000 men as they cross the Alps on their way to Rome in October of 218 BC. Finally you see him defeated by the Roman, Scipio the Younger, at the battle of Zame with 35,000 men dead or captured. Down the leg of Italy you fly until Pegasus pauses over the great amphitheatre of Rome, you give a sigh of sadness thinking that your reward has been paid in full. 'Fear naught,' says Pegasus, 'I am duty bound to salute the gods here, hold on my brother, we must travel fast to Far Eastern lands.'

Giving vent to a whinny the horse soars off again enabling you to feast your eyes on sights that few mortals have beheld, the wondrous panorama of Greece, the gleaming minarets of Istanbul and the shimmering deserts each side of the Persian Gulf. With the deep blue Arabian Sea below you, Pegasus tells how he sprang from the belly of Medusa after she had been put to death by Perseus. Thus born, he flew off to the heavens where he was captured by Minerva and tamed. India looms ahead, your trusty steed compels you to glance northwards and you immediately feel humbled by the awesome high ramparts of the Himalayan Mountains, their peaks jutting high out of the clouds like bright sword blades.

Pegasus continues with his story as he flies over the Indian Ocean, telling you how he had won his spurs in battle. 'Minerva sent me to help a warrior named Bellerophon in his fight against the monster known as Chimera, his forepart was that of a lion, the middle a goat and his rear end a dragon. We fought long and hard but in the end Bellerophon and I were victorious and we slew the fire-breathing monstrosity.' Pegasus went on to explain that this victory led to the eventual defeat of the Amazons by Theseus of Athens. The horse begins to descend and you sense that the journey's end is nigh, you give him an affectionate pat and he snickers with pleasure at being recognised as a fellow warrior. Skimming down the Strait of Malacca the mighty stallion crosses the coast of Malaya, soon bright lights below indicate that you have arrived over the capital city of Kuala Lumpur. With a final flap of his wings, Pegasus hovers above a military airfield situated on the outskirts of the city.

Mars and Minerva appear beside you and you guess that the reward you so richly deserve is about to be presented. The four of you, a god, a goddess, a winged warrior horse and your heroic self are about to join the elite of the brotherhood of fighting men, you are to bear witness to an event which very few people would be privileged to observe. There is movement below, a snort from Pegasus signifies that you should all get closer, Mars signals in agreement and the descent to a more suitable vantage point is made. You make it just in time to see a small convoy of army vehicles discharge its cargo of forty soldiers, the time is 04.00 hrs, the date is 15 August in the year of our lord, 1957. Being by now an experienced soldier you find yourself extremely impressed by the manner in which the troops dismount from the transport without so much as a single word of command. There is no shouting or bawling, no slamming of cab doors or the rattling and crashing of tailgates, nothing, the men simply get off the trucks, grab their weapons, shoulder their heavy packs and file into a nearby aircraft hanger. Once inside, the soldiers form two ranks of twenty men each with about fifteen yards between ranks, they then place their weapons and packs on the ground giving themselves plenty of room for the work that lies ahead of them. Again, you could not but notice that all was accomplished with the absence of any talking and the absolute minimum of fuss and bother.

The troops are dressed in olive green jungle uniforms, they are shod in green canvas and rubber jungle boots and are carrying steel helmets. That's as far as uniformity went in this instance, a closer inspection under the bright lights of the hanger reveals a marked departure from the norm. A quick glance tells you that this is no ordinary unit, definitely not a normal infantry combat formation. No, theirs is not a sea of young faces with slightly older men in command such as you would expect to see in a conventional infantry regiment. In this instance the opposite was the case and the group consisted of older, hard faced, mature and experienced looking men with the odd young face in evidence, nearly all of them sported moustaches with some brilliant examples of the mutton chop variety. Although they wore no badges of rank or military insignia, every man on parade looked capable of commanding at some level or other, indeed, most of them were ex-non-commissioned officers who had reverted to the ranks in order to serve in the unit. An inspection of the men's belt equipment confirms your suspicion that you are in the presence of a very special fighting force. They are wearing extra water bottles and water bottle carriers adapted to contain medical kit and grenades. Ammunition pouches had been modified to suit personal and practical demands and magazine pouches were tailored to meet individual weapon handling styles and techniques. All carried cutting tools such as machetes, golocks or parangs: the inclusion of bayonets and fighting knives supports the suggestion that these men are prepared to get down to business at very close quarters indeed.

You are excused the raised eyebrow as you take in the awesome array of weaponry laid out on the hanger floor. The Bren light machine gun is the supporting fire weapon but it is fitted with a forward pistol grip to assist with firing from the hip in an immediate close-quarter battle situation. The tried and trusted .303-inch Lee Enfield rifle modified for jungle warfare, some American M1 carbines, the Belgian FN rifle and the silenced De Lisle carbine completed the choice of rifles. For more substantial fire power there is the British Sten gun, the Australian Owen gun, the Patchet sub-machine gun and the .45 Thomson sub-machine gun. To provide absolute stopping power up front is the Remington pump-action shotgun and the Browning seven-shot semi-automatic shotgun. For personal protection in extremely difficult and close situations, a selection of pistols have been included in this veritable arsenal, the Browning 9mm automatic appearing to be the favourite. Had you been able to see inside the men's packs you would have found spare ammunition, detonators, primers, fuses, and plastic explosives. In the case of those men who were carrying rifles, spare stripped down sub-machine guns were included for opportune close quarter raids. If the thought had occurred to you that these men had been allowed to choose their own weapons, then think no more, they had. However, their choice had not been random, selection had been based on individual prowess in skill at arms on a particular weapon tempered with the all important question, Is it the right tool for the job?

Whilst you have been busy pondering over who these men might be, they too had been busy drawing parachutes from a store. From another store the troops had been issued with a roll of white webbing 250 feet in length and some odd bits of equipment to go with it.

'Paratroops,' you blurt out.

Pegasus gives a snort, 'Look again, they have no reserve parachutes.'

'Parachutists then,' you concede. Thinking back to their unobtrusive arrival at the airfield, the attention to detail in their form of dress and equipment, and their meticulous choice of weapons; you come to a conclusion. If these men carry that standard of professionalism forward through their given task, then they can only belong to one unit; their exploits are legend, their achievements awesome and they are relentless in their pursuit of excellence. Mars bows his head in reverence for he is their god and Minerva is their advisor and protector. The soldiers preparing for action below are serving with the Special Air Service Regiment and they are about to parachute into the deep jungle areas of Malaya to seek out, and cause the destruction of, an enemy force of Communist Terrorists.

Most people only hear about the SAS operations after the event; your reward is to be in on this one from the start. Mars is willing you to observe one soldier in particular; he is the youngest man on parade. Even so, he has been in the army for four years and has several stints of active service under his belt. He is six feet two inches tall, slimly built and sports a handlebar moustache. His nickname is Fred and he is to be your guide. The god and goddess bid you farewell; Pegasus lowers you gently into your favourite armchair and the great warrior Bellerophon takes your place on the horse's back, he salutes you. They too have gone now, read on dear friend and let the story unfold.

Chapter One

Despite the ungodly hour of 04.00 hrs, Fred was sweating streams, the cool of the night was turning to early morning humidity and the powerful overhead lights were adding to the aggravation. But to explain away the rivulets of perspiration pouring from Fred's sweat glands it must be pointed out that he was suffering from an overdose of a condition known as apprehension, or to put it in a soldier's vernacular, he was shit scared.

Fred was not exactly new to the game of parachuting and it was quite normal, indeed healthy, to experience the proverbial butterflies. This jump though was different; it being his first operational drop with the SAS and his first parachute descent into trees; on both counts it was enough to give anyone the jitters. He was not a newcomer to active service either, he had experienced his baptism of fire whilst serving with a light infantry regiment in Kenya, he then fought in Aden and Cyprus with them before joining the Paras in 1956. Posted to 3 Para he saw more action in Cyprus before taking part in the Suez Crisis, dropping with his Battalion onto El Gamil airfield in Port Said, Egypt. Fred had earned his wings and earned his spurs, he had got his knees brown and it would be fair to say that he was an old sweat.

Now he had gone one step further and had won the privilege to wear the distinctive SAS wings and the coveted winged dagger cap-badge. Fred had gone through hell to get this far, he had dared and he had won Of the sixty-four volunteers who had started out on his selection course, only four had made it into the regiment. Since then Fred had undergone some specialist training in Brecon, another parachute course in Singapore and a jungle warfare training operation in Malaya. For all intents and purposes Fred had made it, but there is always a false crest to every hill and he had yet to make the summit before he was fully accepted by the soldiers of his squadron. To them the slate was clean, it mattered not where he had been or what he had done, nothing counted until he'd bloody well done it with them. They would advise, even teach, they would help and encourage, but Fred knew that these men would not carry him one damned inch. It was the way of the regiment.

Fred looked down at the assortment of equipment spread out before him on the hangar floor, his first job was to prepare it all for the forthcoming jump, a daunting task and one that could not be done single-handed. The squadron had already been detailed off into sticks of four men and Fred was number three in his stick. Each stick was further divided into pairs and Fred's buddy and number four in the stick was a wily old soldier out of the Fusiliers named Bob. They assembled their abseiling gear first; this consisted of a roll of white webbing 250 feet in length and three inches wide. The end of this webbing had to be fed into a metal D-ring, through a belt loop in a canvas contraption called a bikini, and out through the D-ring again, about four feet of the webbing was then pulled through the assembled canvas trunks. The tightly rolled end of the webbing was then stowed away into a canvas valise. With some shorter lengths of webbing that they had been issued with, they set about the task of making an improvised harness for their Bergen rucksacks. They lashed the packs with the webbing rather like tying up a parcel in a criss-cross fashion leaving two lengths each side of the pack that would reach up to the soldier's armpits. Weapons and cumbersome bits of kit that might hamper the men during the jump were also packed into the valise.

At last the job was finished and Fred glanced at Bob who grinned and murmured, 'Let's get it all on then.' The two men helped each other fit their equipment starting with the abseiling gear. The canvas bikini, the bottom half that is, was put on first like a pair of swimming trunks. The valise came next and had to be secured to the body under the left arm by yet more webbing, the four feet of loose webbing being tucked under the right breast pocket of the men's bush jackets. The parachutes were fitted next; first being put on like back packs then careful adjustments made to the harness assembly, especially the leg straps that would take the strain when the parachute opened. A fellow had to be dressed correctly in that area too; otherwise, he could suffer serious damage to his wedding tackle. Now came the heavy Bergen rucksacks, Fred stood astride his pack and tied the two pieces of webbing to his equipment, one each side of his waist belt. Then whilst Bob lifted the 80 lb pack for him he attached it to the top D-rings of his parachute harness with two quick-release clips, thus leaving no room for a reserve parachute. The heat was stifling by the time the men were ready for the Squadron Commander's inspection prior to the dreaded long wait before the Air Force Parachute Instructor's check. The men were allowed to remove the awkward and heavy loads from their chests and sit down on the ground. All were sweating profusely now, so Fred did not feel conspicuous anymore, in fact he sensed that his first session had gone well. He had not made a bloody nuisance of himself but had sought help at exactly the right time. A murmur came down the line; at long last the AF team were ready to start their blitz. The soldiers struggled to their feet and went through the whole performance of helping each other don their packs again. The AF instructors carried out a stringent check of all equipment and when they were eventually satisfied, the order was given for the squadron to proceed to the aircraft. They marched out of the hangar looking more like a mass casualty evacuation than a special task force, swathed as they were in broad bands of white webbing that resembled heavy bandaging. Their tree jumping gear was very Heath Robinson like and the techniques for going into the jungle in this manner were so risky that many of the men might well end up being real casualties. The soldiers of this SAS Squadron were about to perform a duty that was so bloody dangerous that they were not allowed to rehearse for it.

Fred marched out of the hangar into the bright sunlight and his bout of butterflies reached its peak. Men are affected in different ways by this state of nervous flux; for instance, his mate Bob was perfectly all right up to the point of boarding the plane when he became highly strung out until his arrival over the dropping zone. In Fred's case the butterflies commenced from the time he first received the warning order for the drop. He suffered a feeling of dread in the pit of his stomach that remained at a constant level right up until his first glimpse of the aircraft, at which point he went into a blue funk. Fortunately for all concerned, the preparation work was complete and he had merely to follow the man in front of him and adhere to a few simple rules. Even in his sorry state he could hardly cock up the operation at this point.

The column reached the aircraft, a twin-engined Valetta that because of its fat cigar-shaped fuselage and the many odd bits of equipment protruding from the nose area of the plane, was affectionately known as a 'pig'. By now Fred was really suffering in the 90°F heat and was itching in places that he could not damned well scratch, he had to endure yet another check and make some last minute adjustments to his kit before he heard the long-awaited command, 'Tell off by sticks.' The soldiers responded by numbering off from the right, one-two-three-four, One-two-'Three,' Fred heard himself scream as the five sticks comprising his planeload confirmed their order in the formation. In the background he could hear the same procedures being carried out by the other twenty men of the squadron who had peeled off to halt alongside the second aircraft. The order to enplane was given and the soldiers turned to their left in order to face the aircraft door, they would board in the reverse order to which they would jump, the last sticks first. Fred gave a huge shudder, he would never in a month of Sundays get used to the fact that he was going up in this bloody machine and not coming back in it.

'Come on lad,' bawled the cheerful voice of the AF dispatcher as he helped Fred heave himself up the few short steps into the belly of the 'pig'. At that moment Fred had passed the point of no return, the butterflies vanished and the nervous tension was replaced by a rush of excitement and a bloody-minded feeling of chin-up defiance. As he clambered up the sloping deck to his seat he muttered, 'Bloody acceptance ritual, anyone would think this was a Masons' Lodge. I'll show the lot of you just how much I'm worth.' This was Fred's will speaking, the same will that had got him through his light infantry training, had secured his transfer into the Paras, and made possible his finest achievement yet, his entry into the SAS.

Fred's canvas bucket seat was situated on the right-hand side of the plane, he unhooked his pack and placed it between his legs then sat down, not an easy task because the 'pig' was sat on its tail wheel causing the deck to slope away to Fred's left at an acute angle. The door was situated on the opposite side of the aircraft to Fred's position that was only four seats up the fuselage; this gave him a good view out of it. Soon everyone was seated and the aircraft was started, the dispatcher came along the line and hooked the static lines of the parachutes to the strong points located above the soldier's heads. The noise of the 'pig' was deafening and the whole bloody thing shook furiously, at last it started to move and bumped and rattled its way to the take-off position. The engines roared as the pilot increased the power, holding the bucking beast back against the brakes. Whereas the noise had been deafening before, it was now downright frightening and if one's imagination was anything to go by the ancient pile of nuts and bolts would soon be a heap of junk on the tarmac. With a great lurch the thundering, shuddering contraption roared down the runway and the pilot soon had it in the air, the vibrations ceased as if by magic but because the door was still open it remained fairly noisy. At 3,000 feet the aircraft levelled off and throbbed its way to the dropping zone many miles away.

Fred glanced at the man seated on his immediate left; he was the number one of the stick and his Patrol Commander. He was the most experienced jungle hand on the plane having served with the Chindits during the Second World War, this proud man out of the Queen's Regiment with snow white hair was known as Chalky. Bob was sat directly opposite Fred and was going through his own particular kind of hell, coping with the situation by repeatedly tying knots in a piece of cord. Next to Bob, and number two of the stick, languished an individual who had the unsavoury nickname of Worm, this was because he was an avid reader of anything paperback and was seldom seen without a book. At this moment in time he was perusing a 'Dusty Fog' novel under the pretence of appearing cool, calm and collected. The book was upside down. Chalky, Worm, Fred and Bob, in that order, formed a four-man patrol and would be working in a closely knit group living hand in mouth together for three long months.

Fred looked about the plane to see how the others were braving it out. Where men sat near windows they gazed out at the jungle below, escaping that way. Others stared straight ahead thinking of loved ones whilst the more adventurous ate fruit or chocolate and the really cool individuals slept or pretended to sleep. It was an awkward time and if the truth were to be known, every man jack would be glad to get out of the plane. Besides, by the time the squadron arrived over the dropping zone they would all be busting for a piss, an added incentive for them to exit the 'pig'. The men did not have long to wait because the aircraft were indeed approaching the DZ, although they had taken off together they were actually flying about fifteen minutes apart. This was because a mass drop over the difficult jungle terrain was out of the question, if the squadron was to avoid being spread out over miles of one of the most inhospitable countries in the world, then the descents must be made in small numbers, hence the four man sticks.

A movement caught Fred's eye; it was the AF dispatcher standing up to get things ready at the aircraft door. He spoke to the aircrew over his intercom then pointed at the number one of the first stick; he was to jump alone as a drifter to enable the pilot to gauge the wind for the rest of the drop. The dispatcher ordered the man to his feet, checked his equipment and put him to action stations. The lone parachutist was close to the door now, the red light came on and the AF man screamed, 'Stand to the door!' The man took a pace forward so that he was standing right on the edge of the exit, the slipstream catching his facial features and horribly distorting them. The light changed from red to green. 'Go,' commanded the dispatcher as he gave the SAS trooper a hearty slap on the back to encourage him to leap out of the plane. The first man was away and the 'pig' banked in a long turn to make a second approach, the pilot watching the drifter's progress all the time and making fine adjustments to his course. Once again the AF dispatcher pointed his imperial finger, this time at the remaining men of the first stick. 'Stand up. Check equipment. Action stations. Stand to the door.' The green light again, 'Go, three four,' and the stick disappeared from view, three men in as many seconds.

The AF man hauled in the static lines and parachute bags as the aircraft made another circuit. Then with an evil grin on his face he directed the dreaded finger towards Fred's stick. 'Stand up,' he screamed and the four-man patrol complied immediately. 'Check equipment,' he bawled, the men did just that and helped each other don the heavy packs, a difficult job with the plane banking and bumping along its flight path to the approach run. Finally they checked the chin straps of their para helmets and were almost ready to go. 'Action stations,' roared the dispatcher.

'Panic stations more like,' mimicked Bob, his attack of the butterflies had gone now and he was red in the face with excitement and had a crazy look in his eyes. The stick quickly gathered in the parachute static lines, known as strops they dangled from the parachute packs, down onto the deck of the plane and then back up to the aircraft strong-points. Left like that they posed a serious safety hazard and there was a real danger of them snagging on equipment or becoming entangled in the men's feet. Fred picked up his strop and folded it up in a concertina fashion to be held at waist height by the man behind him. He held Worm's strop and passed his own to Bob as they all faced towards the door and began to shuffle along the fuselage. It was hot and bloody confusing as they tried to keep in step, left foot forward and then the right instep against it, rather similar to the present-arms position. 'One-two, one-two,' they chanted to themselves until they halted one step from the exit. The tension was palpable as fear emanated from the soldiers' sweat-soaked bodies, they had to strain every muscle in order to keep upright as the aircraft encountered turbulence in the form of air pockets. The men's hearts sank as the plane dropped like a stone and their legs became glued to the deck as the 'pig' was thrown back up again. At last the red warning light came on and the AF god commanded, 'Stand to the door.' In unison the whole stick responded, 'One-two,' putting Chalky up front in the precarious jumping position where he was hard put to stop himself from tumbling prematurely out of the 'pig'. They were all feeling scared now but eager to get going like dogs about to be let off the leash. A few heart stopping seconds more and then they were given the green light. Everyone concerned was galvanised into action. 'Go,' another step forward as Chalky went out of the plane and Worm moved into the exit. Fred had just enough time to let go of Worm's strop before it could burn his hand off when, 'Two,' Worm vanished from view and Fred found himself standing in the doorway with his left hand braced against the outside of the aircraft whilst he held his right arm tightly over the top of his pack. 'Three,' Fred heard the AF man shout and felt a hand smash into his back. With leverage from his left arm and all the muscle power he could muster from his legs, Fred took a huge lunge into space and broke through the vacuum surrounding the aircraft fuselage. He quickly moved his left arm over his right one to adopt the classic exit position then his legs, being the lightest part of his body, were pushed upwards in front of him as he slid down the slipstream in a sitting position catching a brief glimpse of the tail wheel as it flashed by.

Over the toecaps of his boots he saw Worm's parachute canopy flick forward over his head as it broke free of the static line. In a flash the same thing happened to Fred and he was pulled forward so that he was looking straight down at the jungle for a split second before being jerked violently about as the parachute developed. Fred looked up in time to see his parachute breathe, that is to say, it had fully opened, but was in the process of closing up. His heart missed a beat as he thought his chute was about to candle, but he soon calmed down a bit when the canopy finally blossomed above him.

Fred quickly carried out an all-round observation drill to ensure he was not on a collision course with anyone else, but all was well. He was not spinning and was pleased that he did not have to extricate himself from a situation known as the 'twists': an exercise that could waste valuable time, and time was of the essence.

After the terrific noise and nerve-racking activity aboard the aircraft, the silence, the beautiful experience of absolute peace and quiet was a godsend. This particular phase of a parachute jump is pure bliss and a moment to be treasured, but unfortunately a very short-lived one. It normally takes about forty-five seconds for a man to parachute from a plane at 1,000 feet and land safely on the ground. Fred had jumped from 1,000 feet, but he would not be landing on the ground. He was planning to land on a tree that could be anything up to 250 feet in height. This effectively reduced his descent time by approximately eleven seconds leaving him with only thirty-four seconds of flight time, before he encountered the giants of the rainforest. He had a lot to do and precious little time to do it in.

Fred felt for and operated the two quick-release clips securing the Bergen rucksack to his chest; the pack fell away and was arrested at ankle height by the webbing ties allowing him to stand on the Bergen. This improvised platform would protect his legs when he hopefully crashed into the trees. If he dropped too far below the visible tree line, the parachute could collapse and he would plummet down through the jungle to the ground; a fate too awful to contemplate. He now had to concentrate all his skills on steering the parachute towards the tallest tree that he could see in his general line of flight. It was important that he do this without jeopardising anyone else's plans. He picked out a likely target slightly off to his right and pulled down on his right forward lift-web to steer the parachute towards the tree.

Nicely does it, Fred was thinking when he was suddenly tossed about like a puppet on a string. He had encountered the hot air rising from the jungle. It was turbulent and was causing the parachute to swing violently from side to side, threatening to turn Fred completely over. 'I've heard of bloody thermals,' Fred cursed, 'but this is beyond a sodding joke.' He gritted his teeth and fought the wild oscillations with all his strength in a desperate endeavour to keep his parachute on course for the all-important tree. Fred started to flap because the intended target appeared to be rushing towards him at a rapid rate of knots. But as suddenly as it had started, the turbulence ended and Fred's pulse returned to near normal, but he was fast running out of time. Fifty feet to go and Fred was swinging in a great arc to the right of the gnarled monster, twenty-five feet and back the other way like a pendulum. *This is it,* thought Fred as he prepared for the worse, he closed his eyes and hoped for the best. He heard a loud snapping sound as wood splintered above his head, then his body smashed against the side of the ancient trunk knocking the breath out of his lungs.

He was just regaining his composure when he felt himself falling as his rigging lines slipped down a few feet accompanied by a frightening ripping and tearing noise; but thankfully Fred finally came to rest to find himself hanging straight down the side of the tree, eight feet from the trunk and about 200 feet from the ground. He had achieved his aim of getting 'hung up' in a tree, and although congratulations were in order, he was left with a slight problem regarding the task of getting down from his lofty perch. Because he was suspended well away from the trunk and there were no suitable branches within grasping range, he had nowhere to anchor the abseiling gear from except his own parachute. This was an accepted, and prepared for, eventuality, but it robbed him of a stable platform from which to work.

Beads of sweat were standing out on his forehead as he tried hard to remain in control, Fred thought briefly of swinging the parachute to get himself a purchase around the main trunk but dismissed the idea as idiotic. *Better to accept what I've got,* he thought to himself. 'Into the breach,' Fred muttered as, with a thumping heart and every nerve strung out like violin strings, he prepared himself for the hazardous descent. Pulling the loose end of webbing from his bush jacket, he tied it to the lift-webs of the parachute harness, then taking off his para helmet he secured it in the same place. That done he removed the roll of webbing from the valise being careful not to drop his sub-machine gun and other bits of kit. He dropped the webbing and watched it unravel until it disappeared from view into the foliage below, then he turned his attention to the parachute. The webbing passing around his waist via the bikini formed a step that secured Fred at his present height. To move down he had merely to feed the roll he had just dropped through the metal D-ring, but first he had to be free of his parachute harness. He took a deep breath and turned the quick release box and gave it a hearty tap, with that the four harness straps were released. All seemed well until he had undone the leg straps, then he nearly jumped out of his skin as he fell about a foot and was tilted into the classic abseiling position. Now he was free of the parachute but suspended from it, the slight change in his position had caused him to start swinging; the tree itself was moving all the time, and the combination of both these factors was threatening his already precarious stability. 'The situation,' Fred moaned, 'is definitely hairy.'

There was one more job to do before he could start abseiling down, he drew his Browning 9mm automatic pistol from its holster, cocked it ready for action and put it away again. This was active service he was on and he was descending into enemy-occupied country, it was not beyond the realms of possibility that a bandit might be lying in wait for him below.

The jungle was unusually quiet, the wild tree dwellers silenced no doubt by the arrival of the drifter and the first stick. The primates were there though, Fred could feel their eyes on him and he had visions of them sharpening their claws and fangs in anticipation of an English breakfast.

'Here goes then,' he whispered as he reached down with his left hand to grasp a length of webbing. He lifted it up to waist height allowing it to run smoothly through the D-ring and in turn the bikini. Down he went, and so began his journey to the jungle floor. He carried out the same manoeuvre twice more in order to gain confidence, then he paused to take stock of his situation. His first obstacle seemed to be about sixty feet below him where the trees became smaller and the foliage much denser. Fred took a quick look around to see if he could spot anyone else and was rewarded by the sight of one parachute some five hundred yards to his left. Translated into distance on the ground it might just as well have been in bloody miles. He could not see the parachutist so he had no way of telling if the parachute belonged to one of his own patrol or not.

Fred continued to abseil but this time more rapidly, feeding the webbing through the bikini hand over hand. He was patting himself on the back when a burning sensation in the pit of his stomach forced him to stop; the bloody metal ring was red hot. As Fred writhed about in agony the rigging lines of his parachute slipped through the top branch of the tree, and to the noise of tearing nylon and snapping branches he plummeted twenty feet until he crashed into the jungle canopy, his fall being cushioned by his Bergen rucksack. Fred looked up and saw that it was not all bad news, this time his tattered and torn parachute had well and truly snagged over a substantial fork between the main trunk and a huge branch. Relieved on that score but still thoroughly shaken by the fall, he let the D-ring cool down and attempted to sort himself out, the cocktail of emotions and violent action having drained him of strength. After what seemed like a lifetime of waiting, he was at last ready to continue and he had his work cut out because this was no longer a simple matter of lowering himself down. He now had to contend with the ever-thickening jungle growth and there was an added distraction, albeit a psychological one. The tree population had become used to the intrusion and thousands of birds and monkeys were screeching, hooting and howling; to the unfortunate parachutist the monkeys in particular seemed to be laughing at his every misfortune.

Fred began to pick his way through the branches and vines, an easy run here, a torturous struggle there, but in the main it went without incident if you discount such things as split bamboo, strangling creepers, vicious blood-drawing thorns and millions of man-hating ants. Fred had reached a particularly thick patch of jungle and was thinking that he could not be far from the ground when he suddenly ran out of webbing. The shock to his system was so great that despite the heat he went as white as a sheet, and at his wits' end, he closed his eyes in sheer panic and despair. He really was at the end of his tether, he was hot, bruised and bleeding, bitten half to death by ants, the mosquitoes had joined in the fun and the bloody webbing was running through the bikini totally beyond his control. 'Sodding hell,' he moaned, 'all this for nothing.' His nerves were screaming as he tensed his body for the inevitable plunge to earth.

As if from nowhere he heard a soft voice say, 'Hell is not the place for you my son, open your eyes and behold the kingdom of heaven. Come on now, be brave.' Fred did as the kindly voice bade him to, thinking that he had departed from this world to a higher place. He opened his eyes to find himself staring into the evil, grinning face of his Squadron Sergeant Major, Lofty, who had dropped with the first stick. 'Look down you pillock,' he whispered as he held aside some fern leaves.

Glancing down, Fred started to shake uncontrollably as he saw solid ground only a couple of inches under his Bergen. The webbing ran out of the D-ring at that point, dumping him unceremoniously onto the wet jungle floor. Fred had tears in his eyes as he realised he had done it, and what's more he'd done it with them, the men of his SAS Squadron.

Lofty stayed with him long enough to make sure that he was okay and then disappeared into the jungle to find and man the squadron rendezvous point. Fred could hear the aircraft circling above and the sound of men crashing into the trees all around him as he quickly got out of the bikini and removed his main weapon and other items of fighting gear from the valise. When he had loaded and cocked his Australian Owen gun he made safe the pistol so he couldn't shoot himself in the foot, then he prepared the Bergen for man-packing and hid the swathes of white webbing and the valise in the thick undergrowth. He heaved the pack onto his back and after a brief look at his map and compass he headed for the RV leaving the parachute, abseiling gear and bloody tin hat behind him for the monkeys.

By 14.00 hrs the complete squadron had passed through the RV with, miraculously, no serious casualties. They quickly formed into patrols and troops and marched off to a base camp for the night. At 16.00 hrs the base camp had been established on a hill called Bukit Perloh, Bukit being the Malay word for 'hill'. The base camp and start line for the SAS operation was situated on the state borders of Johore and Pahang.

As the Major commanding the Squadron, nicknamed Caesar because of his roman type nose, gave out his first set of patrol orders he wondered how these tough men would react if they knew that this very dangerous operation had been precipitated by the merest wisp of military intelligence and the hunch of an old wartime Chindit soldier. Deciding that discretion is the better part of valour, he dismissed the Patrol Commanders and got his head down. It was to be an early start in the morning.

Chapter Two

Three months before the SAS drop took place, other events were taking shape within the enemy camp. At the beginning of May 1957 the leader of the Malay Races Liberation Army secretly departed from Malaya for an undisclosed destination. His Quartermaster General, Lai Sing accompanied him. The great guerrilla commander was on a mission to procure desperately needed financial aid, funds with which he could reorganise his beleaguered regiments now eking out a miserable existence in their jungle hideouts. The man delegated to carry the burden of command during his absence was his trusted friend and Paymaster General, Kim Bok.

Kim Bok was running on loyalty. He wasn't being fuelled by good food and drink, not inspired by ideals and the promise of rich rewards, nor was he following a lost cause with blind obedience. None of these things were driving him forward now, he was motivated only by his unswerving loyalty to the two men he loved and revered above all others, his leader and Lai Sing. They went back a long way these three, their friendship cemented by years of bitter fighting against the Japanese during the Second World War and the British since 1948. It was now mid July and two long months had passed by since his friends had marched over the Thailand border in their quest for support. He felt safe enough in his jungle camp high up in the mountainous border country of northern Perak. He had sited the camp so that it actually straddled the border between Malaya and Thailand, because the latter country was neutral in this particular conflict, he could always beat a hasty retreat to comparative safety should things get too hot. The border effectively sealed his back door because he knew that the British would not send patrols into Thailand in order to get around to his rear.

Kim Bok's force of ten men occupied a piece of ground situated on a spur leading up to a 4,763 feet high feature called

Gunong Ulu Merah. The camp perimeter was a mere twelve feet wide and some seventy yards long and was easily defended. The ground fell away very steeply on each side of the spur; any attempt by the enemy to ascend these slopes would cause a hell of a racket, give their position away and they would lose any element of surprise they might have had. That left the only other way into Kim's little fortress, a steep track that followed the spur up to the summit of the mountain with his soldiers barring the way. The forest in this area was known as virgin jungle and consisted of tall trees that blocked out the sunlight with very little undergrowth at ground level. This gave Kim's main defensive weapon, a machine gun, reasonable fields of fire straight down the track. His greatest form of defence though was silence, all he and his men had to do was keep quiet and listen. The guerrillas were permanently hungry, living as they were on a handful of rice a day, water was in short supply and it was strictly rationed. The men were weak and lethargic and needed little encouragement to lay still on the bamboo platforms that they had built for themselves. Camouflaged with the huge leaves of the attap palm, these makeshift shelters, or bashas, were difficult to spot and many a British soldier had stumbled upon such camps as Kim Bok's, the enemy gone with just minutes to spare, alerted by the single snap of a broken twig. This was not always the case and quite often the hunted were caught by surprise and had to turn at bay to fight furiously like cornered animals.

In regard to engaging the enemy, Kim Bok's orders were simple. He was to conserve his ammunition by taking on the British using small delaying tactics, and then only if contact with them was inevitable. The contact drills he and his men had rehearsed time and time again were simple too. If the enemy was heard and not seen, Kim's force would bug out over the Thailand border without making a sound. If the enemy got close enough to be seen, and it was impossible to move without being detected, then Kim's machine gunners would open fire. Hopefully this would force the British to deploy allowing Kim's force to tactically withdraw into Thailand safe in the knowledge that they would not be followed.

Kim Bok's group was not typical of the active service units

normally fielded by the guerrilla army. It was really a gathering of Intelligence Officers from seven of the guerrilla army regiments; the two other men were Kim's bodyguards. In his possession Kim had a set of sealed orders, instructions that could only be opened once he had received word from his leader.

Kim let his mind wander back to his boyhood years to the time he had first met Lai Sing. That had been at a communist party rally held in Lai Sing's home village of Kampong Belukar Panjang situated in the northern state of Kelantan. Kim had been only fifteen years old then and his new-found friend was his senior by two years; they had both been recruited into the party and in the confusion of those turbulent times had found themselves pressed into joining the ranks of the Chinese 8th Route Army. They were soon opposing the much feared Japanese Imperial Army, and by the time this formidable enemy had overrun Malaya and Singapore, Kim had developed into a seasoned jungle fighter and his outlook on life had been hardened by the atrocities his young eyes had been forced to witness. From deep jungle hideouts the two friends served their regiment well, raiding the Japanese lines of communication, derailing trains and ambushing river traffic along the state river, the Sungei Kelantan. Kim's friend was a natural born leader and was soon selected for promotion, with it came a posting to a special unit. He persuaded his superiors to let Kim Bok go with him and they were soon embroiled in the vicious activities of a killer squad, carrying out the assassination of Chinese, Indian and Malay collaborators. In 1943 the duo were appointed as military advisors to the Malay People's Anti-Japanese Army, their job was to help stiffen up resistance to the invaders and to encourage more aggressive action against them.

Posted to the MPAJA's 5th Regiment they came under the command of an officer who was later to become the great leader. The three men formed an unholy alliance that hammered away relentlessly at the Japanese, one day raiding deep into their old stamping grounds of West Kelantan, the next descending from the mountains into Perak, the birthplace of the Leader.

It was during this period that they began to link up with Force 136 and some British officers in order to liase and pool their intelligence regarding the enemy. With the assistance of British intelligence resources, the MPAJA established an important line of communication, a courier route in the form of a secret jungle track that ran the entire length of the Malay Peninsular. It was doubly important because, although the British helped the MPAJA set it up by providing them with details of heavy concentrations of Japanese forces and steering them clear of areas thick with informers, the British themselves never became privy to information regarding the actual route.

Kim Bok's reverie was interrupted by the men about him suddenly sliding into the well-oiled drill of an emergency stand-to; something had alerted the sentry posted at the northern end of the camp. Whispered warnings spread rapidly down the line as the guerrillas grabbed their weapons and took up defensive firing positions. The lean hungry-looking men lay still, their haggard faces drawn in expressions of fearful expectancy, with pounding hearts they waited. Kim moved quickly and quietly to join the sentry; the man made a chopping motion with his hand and pointed up the track indicating that he had heard a snapping sound coming from that direction. Lying on his stomach next to the sentry, Kim had a twenty-yard field of view; a generous distance in the jungle and a definite advantage over anyone approaching the camp. They would have to look down from head height through the tangled mass of vegetation in order to spot a target on the ground at that range. Should anyone walk down the track towards him, Kim would be able to see the person's legs long before he could be spotted himself. 'Yes,' he murmured, 'if there's to be a fight here, I'll have the edge.'

Nothing seemed to be moving out there; whoever or whatever had caused the snapping sound had either stopped dead in their tracks or were being more cautious, perhaps brought back to reality by their own negligence. The jungle noises had not ceased or changed in tempo, a sure indication that any force that might be lurking about was small in number and felt at home in the forest. The monkeys still hooted and howled insanely, millions of insects and birds kept up their incessant din and ants bit savagely without mercy. Despite the high altitude and the fact that sunlight seldom filtered through the trees to the jungle floor, the midday heat was oppressive; it sapped the strength and lowered the men's resistance, sweat poured into their eyes blurring the vision, making observation difficult and misleading. The mosquitoes were omnipresent. The high-pitched hum of their wings buzzed annoyingly in the men's ears, making them cringe with anticipation, before the death dealing malaria carriers plunged their long bloodsucking proboscis into the inviting flesh of their human victims. The guerrillas could only endure this mental and physical torture in silence, to swat at one meant sudden movement and that meant detection by the enemy; a fate that would lead to certain death from a marksman's bullet. Still the men waited, their nerve ends shattered and stretched to breaking point, imaginations worked overtime as fingers twitched nervously on triggers and vocal chords begged for the chance to scream out in order to find release from the terrible tension.

The minutes ticked slowly by as Kim struggled to concentrate on the situation; he was suffering just as much as his men but had to contend with the added pressure that went with a position of command. His gut feeling told him that the threat posed by this particular scare would not come from the British Army. He knew in his bones that they would not cross the border to mount a military operation against him from Thailand, but it would be a mistake on his part to take anything for granted in this close and difficult terrain. The border in these deep jungle areas was inaccurately defined on maps, completely unmarked on the ground and navigational errors were common. Operating this close to an international boundary the British would err on the side of caution and diplomacy; they were though an unpredictable lot who could be very audacious and pure bloody minded at times. In such a mood they might surround his camp by putting out stops to the north, east and west of him, thereby blocking his escape route into Thailand, whilst they attacked the camp from the south. But despite the strain and tension of the moment, Kim just did not have that trapped feeling. He had a hunch that this was something different. *Word from his boss*, he thought, *is long overdue.*

Kim looked intently up the track towards the border, 'Please let it be them,' he whispered in prayer, 'send me a sign.'

Some movement came first, a slight shifting of light and the imperceptible swaying of small branches, not much, but enough to make the sentry bring his rifle completely up into the aiming position. Kim raised his own weapon to a more ready position, his heart was pounding so much that he was sure it could be heard a mile away. *Here goes,* he was thinking when a shrill whistling sound nearly made him jump out of his skin. The whistle quickly changed to a warble that soon degenerated into a coughing croak. The call of the jungle fowl that had silenced the other animals for an instant was not repeated and soon the forest settled back to its normal clamour once more.

Kim Bok's prayers had been answered, that was no jungle fowl out there; the call was a masterful imitation and a warning to him that friendly forces were approaching the camp. He breathed a sigh of relief but did not allow himself or his men to relax their vigilance, to do so could prove to be disastrous. Incoming patrols and visiting units were particularly vulnerable at this point when the thought of rest in a secure camp was uppermost in their minds. Some British patrols were pretty adept at picking up signs and tracking an enemy force back to its base camp where they would watch and listen, recording details of troop dispositions and sentry drills, perhaps they would even overhear the password. Having made this close and highly dangerous reconnaissance they would withdraw to a safe distance and report back to their superiors on the radio; from that point onwards the CT camp would be doomed.

I'll bet my bottom dollar that the British aren't about, he thought, stubbornly holding on to his belief that they would not cross the border to get at him. But if the British had picked up the trail of this incoming party, then they would have had to cross over the border to do so. 'No,' mumbled Kim, 'putting out stops is one thing, going that deep into Thailand is another. But,' he groaned, 'there is always a first time.'

The sentry tensed and his knuckles turned white as he took up the first pressure on his trigger; Kim's eyeballs were almost popping out of their sockets with the strain as he peered through the undergrowth. 'Ah,' he whispered. More movement and the darkening of the background prompted him to follow the sentry's earlier example, he took up the aiming position and focused the foresight blade of his rifle on a spot twenty yards away and waited. Into that miniature world framed within his foresight aperture, onto that sharply defined stage with its hazy backdrop of russet and greens, down onto the hellish, gut wrenching and nerve-racking domain of the hunted; stepped a foot. A foot shod in a mud-splattered brown hockey boot that was the standard footwear of the guerrilla army. One foot became two, and soon there were six; Kim got to his feet, his knees were trembling and his whole body shook with emotion as he greeted the three long-awaited messengers.

His prayers had indeed been answered, word had come; he was not ashamed of the tears that cascaded down his cheeks as he ushered the tired trio to his command post situated in the centre of the camp. Nor could he hide his feelings of relief and joy as he invited the guests to rest their weapons and take off the heavy packs that they were carrying, and sit down. But now was not the time to relax, there were still procedures to be gone through. Leaving the couriers under the watchful eyes of his two bodyguards, Kim withdrew four of his men from their stand-to positions on the perimeter and sent them out on a clearing patrol; two men to the north and the other two southwards. He was clearing his doorstep and reassuring himself that a British Army patrol had not followed his friends in.

Whilst the camp waited anxiously for the patrols to return Kim had ample time to take stock of the newcomers who presented a bedraggled and sorry spectacle. Like the rest of the guerrilla army they were dressed in a mixture of captured or stolen British and Indian Army khaki drill uniforms with the odd item of Malay Police apparel in evidence. The old Japanese Army knee-length puttee was the most popular form of leg protection, the British short puttee made a good second choice whilst the webbing anklet, or gaiter, was worn as a last resort. Belt kit also consisted of an assortment of British, Indian and Japanese equipment with some American gear thrown in. These same countries were the source of supply for arms and ammunition, some French and Chinese weapons were also available. The guerrilla army had home-made weapons too, mainly rifles; expert tradesmen working from their deeply hidden jungle armouries made them.

Kim noticed that the uniforms of this motley looking crew were tattered and torn, splattered with mud and stained black with sweat and grime. Their faces, arms and knees were bleeding from cuts and bruises whilst blood from bursting leeches provided a final macabre touch.

Two of the couriers were conspicuous by the headgear that they wore, peaked khaki caps sporting the red star badge of the MRLA. Of good Chinese stock, both men were well-built and about five feet six inches tall. Kim's eyes shifted slightly to take in the third member of the group, who wore a sweatband around the head, had jet-black hair and dark brown eyes. Despite the dark jungle environment where everyone else's complexion was ashen in hue, it was obvious that this person was not pure Chinese, a slightly darker coloured skin suggesting Eurasian ancestry. At least three inches taller than the other two with long slender legs, not even the bloody and gruesome appearance could conceal a certain air of femininity. Sensing his interest the tall courier prepared to stand up but Kim arrested the movement by giving the silent field signal for everyone to keep still, be quiet and listen out. He glanced at his watch, it was 13.30 hrs, the patrols had been out for over an hour and the period of relief generated by the arrival of the courier group had been short lived. The tension had returned with the deployment of the clearing patrols and had been mounting ever since. Then, like a breath of fresh air, a stirring of hope ran through the camp as the southern patrol came in to report that all was clear. Ten minutes later the other patrol arrived from the north with the same good news, there was absolutely no sign of enemy activity. Still Kim Bok did not allow any relaxation of vigilance, instead, he redeployed the two patrols back to their stand-to positions on the perimeter; there was one more matter to be attended to before he could order a stand-down.

He beckoned for the Eurasian to approach him and held out his hand to receive the proffered tightly bound waterproof package that contained the top secret messages; at the same time Kim's bodyguards covered the two Chinese couriers with fully cocked rifles. In an already tense situation this was a moment charged with danger and could well result in the instant execution of all three couriers. Kim removed the outer cover of the package inspecting it carefully as he did so. He nodded his head and seemed satisfied; the messengers and bodyguards alike breathed a sigh of relief. There were three separate envelopes inside the package, again he painstakingly checked each one, and even Kim was trembling by the time he had finished. He looked at the inscrutable face of the Eurasian, he found the dark brown eyes and pierced them with his own, and then he smiled.

Fantail, a female soldier of the guerrilla army, collapsed in a heap at Kim's feet sobbing uncontrollably. Her colleagues expressed their feelings by grinning from ear to ear whilst they opened the huge backpacks that they had carried so far; both men knew full well that had the package been tampered with in any way, they and Fantail would have been shot on the spot.

What a welcome sight it was to see such luxurious fare as tinned fish, chicken and fruit being laid out on the ground. There was drink too, water bags filled with a rough rice wine called Tuak, and plastic containers brimming with arrack, a more refined rice-based spirit.

As the men filed in from the camp perimeter defences glad of the stand-down, pleased also at the prospect of drinking something stronger than water, Kim got on with the job at hand: reading the mail. 'Let's see what the old man has to say,' he murmured to himself as he opened the first envelope. The news was good, in brief; his leader had managed to procure funds in the form of gold bullion to the tune of five million pounds sterling. But there was a catch: he and his Quartermaster General could only get the gold as far as the Portuguese possession of Macau situated some forty miles west of Hong Kong, Kim was to get the gold out of Macau and smuggle it into Malaya. He was also charged with the responsibility of transporting the bullion inland to a point where his path bisected the old wartime courier route, that by then would have been reactivated by the MRLA's Regimental Commanders. From that point the gold would be taken to a guerrilla stronghold in central Pahang manned by the 10th Regiment; the camp was also the location of the Central Military Committee. To move the heavy precious metal through the thick jungle terrain would be a tough job requiring the possible use of elephants and mules, and of course, the men themselves; a daunting task but one that Kim found exciting. The message concluded by authorising Kim to open and distribute the sealed orders that had been left in his trust.

The second envelope contained more specific orders regarding his particular task, some Malay, Thai and Hong Kong currency, and a letter of introduction to the Leader's man in Macau. The third letter was for the navigators who were to lead the regimental intelligence officers southwards, and re-map the entire length of the courier route; they were Kim's own bodyguards. For the moment Kim had nothing to plan and no lengthy set of orders to write, it was all there in the envelopes and the guides for the first part of his journey would be Fantail and her two colleagues.

He assembled the men and spelt out the situation giving them a brief outline of the overall plan. Then he issued each regimental intelligence officer with a set of the sealed orders that were to be delivered to their respective Commanding Officers. Kim had the sentries changed and went through the whole thing again with them. Finally, he handed his trusty bodyguards their own set of instructions.

Time flies when one is busy and it was now 15.00 hrs with only about two hours of daylight remaining, Kim indicated that everyone should get stuck into the extra food and drink. 'Enjoy it,' he suggested, 'for tomorrow we scatter to the four winds.'

They took him at his word and these bloody hard men became as little children at a party. The rain came at 16.30 hrs drowning out the subdued conversation and the jungle noises as it thundered down onto the great canopy of foliage above.

Fantail, who had drunk too much arrack decided to perform her version of a Dyak bird dance, divesting herself of all clothing as an added provocative touch she leaped stark naked from Kim's shelter out into the pouring rain. When acted out by the native Dyak tribesmen of Borneo wearing animal masks and adorned with bird plumage, the dance could be colourful and wonderfully artistic. Fantail's presentation of it could only be described as erotic, and when she paused between certain postures, it was downright lewd. Her olive-coloured skin was lightened slightly by the cold rainwater that also caused goose pimples to break out all over her body, giving her wet and shiny athletic form a sculptured and marblesque appearance. It accentuated her firm uplifting breasts that trembled at her every move and were the focal point of the all-male audience. With suggestive artistry she contrived to make the rainwater fall from her extremities, her hands, elbows and feet providing a foretaste of what was yet to come; the men gasped as she positioned her torso in such a manner that water jetted from her erect nipples, they groaned as the life-giving liquid cascaded down her back to gush out from between her clenched buttocks. She was driving them mad but not one man attempted to touch this beautiful woman who was known to give freely of herself for the pure love of it. They feared and respected the awesome reputation she had of being utterly ruthless and unmerciful to any adversary. But even that would not be enough to stem the tide of human nature that would surely overflow if this nubile, cavorting female did not bring her teasing antics to a close. Fantail must have sensed this herself because a minute later she concluded the performance with a mind-boggling handstand.

'Well that didn't leave much to the imagination,' chuckled Kim, glad in a way that the dance was over. As Fantail got dressed in the closing minutes before dark, he thought about her.

Fantail had not enjoyed a good start in life, her mother was a dockside whore who had slipped up and become pregnant by a Portuguese seaman in the west coast port of Malacca. Despite much pleading by family and friends, the sailor had refused to marry the young Chinese girl; the Malacca Tongs intervened but to no avail, consequently, the seafarer was found in an alleyway stabbed to death with his private parts sewn into his mouth. Fantail was born six months later, a bastard. She followed in her mother's footsteps selling her body around the waterfront area of Malacca for whatever she could get at the tender age of twelve.

In 1947 Fantail joined the communist party, and through them the guerrilla army, going underground with them in 1948 to help fight the British. She hated anyone who was European, to her way of thinking the British were no better than the scum that had spawned her dead father. With this huge chip on her shoulder Fantail made a perfect guerrilla fighter, despising anything authoritative she discharged her duties like a wildcat and soon earned for herself a reputation bordering on legendary for her bravery and cruel diligence in dispatching the enemy. In one of her exploits she personally flayed a prisoner alive, taking four days to do it. After growing tired of inflicting pain on the poor wretch she left him tied to a tree at the mercy of thousands of red ants; for a long time his screams could be heard from over a mile away. This outrageous incident prompted the British to put a price on Fantail's head, and so concentrated were their efforts to capture her, that it was deemed necessary to transfer the female terrorist to the 12th Independent Regiment that operated out of the more remote terrain of northern Perak and Kelantan. It was there in the rugged mountain regions that she first demonstrated her prowess at imitating animal calls, and earned for herself the nickname Fantail, after the pigeon of the same name.

It was still raining and Kim was alone now, Fantail had gone off to the northern end of the camp for a drink with her courier friends. He stretched out on his bamboo platform and smiled. *Somebody is going to be a lucky man tonight,* he thought as he dozed off.

She came to him in the dark at that time when the rain had stopped and the heat of the day gave way to the coolness of late evening and even the mosquitoes had gone to rest. They fumbled feverishly as they undressed each other and soon they lay naked together on Kim's makeshift bed, their love nest lit only by the floating green spots of the glow-worms and the luminosity of rotting vegetation. The denizens of the night seemed to be sounding their approval as the two lovers embraced and his lips found hers in the darkness and they kissed long and deeply. They were not new to each other, these two, and were eager to rediscover those most secret of places; touching, fondling and caressing until they were both moaning with pleasure and excitement. He made love to her slowly and gently, with infinite tenderness he brought her writhing body almost to boiling point only to let her back down again to a panting, gasping simmer. He coaxed and teased her through this most exquisite of tortures time after time until she begged for release, and he too was fast losing control. Their lovemaking assumed a level of urgency born out of desperation as they strove to snatch this golden moment in time. Bucking and thrusting in a final burst of frenzied passion they threw caution to the wind and gave everything of themselves until their world exploded in a brilliant flash of ecstasy. Slowly their heartbeats returned to normal and they reluctantly released each other; then, completely fulfilled and utterly spent, the two lovers slept; not the uneasy sleep of the damned but the slumber of the contented with its dreams of happy times.

They broke camp the next morning, when everyone was ready to move they formed up on the track that ran through the camp. Kim Bok went along the line of men who were to head south shaking hands with each intelligence officer in turn; once they had marked the length of courier route assigned to their particular regiment they would peel off and report to their respective headquarters. Each regiment would then be responsible for organising the route within their given boundaries. At the end of the line he said a special farewell to his bodyguards Liew and Shen, they had watched over him diligently during these last few months and they had a difficult task ahead of them. They were both older than Kim and had trod this very dangerous path before during the war against the Japanese. If anyone could scout this group safely through the torturous country and map it besides, it was these two old stalwarts. It was an exacting challenge indeed and Kim wished them well with all his heart. He nodded to Shen who was to take point as leading scout; Shen gave the signal to move out and the small column soon disappeared into the jungle with hope riding high in the their minds.

Kim Bok's party then advanced northwards with one of the Chinese couriers leading the way. They crossed the border into Thailand and marched north-north-eastwards towards the railway line that passed through the small town of Tanjong Mat, a gruelling journey through thick jungle of thirty miles: a march where the going was so slow that distance was measured in yards rather than miles, and the average speed at patrol pace was 1,000 yards an hour.

It took seven days to reach Tanjong Mat where they boarded a train, two days later they arrived in Bangkok. There the party split up, Kim and Fantail were to travel on to Hong Kong by air; the two couriers would remain in Bangkok until Kim Bok's return.

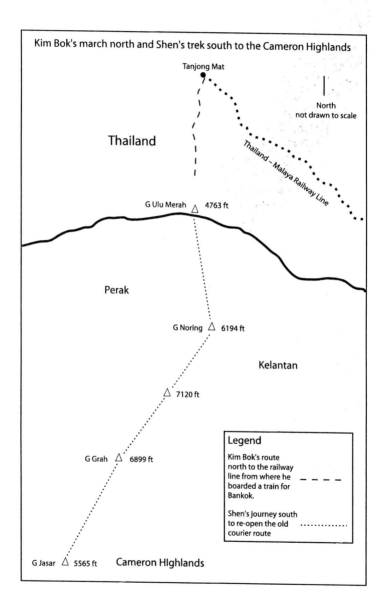

Kim Bok's march north and Shen's trek south to the Cameron Highlands

Tanjong Mat

North
not drawn to scale

Thailand

Thailand – Malaya Railway Line

G Ulu Merah △ 4763 ft

Perak

G Noring △ 6194 ft

Kelantan

△ 7120 ft

G Grah △ 6899 ft

G Jasar △ 5565 ft   Cameron Highlands

Legend

Kim Bok's route
north to the railway
line from where he
boarded a train for
Bankok.

– – –

Shen's journey south
to re-open the old
courier route

....

Chapter Three

The Hermes aircraft took off from Bangkok airport dead on time, its four engines roaring as it climbed up into the blue sky with a good weather forecast to speed it on its way. Kim and Fantail settled down in their seats for the long flight that was scheduled to take seven hours. Kim looked at his watch, it was 09.00 hrs, they should arrive in Hong Kong at 16.00 hrs; add thirty minutes and that meant the plane would touch down at 16.30 hrs, local time. Kim glanced at Fantail with approval, they had purchased some new clothing during their short stay in Bangkok and she looked ravishing in a skintight turquoise dress with a slit cut up one side, this already stunning effect was finished off to perfection by a flower in her hair. Kim was dressed in a coffee-coloured planter's suit complete with a collar and light brown tie. He wore some casual brown footwear with matching socks whilst his lovely companion had opted for a pair of bright green high-heeled shoes but preferred to go barelegged.

As the aircraft droned its way over Laos and North Vietnam, Kim thought about the situation he and his friends found themselves in, he knew instinctively that this was the guerrilla army's last chance of success in Malaya. Deep down he had come to realise that their cause had been doomed from the start, things had simply not gone their way at all. After the war, Kim had continued to serve in the Malayan Communist Party, at that time they were favouring a fairly moderate line hoping to gain influence and control of the Government by rising to the fore like some hideous canker from within. The policy did not work and the age-old ploy of provoking labour unrest was failing. Why? Because in 1948 Malaya was one of the few countries in the world that was actually recovering quickly from the Second World War. The standard of living was fair and improving all the time, there was a light at the end of the tunnel with plenty of work in the offing and the workers wanted to keep whatever money they had earned for themselves. The people were beginning to see the communists in the proper light, not as Samaritans, but as a threat to their well-being; even the powerful trade unions were getting fed-up with communist interference.

As if these setbacks had not been enough to take, the party had yet a bigger pill to swallow. Lai Teck, the Malayan Communist Party leader, had disappeared with all the party funds, and to add insult to injury, the MCP were forced to admit it by going public and issued the famous Lai Teck exposure document. Kim winced at the memory, 'That was two own goals for sure,' he mumbled to himself, remembering the aftermath of that debacle. As a direct consequence of Lai Teck's treachery, Kim's old wartime commander and trusted friend was elected as the new leader of the MCP. What Lai Teck had failed to achieve by taking the moderate line, the new leader hoped to accomplish by force of arms and terror. Accordingly, he raised a communist guerrilla army and appointed Lai Sing to his staff as Quartermaster General. Armed insurrection broke out and Kim once more found himself soldiering in the sweltering jungles of Malaya, this time fighting under the banner of the Malay Races Liberation Army (MRLA). Although only 1,200 men were fielded at the commencement of hostilities against the British, within weeks 5,000 soldiers had rallied to the cause, and by 1951 the fighting strength of the MRLA had reached its peak of 8,000 men and woman, of which ninety per cent were Chinese. Eleven regiments were formed and organised into companies and platoons similar to the British military system. Deployed throughout the Federation, the MRLA posed a considerable threat to the British regime, the guerrilla soldiers were a tough, hard bunch and many of them had experienced actual wartime combat against the Japanese, they were quite a formidable foe. A number of independent companies and platoons sprang up in each state; like bands of marauders they roamed at will and were feared for their vicious aggression. Supporting the MRLA from the onset were about 60,000 members of the underground people's movement, the so-called Min Yuen. They operated in the squatter areas and villages providing food, military intelligence and funds for the jungle units, they also maintained the capability of providing part-time raiders and killer squads. At least half a million rural Chinese either volunteered or were forced into supporting the MRLA.

Thinking of the Min Yuen had brought a smile to Kim's face and he glanced fondly at the sleeping profile of his companion. It was at a Min Yuen rally that he had first set eyes on Fantail, then a sweet young girl of sixteen who had been waving a Min Yuen flag proclaiming, 'Through violence we conquer'. Perhaps sweet is the wrong word because even at that age it was obvious that he was not the first man she had experienced but that mattered not when he had conquered her that very same night. In turbulent, violent and desperate times emotions can run high and the wrong conclusions arrived at from a single night of passion. Was it love, infatuation or pure animal lust? Whichever it was, the chemistry between them was so strong that he recruited her directly into the MRLA's Third Regiment and carted her off immediately to serve with them in the Malacca area.

Kim looked wistfully at Fantail's peaceful face, and at the view of Hainan Island framed in the oval window beside her, and he felt sad as he contemplated the hopelessness of their situation.

The Lai Teck affair had been a bad enough setback to communist advancement in Malaya, but the Leader's error of judgement regarding the British reaction to his use of armed aggression was to prove disastrous; he had completely underestimated his foe. Basing his strategy on the assumption that the British would not be keen to suffer another humiliating debacle similar to the one that they had experienced in Palestine; he judged that the British would pull out of Malaya. They did not. Instead, they dug in and fought back with the ferocity of lions and held their ground with great tenacity. The planters and tin miners did likewise, forming their respective workforces into effective defensive units to ward off terrorist attacks. Then British and Commonwealth troops mounted an offensive that took the war to the terrorists, forcing them to retreat into deep jungle to suffer the humiliation of being beaten at their own game.

Another blow to the leader's plans came in August of 1949. As if to add insult to injury, the British made a move that was enough to goad the terrorist leader into a fury. They appointed the former Inspector General of the Palestine Police Force as

Police Commissioner of Malaya. Assisted by five hundred newly arrived police Sergeants, the majority of whom were ex-Palestine Police and who were granted officer status in the rank of Lieutenant, the Commissioner began to organise and train his 10,000 predominately Malay personnel. He created a police radio-network compatible to that of the military services and developed the new Special Branch. By 1953 he commanded 25,000 regular Police Officers, 41,000 Special Constables and a staggering 250,000 strong Home Guard. In tandem with the military, the police too went on the offensive by deploying twenty-two jungle companies of the Federation Police Field Force, each company consisting of approximately 180 men.

Kim Bok was not a well travelled man and this was his first excursion away from Malaya apart from the odd retreat to jungle hideouts in Thailand. The only policemen he had come into contact with belonged to the Federation of Malaya Police Force. They were part of that worldwide bastion of law and order known as the British Colonial Police Force. Although there were slight differences in each member country's respective dress regulations, insignia, cultures, customs and religions, the force presented a fairly uniform front. A certain amount of voluntary and compulsory cross-postings, due to such things as promotions and disciplinary matters, served to spread and top-up the fount of knowledge within this global police intelligence network. Kim Bok was completely unaware of all this and having successfully escaped from the British in Malaya, he felt safe high up in the sky away from the war. He would have done better to remember that Hong Kong was a British Colony; but this peaceful environment, the new clothes and the sleep inducing drone of the aircraft engines was lulling him into a false sense of security. Hot food, cool drink and a relaxing cigar encouraged this feeling of euphoria to continue until the plane landed at Hong Kong's Kai Tak airport.

With a sensation akin to walking on air, Kim escorted Fantail across the hot tarmac to the arrivals lounge, a gorgeous young woman wearing a revealing uniform ushered him in from the blinding sunlight. As he passed by her the scent of some exotic perfume full of eastern promise wafted up from her provocative figure and heightened his mood of well-being. Once inside the cool air-conditioned lounge his eyes quickly adjusted to the comparatively dim light within. At this point Kim received a short, sharp shock to his system as his gaze focused on two policemen standing only a few yards in front of him, they were British Colonial Policemen. Like a cornered rat, he froze in his tracks and his eyes swivelled in their sockets looking for an avenue of escape, first he glanced to his left and his heart missed a beat at the sight of two more. Then another pair was registered in his brain as he looked right.

Beads of sweat stood out on his forehead and he feared for the worst; the British had trapped him! *No, not this way,* he prayed silently as sheer panic placed him momentarily back in Malaya, *don't take me here like this.* On the brink of reacting foolishly in a manner that would have compromised them both, he was brought back to reality by a dig in the small of his back. Glancing quickly over his shoulder he looked at Fantail's smiling face. 'Cool it', her hard eyes warned; and suddenly Kim was his old self once more, vigilant and outwardly composed.

Apart from a cursory glance at Kim and an admiring look at Fantail, the police showed no interest in the couple and their passage through customs and immigration went without a hitch. Nevertheless, they both breathed a sigh of relief when they eventually settled into the back seat of a taxi. Kim and the driver settled on Cantonese for their conversation and he soon explained that they required accommodation for two, well away from Kowloon and fairly close to the airport. Beaming with pride, bursting with local knowledge and with moneymaking uppermost in his mind the cabby drove them a very short distance by a circuitous route to a destination only one and a half miles from their starting point.

'Here we are,' he said and parked the cab outside a three-storey building in a bustling little thoroughfare with the far from oriental name of Lomond Road. He introduced them to the woman of the house, the ground floor of which was a café, bar and shop all rolled into one.

Whilst he left Fantail to negotiate a one-week stay in a top floor flat, Kim paid the driver an exorbitant fare, reserved he felt sure, for the more gullible of foreign tourists. As the taxi pulled away and Kim turned to rejoin Fantail, he failed to notice the artful cabby grinning a cheeky farewell to his sister. Unable to restrain a giggle, the good lady ushered the bewildered couple up to the flat that consisted of two rooms, then she left them to it and retreated with a flash of gold teeth gabbling away excitedly in her native Cantonese.

Fantail was delighted with her temporary new home and went about the place fussing over every item. Full of excitement she opened and closed drawers and cupboards, she had nothing to put in them but was thrilled to bits. With childlike glee Fantail operated the main light dimmer switch and the huge overhead fan that vibrated and throbbed away rhythmically, and keeping in time with the sound she danced around the parquet floor for a while until she dived upon the enormous double bed. She switched on the bedside standard lamp to give the windowless room a cosy look, never in all her life had she slept in a room such as this.

Meanwhile, Kim had been exploring the bathroom and had discovered that it was equipped with a shower cubicle. 'Come and see this,' he called and started to undress. Fantail joined him and in no time at all they were standing naked together, trembling with emotion; now fully aroused he looked deep into her eyes asking the unspoken question. The bed won and still jumpy from his earlier lapse of concentration at the airport he took her violently, finding bliss and release in her equally ardent lovemaking. Afterwards they dozed off and had they been able to sleep the night through before venturing out into the real world, the destiny of the Malay Races might have been so very, very, different. But fate decreed otherwise and the two lovers were rudely awakened by the rat-tat-tat staccato signature of automatic gunfire. Shocked to the core and thoroughly disorientated they scrambled off the bed in a blind panic groping futilely for non-existent weapons. Slowly they realised that they were not back in the jungle and struggled to throw off the hazy confusion and focus on their present and unaccustomed surroundings. The fog lifted and they gradually became aware of other sounds that accompanied the warlike racket that had disturbed their sleep, music, laughter and the unmistakable sound of happy children filtered up from the street below.

After years of jungle warfare, of being continually hunted down like animals, Kim and Fantail had forgotten what it was like to be normal human beings. They knelt naked on all fours facing each other and wept tears of relief and frustration for almost an hour before they regained their composure and got dressed.

'It's a wedding,' greeted their hostess as they reached the bottom of the staircase. 'Wait one minute,' she shouted above the din of exploding bangers and firecrackers whilst she cleared a pavement table for them, the good lady beckoned for the couple to come outside and be seated. It was a sultry evening and like everyone else they were soon sweating profusely. Despite the high temperature there was an overriding festive feeling in the air, coloured overhead lighting illuminated the street and an abundance of Chinese lanterns adorned walls and doorways.

The noise was terrific and in addition to the pyrotechnics, the crashing of cymbals and oriental music accompanied the frenzied prancing of roaring dragons as they twisted and turned their way in and out of the excited crowds. And all the time grown-ups cheered and sang whilst children shrieked in mock horror.

'Here, I bring you plenty food,' grinned the kind old lady once more displaying an array of gold teeth, 'more when finished, in with rent.' She giggled and went about her business.

'That woman's got enough gold in her mouth to buy an arsenal,' remarked Kim through a mouthful of chow mein. The food was good and the drink pleasant and strong but after watching the fun for an hour, Fantail suggested that they find somewhere cooler and more secluded to have a drink; Kim agreed and they got up to leave.

'Don't be long, nice bed up there,' shrieked the hostess, cackling her way into the back of the café with apron strings flapping.

Coming out of their flat was a mistake, venturing further afield on that particular night was tantamount to disaster. As they walked out of Lomond Road they would have done well to observe that at least five per cent of the revellers were British. They found a nice air-conditioned bar less than half a mile away from their lodgings and were soon comfortably seated at a window table with an ice-cold San Miguel each, enjoying the soft background music and quiet atmosphere of the place. Quiet, that is, until an argument broke out at the far end of the bar from where Kim and Fantail were sitting, an argument between two Englishmen.

The bar staff were quick off the mark and tried to calm the situation down but tension was in the air and the threat of physical violence was very real. The proprietor was taking no chances and quickly reached for the phone; in no time at all both civilian and military police patrols were on the scene. The fracas was nipped in the bud before it could develop into a full-blown fight and the two men, both off-duty British soldiers, were arrested and taken away immediately by the military police. The incident did not spill over to include the two terrorists and they were not involved in any way, Kim kept his cool this time and showed no sign of nervousness at the close proximity of British authority. On the contrary, he seemed highly amused by the whole affair as he sat watching the Hong Kong Police leaving the bar.

He would not have been so happy had he chanced to look at the police patrol vehicle that was parked outside. From it the driver was scrutinising the couple intently, his gaze fixed more on Fantail than Kim, and not for the obvious reasons either. The policeman could see Fantail almost full faced, and as the seconds ticked by and his colleagues seemed to take forever to rejoin him in the vehicle, the driver became more and more convinced of his suspicions but did not react or reveal his hand. He waited until his patrol commander had instructed him to move on, this he did but only for a distance of two hundred yards before stopping again. 'What the hell do you think you're doing?' barked the seasoned old Corporal eyeing his newly appointed Malay driver with utter disdain.

Constable Ibram Rhamsin who was on a temporary posting from the Federation of Malaya Police Force explained his case vehemently. 'That slut back there in the bar is a communist terrorist, she's a murdering bitch and is a member of the MRLA!'

The long-suffering Corporal considered this outburst with

patient interest. 'How do you know, how can you be sure?' he asked.

'Look, when I did a stint with the Federation Police Field Force her wanted poster was pinned up all over the bloody place,' answered Ibram.

'You've got to really convince me before I can act on this,' urged the NCO.

'Well at one time she served with the MRLA's Third Regiment in Malacca and I've helped chase her pretty little arse all over the stinking jungle in that state.' He went on to describe some of Fantail's exploits during her reign of terror there, 'It's her all right, I'll stake my life on it.'

The highly experienced patrol leader listened carefully; he knew all too well the value of observations from the streetwise rank and file. He studied the earnest face of Ibram Rhamsin and the Malayan Campaign medal ribbon he wore so proudly on his chest. 'Decisions, decisions,' he muttered as he made up his mind and grabbed his radio handset. 'Hello Zero, this is Mike Papa 146 message over.' In a matter of minutes his information was being considered by his superiors at police headquarters and by Special Branch in particular. Within an hour, two Special Branch officers were enjoying a drink only a table away from the suspects, whilst another pair kept station in a car just across the street from the bar. Later that night the undercover men tailed the couple to their Lomond Road flat where observation posts were set up to watch the building and quick reaction squads were placed on immediate standby in case the quarry should make a move. By midnight the Paymaster General of the much feared MRLA and his murdering female companion were boxed in by Hong Kong Police surveillance experts. It was the end of a day; a day in which Constable Ibram Rhamsin earned a feather in his cap and the first nail was hammered home in the terrorists' coffins.

The primary task of the Special Branch men was to establish beyond doubt the true identity of the two suspects. They needed good quality photographs to compare with existing ones being sent out from Malaya with detailed descriptions. The surveillance team were contemplating on how to obtain this clear evidence when a golden opportunity was handed to them on a plate by a combination of pure chance and the arrival at Lomond Road of a British Army truck.

The chance came at 07.45 hrs in the form of Kim and Fantail finding a staircase that led up to a sunroof, giving the couple a heaven-sent opportunity to shake off the cobwebs by taking their morning coffee in the fresh air. The building was directly under the flight path of aircraft approaching Kai Tak airport and they stood watching the awesome spectacle of planes roaring low over the rooftops before landing a mile or so away.

The Special Branch men were hopping around in frustration, 'Look at that,' one of them muttered, 'we have the luck to get them out in the open and they face the other way.' But lady luck was still on the side of the righteous and materialised in the shape of a British Army three-ton troop-carrying truck that drove into Lomond Road and screeched to a halt half way along it, a regular occurrence that took place every weekday at 08.00 hrs. The two terrorists had good reason to fear the unmistakable signature of British military vehicles and the sound of one behind them was enough to send them scurrying to the edge of the roof to investigate. They looked furtively over the parapet expecting to see armed troops leaping from the truck but to their astonishment all they saw was a dozen smartly dressed and unarmed soldiers emerging from several of the buildings.

The men checked in with the driver who ticked them off a list before they all boarded the vehicle, soldiers waved farewell to wives and children and the truck was driven off. In order to see all this Kim and Fantail had presented their faces full on to the hidden watchers, the Special Branch cameras clicked and whirred as they captured the suspects on film in classic poses that would have done any professional portrait photographer proud. As for Kim, well he was kicking himself as he realised that out of the thousands of safe dwelling places available to him in crowded Hong Kong he had chosen an area full of family quarters hired out to members of the British Armed Forces.

By midday on the first day of August 1957 the combined efforts of the Hong Kong and Malay Police Forces had positively identified Fantail as the wanted terrorist Constable Ibram Rhamsin suspected her of being. But what really set the wires humming between the two countries was the revelation that her companion was none other than the terrorist organisation's Paymaster General, Kim Bok.

Where paymasters tread the earth money must be close at hand. What had started out as a small observation assignment now escalated into a full-scale surveillance operation. A special task force was set up to keep track of the terrorists in order to determine what their mission was in Hong Kong.

20.30 hrs the same day saw the arrival in Hong Kong of Inspector Tom Nobles of the Malay Police Special Branch, an anti-terrorist expert who was familiar with the case files of both suspects. He was to head the investigation and give it some much needed continuity. He was charged with the responsibility of watching the targets in the hope that they would lead him to bigger fish or unwittingly reveal the true purpose of their visit. His orders from Malaya had been simple, find out at all costs what these two animals are up to in Hong Kong. 'After all,' had been the closing comment from Tom's boss, 'it shouldn't be too difficult to catch them at it, they must be feeling like fish out of water over there.'

Under the watchful eye of Tom Nobles, the plot quickly unfolded with Fantail doing the initial legwork. That night she left the Lomond Road flat and made her way to the waterfront area of Kowloon. Although far removed from her native Malacca she was in her element amongst the seafaring people, their vessels and the bustling harbour-side taverns, shops and whorehouses. In contrast to being like a fish out of water the woman proved to be very difficult to follow and led the watchers a merry dance. She glided effortlessly in and out of the many bars and parlours searching for someone or something, finally after two hours of pub crawling, she latched on to a very young-looking seaman. In no time at all Fantail had the boy eating out of her hand and was practically raping him in public; even the hardened watchers were getting worried about possible reactions from the onlookers to this outrageous behaviour, but the sixteen-year-old youth solved the problem for them all. He had become so worked up that his shorts were bulging at the seams, red faced with embarrassment and with more than a fair share of youthful lust he dragged Fantail along the quayside to his ship that happened to be an ocean-going junk with the sweet sounding name of *Sea Pearl*. The goings on aboard the vessel that night can only be assumed but it was Tom's guess that Fantail probably seduced the young fellow in order to inveigle her way on board the ship for some nefarious reason connected with her task in Hong Kong. Anyway, her ploy must have worked because she came ashore the next morning arm in arm with several other members of the crew in tow.

Meanwhile, Kim had kept a low profile back at the Lomond Road location. For three days Fantail flaunted her femininity and granted sexual favours to most of the crew, gradually she ingratiated herself into the actual ship's company as a cook; once she was on the Captain's payroll, and often as not in his bed, she changed tack. After a particularly athletic bout of lovemaking, Fantail subtly alluded to a conversation that she had supposedly overheard in a bar earlier that day, it concerned a man's interest in hiring an ocean-going vessel for a delicate mission abroad. Bringing all her feminine wiles into play, she cunningly contrived to turn the Captain's thoughts to making money, not a difficult task given that he was a merchant. Fantail accomplished her mission in such fine style that she promoted the Captain's vanity to rise to the fore and he assumed full credit for the whole idea of hiring out his vessel to a completely unknown businessman. 'This fellow,' said the exhausted skipper, 'go and find him again, and please don't lose him this time.'

Fantail could hardly suppress a giggle as she thought, *sucker,* but said very sweetly, 'I'll try not to.'

On the fourth day Fantail returned to Lomond Road, leaving again after an hour accompanied by Kim Bok who was carrying a briefcase. The couple proceeded to Kowloon and then boarded the *Sea Pearl* where it must be assumed that Kim and the Captain came to some amicable agreement because after only a short time Kim Bok left the vessel minus his briefcase. He went back to the lodgings where he settled up, collected his gear and departed from there for good. By early evening he was back on board the *Sea Pearl* as a fully paid up merchant with a signed contract, a contract that authorised the captain to take on a cargo of toys, sculptures and brass-work from the port of Macau.

Hong Kong can be likened to a huge abacus board with each bead representing a faction of the community. When everyone has contributed to the coffers the sum total of the vast amount of collected wealth is Hong Kong itself. Outsiders do not normally come into the calculation, but income extracted from them is counted as a bonus. If you wish to do business in the colony it is wise to seek approval through the clearing houses of the Tongs, it is a way of life in Hong Kong that nobody gets carried, all have to pay their dues. Fantail's exploits had not gone unnoticed by the evil controllers of organised crime, at first it was thought that she was merely trying to make a fast buck by selling her body without paying a fee through her pimp, a crime punishable by facial disfigurement. When it became clear that she did not even have a pimp and that she was servicing only one particular ship's crew they began to suspect that there was more to this caper that meets the eye. The now angry Tong bosses decided to keep a close watch on the junk, and from the very start of their own operation it was glaringly obvious to them that they were not on their own and it did not need a genius to work out who their adversaries were. It has already been mentioned that everyone has to pay into this teeming community and the public services were no exception. Informers were everywhere and reached even into the hallowed halls of the Colonial Police Force allowing the Tongs access to very sensitive information; it took but a matter of minutes to confirm who the other interested parties were.

The cat was out of the bag, the Tongs and Special Branch watched each other as they both observed the *Sea Pearl* for any clue as to what was going on. The ship's captain had not filed any sailing instructions with the harbour authorities yet, so both surveillance teams were expecting the vessel to take on a cargo prior to departure, if that were the intention of those on board.

On the morning of the fifth day they were all caught with their trousers down when suddenly the ship's crew appeared on deck and quickly prepared the vessel for sea. The watchers listening to radio traffic on VHF scanners heard the captain informing the harbour office that he was sailing for Macau immediately, giving them a list of his intended cargo at the same time. A minute later the *Sea Pearl* slipped out of the harbour under the power of twin diesel engines presenting an incongruous picture as she roared away more like a fast patrol boat than an ancient Chinese junk. Apart from an initial bout of panic induced by the sudden departure of the vessel, the Tongs were not greatly worried because they knew the *Sea Pearl's* destination. The evil and dreaded secret society ruled the roost wherever a Chinese community could be found, and Macau was no exception; they had ample time to alert their eyes and ears in the gambling Mecca of the East.

For the Special Branch though it was a different matter, they could not just move a British Police operation into a Portuguese possession. Although Britain enjoyed a certain level of diplomatic licence with the Macau Police, it was not enough to justify barnstorming in brandishing the British Colonial stick; no, the old gunboat diplomacy would not do in this case and a more subtle approach was necessary. The British dipped into their diplomatic bag and called in a few favours from influential people in high places within the Macau government administration. MI6 agents, already in place, were given extra latitude in organising a watch on the land frontier between China and Macau, and the great seaport itself.

To assist their man in Macau, the British sent out an MI6 agent from Malaya, his name was Jeremy Fairburne-Snape of the Foreign Office. Jeremy worked out of Flag House in Kuala Lumpur as a Second Consular Official, he was an expert on the upper echelons of the MRLA and au fait with all things to do with Malacca and the female terrorist named Fantail.

The stage was set, in the gambling capitol that is Macau, rich men chanced their luck in the casinos whilst the Tongs and MI6 played their own dangerous game in the shadowy world outside.

The *Sea Pearl* had departed from Hong Kong at 06.30 hrs and it would take about twelve hours for her to complete the voyage to Macau. During that time, Jeremy Fairburne-Snape had made the rapid move to Macau in an Air force Canberra jet bomber, giving him plenty of time to talk with Tom Nobles over the telephone. Naturally the topic of their conversation was Kim Bok's motive for hiring the junk and they both came to the same conclusion. Considering Kim Bok's position as Paymaster

General and Fantail's extraordinary behaviour on his behalf that cleared the way for him to hire the vessel, it was pretty obvious that finance was the aim of the exercise and that money in some form or other would be included in the cargo. In that part of the world the kind of money that talked the most was gold. Ingots, although heavy, were small enough to be easily concealed; it was also conceivable that the gold could be disguised amongst the brass-work mentioned by the captain to the Hong Kong harbour master.

The *Sea Pearl* docked alongside a bonded warehouse under the cover of darkness at six that evening. Kim Bok disembarked immediately the junk was tied up. He did not leave the quayside, but waited until a chauffeur-driven Mercedes arrived and the leader's man in Macau joined him; he was known only as Chang. They conferred for a while before the chauffeur opened a warehouse and Chang took Kim Bok inside, presumably to conclude some business.

As if by magic, the quay was suddenly swarming with coolies and a couple of mobile cranes chugged up to the *Sea Pearl*. The crew had opened her hatch covers and soon the cargo was being loaded, observed all the time from the murky shadows by the eagle eyes of the British Secret Service and the dreaded Tongs. The ship's hold was small in comparison with the more conventional ocean-going cargo vessels but it seemed like a bottomless pit as crate after crate was lowered into its depths; boxes of toys by the hundreds, dozens of marble statues and huge brass ornaments went aboard. All seemed to be going well when it became obvious that even the experienced stevedores had hit a snag. They were finding it difficult to handle about a dozen boxes that had been lowered onto the deck but not into the hold. These particular containers that were roughly three feet square were obviously destined for another part of the ship and should not have presented the wiry dock-men with any problems. But despite much huffing and puffing, heaving and shoving, they made painfully slow progress and at one point threatened to down tools completely. Amidst all the excited, frantic shouting and gesticulating, only the cool, quiet intervention of the skipper averted a major incident and by midnight the cargo had been squared away. But the commotion had served to focus the attention of the watchers onto the heavy boxes, inflaming the imagination of the Tongs and confirming the suspicions of the British. Had they been able to confer on the subject they would probably have agreed on one supposition, the boxes in question must contain gold.

At 06.00 hrs on 6 August 1957 the captain of the *Sea Pearl* submitted his cargo manifest to the Macau port authorities declaring Singapore as the ship's destination. Two hours later the vessel sailed with Fantail still on board as a crew member.

Kim Bok did not sail with her, he was taken to Macau airport where he boarded Chang's executive *Fokker Friendship* that took off immediately for Hong Kong; there he transferred to the next available flight for Bangkok, where he rejoined the two awaiting couriers.

Despite the excellent assistance received by the British from the Thai Police, they lost sight of Kim Bok and his two companions sometime during his train journey from Bangkok to Kota Bahru, in Malaya.

Jeremy Fairburne-Snape and Tom Nobles met and compared notes at the Hong Kong Police Headquarters before they too did some travelling, flying directly to Kuala Lumpur where they presented their findings to the Government and the Chiefs of the General Staff.

Chapter Four

Field Marshal Colin Petherington, Chief of the General Staff in Malaya, looked around the conference table at the assembled members of his hastily convened extraordinary staff meeting. 'I have gone through the reports written up by MI6 and Special Branch regarding recent events that have taken place in Hong Kong and Macau,' he said. Nodding at Jeremy Fairburne-Snape and Tom Nobles he added, 'Well done both of you.'

'Thank you sir,' they acknowledged in unison.

The Field Marshal tapped out a drum roll on the tabletop with his fingers before he continued. 'Although there is no concrete evidence to go on, I accept that there is reason to believe that the enemy will attempt to smuggle in financial aid, probably in the form of gold bullion?' He paused; his piercing blue eyes making contact with every officer in the room. 'And that ties in nicely with another theory we have concerning a possible escalation of hostilities. I'll let Harry explain that particular snippet to you,' he finished, handing over the stage to Colonel Henry Blunt of General Staff Intelligence.

Harry, a wizened old veteran of the Northwest Frontier, Burma and the Malayan Campaigns, cleared his throat and waved a document in the air. 'This thing,' he announced, 'is a directive issued by the Communist Central Military Committee, a directive ordering the guerrillas to hole up and keep a low profile; hence the unusually quiet spell we are enjoying at the moment. This missive is a subtle piece of work that was obviously leaked out for our benefit. In the vaguest of terms it suggests that a ceasefire and possible surrender talks are on the cards.' Harry paused abruptly.

'But you don't believe it?' quickly questioned the Air Marshal.

'The lull in hostilities is an undisputed fact,' answered Harry, 'but in the light of Jeremy and Tom's report I think that the directive is nothing but a ploy, an attempt at misinforming us. We are meant to call off the hounds whilst they rest and reorganise knowing full well that hard cash is on the way in.'

'And this surrender caper?' queried the Commander of the Naval Forces with a raised eyebrow.

'Not a chance Admiral, oh, they'll commence the proceedings for a ceasefire all right; maybe it will result in talks between the Prime Minister and their top people. But I'll bet my bottom dollar that their plan is to lull us into a false sense of security before they hit us with everything they've got. I know these bastards, they have the patience of Jove and they're playing for time.'

Harry looked pointedly at Tom Nobles. 'I agree entirely,' offered the highly experienced Special Branch Officer.

'Where do you think they'll land the gold?' asked the Field Marshal, after all, I can't see them sticking to the destination declared on the ship's manifest, Singapore, can you?'

'No bloody way,' answered Harry. 'But I have a hunch about all this,' he stated as he walked over to a huge wall-map of Malaya. All eyes were on this man now, when Harry got a hunch it normally meant that the shit was about to hit the fan. He was a legend and had spent his early subaltern years commanding his infantry Platoon up and down the Khyber Pass skirmishing with the fierce Afghan tribesmen. As a Company Commander he found himself defending India's border against the Japanese during the Second World War. In the British advance through Burma he made a name for himself as a tough Chindit fighter with Slim's Fourteenth Army. For the last year of the war, Major (Crazy) Harry Blunt served behind the enemy lines in Malaya with the SOE. At the beginning of the current Malayan campaign he commanded the reformed SAS Regiment. If anyone was capable of getting into the minds of the Chinese Communist Terrorists it was Crazy Harry.

Picking up a pointer he swept it down the West Coast side of the map like a demented swordsman, 'This is out,' he barked. 'Too damned busy and the natives are getting restless and very anti-CT in those developed areas. Besides, to get there they would have to risk running the gauntlet through this lot,' he remarked, slashing across the Strait of Singapore which was a bottleneck for sea traffic.

'Which leaves us with the East Coast,' observed the Admiral.

'Thank Christ we've got a navy,' blurted out Harry, forgetting for a moment to whom he was talking; which explains why this brilliant soldier had been shunted into the sidings as a full Colonel. 'I have a gut feeling that they'll come in through here,' his pointer lunged into the centre of a string of islands stretching twenty miles both north and south of Mersing, a small fishing town in the southern state of Johore. 'It's a good target to aim for and there are a dozen places where they could hide a junk, even the Navy could lose a fleet in there.'

A warning cough from the Admiral brought Harry back on course; and the Field Marshal broke in with a question. 'Ships,' he invited the Admiral, 'how long will it take them to reach those islands?'

'About fourteen days,' came the answer after the old sea dog had done some sums, 'the estimated time of arrival of the largest of them, *Palau Tioman*, will be sometime on 19 August. She's been sailing for two days now so we have twelve days' leeway.'

Petherington gestured for Harry to continue. 'I reckon that Kim Bok did not board the *Sea Pearl* at Macau because he's needed back here in Malaya to organise the reception party and lead the bullion column inland. I think he jumped the train just before the border crossing and is making his way down the East Coast. Remember, the locals living on this bloody awful coastline are very susceptible to terrorism and all that it entails. How and exactly where he'll bring the gold ashore is anyone's guess but the CTs will be very limited in their scope of operations. I know this area well from my SOE days, and don't forget this; so does our friend Kim Bok.' Harry paused for a drink of water. 'Mersing is a small fishing village really with only one road leading into it. I say road, but it's made of nothing more than hard packed mud and chipped stone with the jungle growing right up to the edges, not a proper highway by any stretch of the imagination. And, gentlemen, the road stops at the town because Mersing is a road head.'

'That's the road from Kluang, isn't it?' enquired Tom Nobles.

'Correct, there's roughly sixty miles of it with only four tiny Kampongs along the way. To the north and south of Mersing are miles of impenetrable mangrove swamps; you couldn't do better if you got the Sappers to lay a minefield. There are beaches where small vessels such as sampans can be landed, but sooner or later the gold will have to be manhandled around the immediate outskirts of Mersing, and eventually the one and only road will come into play.' Crazy Harry took a deep breath. 'Even if they do an SAS trick and drive the bloody junk right up to the fishing quay, the Mersing-Kluang road is the key to a quick getaway from the landing point.'

'Getaway to where?' prompted the Admiral.

'Ah!' the old soldier parried, 'that's where my hunch comes in. During the world war I helped these people to set up a courier route that ran the entire length of the country, it's my belief that the CTs are at this very moment reactivating this route in order to transport the gold to a safe place. So gentlemen, whilst we sit on our fat arses watching the soldiers doing endless bloody drill parades because we gullibly believe that the enemy are suing for peace; their troops will be taking advantage of the finest line of communication that I have ever heard tell of.'

'But surely we have the advantage now,' challenged the Air Marshal.

Crazy Harry looked up at the ceiling in horror and prayed to Allah for deliverance. 'The problem is, I don't know the exact location of the courier route but at the risk of sounding Irish, I know where it bloody well isn't. Somewhere between these two places,' his pointer stabbed at Kluang and Mersing. 'This small road is bisected by the old trail; Kim Bok knows where it is, and that gives him the advantage, sir.'

'Touché,' conceded the Air Marshal.

The Colonel plunged into a mass of military intelligence; facts and figures were expounded upon until the assemblage of top brass had a fairly comprehensive idea of where the enemy courier route was thought to be. 'I apologise for harping on about this,' laboured Crazy Harry, pointing once more at the lateral road between Mersing and Kluang. 'But I really do think we need a total commitment in this area or we'll bloody well lose the bastards together with the gold. Moving the gold along that stretch of highway will be most hazardous for them, but it's a short run and they'll go for it; Kim Bok will go hell for leather until he can disappear into the jungle.'

There was a long pause then with a wry smile the Field Marshal asked, 'Where do you think they'll take the gold?'

'Into their main camp somewhere in Central Pahang where they can melt it down in one of their armouries into small negotiable lumps,' came the astonishingly simple answer.

Petherington, who, above all others in the room knew the true value of this eccentric old soldier prompted, 'That's quite a long haul, and a difficult one considering the heavy load of gold ingots?' a raised eyebrow invited a response.

'I'm guessing that he'll use mules and perhaps elephants, man-packing is an option but he'll have to draw heavily on the CT's 9th Central Johore Regiment for that and time is against him there. They have no radio communications set-up to speak of, and their right hand doesn't know what the left one is doing half of the time. The bush telegraph will come into play once Kim Bok appears back on the scene but good organisation will be difficult to achieve. It might take them a little time to get their act together; but of one thing you can be sure, once these tenacious bastards get to know that the gold is on the way they'll fight like hell to keep it.' Crazy Harry smiled and squared his shoulders, 'But they're not going to get it, are they, sir?'

'No Harry, they damn well aren't,' stated the Field Marshal with absolute conviction. 'Gentlemen, this is my plan.'

By the end of that day, 7 August 1957, a signal went out to the British Air Force base in Hong Kong. They were given the responsibility of carrying out high altitude surveillance of the junk *Sea Pearl*; their limit of exploitation was a position due west of Da Nang in Vietnam. From that point onwards, aircraft from Air Force bases in Malaya would cover the vessel.

The next day, British Commandos embarked aboard several warships from the Naval Base in Singapore. By the ninth, they had been secretly put ashore to occupy observation posts on the islands off Mersing; a headquarters unit was landed on Palau Sribuat. Three frigates were deployed to patrol a screening area 100 miles northeast of that island.

The tenth of August saw the deployment of two Gurkha rifle battalions to covertly watch the sixty-odd miles of road between Kluang and Mersing. At the same time the Commonwealth Brigade was committed to the jungles of North and Central Johore, two Battalions to ambush the area immediately east of the railway line from Kluang to Segamat, with the third Battalion held in reserve as a rapid reaction force.

On the twelfth the responsibility for watching the *Sea Pearl* switched to Air Force Squadrons based in Malaya as the vessel sailed serenely past Da Nang completely unaware that she was the focus of so much attention.

These preliminary moves in the military chess game were completed when the SAS Squadron was parachuted into South Pahang on 15 August 1957.

The plan was simple, the gold shipment was to be allowed into the country and the enemy force followed in the hope that they might lead the British to the main CT camp, which was also thought to be the headquarters of the Central Military Committee. The Gurkha Rifles watching the Mersing-Kluang road would receive ample warning of the enemy's approach from the commandos manning the island observation posts. Once the Gurkhas had picked up the trail they would monitor the terrorists' movements to the courier route, at which point a follow-up operation would be mounted. The tough men from Nepal were to track the communists northwards to their long concealed lair; leaving ambush positions in their wake to catch and silence any enemy couriers that might be using the old trail from the south. The mission of the Commonwealth Brigade was to block off any escape routes in a westerly direction should anything go wrong with the Gurkhas' extremely difficult task. The thick mangrove swamps would deter the CTs from fleeing eastwards but should some of them succeed in reaching the coastline, the commandos would cut them to pieces. The SAS drop was a far-sighted attempt to locate the hiding place of the Central Military Committee well in advance of the Gurkha operation. This was for two reasons. Planning was the first; it would take up much valuable time to plan and execute an attack on the scale envisaged by the Field Marshal. If they had to rely on the enemy gold column to lead them in, the wily foe might well move on whilst the attack deployment was taking place. The second reason was that if the enemy column got the slightest inkling that the British were pursuing them they would abort the operation as such and the camp would probably never be found. Should the SAS be successful they were to carry out a close reconnaissance of the enemy dispositions and then act as guides to lead in the assault troops.

The trap was set, whilst the SAS began the arduous and painstaking job of detecting the slightest signs of enemy activity in the rugged area thought to conceal the hub of terrorism in Malaya, the rest watched and waited.

The British though had overlooked a major player in this dangerous game, the Tongs. During the Field Marshal's staff meeting at Flag House in Kuala Lumpur, a passing reference had been made to them. Special Branch in Hong Kong and MI6 in Macau had noticed them, of course. But the consensus of opinion, except for Crazy Harry that is, was that once the cargo of gold had sailed clear of Hong Kong and Macau territorial waters, the Tongs would drop out of the chase; 'Not so,' had been Harry's last word on the matter; he was right.

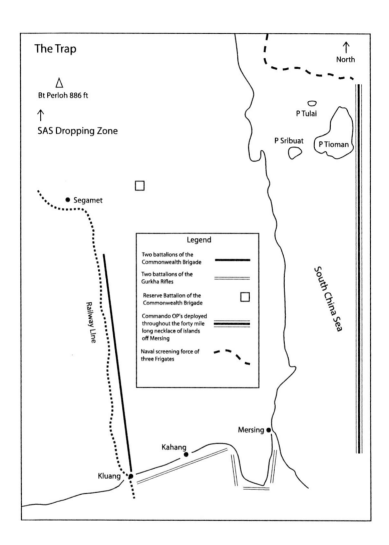

The Trap

△
Bt Perloh 886 ft

↑
SAS Dropping Zone

● Segamet

P Tulai

P Sribuat

P Tioman

South China Sea

Railway Line

Legend

Two battalions of the Commonwealth Brigade	▬▬▬
Two battalions of the Gurkha Rifles	═══
Reserve Battalion of the Commonwealth Brigade	☐
Commando OP's deployed throughout the forty mile long necklace of islands off Mersing	▬▬▬
Naval screening force of three Frigates	▬ ▬ ▬

Mersing ●

Kahang ●

Kluang ●

↑
North

The all seeing, far-reaching Tongs had not given up and were not likely to as long as there was the slightest chance of them getting their hands on solid gold. They did not have the resources of the Hong Kong and Malay Governments, nor were they privy to information regarding the British military operation currently being set up in Malaya. But they did have some feelers into the Hong Kong police and had come up with the name of the female terrorist, Fantail, and her connection with the port of Malacca; a location where the Tongs had considerable business interests. They immediately jumped to a conclusion and unlike the British were of the opinion that Fantail would take the cargo of precious metal through the Strait of Singapore and into the ancient seaport of Malacca itself. Despite the fact that nobody involved in the huge surveillance operation in Hong Kong and Macau had actually seen the gold, they did not doubt for one minute that it was on board the *Sea Pearl*. After all, they could not imagine the British devoting so much time and effort on mere peanuts.

The Tongs' business interests in Malacca were left very much in the capable hands of a local criminal and gangland boss of long standing, Mr Lin Tan. It was through him that the Tongs believed that they would eventually succeed in tracking down and stealing the gold bullion.

Mr Lin Tan was a native of Malacca; he was born in 1927 of Chinese parents who came from the South China Sea island of Hainan. The people of Hainan have provided Malaya with an excellent stock of shopkeepers, domestic servants and small-scale planters since the Napoleonic wars when the western trade routes were opened up and the British commenced their rule of the Malay states. The Hainan islanders are well-bred and proud people but every society has its fair share of misfits and failures, Mr Lin Tan was one of them. He did not follow in his father's honourable footsteps. Perhaps, this was because he was in his early teens when the Japanese invaded, overran and occupied Malaya during the Second World War, an event that changed the lives of millions of people. The boy had survived those terrible years and when it had seemed that peace had at last arrived for good, the country once more erupted into violence as the Communist powers tried to wrest control of Malaya from the

British. Whatever the reasons, Mr Tan had turned to crime dragging his younger brother with him. He had been only twenty-one years old when the Communist Terrorists had began their violent onslaught in 1948. Even so, he was soon climbing the ladder of success to reap the harvest from the black market trading that runs rife in any theatre of war. Mr Tan was good at his job; he was respected by his fellow criminals and trusted by the Tongs. Two important factors that earned him rapid promotion within the ranks of the underworld; now in the year of 1957 he was a rich man and the undisputed boss of the Malacca riverside gangs.

Compared with the Chinese Tongs of which he was not a member, merely a tool, he was small fry but still a force to be reckoned with and a valuable asset to them. Like all rich men, Mr Tan craved to increase his wealth. He was greedy and the very thought of losing a source of income was enough to send him into a panic-ridden frenzy. Mr Tan was facing just such a crisis now, a problem caused by two separate sets of circumstances. The first was the relentless pressure against the Communist Terrorists by the British Army and the Federation of Malaya Police Force; this was seriously hampering his movement of contraband goods out of the Port of Malacca. Also, road blocks and control points were preventing his gangs from carrying out the lucrative business of hijacking lorries.

Lin Tan looked out of his third-floor office window at the potpourri of faces streaming to and fro like ants below. He thought about the second cause for his anxiety; it was the sad fact that he would never again see his brother's face amongst them because he was dead, a victim of a terrorist ambush. This personal loss was proving difficult to come to terms with, but much harder to bear was the loss of income from his late brother's smuggling operation in nearby Port Dickson. Mr Tan was fed up with the British Army; angry over his brother's murder and very worried, for although he had profited from the spoils of the war being conducted by them he had never become directly involved with the terrorist movement. But with the recent murder of his brother, all that was about to change because Mr Tan had two things on his mind now, money and revenge; he was pondering over the latter when his phone rang.

He picked up the receiver and listened to the caller intently for a full five minutes with a look of utter disbelief on his face; then sputtering an inarticulate form of acknowledgement, he hung up completely dumbfounded. It was as if his prayers had been answered; the caller was none other than the Tong mandarin of all Malaya. He had given Mr Tan strict instructions to be on the lookout for a specific cargo believed to be on its way to Malacca by sea, the estimated time of arrival being in roughly three weeks. The actual word gold was not mentioned but the perceptive old crook was no fool and knew good news when he heard it. He was also aware that he would never get his hands on the hard stuff but it was an odds-on certainty that his cut would be a considerable amount. Mr Lin Tan made some phone calls to alert his army of informers amongst the rank and file of the Malacca political, industrial and public services; one such service being the Police Force.

When finished, he glanced up at his ornate wall clock, it was a quarter to twelve. *A little early for lunch,* he thought, *but under the present circumstances I might as well combine business with pleasure and have a trip out.* Lin Tan inspected his handsome appearance in a full length mirror, at five feet six inches tall he cut a compact and dashing figure dressed as he was in a light blue sharkskin suit with a matching shirt and dark blue tie. He picked up his black ebony stick with its silver knob and ferrule, then made his way outside to his blue Mercedes car; his stick and black patent leather shoes flashed in the sunlight and caught the eyes of passers-by.

He took the coast road to a village seven miles north of Malacca called Kampong Masjid Tanet, the Kampong had recently been declared safe from communist influence and the security barriers and gates that had surrounded the place for years had been removed. Although military and police patrols were still very much in evidence, Lin Tan had an uneventful journey. On arriving at the outskirts of the village he paused outside the police station for a second to sound his car horn three times. He then drove on until he came to a breeze-block and tin sheet construction that served as a bar and mah-jong parlour. Masjid Tanet was a predominately Malay village but this particular pleasure centre had been diplomatically reserved for the Chinese workers from a nearby rubber plantation. Lin Tan was a regular visitor to the bar and the wily clientele were aware of his underworld activities, but this knowledge was never reflected in their inscrutable faces. Besides, the gangland boss always left a drink for the house before he left, and was kind and generous to the many children who crowded around his car.

Mr Tan spoke softly to the proprietor who ushered him into a private room at the rear of the premises; a waitress laid a table for two and took Lin's order for a curry dish and some ice-cold Anchor beer. Then the arch villain settled back in his chair to await the arrival of his visitor.

Sergeant Abdul Hassan of the Federation of Malaya Police Force marched out of his police station looking as smart as a button stick, inwardly though, he was not feeling as proud as his immaculate turnout suggested. Abdul had done well to make the rank of Sergeant at the age of twenty-six with only eight years service under his belt. As he strode purposefully through his home village of Kampong Masjid Tanet, he reflected on that short but eventful period of his life.

He had been an adventurous boy with the blood of his fierce ancestors coursing through his veins; they had been firstly Malay sea-gypsies living as fishermen and then later with the eastward advance of Indian commerce, pirates. The fuel was there like a fire waiting to be kindled. His chance came in 1948 when the Malayan Emergence had begun and the Chinese Communist Terrorists went berserk, blowing up tin mines, slashing rubber trees and killing workers. Abdul had rallied to the call and volunteered for service with the Home Guard. He would never forget that day when together with six other young men of his Kampong, he had lined up for inspection by a Malay Police Sergeant. The man was smart and resplendent in his distinctive khaki drill uniform that was topped with a magnificent bush hat similar to those worn by Australian troops. That day Abdul fell in love with that hat, he just simply had to have one. He worked hard until he was eighteen, taking part in minor Home Guard operations against the enemy and protecting his Kampong from attack and brutal attempts at intimidation. On his eighteenth birthday he asked his parents if he could join the Police Force. They could barely afford the loss of his labour on their small farming and fishing business and because his mother was ill his father had become dependant on Abdul's youthful strength to eke out a living. But in the end his parents gave way to that great Malay characteristic, pride, and gave Abdul their blessing.

Within days he was called up and went off to become Constable Abdul Hassan, a success story so far but not for long. After his basic training he was posted to Malacca where he found himself patrolling the tough riverside area. There, in the most volatile part of the great seaport he made many friends but unfortunately for him, the wrong kind of friends. As his mother's condition got worse and his father had to neglect the business in order to care for her, debt reared its ugly head and the father had to turn to his son for help. Not wishing to let down his parents in their hour of need Abdul did something that no policeman should ever dream of doing, he borrowed money; to make matters worse he borrowed it off the underworld con men that he should never have made friends with in the first place. Constable Abdul Hassan, the upstanding model policeman, was well and truly hooked. He was prompt with the offer of his first repayment but his so-called friends waved him off saying that there was no urgency; they failed to inform the naïve young fool that the interest on his loan was already rocketing sky high. Within four months he was hopelessly in debt and forever in the clutches of the crooks headed by a character named Mr Lin Tan. Over the years they had used Abdul's position of trust for gain, nothing big mind you, but enough to keep themselves well informed and that one important step ahead of the law; to them Abdul was nothing more than an early warning system.

The man in question flicked some dust from his uniform with his swagger cane, adjusted his beloved bush hat and entered the mah-jong parlour by the back door; he was greeted by a waitress and conducted into the august presence of Mr Lin Tan.

'Sit down my good friend,' greeted Lin, 'I have news that could benefit us both but let's eat first.' He smiled, indicating the loaded table.

They were half way through the meal before Mr Tan explained the situation to his companion, holding back nothing including his thoughts about the gold. He had a soft spot for this likeable policeman and when he had been posted back to the village of his birth as Station Sergeant, Lin had actually cleared all the man's debts. He still controlled the reins with thinly veiled threats of exposure, not to the authorities but to Abdul's father who was blissfully unaware of the situation.

'You see my boy,' continued Mr Tan, 'the information that I require concerns military operations being carried out against communist forces in the Malacca area.' He paused to let his statement sink in. 'If my Tong friends know about the existence of this fortune then it follows that the British must be on the track of it too. If that is the case their operations in Malacca will be a pointer for both the landing place and the approximate time of arrival.'

'Well I'm not so sure about all this,' retorted Abdul looking decidedly worried. The gangster, mistaking his friend's concern as a reluctance to get involved in British Army operations butted in, 'Look at it this way, by hurting the terrorists you will in a way be doing your duty as a member of the security forces. At the same time the information will help me avenge my brother's death and all this will bring you financial gain. You can't lose man.'

Abdul was getting quite agitated now and his frantic attempts to get a word in edgeways had been reduced to an inarticulate splutter that sprayed grains of rice over his host. Mr Tan seemed unperturbed by this disgusting display of table manners as he took a swig of his beer; he would let Abdul mull the subject over for a while. But the policeman had found his voice at last. 'Mr Tan,' he fairly shouted, 'you don't have to explain all that to me because I'm more than willing to help you. It's just that I've got news for you too, I was going to call you when I heard you sounding your car horn on the way in.'

'News, what news, boy?'

'Before I answer that question let me point out that there is hardly any military activity going on in the whole of Malacca, the odd internal security patrol with a road block thrown in here and there; it's almost as if they're having a rest. If the British do think the stuff is coming in through the Port of Malacca then they are playing it pretty cool, but,' the policeman paused to avail himself of a drink.

'But what?' prompted Mr Tan, his shifty eyes lighting up.

'But there is something big going on in Pahang and Johore, my source says that they're pouring thousands of troops into the area and they've dropped some SAS blokes into the jungle. Marines and the Navy have been drafted in as well.'

'Normally,' answered Mr Tan, 'that sort of information wouldn't be of much use to me, it being outside of my patch so to speak.' He looked sharply at Abdul. 'Why would you want to contact me about that, what's the connection, boy?'

'The connection is the female terrorist we all know as Fantail, she's forever linked with Malacca and the British are committing whole brigades in order to catch her.'

'Bloody hell,' was all that Mr Tan could manage to say.

Abdul looked furtively around the room frightened that the walls might have ears. 'I think,' he whispered, 'that the Tongs have got it wrong. The gold, if that is what it is, is not coming our way at all.' Mr Tan's face had turned as white as a sheet at the thought of having to tell the Tongs about that. Abdul's information on its own was but a useful snippet, something that might come in handy at a later date, but combined with what the Tong Chief had told him, it became a prime item of intelligence. In the light of what Abdul had said, Mr Tan urgently needed to talk with his Tong masters, it would be a very dangerous meeting indeed; they might kill him for doubting their judgement concerning the entry point of the mysterious shipment. On the other hand if he failed to inform them of Abdul's news and they found out later from some other source they would definitely kill him. Mr Tan shuddered at the thought as he spoke to Abdul. 'Your source didn't mention anything about gold?'

'Not once.'

'Right, I'm going to the Tongs with what we've got so far; I want you to get on to your mole, he must find out if all these troop movements are in any way connected with this expected cargo of gold.' Mr Tan brought the luncheon meeting to a close.

As he drove out of the village he wondered who Abdul's source of information was, it had not seemed of much importance before now, but given the calibre of the latest communication; the man, or woman, must have access to people in very high places.

Abdul marched back to the police station and immediately shut himself into his office telling the duty constable that he was not to be disturbed. Picking up his telephone he dialled the number of his informer.

Simon Belchard was exhausted and it was only two thirty in the afternoon. The cause of his weakened state was lying next to him in his bed half-asleep and slowly recovering from their latest bout of lovemaking, the fourth such amorous encounter that they had enjoyed since eleven that morning. It was stifling hot and both their bodies were covered in a thin film of perspiration. He was tracing patterns down her back with his forefinger and when he had reached the cheeks of her buttocks he felt the muscles twitch and tremble under his hand, a sure sign that she was becoming aroused again and would soon be demanding attention. Simon was contemplating what page of the *Kama Sutra* they had reached when his thoughts were interrupted by the jangling of his telephone. He got out of bed to answer it.

'Be quick,' the woman panted, 'I need you, lover.'

'Back soon,' he assured her as he hurried away to the study at the far end of his bungalow. He listened carefully to what the caller had to say. 'I'll get back to you this time tomorrow without fail,' was all he said in reply. 'Now I've got my work cut out,' he murmured to himself, 'but it could prove to be most enjoyable.' He chuckled as he returned to his bedroom. The sight that met his eyes as he entered the room was enough to make his blood boil, and it did, bringing him to an instant, rampant arousal. The woman was on her hands and knees with her back arched as she presented herself like a wild animal; he took her like that until he was sure that the sound of their lurid and tempestuous lovemaking could be heard in the next house. Like a master conductor he brought the performance to a grand closing crescendo and they both collapsed in a heap amongst the soiled linen. Afterwards during that period of tranquillity when he knew she was most susceptible to suggestions, he made a casual reference to their conversation of the day before. Nothing direct, just the merest hint of a fortune in gold bars and the untold wealth it could bring.

'Gold bars darling,' she giggled. 'How absurd you can be sometimes,' were her last words before she fell asleep. But her lover knew that he had said enough to do the trick, when the time came she would unconsciously gather in the intelligence that he required.

He woke her up after an hour because she had to drive to her family home in nearby Gemas, a distance of only fourteen miles but best done before darkness fell. 'Come on Fiona,' he urged, 'duty calls and all that.'

'Duty,' she answered, 'that's all sleeping with him is, a damned duty.' She staggered out to her old Morris and waved madly at Simon as she drove away. He watched her until the car disappeared from view; her husband was a minor government official who worked in the capital. A good thing really because the man seldom came this far out from his work allowing Fiona and himself to have a trouble free affair. This past week though, the unsuspecting spouse had been home more than was usual because of a recent trip abroad. Simon went inside to his study and settled down into a comfortable armchair. 'Bloody Tongs,' he sighed, 'what have I let myself in for?'

Simon Belchard was of military stock. His father had served with the British Army in France during the First World War and had miraculously escaped without a scratch. Soon after the Armistice had been signed, Belchard senior had been given command of a battalion that had been promptly posted to India. In 1919 at a place called Poona he had sired his only son, Simon.

At the tender age of twelve Simon showed his first interest in the fair sex and revealed his true colours. One evening at dinner he was caught sliding his hand up the skirt of a serving girl, his parent's were shamed and the guests horrified. The wench was dismissed; Simon was sent home in disgrace.

His second encounter with the female gender was a more serious affair and it occurred whilst he was attending school at Harrow. This time he had gone the whole hog and had been caught having sexual intercourse with an innkeeper's daughter, by the girl's angry father. Simon had received a thorough thrashing and only his brilliant record of academic achievements had saved him from expulsion.

He continued to pursue his obsession with the opposite sex with vigour and experienced some pretty close shaves with angry parents and husbands alike. The Second World War came along none to soon for Simon's safety and he found himself passing out of the Military Academy with a commission in a Home Counties regiment. Posted to the Far East he served with distinction in India, Burma and Malaya.

Belchard junior served in the Army only for the duration of the war, giving up a promising military career he swapped uniforms and joined the Colonial Police Force. He first served with them in the hotbed situation in Palestine where he was soon up to his old tricks. He was also finding out that fighting the Japanese had been mere child's play compared to dealing with mature, disgruntled spouses. One night he attended a residency function and bedded down the wife of a senior American Diplomat, the affair was not discreet and Simon found himself on the mat; as a consequence he was posted to Kenya.

This was a wrong move by the authorities because the long hot days, drink and boredom was enough to make the ladies of the British Colonial Aristocracy look for diversions. They found one in Simon and he was soon servicing several of them, unfortunately for him one of the ladies concerned was the wife of an Army Captain who was serving in the King's African Rifles. The angry soldier driven to distraction by this act of ungallant behaviour actually challenged Simon to a duel. The duel being against military rules and regulations was not fought but our friend was rapidly moved to Hong Kong.

There he really excelled himself by taking his amorous indiscretions outside the British circle of society by entering into an affair with a Chinese banker's wife. He was threatened with the might of the Tongs and once again found his position untenable. His superior officers gave Simon one more chance and transferred him to the Federation of Malaya Police Force.

Simon was now thirty-eight, just past his prime maybe, but

still a handsome fellow being six feet tall with the square upright carriage of a military man and sporting a fine waxed and curled moustache. He cut a distinguished figure when dressed in his police uniform and mixed in well with the military and embassy staff that he rubbed shoulders with. His position within the force was a fair one considering his stormy background; he was an Area Inspector with his headquarters stationed at a town called Rompin that was situated in the State of Negri Sembilan. It was a recent appointment following a period of temporary duty in the Malacca area at the village of Kampong Masjid Tanet. Whilst serving there, he had made the acquaintance of a character named Sergeant Abdul Hassan. They had become friends and all went well until Abdul found out about Simon's affair with a Government Official's wife. Things turned sour then and Simon and Fiona came to realise the truth in that old saying, 'familiarity breeds contempt'. What had once seemed like a natural thirst for knowledge on Abdul's part now turned out to be downright demands for information as he proceeded to ruthlessly blackmail his superior officer. Today's telephone call had been from Abdul and it had revealed him to be in a blind panic, that on its own was dangerous enough; but mention of the dreaded Tongs being somehow involved threatened certain disaster. Deep down, Simon knew that it was only a matter of time now before his antics with Fiona became public knowledge, and together with any proof that he was mixed up with the Tongs, would be the end for him. The writing was on the wall and he wondered how he was going to cope with it. For the time being, Simon decided to play along with the game and see if there was a way out of this bloody awful mess with some sort of honour.

Jeremy Fairburne-Snape flew home that night in an Air force Beaver aircraft from Kuala Lumpur. It was only a short hop to the military airstrip at Gemas and he arrived just before last light. A chauffeur-driven car picked him up and he was taken to his own private residence. It was dark when he walked up to the front entrance, the lights were ablaze and the place looked warm and friendly. A voice called to him from a reception room. 'Is that you, Jeremy darling?'

'Yes my dear, the wanderer returns,' he answered as his wife came running into his arms and he embraced her. 'Oh Fiona my love, how I've missed you.'

Early the next evening, Mr Tan received the information that he had been waiting for; the British were indeed lying in ambush to intercept a consignment of gold bullion. The exact dispositions of the British troops were not known, so the landing point could only be guessed at. But British Naval activity had been observed off Kuala Pahang, the mouth of the mighty Pahang River.

Chapter Five

Caesar's SAS Squadron was now five days into the operation and all ten of his four-man patrols were active along the streams that trickled into the Sungei Jeram, a river that drew its water from the two main features in his present area of responsibility. They were the 1,718 feet high Bukit Chermingat and its smaller sister, Bukit Bertangga of 1,539 feet. Caesar's patrols had already cleared the area for ten miles north of the dropping zone and were getting into their stride, adapting quickly to Caesar's patrol strategy that was based on one thing, water. In jungle warfare water is precious, and although it rains every day in Malaya and soldiers fighting in a jungle environment are permanently soaked to the skin, drinking water in any useful volume is bloody difficult and dangerous to get hold of. Control of high ground is a factor that dominates the thinking of professional soldiers in any type of warfare, the jungle being no exception. In such close country it is also much easier to travel along the high ridgelines and spurs. Water is available on these features from giant vines and some bamboo, and rainwater can be collected from canvas and vegetation traps. But if you require a substantial resupply of the life-giving liquid it will be necessary to come down from the hills to get it, and therein lies the problem. In the low lying valleys and re-entrants the jungle grows thicker and it is very difficult to move through it without making a noise, it is a slow and time consuming task. Getting down to a water point and then returning back up to the safety of the high ground afterwards is a chore that befalls some poor sod at the end of every day's hard slog. The men whose lot it is to form a water party will be dog tired and ready to drop; it is a time when even the fittest of men are vulnerable and prone to making mistakes, errors in skills and judgements that can put lives in jeopardy.

If Crazy Harry's theory was correct, the CTs would be working their way south from the highlands of North Malaya; the

SAS men were slowly patrolling northwards to meet them, not to do battle, but to observe their movements and record the enemy strengths and dispositions. The role of Caesar's men on this operation was primarily one of reconnaissance, they were to locate and then stalk the enemy to their hidden camp. Sometime or other, the CTs would have to come down to a watering hole; and that is when Caesar's SAS troopers lurking in the low-lying and stinking wetlands would catch the bandits off guard.

★

Shen and Liew, whose column had broken company with Kim Bok's party twenty-six days earlier, came to a halt on a spur running off the south side of a hill called Bukit Chermingat situated in South Pahang. Shen ordered the small group of men, now reduced to four out of the original nine, to form a tight defensive circle whilst he collected his thoughts and gave everyone a well-earned rest. They were descending from the high ground towards Tasek Bera, a particularly nasty swamp that lay at the bottom of the hill; by mutual agreement, they had all opted to have a good night's rest before attempting to cross the formidable twelve-mile obstacle.

Shen looked at the tired faces of his companions and wondered how their departed friends were faring further north. *I hope they all made it back to their regiments,* he thought as he relived the journey in his mind.

From their starting point high up in Kim Bok's mountain retreat they had taken a roller-coaster route through the rugged terrain of North Perak to the 6,194 foot high peak of Gunong Noring that straddles the Perak-Kelantan State border like some huge sentinel. From there they had dropped off the unit representative of the 12th Independent Regiment that was responsible for operations in North Perak and Kelantan. The next to go was the 5th Regiment's man who descended from the hills around Gunong Grah to report to the Colonel that lorded over the bandits of Perak and West Kelantan. Skirting to the west of the Cameron Highlands area, Shen and Liew led the party forever southwards but slowly curving east into the state of Pahang, dispatching the Intelligence Officers of the 1st Selangor and the 2nd Negri Sembilan regiments on the way. They crossed the railway line just north of Mentacab, and the mighty Pahang River at Temerloh. Heading due east from there, they crossed it again at Kampong Keatau where they said goodbye to their 10th Regiment friend. He was to continue eastwards until he reached the main CT camp and the headquarters of the Central Military Committee that was located about twenty miles away in the Chini Lake area. Shen's little force now consisting of himself, his friend Liew and an officer each from the 4th and 9th Regiments, marched out of the low, waterlogged area of the Pahang River and headed south. They ascended to 1,539 feet over the summit of Bukit Berangga, down the other side and back up again to navigate around the peak of Bukit Chermingat. Now on the south side of that hill, the tired guerrillas had come to rest.

Shen looked at his watch, it was 15.00 hrs, time to send out a water party; he and the man from the 4th Regiment had done it yesterday so it was Liew's turn to take the fellow from the 9th. Shen clicked his fingers once; there was no need to say a word. Liew and his companion collected together all the water bottles and canvas water carriers and quietly commenced their descent eastwards towards the Sungei Jeram or one of its tributaries. They were hoping to come across one of the latter to make their task a shorter one.

Liew led off carefully, picking his way down the steep slope, it had not started to rain yet but the going was still difficult and both men were already slipping and sliding and it was making them lose their balance. They were forced to grab hold of small tree trunks in order to stop themselves falling and this caused the trees to shake. In addition to making a noise, the movement was telegraphed upwards, the higher it got the more vigorous it became; a sure indication to a vigilant enemy that a foe could be approaching.

It took half an hour for them to reach the bottom of the hill where they found a dried-up streambed. Liew paused there to listen and tried to work out which way the water would have flowed had it been there. This was not an easy task because he was navigating with only a sketch map and had no compass, and the visibility was down to four yards. He decided to follow the streambed in an easterly direction and was elated when it sloped downwards, not long after that the wise old jungle veteran heard the musical sound of trickling water. Liew lost track of the streambed in a jumble of rocks but came upon the actual stream about five minutes later, it was not the Sungei Jeram, Liew had found his hoped for tributary.

It was six feet wide with a steep bank on the home side, Liew climbed down four feet to the slowly flowing water but slipped as he did so and that caused him to bang a bamboo water carrier against a tree. He froze for a whole minute to listen out for any reaction to the muffled 'bonk-like' noise. The jungle sounds had not changed so Liew indicated that his partner should pass down the water carriers to be filled. The task was soon completed and he started to climb back out of the stream only to find that his left foot was stuck in the mud. Liew beckoned for the other man to give him a pull out, with an alarmingly loud squelching sound Liew was suddenly free, but his hockey boot came halfway off and water cascaded from it back down the bank. Momentarily panic-stricken, the terrorist scrambled to safety leaving far too many signs behind him. The panic bout over, Liew quickly regained his composure, adjusted his boot and led the way back up the hill.

★

Because he was doing a stint as leading scout at the head of his four-man patrol Fred was armed with a shotgun, his Owen gun being stowed away in his Bergen. The patrol's task was to scout all the streams that led into the Sungei Jeram from the western side of the river, or Fred's left; he was following such a tributary now. It was a bloody awful job and because the jungle was so thick in many places along the stream much of the patrol's time was actually spent in the water. This was the case now as Fred decided that he could not negotiate the tangled mass of foliage ahead of him. Any CTs seeking access to the stream at this point would have been in the same boat and could not have left any sign on the bank for Fred to find. He led the patrol through some razor-sharp palm leaves and over a pile of slippery moss-covered rocks down into the water. It was not very deep but one had to be careful of the odd bottomless hole.

The going was slower even than patrol pace because of the overhanging vines and branches that blocked the way, and walking through water is bloody hard work and makes a hell of a racket. The patrol had been checking out this particular stream for over an hour, they had turned left at the junction with the main river and had followed the left bank most of the way with the occasional excursion into the water. Except for pig tracks at the more accessible points, there had been no visible signs of life. In general, the bank of the stream had been steep-sided, it looked almost as if navvies had cut it out and it was obvious that any ground below four feet from the edges would be flooded during the monsoon season. Fred had reached a point where the stream was about six feet wide, for the most part, the water was ankle deep and both banks were at shoulder height. His task of observing the stream's access points was proving to be a difficult one, due to the gymnastics he was required to perform, in order to negotiate the many obstacles that lay in his path. Whilst clawing his way through the confusing mess of thorn-covered palms without making a sound or climbing over, and in some cases ducking under overhanging vines and branches, he simply could not concentrate on the job of tracking properly and felt very vulnerable. Getting through or around each obstacle required an extreme physical effort not helped in the least by the heavy load that he was carrying. Normally, patrols would operate from a troop base camp and work out of it carrying a few days' rations in a small pack. But this job required them to take all of their kit with them, so spread out on the ground was the squadron.

Patrolling with an 80 lb Bergen on his back was a terrific challenge to Fred's stamina in itself. After each Herculean effort, he had to stand perfectly still in order to listen out, and then to continue with his minute study of the ground ahead of him, and to his right and left for signs. Whilst doing so he had to put all his trust in the man behind him to watch both his back and the jungle wall just above his head and to each side of him; all in all it was a mental nightmare and a strength-sapping chore.

Fred was just straightening up after ducking under a creeper-draped branch when he froze, still in a crouching position he cupped his right hand to his ear indicating to Chalky that he had heard something; the Patrol Commander repeated the signal and all four men stood like statues with ears and eyes straining. The noise Fred had heard sounded like a muffled thump, not unlike wood against wood and could have been made by a falling branch landing on log. Fred waited three long minutes, but heard nothing more except for the uninterrupted racket that was the jungle norm. Although he felt excitement welling up inside of him and his heart was thumping like mad, he did not sense any immediate danger so he gave the signal to advance and gingerly continued up stream with his eyes nearly bulging out of his head. He was approaching a left-hand bend and had to kneel down to select his next few steps when another sound invaded his senses. *Bloody hell,* he thought as he froze once more and gave the signal again.

This time it sounded like a snort or a grunt, 'Maybe it's pigs wallowing in the mud,' he whispered hopefully but knew in his heart that it was something different. Fred was really keyed up now; alerted twice in five minutes was too much to let go, he must heed his sixth sense that was sounding warning bells in his skull. Because of the deadened nature of the sounds, he thought perhaps they might have been made a fair distance away. Deciding to advance a little further he looked behind him to make sure that he had Chalky's attention then gave him the thumbs down sign, the field signal for enemy forces. He followed this with another silent communication, this time circling an eye with a forefinger and thumb informing Chalky that his scout was going to move forward on his own to carry out a close reconnaissance of the area ahead. Chalky in turn gave the same two signals to let the other men know what was happening. Fred was elated, that action by Chalky indicated to him that the man did not doubt his judgement and he was letting the new leading scout have his head; this measure of trust from the Second World War veteran was a terrific boost to Fred's moral. It gave him added confidence as he inched his way forward with renewed determination and stealth. Very slowly he moved, hardly going as fast as the water that was trickling against his legs, the tension was almost mind bending as he tried to block out the normal jungle clatter and concentrate on unusual or man-made sounds. But it was not noise that gave him the first positive clue to the presence of CTs, it was movement. Fred had just rounded the bend when something caught his eye, he was perspiring like mad and the sweat was stinging his eyes that were already being strained to the limit. The seconds ticked by, the tense atmosphere was suffocating and sickeningly cloying and the closeness of the surrounding jungle frightening and claustrophobic. A new sound had joined the din of the wilds that seemed to have increased in volume, it was the deep resonate throb of his own heart; and try as he might he could not make out what it was that had alarmed him.

There is an old proverb that goes 'You cannot see the wood for the trees' and it came to Fred's aid now. The scout had not moved a muscle since the tiny motion had caused him to freeze in his tracks. He had been focusing his powers of observation on a distance of about five yards plus, trackers seldom look straight down at closer ranges until they have spotted something worthy of their attention. There is a pattern to the seemingly chaotic jungle floor and a good scout can spot disturbances in it easily. Fred could detect no sign of enemy movement ahead of him in this instance; *besides*, he thought to himself, *it's nearly all bloody water.*

He was beginning to shake with the sheer effort of concentration and almost jumped out of his skin when a flicker of movement flashed in the corner of his eye, Bloody mosquitoes, flitted though his mind but no, something was moving, albeit very slowly. Fred turned his head equally slowly to look at the left bank, there, at only an arm's length was a twig. It is not unusual to find a twig in a jungle full of wood but this particular half-inch long specimen was being carried downwards by a trickle of water that was flowing through the cracked surface of an otherwise dry bank, the water should not have been there. As if mesmerised by the object he followed the progress of the twig until it entered the stream and was taken away by the current, at this point he discovered that the water in the immediate area of the minute waterfall was discoloured by mud.

Closer scrutiny of the bank revealed grooves in the earth and damage to the undergrowth, clear evidence that a human being had recently climbed in and out of the stream, *and*, thought Fred, *had made a fine old mess of it.* He could hardly believe his own eyes, it was phenomenal, at this very early stage of his first SAS operation he had found a freshly used enemy water point. This brief feeling of euphoria soon disappeared as the already hostile atmosphere of the jungle took on a very real aspect of deadly menace. It did not need a genius in military tactics to work out that if the tracks were fresh, then the enemy must be pretty damned close and that raised a few questions. Was he about to be shot? It now seemed to him that there was a bandit behind every tree and that every bit of shadow might conceal a machine gun position. Was this an ambush, were the enemy waiting for more men to walk into the killing ground before opening fire?

The options flying around inside of Fred's head were mind-boggling and lesser men might have panicked but his years of tough training and military discipline came to his rescue. In a split second a flash of inspiration explained the noises that he had heard and he guessed that a terrorist had fallen down the bank banging some equipment on a tree on his way down. He had then got stuck in the mud, and what Fred had thought were snorts was, he now supposed, the squelching sound of the man extracting himself from the sticky morass. Further to that, the muffling effect that he had attributed to distance was the bend in the stream masking the sound. Fred realised two things instinctively, the first was that having made a noise, the terrorists would want to bug out and put some distance between themselves and the water point just in case they had been heard. The second point was that although he had come bloody close to doing so, it was not he that was panicking; it was the foe.

All of these fears and thoughts had flashed through the scout's mind in but a few seconds; it was time for him to act before the terrorists got too far ahead of the SAS patrol. *I must get this info back to Chalky,* he thought. Hoping the streamed was not going to hold him fast he attempted to move and breathed a sigh of relief as his feet came smoothly free of the bottom, then he commenced the difficult task of withdrawing backwards to the bend in the stream. It was a bloody hair-raising feat trying to concentrate on his front whilst attempting to remain upright with the Bergen doing its damnedest to pull him onto his back, but slowly with infinite patience he made it. Once there he felt safer because he was once more within sight of his mates who were now covering his movements. Comfortable in that knowledge he turned around and stalked back to Chalky to make his report without any further shocks to his nervous system.

Chalky took the report on board calmly and made an instant decision, he wanted to look at the water point himself before committing the patrol to any follow-up action, but from the top of the bank. The patrol scrambled up the steep incline with Fred leading the way, and then they followed him on all fours to the target area where Chalky immediately posted Bob and Worm as sentries. Taking Fred with him, Chalky carried out a thorough reconnaissance of the scene of enemy activity encountering no difficulty in finding two sets of tracks, one set leading down to the stream and another, much clearer set heading away from it. Chalky was in no mood to muck about so with a gleam in his eye he regrouped the patrol and informed them of his intentions. He had decided to follow the enemy tracks until it got dark, then at first light the next morning an attempt would be made to locate the enemy camp. 'They can't be more than twenty minutes in front of us,' he whispered as he signalled for Fred to proceed.

As he started to track the two men away from the stream towards the high ground, it started to rain. *That's all I bloody well need,* he grinned to himself. For this was a very different Fred that was leading the way forward now, a man with more confidence in his own ability; and one that knew from the body language of the rest of the patrol, that they had completely accepted him.

★

Liew had been praying for rain, he wanted to go faster and the rain would cover the noise that he was bound to make by doing so. As if the gods wished to please him, the wind began to rustle the trees furiously and Liew heard the mighty roar of an approaching downpour. To make haste in the jungle went against all of Liew's training and his normal sense of logic but an overriding feeling of doom, a deep foreboding of danger, was urging him to rush back to his friend Shen as soon as possible. The rain came as he climbed out of the old dried-up streambed and started the ascent of Bukit Chermingat, the noise was deafening and the two CTs threw caution to the wind and literally clawed their way frantically up the steep hill. They were exhausted and their tired legs took the least line of resistance, and as a direct result of their frenzied flight of folly Liew lost sight of the downward track and veered off to the left hitting the spur much further down the hill than he had intended to. This caused him to miss Shen's position by a hundred yards or so. Realising that he had made a major navigational error Liew turned right and headed northwards in order to make good his mistake, eventually he rejoined Shen with only thirty minutes of daylight to spare.

Liew was surprised to find that his leader had not made camp but was sitting on his pack strumming impatient fingers on a map case. He seemed a little taken aback at the sight of his number two approaching from entirely the wrong direction but if he had any thoughts on the matter he kept them to himself for the time being. A very tired Liew reported in, he tried to explain his fears to his old friend but Shen cut him off curtly. 'We're moving further down the spur to find a bit of flat ground to camp on, dish out the water and let's get moving.'

'But I've got this feeling,' Liew tried again to explain.

'If you're worried about the bloody British,' Shen cut him off, 'then we're better off away from this sodding great track. Lead the way down, now!' Hurt by Shen's uncompromising attitude and with his guts churning with dreadful apprehension, Liew led the terrorist group southwards towards the Tasek Bera swamp.

★

Fred's success at finding the water point had triggered off something in his makeup, a built-in gift that had remained dormant until now. He was still not aware of it, but Fred was a natural born tracker and one of those rare souls that are at home in the jungle. He had learned woodcraft as a boy, trapping and snaring with the best of poachers in his native Somerset countryside. As a Light Infantryman he had been required to excel in field craft just to stand the slightest chance of getting through his basic training. In Kenya he had taken a keen interest in tracking but before anything could become of it, his battalion had been rushed to riot-torn Aden. During his three-week jungle training operation with the SAS, Fred had shown great promise as a combat tracker and had successfully followed all the trails that had been laid down for him. But it had taken a real test to bring this natural aptitude to the fore, the skill to spot the signs, the inquisitiveness to look deeper, and above all, the courage to move forward and investigate. It was worlds away from poaching for game, this following a live quarry that could be every bit as clever as yourself, and had the capability to shoot back.

Fred found no difficulty in following the double set of tracks and the rain that before this particular day he would have considered to be a bloody nuisance was now part of his armoury, it was cooling him down and that enabled him to think more clearly. The sound of the rain thundering down onto the jungle canopy made it impossible for him to hear any likely enemy activity, for exactly the same reason; they would not be able to hear him. This did not mean that Fred was about to speed up the chase, no, he was not going to fall for that one. If anything he actually slowed the pace down to take advantage of the racket to shut his ears, so to speak, to heighten his powers of visual observation and concentrate on the enemy's ground scent. Under this heaven-sent cloak of distraction, Fred hoped to find every bit of sign that the terrorists might negligently leave.

Shortly after leaving the water point and heading in a westerly direction, Fred came upon a jumble of rocks that were almost blocking his path, he could easily have lost the trail there and then if he had been rushing the job. But he found some slight scuffmarks on the moss-covered mounds and eventually found the dried-out streambed; only it was not dry anymore because the heavy downpour had filled it up and the water was flowing towards Fred. Looking down he could see that the stream disappeared below the ground through the base of the rocks at his feet, the scout guessed that by midnight the small waterway would have dried up and the whole process would begin all over again tomorrow. The enemy tracks were naturally being washed away before his eyes but instead of getting all exasperated over the matter he surveyed the situation coolly and put himself in the enemy's shoes. Again he guessed that they must have come upon this track-like gully and had followed it to the water point. He surmised that the enemy party had come down off the high ground to his left, and it followed that they would have to go back up more or less the same way. Fred made his decision: he would follow the watercourse until he found the enemy's entry and exit points, concentrating his main efforts on the left-hand side.

He advanced against the fast flowing torrent with great care and by dint of much diligence he was rewarded after only ten minutes by a sign. It was only a large leaf that had been reversed by someone brushing aside a sapling, but the underside of most leaves are much lighter in shade than the surface normally presented to an observer. This one was standing out like a Belisha beacon as the heavy raindrops knocked it about. It was enough to make Fred try harder and he was soon hot on the trail once more, taking the patrol out of the water to begin ascending the side of Bukit Chermingat.

The first thirty yards after breaking away from the low ground to tackle the hill were still a challenge with not much to see at all. A bent twig here, a piece of stripped bark there and he found one indentation in the soft earth on the far side of a fallen tree indicating that one of the men had lost his balance. From that point onwards it became obvious that the bandits ahead had lost their cool, they were rushing through the jungle leaving a trail that even a blind man could follow and as the gradient got steeper they compounded their errors giving Fred plenty of clues to follow up. In the odd places where clear footprints had been made in the mud he was able to determine by their characteristics that the men were not carrying packs. From that useful clue he had deduced that the terrorists were probably making for a rendezvous where they would have left their packs, or were heading for a more permanent base camp. Many of the gouges and prints in the ground had not yet filled with water which meant that the enemy must be bloody close by, the tracker noticed that despite their haste the bandits were taking two steps back for every one forward.

Fred stuck to his slow, methodical and cautious patrol pace but even so he was gaining on the duo of spooked CTs. He plodded on and when he had estimated that the patrol were well over two-thirds of the way up that particular section of the hill, he hit a problem, the trail he was following had split. After closer examination of the signs he could see that the two men had stopped following their original course and had veered off to the left. Fred signalled for Chalky to come forward and have a look.

The Patrol Commander studied the mess of tracks for a few seconds. 'Let's follow what we've got for certain,' he whispered, 'whatever these two bastards are up to they're bound to lead us to the others eventually. Perhaps their packs are being taken to a prearranged rendezvous or maybe the fools have wandered off course momentarily.' He paused, scratching his head thoughtfully. 'A lapse of concentration tempered with panic perhaps?'

'I'll go for the latter,' answered Fred softly with an evil glint in his eye, 'we've got them worried, I can feel it in my bones.'

'Carry on the good work Big White Hunter,' grinned Chalky. But in a more serious vein he added, 'Remember this, if we've got them running scared then they must suspect that we're here too. And that my boy is bad news for us because we are supposed to see without being seen!' Chalky watched as Fred continued with his task and noted how easily the new man seemed to glide through the close tangle of jungle growth; all his movements were smooth and stealthy and well thought out in advance. Fred was now using the jungle instead of fighting it; it was a far cry from his performance at the beginning of the operation when Chalky had taken him under his wing. Fred had improved at every step of the way and did not need anything explained twice. Chalky, who was an expert in the very tough and individual art of jungle warfare and one of the regiment's finest combat trackers was more at home in the jungle than he was in his mother's house. It takes one to know one and the old campaigner recognised that at long last it had clicked for Fred. To find two such men in a squadron was an asset, in a troop it was bloody unusual. But in the same patrol, well, it was just downright phenomenal; and very bad news for the enemy.

The CTs tracks continued to avoid a direct route up the hill taking a diagonal path with a definite left-hand bias. *They're all in,* thought Fred, *if they keep to this curved course we'll all end up back at the bottom of the bloody hill.* Suddenly he froze in his tracks, he knew not why; he just came to a halt in mid-stride as an ice-cold shiver ran down his spine. 'Someone has just walked over my grave,' he whispered to himself. Some extra inner sense forced him to look to his right and upwards; he strained his eyes, trying to pierce through the wet green wall but could see nothing past five yards.

Had he heard a noise? Not bloody likely with this racket going on, he reasoned and took up the trail once more. So acute had the left-hand bias become that when Fred reached the spur-line he was literally walking along it in a downward direction for a couple of paces before he realised it, he had hit a kind of Y-shaped junction that was just discernible to the tracker. For a split second Fred thought he had lost the scent, he stopped and slowly turned around to look back the way he had come; his glance took in the more established trail of the main spur. Fred knelt down to increase his field of view, you can see further in the jungle when your eyes are closer to the ground, and there it was. Now he could see that the pattern of leaves had been disturbed, like scuff marks on a badly painted surface; his heart turned cold as he came to the conclusion that the bandits had turned right onto the spur almost doubling back on themselves in the process.

The tracker knew with utter certainty the true significance of the strange experience of a few minutes ago and the very thought of what must have happened was enough to make even the most seasoned soldiers want to crap in their pants. The SAS patrol and the terrorist water party had passed each other by at a range of less than twenty-five yards. 'Hairy isn't the word for it,' mused Fred. They were very close on the enemy's heels now, much closer than he and Chalky had estimated; once more he summoned his commander up front to confer.

Chalky looked at the narrow angle between the track that they had just followed and the one leading away towards the summit of Bukit Chermingat, catching Fred's eye, he let it be known that he fully understood. 'That,' he murmured grim faced, 'was a bloody close shave, a contact now would bugger up Caesar's plans for sure.' He was again reminding the scout that they were a reconnaissance patrol and a clash with the terrorists was to be avoided at all costs, they were the eyes and ears of thousands of troops.

There was now only about half an hour of daylight left with a lot to do in a short space of time, Chalky grouped his patrol together and spelt it out. 'So far we know that we're on the trail of two men, fact. They are travelling light, another fact. Now I'm guessing that they're making for a base camp to join their mates. I don't know the fighting strength of the enemy force ahead. I haven't a clue as to the whereabouts of their camp, but Fred and I reckon it's along this spur and pretty damned close at that. Our task is to establish if they're sticking to the spur or just crossing over it, we'll follow the tracks for fifteen minutes or until they drop off the feature, whichever comes first.'

'So whatever happens we'll be spending the night up here?' queried Worm.

'That's right,' confirmed Chalky, 'if they do have a camp further up the spur we may hear them during the hours of darkness when they think they're safe. If they drop off the feature tonight then we'll definitely hear them crashing about.'

'No camp for us then?' moaned Bob.

Chalky looked at his tired men, the strain beginning to show on their faces. 'No camp, no brew-ups or cooking and smoking is out. They're too bloody close for comfort. Now let's get going, we're running out of light.'

Fred took the lead once again, the rain that had cooled him down at first was now freezing his nuts off and he was shivering uncontrollably, he was definitely not looking forward to spending the night in his wet gear. It was but a fleeting thought, the close proximity of the enemy brought his mind back to the job at hand and he advanced slowly, studying the ground intently. He especially concentrated on the left-hand edge of the spur for any signs of a departure from the high ground in that direction.

The minutes ticked by seeming more like hours, Fred was on his last legs and every muscle in his body ached like hell; he was also beginning to see spots before his eyes, a sure sign that tiredness was taking its relentless toll. The tracks continued to lead him northwards up the hill, the light was fading and the normal gloomy shade of the jungle was taking on an ominous and evil hue; time was running out.

Fred paused as the green veil of tangled growth thinned out and he was suddenly able to see at least fifteen yards straight to his front, it would have been further but a huge tree was obscuring his vision. The track became wider at this point too, as if to accommodate the enormous buttress-like roots of the forest giant. Fred knelt down and looked at his watch, the allotted time was up and he estimated that it would be dark in under a quarter of an hour.

The tree offered the patrol a convenient haven for the night where each man could fit into a buttress giving him ample protection for his back. Knowing that Chalky would need all the available time to organise the night routine, he turned around to signal him forward; but Chalky anticipating the scout's intentions was already on his way. He took in the situation at a glance and whispered, 'Trust you to find some bloody armchairs, go and check them out and the track for twenty yards past them. I'll wait here, if it's all clear signal from the tree.'

Fred acknowledged, thinking, to find a sense of humour at a time like this shows the true measure of the man. Fred advanced towards the tree with his pump action Remington shotgun at the ready.

Chalky watched his back and the left flank, covering him with a 9mm Australian Owen sub-machine gun. Five yards behind Chalky and responsible for the right flank was Bob armed with a short No. 5 .303-inch Lee Enfield, the so-called jungle rifle. Worm, carrying his trusty American M1 carbine, guarded the rear in that most hated of positions in a single file formation, tail-end Charlie. If Fred's job up front was nerve-racking; then Worm's task could only be described as downright spooky.

Fred had hardly taken five paces before he suddenly felt like death warmed up and had to pause with one foot still off the ground; so heart stopping was the feeling that something was not quite right. The tracks made by the CTs led around the left-hand side of the tree. He had been in the process of planning on how to negotiate the obstacle presented by the extra large tree roots and the steep edges of the spur when the strange feeling had hit him. He steeled his nerves and willed himself to move, with a tremendous effort he placed his left foot forward; at that precise moment he was confronted by the upper half of a man who was approaching him from the other side of the tree roots.

Liew, still smarting from Shen's offhand treatment of him, was rushing things again, undoubtedly encouraged on his way by the fact that he was proceeding downhill and was keen to find a suitable piece of ground where he could get a good night's rest. But for the life of him he could not understand why his friend wanted to move at all, especially at this time of day when it was going to be dark long before they could get settled into a camp. To Liew's further annoyance, the three men behind him were not following his example and were hanging back making it necessary for Liew to stop and start in order to maintain visual contact. In his frustration he was spending as much time looking backwards as he was forward.

Liew was about to pass around a big tree that he had noticed on his way up the hill, he glanced to his rear to check that the others were still in sight, they were. Satisfied, he faced the front again to look over the three-foot-high tree roots that were barring his way and found himself peering straight down the gaping barrel of a shotgun.

Liew felt no pain, just a numbing thump in the area of his midriff. He was attempting to get his own weapon up into action when the lights went out in his life, forever.

Now that he had come face to face with the enemy and the element of secrecy and surprise had been lost, Fred swung into action like the well-oiled fighting machine he was. He performed weapon handling drills and physically exacting tactical manoeuvres with a speed and efficiency that was awesome to behold. At the point of visual contact, the butt of Fred's shotgun was positioned under his right arm at about waist height. He immediately clamped it into his side with his elbow and pointed the weapon at the terrorist using his left hand. In the same split second he fired his first shot from the hip shouting, 'Contact front' as he did so.

The twelve bore ammunition, consisting of nine steel balls packed within a cartridge case in three separate layers of three balls each, erupted from the muzzle in a triangular pattern of hot metal that upon reaching the target had spread into a twenty-two-inch group. The shots blasted into the man's abdomen nearly cutting the enemy soldier in two. Faster than the eye could follow, Fred's left arm pulled back and powered forward the pump action of the shotgun, ejecting the spent cartridge and inserting a new one into the chamber. In the same blurred lighting action he brought the Remington up into the aim and fired a second shot, this time hitting his adversary in the neck and breastbone area. Immediately he felt the recoil of that second round, Fred dived to his left in order that Chalky who was pounding up behind him could take up a firing position.

Chalky had seen Fred stop and sensed his apprehension but could not see anything because the scout was blocking his view, however, the wily old soldier guessed that all hell was about to break loose. In anticipation he had slipped off his Bergen and was on the move as Fred erupted into a flurry of action. The patrol commander saw a figure slumped over a buttress with his head bent forward, taking no chances he fired a short burst of three rounds from the kneeling position. The stubby 9mm bullets shattered the terrorist's head and blew his body over the tree roots and out of sight. Chalky fired two longer bursts one each side of the tree, then he too jumped to his left making room for Bob.

As yet the enemy had not returned fire. *Probably because they can't see us through that bloody tree,* Chalky reasoned, *and now we've got the same problem.*

Bob came up into line closely followed by Worm. Chalky waved them onwards, 'Get to that tree, Bob left, Worm right. Put some fire down quick.'

The two men hardly broke stride as they forged ahead to take up firing positions in the very buttresses earmarked for their night's resting place. The jungle reverberated with the heavy thump of Bob's .303 and the lighter crack of Worm's carbine, they were firing for effect and were soon rewarded by the sound of someone yelping in pain as some of the bullets found their mark. Bark started to fly as the CTs began firing back; the engagement had been in progress for a mere thirty seconds.

Fred, of course, had opened the contact with his Bergen still on. As soon as he had hit the deck he extricated himself from the harness and cocked the shotgun ready for more action, it took but a couple of seconds; by the time he was finished, Chalky was lying beside him and Fred looked at him for guidance. That cool individual indicated that Fred should move forward until he was in line with the others but down off the spur a little to cover the steep slope. Fred slipped over the edge until his head was level with the track and some five yards to the left of it. From the corner of his eye he noticed Chalky start to crawl forward, taking this as his cue he too advanced from root to root until the patrol's formation had changed from single file to extended line, albeit a pretty tight one. He could see the tree but not the individuals around it, and only the staccato bursts of the Owen gun told him that Chalky had drawn level with the others. Fred wedged himself into a standing position between a tree trunk and the steep, slippery contour of the spur and waited at the ready, butt in the shoulder with the muzzle slightly lowered allowing him to observe over the top of his weapon sights.

The incoming enemy fire was now fast and furious but all seeming to come from single-shot weapons, either that, or they were making a damned good job of concealing the fact that they had automatics; a ploy that often forced an adversary into making a fatal tactical error. Fred dismissed the latter theory; he had a gut feeling that they were dealing with a small force, probably the same strength as the SAS patrol. As for armament, well the bandits seemed to be scraping the barrel because although the snapping sound of the bullets passing overhead gave no indication of what weapons were being fired, Fred had no trouble recognising the metallic clicking noise of at least two bolt action rifles. And amidst the thumping of discharging firearms, he could detect the flat crisp report of a pistol, suggesting that this particular bunch of CTs were hard up for carbines and sub-machine guns.

The crashing of undergrowth as one of the terrorists attempted to flee across the SAS man's field of fire interrupted any further thoughts Fred may have had on the matter. For a fleeting second he saw the CT's face and immediately opened fire with a couple of quick rounds. In addition to hitting the unfortunate bandit, the shotgun pellets also shredded the thick foliage and cleared a path through the close cover to expose the target for Fred to finish off, he did so with two well aimed shots. In the unlikely event that the four rounds of twelve-bore ammunition did not kill the enemy soldier, then his fall did, because Fred heard the gruesome sound of his neck snapping as the man's head jammed in the fork of a tree. The short but furious battle of the Bukit Chermingat spur ended as abruptly as it had began, both sides ceasing fire as if by mutual agreement.

Steam generated by the frenzied excitement of the fight rose in clouds from the soldiers' sweat stained and rain sodden clothing to mix with the thick smoke and acrid stench of cordite fumes, effectively hastening the onset of dusk. In the fading light Fred crawled the short distance to the giant tree, a simple enough task but if attempted in complete darkness, an extremely hazardous one. In the short time available to him, Chalky organised the retrieval of the patrol's rucksacks and put Worm to work erecting the all important radio antenna, another task that would be well-nigh impossible to perform after dark.

Under normal circumstances, following a contact a very wary check would have been made of the suspected enemy dead. For this the men would work in pairs, one man providing cover whilst his buddy confirmed the kill and searched the body for maps and any other kind of documents. Captured arms and ammunition would also be gathered in at this point. Why a wary check? Well it is a common practice for these fanatically brave terrorists to feign death when riddled with bullets and mortally wounded. A favourite ploy is to lie on their stomachs clutching a hand grenade beneath themselves, the safety pin having been pulled. Then on hearing the approach of a clearing patrol or mopping up force the man would roll over exposing the grenade in the hope that in the closing seconds of his existence he might take some of the foe with him. In this instance Chalky did not have the time to carry out the proper procedure. He knew damned well that the enemy soldier engaged by the tree was definitely dead and he was prepared to take Fred's word for it that the other bandit too was no longer of this world. The SAS men threw the body of the former down the slope to join 'he of the broken neck'; both corpses would be attended to in the morning. It was completely dark now and there had been no sound of any enemy activity since the engagement had broken off, Chalky guessed that the bandits too realised the utter futility of moving in the jungle at night.

The whole patrol was now sitting in their allotted buttresses facing outwards from what was possibly the tightest defensive circle of all time. Rucksacks were positioned between the men's knees with their weapons resting over the top of them, very uncomfortable positions that these hard men would have to endure until first light. Soaking wet, dog tired and still hyped up from the brief but bitter action that they had fought, the four men steeled themselves for a sleepless night.

Bob had been busy doing his thing with the radio, getting the antenna looped over the highest branch possible and establishing communications with Caesar's HQ. He had also sent a contact report that effectively imposed radio silence on all other stations operating on the squadron net. Being that late in the day, the nine other patrols would have set up their radios before the engagement and would have heard Bob's brief message of 'Contact, wait out.' They would be waiting eagerly in the wings for Chalky's expected update on the situation and Caesar's decision on what to do about it.

When all appeared to be settled, and after a reasonable period of stand-to, Chalky took over the radio headset and Morse key from Bob. He tapped away in Morse code for nearly five minutes, the key making only the slightest clicking sound. He explained the situation fully to his commander giving only the bare facts with no added suppositions. The reply came through and because Chalky was wearing a headset, no incoming signal was audible. Using this method of communication together with silent field signals and only whispering to each other, SAS men often spent an entire three-month operation without uttering a single word aloud. In jungle warfare silence is golden and Chalky having received his orders was left with the problem of issuing his interpretation of them to his men, this task to be done quietly and in complete darkness.

Under the circumstances Chalky opted to issue a brief warning order with just enough specific detail to get things moving in the morning. He accomplished this by manoeuvring his wiry body around each buttress in turn and whispering into the occupant's shell-like ear; Fred was the last man to receive Chalky's pearls of wisdom. In general the patrol was to carry out a follow-up whilst the tracks were still fresh, first though the dead bodies and captured weapons had to be hidden until a back-up patrol could occupy the position. But just in case something should go wrong with that plan or the recovery of the bodies should prove to be a lengthy business, some form of identity had to be obtained at the scene. That was where Fred's specific orders came in, he was to collect items of identification from the bodies at first light, a task that he was not exactly looking forward to but he would face it when the time came.

Fred wriggled his arse around to contour himself into the rain sodden and rotting vegetation that lay between the tree roots. The rainwater was cascading down the huge old tree trunk, the thick bark channelling it into minute waterfalls that were soaking his back, whilst all the time there was no respite from the drip-drip-drip-drip of large droplets landing on the top of his jungle hat. Yet more rain was rebounding off the leaves that carpeted the jungle floor to splash into his eyes, an irritation that was setting his nerves jangling; like the sands of the desert there was no escaping from it.

The rain stopped at 20.00 hrs, the patrol had been sitting still for over three hours now and the slight rise in temperature that always came after the rain was a welcome relief. The cold and discomfort had kept alive the high that Fred had experienced during the contact, the warmth that was now seeping into his bones and tired muscles was bringing him down and he felt drained and utterly exhausted. His eyelids felt heavy and were closing of their own accord as sleep threatened his resolve to remain vigilant.

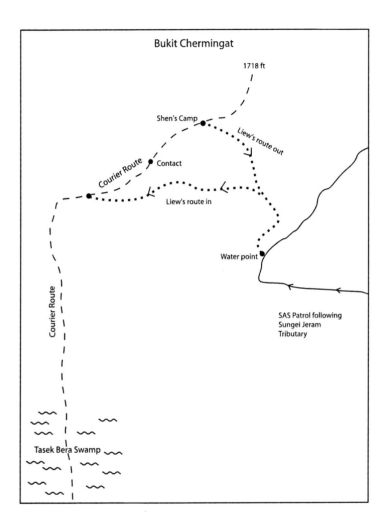

Bukit Chermingat

1718 ft

Shen's Camp

Liew's route out

Courier Route

Contact

Liew's route in

Water point

SAS Patrol following
Sungei Jeram
Tributary

Courier Route

Tasek Bera Swamp

There is no gain without pain, they say, and with the warmer conditions came the mosquitoes, hell-bent on making up for lost time. They dive bombed Fred with the precision of Air force fighter pilots and the malevolence of Lucifer himself, in his present predicament there was no protection against them. Under normal patrol routine they would have stopped in time to erect themselves two-man bashas using one man's poncho as a tent-like shelter and the other man's as a ground sheet. The men would have changed into dry clothing and erected makeshift mosquito nets made out of silk airdrop parachute panels. As an optional extra the men could anoint themselves with army-issue mosquito repellent, not recommended by most soldiers because the bloody things loved the stuff. But none of these comforting measures was possible for Chalky's patrol that night. Fred had to counter the concentrated mosquito offensive with quiet stoicism. To reduce the target area he had rolled down the sleeves of his bush jacket and buttoned the neck right up to the throat. He had placed his camouflaged face veil over the top of his jungle hat so that it hung down to cover his head and shoulders, hopefully this would stop at least half of the mosquitoes from getting through. Because of the awkward sitting position he had been forced to adopt, his clothes were stretched tightly over his upper arms and legs, thus enabling the intrepid mosquitoes to easily penetrate the thin material and get at his skin. The winged devils led Fred a merry dance, plunging their spear-like proboscis into his flesh, an arm here, a leg there and bloody mosquito bites everywhere. And when they did manage to get through his defences to attack his head he was driven half crazy by the harrowing experience. At first it was the high-pitched humming of their wings that got to him, it made his hands and feet itch with trapped tension and he felt impotent against the tiny invaders, he wanted to scream out in anger and frustration. But it got worse as the attack escalated into the final assault phase, the buzzing became a deafening, nerve-racking screech, then silence, the dreaded period of absolute quiet before the mosquito made physical contact. 'You bastard', Fred felt like crying out, but with tremendous will power he kept his trap shut. It was not so much the pain when it came; it was the anticipation of it that did the most damage to his nervous system.

Because it was dark a gentle swatting was possible but the backs of his hands soon got covered in bites and became quite swollen. Perhaps this systematic onslaught was a blessing in disguise because it kept Fred awake and the distraction alleviated other problems.

The mosquitoes made a tactical withdrawal at midnight when it got too cold for them, the bombardment ceased and they flew off to their filthy breeding grounds. Immediately they had gone Fred became aware of the drip-drip-drip-dripping again, this time it was the rainwater filtering down though the tree canopy long after the rain itself had ceased. *Bloody hell,* he thought, *now it's to be a water torture.* In tandem with the aggravating dripping sound came other jungle noises as the denizens of the night made their presence felt. But what and where was hard to guess, it played havoc on the nerves.

On a dark night in the jungle imagination plays evil tricks on the mind and pessimism leaps to the fore. Fred sniffed, for the first time that night he caught a whiff of the stench that was emanating from the two dead bodies lying only a few yards away from him. A loud snapping sound came from that direction, alarmed, Fred recoiled in horror at the thought of what might be going on out there and banged his head against the tree into the bargain. 'What the hell was that?' he felt like saying, but buttoned his lip instead, then he calmed down a bit and regained his composure. *Could be a pig eating the bastards,* he mused, *or maybe a bloody tiger.* But did the sound come from that direction at all? It was difficult to tell in the dark. Now rustling noises made the hackles rise on the back of his neck and mind-boggling images of snakes, scorpions and centipedes made him shudder in fear.

Whilst the jungle noises wreaked havoc with Fred's nervous system, the glow-worms came along to play games with his vision; they danced about like grim green spectres in the company of more luminosity from the rotting vegetation that was strewn about the jungle floor. Fred glanced down at the luminous dial of his watch and found that it was only 01.30 hrs. *Christ,* he thought, *roll on the bloody morning.*

There was a terrific crack as some ancient tree split down the middle, then loud creaking sounds and almost human-like groans

107

echoed through the jungle as the tree fell to the ground with a tremendous crash taking many smaller trees with it. The din was frightening and Fred wondered if the bloody thing was going to land on top of him; it was anybody's guess as to the proximity of the danger. Primates leaped for safety and vented their fury by screeching madly and howling with rage. Other creatures joined in, and it was well over an hour before the jungle settled down once more. He looked at his watch again, only 03.00 hrs. He jerked his head up sharply in response to a snapping of undergrowth straight in front of his position, and pretty damned close at that. The image of the luminous dial of his watch was still imprinted on his eyeball and blended in with the vision now before his eyes – thousands of little green dots.

In his present agitated state Fred had an alarming thought, What if some of those dots out there were coming from luminous watch dials, if so, how many men were stalking around wearing the bloody things? No, that's a preposterous suggestion. Or was it?

What saved Fred from becoming a gibbering maniac that night was pain, the excruciating agony that comes with cramp. Spasms of it tortured his feet and leg muscles, it was not as if he could stand up and exercise the cramp away, he was well and truly stuck with it. With the pain came the realisation that it was cold, nay, bloody freezing was more like it. Fred started to shiver uncontrollably and his teeth chattered away like castanets to such an extent that he had to stuff a corner of his camouflaged face veil into his mouth to stop the noise.

Fred had now reached the point where his back was against the wall, so to speak, and that great factor of SAS mystique came to the fore, sending Fred onto the offensive with his will. He used it to combat the pain, he cursed it, and he goaded it to get worse and dared it to break his bones. Fred gritted his teeth and willed the agony into exquisite bliss and slowly but surely, with resolute determination, he fought off the pain and eventually won the battle of mind over matter.

By first light the cramp had gone; the glow-worms had gone too, and the only green dots visible were those on the face of his watch. It was 06.30 hrs and slowly the silver-grey outline of foliage cloaked in the early morning vapour began to appear. The nocturnal creatures had gone to bed and the music of the night had ceased; the jungle was waking up and the inharmonious clatter of the day was about to commence. And so ended a not so typical night in the life of a British soldier at work in the jungle.

A new day was dawning, in military terminology that translates into 'first light'. It is the particular time of day that soldiers are supposedly still half-asleep and thoroughly disorganised. Military Commanders the world over deem it the ideal moment to attack a foe. To combat that strategy, the British Army rouses its troops well before first light to adopt all-round defensive positions in order to be prepared for a dawn attack. This well rehearsed drill, that is also carried out at last light, is known as a 'stand-to'.

The SAS patrol had not changed its formation in any way and the men were still sitting statue-like in their respective buttresses, the highly trained soldiers did not need telling what to do; they had automatically put themselves on full alert ready to repel a possible CT attack. They had no way of knowing the strength of the enemy force, it was impossible to guess what they were up against; there could be as few as a four-man group or there could be bloody dozens of the sods. If there were that many and they did mount an attack the SAS men knew that they would not see out the day, but by hell, they would sell their lives dearly.

There is no set time for the duration of a stand-to, individual commanders on the ground set it, in this case it was Chalky. In Malaya the transition from night into day takes about fifteen minutes, so by 06.45 hrs it was completely light. The CT attack did not materialise and Fred sensed that Chalky would soon signal the stand-down, in anticipation of that the scout geared himself for his first task of the day.

The collection of some form of identification from the two dead terrorists was necessary because both the military and civil security services held records of all known terrorists. The guerrilla army had an official order of battle and regimental nominal rolls of their soldiers. In order to cross dead terrorists off of the list, operational troops serving in the deep jungle were required to produce identification from their reported 'kills'. The records held by the authorities, of mostly the hard-core element from the Chinese 8th Route Army, included photographs, fingerprints and personal details that described tattoos, temperaments, habits and mannerisms. In theory the intrepid new SAS man was to obtain photographs or fingerprints of the dead men. In 1957 the kind of photographic equipment that was likely to be issued to troops was along the same lines as the Box Brownie camera. They were small, compact and light, simple to understand and operate but were not waterproof. More to the point, they were definitely not soldier-proof. Carried about in a soldier's pack for weeks on end, the fragile piece of equipment was easily damaged, that, together with the damp and humid conditions often put paid to the sensitive film. On a three-month long SAS deep-penetration patrol it was unlikely that an issue camera would last the pace. Anyway, it is Sod's Law that should a camera survive the inevitable battering there is no guarantee that there will be a face left to photograph. That left another non-starter, fingerprinting, is it even worth thinking about? On one hand an official form had to be prepared for the job using an inkpad and roller, this task to be carried out in a dripping wet jungle environment under battle conditions. On the other hand, there is a dead body probably covered in blood and other matter, soaking wet from the elements and urine, and soiled by excrement. In this particular instance the body would be difficult to handle due to the onset of rigor mortis; the execution of this task must be left to one's imagination.

Chalky got to his feet signifying the end of the stand-to; the watching and waiting was over and it was time to get going. As previously planned, Chalky advanced twenty yards up the spur to guard the point. Worm backtracked the same distance down the feature to watch the rear; Fred covered Bob whilst he gathered in the radio antenna and packed it away. Then the two men reversed roles with Bob protecting Fred as he approached the dead bodies. The stench was now overpowering and the corpses were crawling with ants, and leeches were striving to extract the last drop of blood from the opportune feast. Fred negotiated the steep, slippery side of the spur and considered the nearest dead CT, the first of the two men that he had shot. He weighed up the options, the head was missing completely, which explained the snapping and crunching sounds of the night; thus solving the problem of choice.

'No head, no photograph,' Fred whispered to himself. 'So it's to be a fingerprint job then,' he decided. The scout had shrugged off his earlier reluctance to perform this particular chore, now that it was inevitable he went at the task with determination and ruthless efficiency. He looked back to ensure that Bob was covering him before propping his shotgun up against a tree. With both hands now free he prepared the corpse for the work ahead, first he pulled at the dead man's right arm until he could wedge it at the wrist in the fork of a split sapling. Due to rigor mortis setting in, the limb kept springing back out and Fred had to secure it in place with some thin vine. Satisfied with his crude workbench he now proceeded with the operation itself. Drawing his razor sharp parang, a short Malay cutlass, he executed one well-aimed swipe and cut off the hand at the wrist.

'One set of fingerprints,' he chuckled evilly as he packed the severed limb into a polythene food bag for preservation. The bag had been brought along especially for the task instead of a camera and a fingerprint outfit. It might be some time before it could be passed on to the powers that be, but once in their possession it became indisputable evidence. He put the gory package down next to his shotgun and turned his attention towards the second body. This one was lying face downwards with the broken neck still trapped in the fork of a tree about three feet off the ground, the back of his head was intact and presented at an inviting angle. Fred had an irresistible urge to lop it off but curbed the impulse; instead, he lifted up the head to look at the face, or rather, what was left of it. The features had been obliterated by the shotgun blast and finished off by the creatures of the night, ants were picking clean the eye sockets and nose cavities, the lower jawbone had been shot away and yet more ants were working frantically around the exposed windpipe. Fred dropped the head in disgust, 'Too bloody heavy to carry anyway,' he muttered.

The right arm was broken and twisted in such a manner that it hung down the tree trunk palm outwards as if beckoning. With a backhand slash, Fred cut into the wrist arresting the blade before it could impact the hard wood and make a noise, then he silently finished the job by sawing through flesh and sinew that was still holding the hand to the shattered arm. The hand went into a separate food bag and that brought the grisly task to an end. Fred looked around at the blast-damaged foliage and the shot-scarred timber, it was obvious that a fight had occurred here and all the camouflage in the world would not hide the fact. He decided to leave the bodies as they were, positioned a good twenty yards below the main track they would be hard to spot anyway. The weapons though were a different matter, they had to be hidden so he collected them in: a .303-inch No. 3 Lee-Enfield rifle of Second World War vintage and a .38 Smith and Wesson revolver, both weapons were empty and Fred could find no spare ammunition. Nor were there any sign of documents or maps.

Fred carried the two weapons and the hands up to the edge of the spur and laid them on the track, then recovering his shotgun he clambered up the torturous slope and rejoined Bob. The track was so narrow at that particular elevation that there was nowhere really suitable to hide the captured arms except up in the trees. He pulled down and bent over a stout but springy sapling and secured it to a convenient branch with some vine. That done Fred was able to tie the weapons to the top third part of the young tree, then he released the ties allowing the sapling to spring back into its original position taking the rifle and pistol up and out of sight into the foliage above. Finally he rearranged some small branches to form indicators at about head height, to the untrained eye nothing appeared to be amiss, but to the advancing SAS patrols it was as clear as any signpost: 'Bodies down, weapons up'. Fred quickly stowed away the severed hands into his Bergen rucksack. *I'd better not put them in with my grub,* he mused, *or I'll end up cooking the bloody things.*

It was time to go and Fred gave Bob the nod; he in turn signalled to Worm and the three men moved up the spur towards Chalky leaving the ancient battle-scarred tree behind them. The patrol regrouped into the previous day's order-of-march with Fred leading the way as scout.

At first it was not so much the case of tracking the guerrillas but more like following a trail of frantic activity and destruction. Trees and undergrowth had been ripped to shreds by gunfire from both sides; blood stained the ground and some foliage here and there, and everywhere there were signs of enemy movement such as footprints, discarded items of kit and empty cartridge cases. Fred soon came upon the spot where the CTs had rested the day before, prior to the engagement.

From the tracks and other signs Chalky was able to put together a picture of what must have happened from the enemy's point of view, and it explained away the head-on clash. 'Bloody bad luck for them, and us too,' he whispered to Fred.

'Yeah,' replied the scout, 'any other night and they would have just kipped down here!'

Chalky signalled for the patrol to continue; Fred cautiously picked his way forward and after about fifty yards he discovered that the bandits had taken a ninety-degree turn to the left, the enemy were fleeing down off the spur in a westerly direction. The chase was on and Fred was hot on the trail, the follow up proper had begun.

An hour later, the patrol reached a small stream and the ground rose steeply on the other side of it. In the damp earth, each side of the streambed, Fred found some well-defined tracks and was able to determine from them that one of the men was using his rifle as a walking stick and was obviously the wounded bandit. But strangely enough it was that man who appeared to be leading the way; the other bandit seemed to be weighed down with kit and was making heavy going of it. In the deeper imprints that were leading out of the stream where a substantial amount of water had been displaced, some of it was still trickling back into the depressions. Fred guessed that the bandits had bugged out from Bukit Chermingat dead on first light whilst he had been busy with his gruesome chore, and as a result the enemy soldiers had stolen a march on the SAS patrol of at least an hour.

All that day the patrol pursued the enemy using Fred's tracking skills and Chalky's guile. They were catching up but the scout had to curb the impulse to close in for the kill. Chalky, always the iceman, held him in check like any good dog handler. The ploy was to monitor the guerrillas' progress to see if they were following a particular bearing or were just fleeing in panic, getting too close to the CTs might alarm or provoke them into resorting to the latter.

By 15.00 hrs Chalky was satisfied that he had cracked it and ordered the patrol to bash-up for the night. This time they were able to follow the normal routine, and whilst the other three men went about the business of making camp, Chalky did some plotting on his map. Drawing a line through the general axis of the enemy's advance he calculated that they were heading for a place called Triang. Their route would be fairly straightforward except for one major obstacle, the Sungei Bera. 'That,' he whispered to himself, 'will be the end of the road for them.' By the time he had finished, Bob had set up the radio and was soon sending Chalky's situation report to Squadron Headquarters.

Caesar received Chalky's report only minutes after his signaller had got himself organised. Soon the airwaves were busy as he sent out instructions to all his patrols. In effect he had ordered the whole squadron to the Bukit Chermingat area, the Squadron Commander also sent Chalky's report verbatim to Brigade HQ.

By 16.00 hrs the next day Caesar's squadron were all deployed on or around Bukit Chermingat, Caesar's own four-man patrol occupying the summit; in tandem with the SAS movements, the Brigade Commander had initiated a blocking move in this deadly game of chess.

★

On 21 August 1957 the reserve Battalion of the Commonwealth Brigade was deployed to various road heads by trucks, and in some cases, helicopters. From these remote access points, the Australian infantrymen marched to a series of ambush positions along the winding river-line and complex tributaries of the Sungei Bera. Their orders were to kill, or if possible, capture the two CTs; at all costs they were to be stopped.

★

On the third day of the follow-up, the 22nd, Chalky's patrol had tracked the enemy to within 1,000 yards of the Sungei Bera. If the

CTs kept to the present bearing they would hit the river at a point where it crossed at right angles to their path. Flowing into the river on each side of the fleeing men were two tributaries that formed a natural trap with the river as a baseline. The CTs were showing no signs of awareness that they were being followed, and of course, they were completely oblivious to the fact that they were approaching over eight hundred tough Australian troops. Chalky knew that by the middle of the morrow it would all be over, he was also aware that he and his men would shortly be facing a situation that was all too familiar to SAS soldiers; that of facing the firepower of friendly forces.

★

Shen was dying and he knew it. Whether his end would come solely from the ghastly wounds that he had already received or from the fight that was yet to come was open to conjecture, but die he surely would.

Shen had got 'the one with his name on it' shortly after he had heard the first two shots fired at Bukit Chermingat. The booming of the shotgun told him all too clearly that his lifelong friend Liew was dead, and that had shocked him to the core; it also gave him a clue as to whom he was facing. When only a split second after the first volley a storm of 9mm bullets had buzzed angrily about him like enraged hornets, and he was hit by two of them, he was convinced that he knew who they were. His worst fears were confirmed when two more weapons joined in the fray almost immediately: four men, and all firing effectively within seconds. Shen knew of only one unit in the British Army that were deployed in such small numbers and could be that quick off the mark, they were the madmen who dropped from the sky into the trees. They roamed the jungle for months at a time, carried big packs, wore beards and called themselves the SAS. Shen's thoughts had been interrupted by two more thunderous reports from a shotgun and he knew instinctively that whoever was on the receiving end of that lethal charge had perished too. In the closing moments of daylight he had signalled a ceasefire; as if in agreement the British had followed suit a few seconds later.

With the breaking off of the action came the pain, the cruel, excruciating pain of gunshot wounds. He had been shot in the right shoulder and upper arm, no bones had been broken but a bullet was lodged in his shoulder and that wound was bleeding profusely. He had no medical kit so he staunched the flow of blood with improvised dressings made from leaves and tree bark that he tied on with strips of cloth torn from his bush jacket. All this was achieved in complete darkness, in utter silence and only yards from a deadly enemy; such was the measure of the man. Shen prayed for death many times during that long, pain-ridden and nerve-racking night but daylight eventually came, and with it the hope of escape.

Shen and his fellow terrorist had managed to creep away undetected at first light and were soon descending the western slopes of Bukit Chermingat. Shen was too far gone to carry any weight so he handed over his pack to the other man at the first opportunity but insisted on leading the way. The Chinese are renowned for their pride, stubbornness and endurance, the next four days in the lives of the two terrorists proved that beyond a shadow of doubt. It was a hellish march where they first had to cross-grain their way through steep-sided re-entrants and then negotiate the edges of the leech-infested swamplands of Tasek Bera before approaching the Sungei Bera itself. The pain from Shen's wounds was driving him crazy; whilst his companion suffered a different kind of agony caused by the enormous load he was carrying, but nonetheless, just as painful and equally mind bending.

They suffered mental torment too, for although he had detected no sign of it, Shen guessed that the SAS hounds must be hot on his tail. They were living on a nervous knife-edge of tension, not knowing how far behind them the tough parachutists might be or what fiendish fate the British had in store for them ahead. Psychologically Shen was experiencing a feeling of dark foreboding, for the SAS to bump into them on the actual courier route was more than a mere coincidence and Shen had a feeling that things had gone terribly wrong at Kim Bok's end. The two guerrilla fighters endured all this on a few grains of rice and less than a pint of water, it was a Herculean effort that even the pursuing SAS soldiers would have been hard pushed to match.

At the end of that fourth day Shen and his exhausted friend huddled together like babes in the wood knowing deep down in their hearts that they would be very lucky to see out another full day.

The SAS men were closing up on the CTs. Chalky guessed that they could be no more than a hundred yards behind their quarry; at times he could hear the terrorists stumbling about the jungle. By 16.00 hrs the patrol had reached its limit of exploitation, they could go no further. Chalky had Bob set up the radio, then with about the same distance as your average telegraph pole between himself and the enemy, he sent the grid reference of his position and the estimated location of the two CTs. The grid references were accurate to within one hundred yards; in effect, friend and foe were in one and the same place. Chalky decreed that there would be no building of bashas, no cooking or smoking; like that first night back at the old tree, the SAS men sat back to back and kept silent vigil.

Shen woke up to the spinning world of the sick and disorientated, he felt dizzy and weak and could not collect his thoughts or co-ordinate any bodily movements. The two hunted men lay comatose until the sun rose high in the sky and the midday heat put energy back into their bones. The desperate duo staggered to their feet and for a long moment looked deep into each other's eyes, by some unspoken but mutual agreement they discarded all their equipment except for weapons and ammunition. Shen had long since destroyed the written instructions that he had received from Kim Bok but he still had the sketch maps of the courier route. He now mashed them into a pulp and buried the bits. Then with weapons held at the ready, the two men advanced proudly to meet their fate.

A first light on the fifth day, the SAS men fanned out to form an extended line with about ten yards between each man; crawling towards a slight rise in the ground, they took up firing positions. Using the advantage of increased visibility at ground level they were able to cover a front in excess of fifty yards allowing for the field of fire of the two flank men. Their mission was to stop any attempt by the enemy to withdraw from the impending action by the waiting Australian infantrymen who, of course, would be firing straight towards the SAS patrol; squirming themselves flat to the ground, Chalky and his men watched and waited.

The Commanding Officer of the Australian Infantry Battalion had deployed two of his companies into the ambush area, keeping a third back at a helicopter landing point in reserve. On the face of it, two companies of men to deal with a couple of terrorists might seem a little heavy-handed but in the limited visibility of the close country, the jungle swallowed up soldiers like some huge green monster. Commanders never seemed to have enough men to put on the ground. Each ambush was of a platoon strength, that is to say about thirty men, and there were six of them in all. The soldiers of No. 4 Platoon of Bravo Company had mounted one such ambush.

In No. 1 Section of that platoon a big-boned, taciturn man known to his mates as Shovel, manned the Bren light machine gun. He was so called because it was said that he could dig himself a slit trench with his enormous lantern jaw. An old soldier, he had fought in the Korean War and had completed one and a half stints of active service in Malaya. A man of infinite patience, he had spent most of the last three days teaching his No. 2 on the gun not to fidget.

'Strewth man,' he had been forced to advise in a whisper, 'why don't you send a bloody message to the commie bastards.' The boy, for despite the macho uniform, rifle and equipment, that was what he was, listened and learned. He also secretly wished that he could serve the whole of his time with this bloke, then perhaps he would see the end of his National Service in one bloody piece.

They had been told of the British encounter four days previously and by a combination of transport and boot leather had made it to this god-awful place to lie in wait for the enemy. The boy glanced at Shovel and thought, *The sun is well past its zenith and if those Pommy SAS bastards have got it dead to rights then the CTs should have made a move by now.*

The muscles of Shovel's face twitched and slowly, oh ever so slowly, he brought the butt of the Bren gun up into his shoulder. The air became electric with tension but the veteran was outwardly calm and his eyes were hard and piercing.

He's heard or sensed something, pondered the young shaver, his hands were trembling with nervousness but he had an excited look in his eyes and he followed Shovel's example and concentrated on the ground to his front.

Shovel moved the change lever of the gun to 'R', for repetition, so that it would only fire single rounds; ambushes are always sprung by a singe shot. Burst from automatic weapons can be unreliable due to stoppages and misfires, such an occurrence at a crucial time like this would confuse the issue and the element of surprise would be lost. The slight swaying of a sapling was enough to make both men take up the first pressure on their triggers.

★

The rubbery textured form of the leech stretched its worm-like body upwards, the lower extremity being firmly anchored by suckers to a fallen leaf that lay on the damp russet mat of the jungle floor. The creature swayed from side to side like a snake under the spell of a charmer's flute, its upper end was also equipped with suckers that probed the air for the scent of any approaching prey. It awaited the chance to attach itself to a source of food, for the minute predator yearned to gorge on the life-giving liquids of its victims in an attempt to quench an insatiable thirst. An abundance of water was nearby and the ground was well marked with spoor, the leech knew that there was plenty of common food in the offing but it sensed the presence of a much favoured delicacy that flowed through the bodies of those that walked on their hind legs only. To the higher order of earthly creatures they were known as the Upright Ones. The problem was that this strange species cloaked their lower limbs in a kind of thick skin that could not normally be penetrated by the leech's sensitive suckers. To get at the soft skin and the red juices that flowed through it entailed crawling up the animal's legs, an exercise fraught with danger. To follow this path would lead to certain detection resulting in death by burning from the smoking sticks that the creatures carried in their jaws, or an equally horrible end from the liquid that they sometimes rubbed on their bodies. The answer, the leech knew, was to climb above the upright beast and drop onto the most vulnerable and lucrative parts of the unsuspecting quarry using the thick jungle foliage as camouflage. A daunting task, but considering the plentiful supply of prime fluid from behind the victim's ears and around the throat, the rewards were well worth the effort.

The leech began its laborious journey by crawling across the carpet of leaves in search of a hanging creeper or vine that would guide it aloft. Perhaps crawling is the wrong expression; cart wheeling would be a more apt description of its movements. For the leech to travel, it had first to stretch its free end as far as possible in the direction that it wished to go, and then anchor that end down with its suckers. Having completed that exercise the leech could release the other end and adopt an upright, all round observation and sensory posture for a second or two before repeating the whole operation all over again. And so, head over heels, it proceeded on its way: dunk – release – up, and observe – stretch – dunk and so on. As both ends of a leech are almost identical it would be fair to say that it could never be quite sure whether it was standing on its head or its arse.

It was noon by the time the intrepid vampire had reached a suitable leaf that was hanging from a branch about six feet from the ground. The heat was stifling and the leech was glad of the rest after tackling the difficult highway of mosses, lichens, ferns, palms, thorns and wet, slippery saplings. It was also exhausted from running the gauntlet of other predators especially the winged kind who had the infuriating habit of flinging leeches great distances like discarded chewing gum after discovering that the elastic creatures were inedible.

The leech adopted its alert posture and immediately picked up the signature of many of its own kind. But the predominate scent that rode the hot air waves, the one that made the leech's senses reel with pleasure and its suckers and jaws drool with anticipation was that of the Upright Ones. Many, the leech sensed, were nearby and static but others were on the move and getting closer by the minute. The pitiless heart within the loathsome, disgusting hunter beat faster as the time came for it to move in for the kill. The revolting form of the leech, whose only warmth in life came from the fluids that it drank from its victims' arteries and veins, moved to the edge of the leaf and prepared itself for the drop.

Now at the point of no return it had a sudden panic attack as it remembered, that like the birds, the Upright Ones had irritating traits too. Having detected the presence of a leech upon their bodies the more daring of them would pull it out leaving one end still embedded in the flesh by its suckers to die and rot. The beasts would then play with the long free end stretching it almost to breaking point before tying it in a knot; the writhing leech would then be rolled into a ball and flicked away in utter disgust.

The scent of food was now so overpowering that it cancelled out the panic and fear, indeed, the leech could not remember the last time that the air had carried such a strong stench of the red liquor that it existed on. Suddenly the Upright One was directly beneath the leech and stationary; the leech let go and began its free fall towards the target area between the ear and the head where it hoped to get wedged in. It was on course and prepared its suckers for the landing, being so light it was unlikely that the quarry would feel the impact, the danger point would be the instant that it inserted both sets of slavering jaws and suckers into the soft inviting skin. But so adept was the leech at this particular skill that it was doubtful if the Upright One would be aware of it.

Still on track, it was distracted by a loud screeching noise caused by the wings of an evil disease-carrying insect, faster than the leech could see, the winged creature flew straight into the Upright One's ear. The upright beast reacted instantly and slapped at the threatened organ with its paw, tilting its head to one side as it did so. The leech missed the target and fell to the ground where it wriggled about in frustration and anger. A sound like a clap of thunder, followed quickly by several more stirred the leech into even greater fits of frenzy, and as the noise rumbled and echoed away into the distance, a huge weight pressed down on the hunter blocking out the light and soaking it in a thick warm substance.

The leech drowned in the very liquid that it had worked so hard to obtain, blood.

★

A flash of movement caught Shovel's eye, he knew not what it was, but instinct told him to fire anyway, and this he did by loosing off a single shot followed by several bursts of two to three rounds. His action precipitated rapid fire along the entire platoon front of 100 yards. The jungle reverberated to the sound of light machine guns, sub-machine guns and rifles. Booby traps that had been laid in dead ground were exploded and trip flares to assist in night firing were set off too. Foliage and small trees were cut or blown down in great swathes by the sheer intensity of this sustained volley.

Not all men could fire at the same target as Shovel; indeed, each soldier had his own arc of responsibility that was marked out with pegs sited in front of his position. Both by day and night those pegs, or stops, would physically limit the distance left or right that the soldier could traverse the barrel of his weapon, the ploy was for that soldier to concentrate all his efforts within his restricted field of fire. All arcs were interlocking so that the whole platoon front was covered by a wicked crossfire. Accuracy was not the name of the game here, firepower was. It has been said that for every man killed in action during the Second World War a million rounds of ammunition was expended. Well, the Diggers in this particular ambush were doing their damnedest to uphold that theory, one would think that nobody could survive such a devastating onslaught, but they did.

★

Shovel's first shot hit Shen in the stomach, and the burst that followed blew his arm off. The second burst removed his head and needless to say he was dead before he hit the ground. The accuracy of those first shots and the split-second pause before the rest of the ambush responded allowed Shen's colleague to dive for cover but he collected a slight head wound in the process. In the brief moment that he was in the prone position the terrorist was presented with an opportune target in the form of an enemy soldier who had broken cover, he took a snap shot at the man and had the satisfaction of seeing him go down. It was the one and only shot fired by the CTs during the engagement.

When the trap had been sprung the young Australian soldier was able to fire only two shots from his rifle before he was required to carry out his duties as Shovel's No. 2 on the Bren gun, in this instance it was to change magazines. The gun stopped, Shovel had fired twenty-eight rounds. He cocked the gun and quickly knocked the empty magazine off; the boy deftly replaced it with a full one, the first change had gone without a hitch. The gun stopped again, the same drill was carried out but this time the No. 2 fumbled the change and the full magazine fell to the ground on Shovel's side of the gun. The boy reached over the Bren to retrieve it and the underside of his left forearm came into contact with the red-hot barrel. He screamed out in agony and, completely caught off guard, rose above his cover for a second; and one lousy second was all that it took for a bullet to enter his brain through his right eye; his National Service had been terminated.

The Platoon Commander gave the order to ceasefire but because of the horrendous racket it took some time for it to become effective. The lone CT took full advantage of this period of confusion to crawl away from the killing ground. When he thought that enough distance had been put between himself and the enemy he stood up and ran; it is foolish to run in the jungle, especially in panic. The hostile environment seems to sense distress in an individual and gangs up on the unfortunate being, deploying its arsenal of vines, creepers and thorns. One such thorn grows on the very end of the leaves of the attap palm and is known to the troops as 'wait a while'. The tiny, razor-sharp barbs of one of these plants had caught up in the fleeing man's upper lip and his right eyebrow, holding him back and causing him great distress; some had become entangled in his hair and were aggravating his already painful scalp wound. The half-crazed terrorist was also trapped by a mass of hanging vines and was going nowhere fast. Wild eyed and at breaking point he found himself looking over the top of a moss-covered fallen tree; resting on the top of it and pointing straight at his head was the muzzle of a shotgun.

What Chalky had first thought was a rise in the ground, was in fact, a huge fallen tree that was now covered in moss and fungus; it was also the probable home for dozens of scorpions and centipedes. It gave the patrol the advantage of some elevation, cover from view, but very little cover from fire. The SAS men had waited all morning for the ambush to be sprung lying as flat as they could behind the giant log, they were ready to spring up and adopt firing positions as soon as the Aussies ceased firing. When the ambush opened just a little after midday, the suddenness of it was enough to shock the nervous system, and even the tough SAS soldiers nearly jumped out of their skins. The ear shattering rattle of automatic fire and the crump-crump of exploding grenades together with the snap-snap-snapping of bullets passing overhead was an experience never to be forgotten. Add to this the hissing of burning tracer and the whining of ricochets that collected foliage, wood splinters and bark, turning the natural substances into a vicious hail of shrapnel; and you have hell on earth.

Now that battle had been joined, so to speak, there was no need for the Aussies to remain mute so the verbal orders for the ceasefire when they came were given with some stick and were quite audible to the SAS men. By the time Fred had judged it prudent to unglue himself from the jungle floor, he could already hear the sound of someone crashing around and heading his way. Then like a fiendish apparition from the pit a blood-soaked head appeared before his eyes and seemed to hang there as if in suspended animation. The fact that the man was hopelessly hung up in a tangled mass of jungle vegetation and that there was a requirement for a prisoner to be taken saved the wretched terrorist's life for the time being because Fred did not open fire. Had he done so it might have invited a barrage of returning fire from the now hyped-up Australian soldiers, that possibility and the threat of an almighty cock-up had now been averted.

The wounded terrorist was by now a gibbering wreck and was wailing like a banshee. There were a few tense moments when it was feared that a trigger-happy rifleman might take a pot shot towards the noise. Chalky who had crawled up to Fred's position summed up the situation in a glance. 'Let's go for it,' he said cupping his hands to his mouth. Then in a rare display of the spoken word the SAS Patrol Commander shouted the password, 'Beehive! Beehive! Beehive!' After which he volunteered the information, 'Four men, one prisoner, coming in!'

'Advance in single file, weapons pointed straight up!' came the authoritative reply from the Aussie Platoon Sergeant. The SAS men cut the wounded bandit free from the vines and thorns and led him up to the Australian lines where he was duly handed over and taken in tow as a prisoner of war. Fred handed over his grisly evidence much to the amusement of the Aussie troops and then the exhausted patrol gratefully accepted a brew-up from the elated Diggers.

As part of a battalion combat group, the triumphant ambush party had ample back-up and excellent lines of communication including a well-tried casualty evacuation system, but first the two bodies of friend and foe alike would have to be carried out to the nearest road-head or helicopter landing point. After that the remains, including the hands, would be taken to Kuala Lumpur. Within days, the forensic experts would produce the true identity of Shen's corpse and that of the men who had once owned the hands.

The platoon medic was already patching up the prisoner who had been pronounced 'fit to march'; not that anyone would have carried him anyway. From the exit point he would be taken to a police location and handed over to them to face legal processing and inevitable interrogation; and his response to that would determine his fate.

As Chalky swigged down the last of his tea he smiled wryly. The SAS team did not have the luxury of an administrative tail such as the Australian troops enjoyed. They worked in isolation like the nomads that they so much resembled, seeking out the quarry and herding them into traps laid by military formations far better equipped to deal with all those other mundane problems.

The Australian platoon were now going through their reorganisation drill, checking weapons, expenditure of ammunition and redistributing it where necessary. Casualties had to be logged and the smallest of injuries treated, a minute cut in the jungle can develop into a festering major wound in less than a day. Equipment used to set up the ambush had to be retrieved and the platoon put back into a state of readiness. In these hectic times a good platoon Sergeant is worth his weight in gold; and by the time the young platoon Commander had plotted his route for the march out, the Sergeant was able to inform him that the platoon was ready to move. And move they had to in case of an enemy counter-attack or some retaliatory shell or mortar fire. The Aussies pulled out taking their still-dazed prisoner with them; each and every one of these rough individuals shook hands with the SAS patrol as they passed by.

The SAS men bugged out too, making a 'heads down arse up' bash of 2,000 yards to take them out of the area. At 15.00 hrs with still an hour and a half of daylight left, they stopped and made a decent camp for a change, and for the first time in five days they ate some hot food.

As Chalky spooned down his mess tin full of steak, peas and onions flavoured with curry powder and soggy Oxo he pondered over the situation. No matter which way he looked at it the conclusion was that he had made an almighty cock-up of the job, his small force was a reconnaissance patrol, nothing more, and nothing less; their task was to find the enemy, not to fight them. In war the best laid plans go awry due to the slightest unforeseen incident, and had the bloody CTs just kipped down for the night where they were instead of moving on things might have gone to plan. He knew that it was not his fault but it stuck in his craw. However, there was some consolation in the fact that once his patrol had been committed to action they had acquitted themselves well. He was also pleased with how he had accurately predicted and plotted the enemy's movements, so enabling the Australian troops to reach the correct map references at the right time. As for Fred, well he had proved himself to be a worthy member of the elite. He was in a class of his own and could walk tall amongst giants.

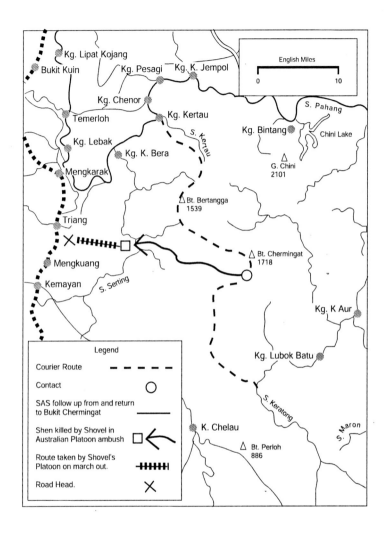

Legend

Courier Route - - - -

Contact ○

SAS follow up from and return
to Bukit Chermingat ——

Shen killed by Shovel in
Australian Platoon ambush □ ←

Route taken by Shovel's
Platoon on march out. ++++++

Road Head. ×

Chapter Six

It took Shovel's platoon four days to march out of the jungle, a long hard slog to reach the rendezvous with the transport that met them at the nearest road-head. The platoon had made slow progress because it had been necessary to carry Shen's body slung on a pole like some beast that had been shot on safari. They had carried the body of their comrade, the boy, on an improvised stretcher made from two more poles and one of the men's ponchos. Despite the arduous nature of the task, the tough Australian infantrymen made it in high spirits.

That indispensable functionary of infantry life, the Company Quartermaster Sergeant, met them at the road-head. This man, better known to the rank and file as 'Colour', short for Colour Sergeant, issued each man with a can of lager with which to wash down a steak sandwich that had the same dimensions as a doorstep. The prisoner was offered the same fare but declined to accept Colour's hospitality; he would go to his grave without understanding the rough Australian humour and their tolerance of him as a prisoner of war. It puzzled him because apart from the odd shove in the back to make him keep up on the march, they had not mistreated him in any way. On the contrary, they had offered him cigarettes and always included him in their brew-ups and cooking. *Where was the Western decadence,* he wondered, *why are they not torturing me?*

After a suitable break, the soldiers were ordered to board three troop-carrying trucks that Colour had led to the remote dead end; the prisoner was made to travel in the first vehicle with Shovel's rifle section. Sentries were posted at each corner of the open trucks with clear arcs of observation being given to each man; the Platoon Sergeant went to every vehicle in turn to check that things were okay. The platoon was cock-a-hoop over their success but it would not do to become complacent in this ambush-ridden country. When he was satisfied that all was in order that august person reported back to his young Platoon Commander and then climbed aboard the rear three-tonner. The convoy moved off; behind the leading vehicle came the second rifle section and the platoon headquarters group. Next in line was a one-tonne ambulance carrying the two dead bodies, followed by Colour in his three-tonne truck that was also towing a water-trailer. Bringing up the rear was the third rifle section, and as always, the trusty Platoon Sergeant.

For over an hour the convoy whined and growled its way along the twisting, slippery and deeply rutted cart track. The fact that the mapmakers in all their wisdom had had the temerity to call it a road was the subject of many ribald comments from the jungle weary, tensed up troops. Parts of this questionable route were overgrown with secondary jungle and in many places it seemed as if they were driving though a tunnel.

This was indeed perfect ambush country with the main threat coming from anti-tank mines sited to explode under the leading vehicle. The prisoner was very aware of this fact and his apprehension was visibly evident. *Ah, perhaps their torture is more subtle than ours,* he thought nervously. As well as killing some of the soldiers, the mine would cause utter confusion and the terrorists would take full advantage of this to shower the convoy with hand grenades and hosepipe it with a withering crossfire. It was a bone-shaking, nerve-racking ride but luckily for all concerned, an uneventful one, and when at long last they reached a road with a tarmac surface they all breathed a sigh of relief.

The road was also heavily patrolled by armoured cars and two had been allocated to the convoy as escorts for the remainder of the journey south to a town called Rompin. Whilst the platoon had been enjoying their food and drink at the RV, the Platoon Commander had informed his superiors of the platoon's estimated time of arrival at the Rompin police barracks. This information would have been passed on to the Federation of Malaya Police Force who manned the training camp there; and they would be expecting the convoy of tired Australian troops, and of course, the prisoner.

The army was duty bound to hand over all prisoners of war to the civilian police, and in particular, to the Special Branch whenever possible. In this case Special Branch would no doubt be waiting to question the prisoner having been given ample warning of his impending arrival. Once they had positively identified the prisoner of war as a terrorist he would be charged with offences under civil law and the matter would be taken out of military hands altogether. In many cases, the terrorists were given the option to cooperate with the Security Forces; those who declined the offer to turn on their comrades faced the prospect of hanging for their sins.

The convoy passed straight through the small town of Rompin that was situated in the state of Negri Sembilan; three miles south of the town the vehicles turned left and after a further couple of miles arrived at the barracks. Constructed especially for the Emergency it resembled the typical Second World War German prison camps as often depicted in films, complete with watchtowers, barriers and miles of barbed wire fencing. It was a police recruit training establishment and the men were housed in neat rows of wooden huts that were clad in frames of attap leaves and wooden shutters acted as windows. Just inside the gate was a whitewashed, breeze block building that housed the guardroom and the administrative offices; it was also the Rompin Area Police Headquarters.

The dirt-grimed, bedraggled diggers looked like country cousins when compared with the immaculately turned out Malay policemen on gate duty outside the guardroom. Brass shell cases sparkled in the sun as they stood sentinel-like on the polished verandah, whilst the Union Jack together with the Federation of Malaya Police Force flags fluttered proudly from their white painted poles. As the convoy drove into the camp to park up on the barrack square the policemen regarded the troops with open admiration; whilst the Aussies responded in their customary crude style of rough military humour. 'Good day you bullshitting bastards,' was considered to be a polite form of greeting. Whilst, 'Where's the bloody bar then?' constituted a reasonable enquiry.

There was a short delay in the proceedings whilst the duty police Sergeant informed the senior officer that the convoy had arrived.

'He won't be long, sir,' apologised the sergeant addressing the

Australian subaltern, 'he's just leaving his bungalow now. Lives on the outskirts of town you know.'

Fifteen minutes later the officer in question arrived to take over the prisoner. 'Good afternoon,' he greeted, offering his hand to the army man, 'Simon Belchard's my name, where's this murdering blighter then?' The prisoner was brought in from the transport and formally handed over to the civilian authorities and duly locked away in a cell. Shortly after that the Australian troops departed for Segamat to be redeployed.

Simon Belchard was not a happy man. He was under constant pressure from the Tongs via Abdul and Mr Tan for this damned information regarding British military operations taking place in Pahang; the overriding question being asked by the Tongs was, 'Are the activities in any way connected with the gold bullion?' The answer was simple, he did not know, the well had run dry and nothing was coming through from his source. Simon desperately wanted a way out of this terrible mess and his mind was torn between his desire for Fiona, his loyalty to the service, and of course, the lure of precious metal.

The terrorist had been brought in from the Pahang-Negri Sembilan border area, he surely must know something of what was going on up there. Simon thought long and hard before coming to a conclusion. *Perhaps,* he mused, *I could steal a march on the establishment and really get well in with the Tongs. They have me dead to rights and pose the biggest threat to me and they will never let go if I cross them.* When considering his affair with Fiona he thought, *If I come clean with the Commissioner I'll lose her for sure. By working for the villains I get to keep her and I'll get bloody well paid for it too, not to mention possible monetary gain from the gold venture.* And so it was that Simon Belchard continued to go down the left-hand path.

★

The Field Marshal was clearing his desk for the day when his phone rang; it was Crazy Harry Blunt. 'I've just heard from the task force commander sir, the Aussies have just handed over the CT to the police in Rompin. The message is timed at 15.30 hrs.'

'Thank you Harry, come on over to my office and bring Fairburne-Snape and that Nobles fellow with you.'

A short time later the trio was sat around a table looking expectantly at Petherington.

'Snape and…' the Field Marshal paused awkwardly looking at the two security men.

'Tom Nobles sir,' volunteered the Special Branch man.

'Ah yes, quite. Well the pair of you are to organise the interrogation of the prisoner who is now lodged at the Rompin Police Barracks. When can you start?'

'We can start tonight sir, but Tom here has some thoughts about that.'

'Thoughts, what thoughts?'

'I'd like to wait for the pathologist's report on the CT's remains first,' said Tom, answering the question for Jeremy.

'Yes,' resumed the MI6 man, 'a positive ID of these men and a direct link between them, Kim Bok and his woman would give us a definite edge at the onset of the interrogation proceedings.'

'And,' concluded Tom, 'forty-eight hours in a hot cell is a good way to let him sweat it out a bit.'

'Agreed,' nodded the Field Marshal, 'now let me bring you up to date on some other developments.' He gave them a comprehensive situation report concluding with, 'The SAS Squadron Commander… ah, Nero?'

'Caesar sir,' laughed Crazy Harry.

'I see,' grinned the military chief with a twinkle in his eye. 'Well the bloody emperor wants to backtrack the CTs to see where they came from before the contact – he thinks he's found the courier route?'

'I'd put my money on it,' remarked Harry. 'It would be a breakthrough if he's right,' said Jeremy with enthusiasm. Tom Nobles did not comment but he had a thoughtful look on his face; this prompted Harry Blunt to ask, 'What's up Tom?'

'I'm not sure yet,' Tom replied, looking at the wall clock behind Petherington's desk, 'can I use your phone sir?'

'Be my guest,' came the instant reply. The call took only a few seconds and when he had put the receiver down he was grim-faced with anger. He did not need any prompting to announce,

'That was my office I just phoned and…' he took a deep breath, 'Rompin have not yet informed us about the prisoner.'

'But he's been there for over two hours now,' observed Jeremy completely appalled.

The Field Marshal nodded at Harry, 'Get on the blower to the Commissioner's office and find out what bloody idiot is in charge down there. Get some background on the man, and keep Rompin out of it for the time being.' Harry dashed out to another room and Petherington ordered some tea and wads.

At 18.00 hrs the Police Commissioner himself joined the group gathered together in the army chief's office. An hour later everyone in the room knew more about Simon Belchard's sexual exploits than he did himself. This did not include his current liaison with Fiona Fairburne-Snape but the writing was on the wall.

'I shouldn't have taken the man on,' confessed the irate police chief. 'Bad judgement on my part,' he admitted.

'The thing is,' pondered the Field Marshal aloud, 'what the hell's he up to, what's his game?' He fixed his piercing gaze on Jeremy, 'You're the bloody spook man, give us a clue.'

Jeremy had no firm theory to expound upon so he suggested that they stick to the planned timescale of forty-eight hours. 'Let the prisoner sweat it out as agreed. If this man Belchard is bent or being got at, or both, the forty-eight hours worth of rope might be enough to hang him,' concluded Jeremy.

'Okay,' agreed the Field Marshal once more, 'then we'll do just that.'

★

The prisoner had not uttered a word. He had been stripped of his filthy clothing and given a Malay sarong to wear around his waist, someone had produced a pair of flip-flops so he was comfortably shod too. Simon had offered him some hot food and drink, even a shower and a hint that female company might be arranged. But the man refused to respond to this kind and considerate treatment. Simon continued with the soft approach throughout his first session of interrogation; a practice that should have been delayed until the arrival of MI6 and Special Branch. Simon knew all too well that he was way out of line here. After two fruitless hours he had the prisoner taken back to his cell not having extracted one single word from him. He was contemplating on what to do next when a Sergeant came into his office and handed him a small scrap of paper. 'We found this in his trouser pocket sir.'

Simon took the proffered soggy mess and spread it out on his desktop, written on the paper but hardly legible was a set of numbers arranged in four groups of ten digits each, all of which were meaningless to him. He marched into the prisoner's cell brandishing the obviously coded message, and confronting the man with it he barked, 'What's this, what's it mean?'

The terrorist responded at last but only to shake his head, his expression was blank. Inwardly though his heart sank for he remembered the note well, his mind wandered back to the moment in time when he and the 10th Regiment Intelligence Officer had said farewell at Kampong Kertau. On the point of leaving, the man had handed him the memo, 'Here take this,' he had asked, 'and destroy it for me?' In one of those rare moments of negligence he had stuck the piece of paper in his pocket and had completely forgotten about it. He knew exactly what the coded numbers meant, he felt ashamed of himself but resolved to hold out for as long as possible to give his friends some time; a futile gesture but an honourable one.

Simon did not ask the question again, instead, he left the cell and summoned two burly constables to his office. Both of the men had families that had suffered at the hands of the Communist Terrorists. He had chosen them well and knew that they would not shirk their duty.

'Go and soften him up a bit,' he ordered.

'Yes sir,' they replied as they retired from his office.

The two policemen took the prisoner to an open area at the end of the building that served as the ablutions block where they beat him with their fists and gave him a good kicking with the heavy army-issue boots that they wore whenever he went down. Every time he lapsed into unconsciousness they revived him with buckets of water, repeating this process over and over again for an hour, then they tied the man to a chair. He had not spoken a word nor cried out in pain, but despite the strong smell of disinfectant that permeated the air of the combined washroom and toilet, it was evident from the overpowering stench coming from the battered terrorist that he had voided himself.

The policemen went to fetch Simon who had been busy copying the numbers from the scrap of paper onto a blackboard. He instructed the constables to erect the board in a corner of the washroom where the prisoner could see it clearly.

'Has he said anything at all?' Simon enquired.

'Not a thing sir,' they both replied at the same time.

Using a pick handle as a pointer, Simon rapped the blackboard with it and addressed the prisoner, 'I'll ask again, what do these numbers mean?' He emphasised the question by banging the board on each group of figures.

The terrorist did not reply; he just stared straight through his antagonist. Again Simon rapped the board and asked the same question, the result was the same too – negative.

Addressing the two policemen this time he ordered, 'Get an empty fire bucket.'

When the bright red receptacle was produced he instructed the men to place it over the prisoner's head like a helmet, then he gave the bucket a swipe with the pick handle. Although no contact was made with the man's head, the noise within must have been terrifically loud and painful, rather like being inside a bell. He offered the pick handle to the constables. 'Hit that bucket every ten seconds for an hour,' he said. 'Take it in turns, it gets tedious.'

When the hour was up and the bucket had been removed from the man's head even the bitter-minded tormentors were shocked by his appearance. His face had swollen up like a balloon and blood mixed with other matter was trickling out of his ears and nose; the man's eyes were bulging out of their sockets and had a wild look in them. Simon resumed the interrogation asking the same question over and over again but he met with absolutely no success.

More than a little cross, Simon changed to another method of torture. He had a charpoy, a low bed made from wood and rattan, brought in and had it placed so that one end of it was positioned under a water tap. 'Strap him to that so he cannot move his head,' he barked. When the man was securely lashed up in the improvised straight jacket Simon continued, 'Now turn on the tap until the water drips onto his forehead every five seconds. I'm going to have a sleep in my office, wake me up if he starts talking.'

The night wore on and the seconds ticked away past midnight and into another day. Drip... drip... drip... it went on relentlessly for hours on end; each drop of water sounding like an explosion inside the terrorist's skull as it impacted his forehead. At three in the morning, the prisoner started to scream, long blood-curdling shrieks of mental agony that seemed to last forever putting everyone on edge until Simon brought it to an end by turning off the tap. 'Leave him be until 06.00 hrs,' he said and returned to his office.

At precisely that time Simon looked down at the terrorist, his eyes were clear but his head was still swollen. Simon spoke, 'You know what I want.' He repeated the question several times in English, Malay and several dialects of Chinese. 'Come on man, what do the numbers mean? There's no need for all this suffering.' But the prisoner's eyes said it all, 'Go to hell.'

Simon Belchard was now thoroughly pissed off and had one of the constables fetch in a wok and a towel, then placing the latter over the stubborn man's face he poured a wok full of water over the cloth. The water prevented air from filtering through the towel thereby making in impossible for the terrorist to breathe through it. His desperate attempts to do so only made matters worse because the towel was being sucked into his mouth. Still the policeman poured the water; he poured it slowly until the writhing, struggling figure lapsed into unconsciousness. The man had effectively experienced drowning.

'Revive him quickly,' ordered the officer curtly.

And so it continued, revival-question-cloth-water-blackout, and so on until that particular form of torture also proved to be fruitless.

The Police Inspector was fast losing his composure and the two constables their enthusiasm; it was now well past ten in the morning and the temperature was already in the high eighties.

'Leave him out in the sun to bake for a bit, then we'll show him a thing or two,' boasted an irate Simon. And so ended the water torture.

Over two hours later at 13.00 hrs, Simon issued the two constables with a bamboo cane each. The prisoner was still immobilised on the charpoy, he was nearly insane and blinded by the sun.

This time there were no questions, 'Give him some stick with those canes,' came the command. The constables lashed at the soles of the prisoner's feet and so began the old eastern punishment of bastinado. The terrorist began to shriek almost immediately but stuck it out for an hour before he broke. At first his torturers did not recognise the pitiful croaks and sobs as actual words but slowly they became discernible to them. Amidst the howling and soul-wrenching cries the tormentors heard the words, 'China, China, China. Piggi jalan Chinaaaaaaaah!' he screamed. 'China, piggi jalaaaaan,' the man sobbed. Over and over he screamed, howled and sobbed the same thing.

The word China spoke for itself. In Malay the word piggi meant go and jalan was road. China, go road. It meant no bloody sense at all to the three torturers, especially now that they had lost their self-control and all sense of reasoning. But out of the fog Simon had an inspiration, 'Cut his hands free,' he ordered, 'sometimes the hands can do the talking.' The two constables untied the mans hands; and he sobbed with relief because he thought his ordeal was over, he had told them all that he knew.

His relief was short-lived, the bamboo canes lashed his feet harder than ever; he screamed louder and using his hands to emphasise his meaning, the terrorist pointed at himself with his right hand and cried, 'Chinaaaah.' With his left hand he pointed away from himself and screamed, 'Piggi jalaaaaaaan.'

Because the man was lying on his back he was actually pointing upwards, and Simon Belchard totally misconstrued the message. He took it to mean, 'I'm Chinese, you can go to hell.' Simon now completely lost control of himself and bellowed, 'It's you that's going to hell, string him up by his thumbs.' He screeched fairly dancing with rage, 'Get a pick handle each.' He added, 'I'll break him yet, even if it's into little bloody bits.'

The gibbering bandit was dragged from the charpoy and

strung up from an overhead water pipe. All three men beat the prisoner with their heavy pick handles, his screams gradually decreased until they were but pitiful mewling sounds and finally after only fifteen minutes they too stopped and there was nothing but silence. But the frenzied trio continued to rain down blow after blow onto the broken man, they beat him long after he was dead and only utter exhaustion stopped them in the end.

Inspector Simon Belchard was in big trouble, the enormity of his crime now dwarfed his earlier indiscretions and they had been bad enough. The authorities would throw the book at him for this; he had compounded his catalogue of errors by instructing his two helpers to put the smashed up body of the prisoner into a solitary confinement cell. Then to cap it all he issued instructions to the effect that only he was to have access to the prisoner, up to that point Simon and the two constables were the only three people who knew that the man was dead.

To satisfy any curiosity from the duty policemen he personally delivered some bread and water to the cell. On his way out he called over his shoulder, 'You'd better get that down because that's your lot until tomorrow morning.' That was his last word on the matter, he locked the cell, kept the key and went to his office. Nobody thought to question him about taking a key away from the guardroom, after all, he was an inspector.

Sitting in his office he was slowly coming down from the high that he had got from inflicting pain on the late prisoner to face stark reality. In the sober light of day he tried to pick a way through the maze that was his dilemma, but it was hopeless. If he were to confess to his superiors now he would really be in the shit, if he did not they would still bag him anyway, it was only a matter of time. He decided to brazen it out for a little longer in the hope that the Tongs might extract him from this disastrous predicament if he were to produce the goods. He picked up the phone and dialled a number. 'Ah, Abdul my good man. There's been a breakthrough of sorts.' And he went on to explain the situation to the blackmailing sergeant leaving absolutely nothing out.

After finishing the call and feeling decidedly as sick as the proverbial dog he looked out of his office window that overlooked the barrack square. Normally anyone on or near this hallowed ground would straighten themselves up and march smartly to attention. They would avoid the area completely if possible and nobody would ever dream of hanging about the place. But at this particular moment people were doing just that, policemen, on and off duty alike were actually loitering around in groups and staring at the headquarters building. He thought briefly of gathering together a group of senior ranks to disperse the curious policemen but dismissed the idea; it would only help to further undermine his already waning powers of authority. No, enough was enough, it was time to make himself scarce. He drove out of the barracks at precisely 15.30 hrs, a full twenty-four hours after first setting eyes on the dead terrorist.

During that eventful period he had completely forgotten that Fiona was due to visit him at the bungalow at 14.30 hrs that very afternoon, that was an hour ago and he was already late. She had a key and his servants could always let her in but knowing Fiona and her moods she was probably pacing up and down fuming with frustration. *All the better,* he thought, *I like them when they're wild.*

The late afternoon session with Fiona did not go well at all, he could normally satisfy her every demand and then some more. His first performance was physically successful in that he managed to bring Fiona to a climax but it lacked his usual enthusiasm and otherwise masterful touch; he just simply had too much on his mind. She coaxed and caressed him but try as she might Fiona was not able to find that spark in her distressed lover to rise to the occasion, it was useless.

She was as mad as hell at this lack of response and crying tears of frustration she accused him of having another woman. 'That's why you can't get it up,' she wailed in despair, 'who is the bitch?' Then like a demented wildcat she attacked him, scratching, slapping and biting. 'Come on you bastard,' Fiona screamed, 'I'll get it out of you!'

Simon did not try and defend himself; instead, he broke down and cried with deep body-racking sobs of pent-up fear and emotion. This unexpected reaction had a steadying effect on Fiona and she ceased her tirade against him and became as a mother figure, cradling his head to her breasts and stroking his hair fondly. Simon let everything pour out in a torrent of inner cleansing, confessing to all except his part in the death of the prisoner.

Fiona got back to her home in Gemas at eight that evening, an hour before her husband arrived home from his office in Kuala Lumpur. Jeremy was somewhat surprised at the greeting that he received from Fiona. Instead of the obligatory peck and the affectionate cuddle he was afforded the whole treatment, a long lingering, tongue probing kiss, her fingers dug into the back of his neck as she moved her hips suggestively against his groin. A long time had passed since he had been treated thus and it aroused him immediately so that Fiona could feel his hardness despite the clothing that they wore. *Success at last,* she thought as her now rampant husband dragged her upstairs to the master bedroom.

It was like their honeymoon all over again, they tore at one another's clothing until they were both completely naked, there was no foreplay so great was their need for each other. He forced Fiona onto the bed and covered her with his body, finding her warmth and joining with her in a lustful and tempestuous union. His ardour of earlier youth was rekindled and he dominated the writhing, quivering form of his wife. Fiona's response was so vigorous that her contortions threatened to force them apart but somehow the couple managed to maintain contact. The frustrations of the day had heightened Fiona's sexual chemistry to such an extent that she was experiencing a fireball of almost painful pleasure welling up inside her, so intense was this feeling that she bared her teeth in anticipation. He felt it too and before her wild biting and scratching could defeat his male dominance he intensified his efforts to match hers and Fiona reached a screaming, back-arcing climax with him. So complete was her release that it drained her and she collapsed by Jeremy's side whimpering and gasping with pure ecstasy.

They lay quietly for a while, dozing as one does after lovemaking, then Fiona started to gabble on about everything under the sun. She always did this and he never really listened to her pillow talk, it was nearly all inconsequential rubbish anyway. Then uncommonly soon for him he felt himself becoming aroused again. *Ah,* he thought, *this will shut her up.* Then he sat bolt upright at something she had just said. 'What's that?' he blurted out but remembering that he was an MI6 agent, he modified his tone of voice. 'Fiona dear,' he asked soothingly, 'I didn't quite get that, did you mention something about Rompin?'

'Rompin darling, did I?' She had been brought up with a start.

'Yes you did, pet,' he suggested, his obvious sexual desire now visibly wilting. 'Not far from here is it?' he prompted.

'No, it's only about thirteen miles up the road towards Kuala Lumpur, half an hour by car. I do the…' she tailed off.

'You do what love, go on, do finish what you were going to say.'

Fiona knew that she had slipped up and was getting edgy. She had no qualms about revealing the information regarding Rompin to Jeremy; it meant nothing to her. It was the source that had to be protected and her affair with Simon had to remain a secret so she quickly searched her memory and drummed up a name before answering. 'I was going to say, before you so rudely interrupted me, that I drove over to see Cynthia today. You know, that planter chap's wife, Banks I think their name is?'

'Oh yes, I remember them, nice people.' Jeremy did not know them from Adam but he encouraged Fiona to continue, 'Something special was it?'

'No, not really. It's just that I get so dreadfully bored sometimes.' Then thinking to satisfy Jeremy's curiosity she told him all, inventing a reason why her friend Cynthia should be privy to such a morsel.

'Well I'll be damned,' remarked Jeremy calmly. 'Whatever next,' he feigned; inwardly though he was both shocked and seething with anger. Her story or the bit concerning her pal Cynthia was plausible enough but he did not believe a word of it. It was perfectly clear to him that her confidant was a man and that she had come by the information whilst lying in his bed. Her sexual favours towards him on this night were a rarity, he deduced that all had not gone well for Fiona on her latest assignation and she had not been satisfied. Jeremy did not press her further on the subject but fell back into his pillows utterly deflated. His thoughts went back to the first time he had met

Fiona and to a little later on when he had married her. He could hardly but notice that as far as sex was concerned she was insatiable, to the more outspoken of her associates the term used was probably nymphomaniac. They had been tempestuous times, she had drained him nightly and daily whenever she could catch him with his trousers down, so to speak, and he had been hard pressed indeed to keep up with his work. The situation had gotten so out of hand that it was he, not her, who had to cry off with the proverbial headaches. Fiona took these rejections on the chin and slowly her demands eased off, indeed, she turned the tables completely around and it was now Jeremy who had to make the advances.

For a spy Jeremy was very naïve in some respects, he had put Fiona's earlier excesses down to youthful exuberance and considered her later restraint to be the behaviour of a lady settling down to a steady and healthy marriage. Jeremy bit his tongue to stop himself from crying out, *Oh what a bloody fool I've been.* He screamed inwardly, *I can see it all now as plain as day.* Yes, he had been a silly bloody fool all right. Fiona had only stopped pestering him sexually because she was being serviced by others. *Oh bloody hell,* he thought, *how many was it?*

Casting his mind back to the many embassy and other functions that they had attended, he could remember the admiring glances and ready smiles that were directed at them. They had cut good figures and projected an image of happiness and success and it had done his ego good to think that they thought so. Now, with hindsight, he realised that those smiles were probably sniggers of derision and the thought that must have been uppermost in their minds was that he was a complete arsehole. Then there was the chauffeur who was responsible for servicing the couple's private cars as well as driving Jeremy about. The man was constantly going on about the mileage on Fiona's old Morris; Jeremy had taken no notice at the time, putting it down to the driver's natural whining, complaining character.

In his hour of enlightenment Jeremy could see that the chauffeur's observations made sense. *What was it now,* he mused, *thirteen miles, a round trip of twenty-six miles.* Knowing Fiona's sexual appetite he surmised that it was probably on a daily basis. No wonder the man had been worried, call it thirty miles a day on embassy fuel. Jeremy thought sadly, *I'll have to come clean about all this, of course, and when this caper is over I'll tender my resignation.* First though, he would offer to assist in finding out whom, amongst other things, was milking Fiona. In addition but more importantly he needed to unmask this wife-stealing bastard and get him to reveal for whom he was working. Of one thing Jeremy was quite sure, Fiona's infidelity was purely sexually motivated and he did not believe that she had the slightest notion that she was being used. Jeremy looked at her, she was sleeping soundly now, so he got quietly out of bed and crept downstairs to his study. Using his red emergency telephone to the embassy he dialled a number, 'Give me Field Marshal Petherington please.'

The atmosphere in the Flag House conference room was frosty to say the least. Upon receiving Jeremy's telephone call at the unearthly hour of midnight the somewhat irate Field Marshal immediately instructed an aid to call in the Chiefs of Staff, the Security Services and the Police Commissioner. These busy men had come from far and wide in order to reach the capital, the last man to arrive being the Admiral who had travelled all the way from Singapore. By 09.00 hrs they were all present and seated ready for the blitz. Petherington was in a filthy mood but started the meeting on a bright note by complimenting the Air force on their diligence, 'As you know we lost track of the *Sea Pearl* on the fifteenth. But because of some excellent plotting work done by the aircrews we now have her in our sights again. But the vessel was pushed back off course and it is unlikely that she'll arrive off the island of Palau Tioman until at least the thirtieth, that's twelve days late.' He looked at both the Commonwealth Brigade Commander and the Admiral, 'A long wait for your men I'm afraid.' In a more apologetic air he reflected that it was bad luck that the SAS had bumped the enemy so soon. 'But all is not lost, the SAS have found more signs of enemy activity but say that no guerrilla force could have been in earshot of the Bukit Chermingat engagement. Coupled with the fact that all four of the bandits involved have been accounted for, the Squadron Commander is led to believe that the Guerrilla Army

Headquarters has no idea that they have lost these men.'

Petherington paused to clear his throat, then with a deceptively smooth voice continued. 'The three armed services have really pulled their fingers out on this one and by dint of much hard work are ready to pounce on the enemy whichever way he turns.' He took a deep breath, 'I'll not have their efforts jeopardised,' he looked daggers at the Police Commissioner and Jeremy Fairburne-Snape, then shouted so that all of Kuala Lumpur could hear, 'by a faction amongst us that can't get their bloody act together.'

The raised voice surprised even Crazy Harry who grinned wryly.

'We have,' spluttered the Field Marshal, really warming to his task, 'a police Inspector whose brains seem to be between his legs, and the wife of an MI6 bod who is compromising the agent on a daily basis. Without, mind you, the silly sod having the slightest inkling that anything is amiss. Christ, give me the plain old redcap any day!'

The room went quiet and military personnel seemed to close ranks as they looked at the Security Services men with disdain. His outburst over Petherington's attitude changed and he once more became the masterful man-manager.

'We are a team,' he continued, 'and it as a team that we are going to overcome this problem, got it?' He directed his fiery gaze at the fighting service's top brass.

'Yes sir,' they all complied like so many puppets on a string.

'Good, then let me put you in the picture.' He gave them a detailed account of the god-awful mess as he knew it concluding with, 'In a nutshell we have a police officer who, for reasons unknown to us at the moment, has failed to confirm his receipt of a prisoner of war from the military. In addition to this the wife of Jeremy here has knowledge of the prisoner, which she shouldn't have, and says that the man has been interrogated; and has talked.'

'It's pretty obvious to me that she got all this stuff directly from Belchard himself, this Cynthia business is nothing but a load of old codswallop,' broke in Harry, whilst the Field Marshal took a drink of water wishing that it was something a little stronger.

'I'll go along with that,' added the Police Commissioner. Tom Nobles nodded his head in agreement; and Jeremy looked down in shame. The military bosses just stared.

Noticing Jeremy's obvious embarrassment Petherington said, 'I must confess that I agree with Snape's point that he thinks his wife is a mere dupe, just an unwitting pawn in a much bigger game. But gentlemen, we must find out who the prime movers are.' He looked directly at the Police Commissioner, 'Claude, you and Tom Nobles are to deal with the Rompin end of things, get whatever information this Belchard fellow has acquired back to me soonest.' The two men nodded in acknowledgement. 'Jeremy, you with Harry acting as an aide are to mount a misinformation operation that will be dependant on what we get from Rompin,' he sighed heavily before continuing, 'and Jeremy old fellow, we'll use your wife and try to turn this whole thing around to our advantage. You never know, it could lead to an honourable way out for the both of you.'

At that moment an aide rushed in and handed the Field Marshal a message. Petherington quickly read it then looked up. 'This,' he said waving the missive in the air, 'is from Rompin, let me read it to you. "I have a captured terrorist in custody. But there is a problem." The message is signed by Simon Belchard.' He then, placed the message carefully down on his desk.

'He'll have a bloody problem when I get down to Rompin,' threatened the Commissioner.

Tom Nobles grinned. 'Steady on Claude old chap,' laughed the military chief.

Claude Rysdale and Tom Nobles arrived at the Rompin Police Barracks at 14.00 hrs that very same day, nearly forty-eight hours after the Australian Army had handed over the prisoner. Inspector Simon Belchard who ushered the two men into his office expecting nothing but the worst met them. He offered the Commissioner his seat at the desk and it was duly accepted. Tom grabbed a chair and seated himself to one side of the desk so that he could see the faces of both men, a strategy that he and Claude had agreed upon beforehand. Simon remained standing before his supreme boss with a look of trepidation on his face; fully aware that he was under intense scrutiny by the Special Branch officer from his vantage point on the right-hand side of the tiny room.

'Relax,' opened the Police Commissioner, 'sit down, go on, I insist.' He waited until the slightly puzzled Inspector was seated then continued. 'Inspector, there is no denying the seriousness of your position, disciplinary measures will have to be faced on your part, of that there is no doubt. However, the severity of the punishment meted out to you depends on your motives for committing this enormous breach of conduct.'

Whilst that was sinking in, Tom Nobles took over. 'This is only a preliminary enquiry, of course, you're not facing any charges yet. Do you understand?'

Simon who was looking thoroughly bewildered nodded; he had not expected this soft touch.

'Inspector,' Claude resumed kindly, 'in your own words if you please.' Simon had decided to push his luck to the limit and confessed to all but his involvement with Abdul, Mr Tan and the Tongs, and of course, Fiona. He took full responsibility for the treatment of the prisoner and his subsequent death.

'Are you telling us,' asked Tom Nobles, 'that this regrettable affair is down to your desire to look clever and it all went pear-shaped because you and others were bloody over zealous in your interrogation methods?'

'Yes sir,' answered Simon meekly.

'And there are no outside organisations motivating your actions, you are not being got at?' pressed the Special Branch man.

'No sir, none.'

'You're not being blackmailed?'

'No,' lied Simon.

'A woman then, a honey trap?'

'No bloody woman,' snapped the Inspector losing his cool and displaying his weakness. Tom stopped it there, he already knew that the man was lying, not to have asked at all would have aroused Belchard's suspicion. To push him further would be to overplay their hand and they needed the Inspector's unwitting assistance if they were to expose the prime movers in this dangerous game with high stakes.

Commissioner Rysdale held out his hand, 'The piece of paper

please,' he demanded. He looked at the small page of figures for a moment before passing it to Tom. 'What do you make of those numbers?' he asked him.

'Could be encoded map co-ordinates similar to what the military call griddle, my cipher blokes will crack it in minutes.'

The Commissioner looked pleased; Simon pricked up his ears. Claude addressed Simon, 'These words that you said the man spoke, what were they?' He strummed his fingers on the desk waiting for an answer.

'He said China, then Piggi and Jalan.'

The Commissioner wrote the words down; Tom Nobles quickly said, 'So because you thought that he was telling you to bugger off down some road or other—'

'He was telling me to go to hell,' interrupted Simon.

'All right then, because of that you beat him to death?'

'Not deliberately,' defended the Inspector, 'it was an act of negligence. Temper and rage yes, murderous intent no.' There was a hushed silence.

That, thought Tom, *is probably the truth.*

Claude coughed, 'Belchard, I'm half inclined to believe you. I am prepared to set aside criminal charges for the time being, I have inherited this problem from you and I need your co-operation to solve it.'

'Of course sir,' Simon answered the unspoken question.

'Quite, well, due to the importance of a military operation now currently in progress in the area where the terrorist was captured,' Claude paused to let that little snippet sink in. 'We'll have to keep this incident under wraps until the Army has finished up there in Pahang.'

'You can count on my discretion sir,' grovelled Simon.

I'll bet we bloody well can, thought Tom.

Claude addressed the Special Branch man. 'Get the body out of Rompin and up to Kuala Lumpur, I want the lab to identify the remains from records.' Fixing his eagle eye on Inspector Simon Belchard he brought the brief enquiry to a close. 'Well man,' he encouraged, 'we'll get through this thing together. It's time to close ranks, chins up and loyalty to the service, eh inspector?'

'Yes sir,' answered a very bewildered and relieved Simon as he escorted the Police Commissioner out to his transport. Malaya's top policeman did not return the Inspector's salute.

On the drive back to the capital Claude said to Tom, 'Slimy little bastard isn't he?'

'A total shit,' answered Tom, 'I could crack him in a day.'

'Easily, I'm sure, and we'd get the job done just the same but?'

'Yeah, I know, it'll lead to a long drawn-out procedure and we haven't got the bloody time.'

'Quite right, we need that nasty little sod and we'll use Fiona as our conduit; the legal beavers would only bugger up that sort of ploy.' Tom laughed, never had he thought that he'd hear a statement like that coming from a police chief: We cannot do it that way because it's too legal.

Deep in the cellars of Flag House in the capital city of Kuala Lumpur the Special Branch cipher men went to work on the piece of paper found in the dead prisoner's clothing. After a few hours of overtime they had broken the code and by 22.00 hrs their report was on the Field Marshal's desk. The Staff Meeting had been reconvened and everyone present was eager to hear the news. A blackboard had been set up and a map of the Pahang operational area was pinned to the wall next to it.

'Gentlemen,' announced Petherington, 'I'll let Harry take you through this.'

Colonel Crazy Harry Blunt, forever the eccentric, took the stage brandishing his staff pointer like a sabre. 'It,' he said nearly losing the end of the pointer in the overhead fan, 'took Tom's cryptic maniacs but a short time to crack the code. The message isn't, as we first thought, a list of map co-ordinates. The figures are grouped in four separate blocks of four digits each and have been identified as map sheet numbers, so we weren't too far off the mark. There are four maps in all and I must point out.' He lunged at the map. 'If you'll excuse the pun, that the centre of the area covered by those maps is here.' The whole room was looking at the point where Harry had actually pierced the map. 'It's the Chini Lake area,' he said softly. He walked over to the blackboard and wrote down the word Chini. 'I put it to you that the word being uttered time and time again by the tortured prisoner was

Chini, and not China like that silly bloody copper thought it was.'

All the military men grinned; Claude winced and Tom Nobles ducked as Harry's pointer whizzed over his head. He continued 'Now we all know, that if we point down a road and say, "Piggi Jalan", your average chap will toddle off down that particular road like a good little soul. If I point at myself with the other hand,' he paused for effect. 'I would be saying that "I am going down that road", or, "I will take you down that road". What the terrorist was telling that fool Belchard was, "The numbers mean the Chini Lake area and I will take you there". God give me strength,' said Harry and took a drink of water. He stabbed at the map once more to emphasise his point. 'Chini,' he screamed pointing at himself, 'Piggi Jalan,' he echoed, 'I'll take you to the camp.' Harry's audience, except for the Field Marshal who already knew, were stunned by the news. 'But there's more,' Harry continued, 'because of that policeman's act of folly we have lost the opportunity of learning the exact location of the enemy's headquarters; now we will have to search all four map squares in that area of stinking jungle.'

'But we've been given a clue, surely that's a bonus?' remarked the Commonwealth Brigade Commander.

'Yes,' agreed Petherington, 'and that SAS chap Augustus is getting pretty close now.'

'Caesar sir.'

'Ah yes, Caesar it is.'

'And talking of the SAS,' said Harry actually dislodging Jeremy's monocle with a vicious backslash.

'Put that damned sword away,' laughed the Field Marshal, 'before you decapitate someone!'

Harry complied much to the relief of everyone present. 'As I was saying,' he continued quite unperturbed, 'the enemy group that the SAS bumped would not have led them to the camp; the CTs were actually marching away from it.'

'How do we know that? questioned the Admiral.

'Because we now know the identity of all four terrorists involved in the SAS action. Two of them are known to be close associates of Kim Bok the Paymaster General, they're probably his bodyguards. They were also old Second World War veterans and it's an odds-on certainty that they knew the wartime courier route like the back of their hands. It's my guess that they were acting as guides.'

'And the other two?' prompted Claude.

'They were both Intelligence Officers, one each from the 4th and 9th Regiments. Those units are responsible for south Johore, and central Johore respectively.' The significance of what Harry was saying was getting through and he hammered the point home. 'If the SAS chaps backtrack that group from the scene of the contact, and knowing them, they're probably already doing so, they'll find evidence along the way indicating that individuals, all Intelligence Officers, have dropped out of the column at strategic points not far from their regimental areas. I'll bet my life on it,' said Harry taking a breather.

The Field Marshal smiled. Crazy Harry was on his hobbyhorse now; he was not in the room but deep in the jungle living out his theory with the SAS patrols.

'I'm telling you,' expounded the legend of jungle warfare, 'get those SAS devils to trace that party back to the last drop off point. The man who left the column there will have headed east towards the Chini Lake, and that gentlemen, is the domain of the enemy's elite: the 10th Regiment.'

The Field Marshal accepted Harry's appreciation of the situation as being sound but a nagging doubt was creeping into his mind. Not about the location of the enemy camp because he was confident that Harry was on the right track there. Nor was it the final destination of the gold shipment, no, it was the landing point that was worrying him. He addressed Harry nodding at the map as he did so. 'If they do indeed have their main camp in the Chini Lake area, why wouldn't they bring the gold in through Kuala Pahang and then up the river to the lake?'

'Draught wise,' answered Harry, 'they could get the junk upriver for about forty miles but,' Harry looked towards the Admiral. The senior service man took up the challenge. 'The thing's tidal, of course, and it's a virtual minefield of sandbanks. Because of the wicked tidal streams generated by the ebb and flow of the river, I'd say that they'd need a top-notch river pilot for the job.'

'What about these 10th Regiment blokes, asked the Brigadier, 'some of them would know the river pretty well surely?'

'Like the back of their hands,' answered Harry, 'but they're only small-boat men, sampans and the like. Handling a dirty great junk up that treacherous river is another kettle of fish, they would be out of their depth and high and dry on the sandbanks in no time at all.'

'And?' encouraged Petherington almost convinced once more.

'And there is the river bank population to consider. There are seven main villages along the route plus dozens of small river dwellings similar to Dyak long houses but tiny in comparison. I can tell you now that the majority of these people are Malays and have no time for the communists at all. But the guerrillas do have some sympathisers in the Kuala Pahang and Pekan areas. Honestly sir, I really do think the Sungei Pahang is a no go on this one.'

'There's another point connected with your comments about the riverside locals,' said Claude, 'if they do bring the gold in that way then secrecy is out of the window.'

'And,' butted in Jeremy, 'if they make it obvious and we do nothing about it, they'll guess we're on to them anyway.'

'Yes, then bang goes our secrecy,' added Tom.

'Hang on, hang on chaps, let's not get ourselves in a buggers muddle over this. I've got the message, right?' said the Field Marshal with an evil glint in his eye. Harry who was conversant with that look knew that the old campaigner had a cunning plan up his sleeve to put before them.

'I have a plan,' announced the Army Chief.

Harry grinned and chalked one up.

'First of all we don't know who this Belchard chap is passing his information back to. We have to assume that he learned about the gold from his latest bit of fluff,' Jeremy went red in the face, 'who must have got it from her husband Jeremy here.' The MI6 man was now sweating with embarrassment. 'Because the information involves gold and that would more than interest a criminal organisation we must further assume that Belchard is being blackmailed for some reason.' He did not hurt Jeremy by stating the obvious. He continued, 'Right,' 'no matter who they may be or how big an organisation they are the most they can be to us is a bloody nuisance. A thorn in our side if you like, but big enough to compromise our operation if we don't pull it out. My plan is to create a diversion to keep them away from the Mersing area and lure the sods towards the Chini Lake but confine them to the river-line somehow. They should be out of harm's way there because I don't think the enemy camp is near the lake. Harry?' he invited.

'I agree, it will be on or close to this mountain,' he pointed at the map, 'Gunong Chini, it's some ten miles south of the lake.' He stopped before he could steal the Field Marshal's thunder.

'With this as yet unknown faction being kept busy on the lake or on the river close to it, I can see my way clear, Claude, to offering up this criminal element to you.' A buzz of excitement ran round the room. 'Jeremy and Harry, leak out through Fiona that the gold shipment is coming in through the Sungei Pahang. Drop the name Chini Lake as a carrot and leave it at that.'

The two men acknowledged with a nod.

'Navy?'

'Yes sir,' responded the Admiral. 'If the guerrillas leave that junk intact I want the SBS to board it and be prepared to sail the bloody thing up the river.'

'And if,' the Admiral started to say.

'If they destroy it I want another like it stood by to take its place, name and all. Get one from somewhere and train your SBS chaps up on it.'

'I will indeed,' remarked the Admiral rubbing his hands together in glee.

'Claude,' barked Petherington, 'place one of your Field Force Companies under command of the Navy. They're to be attached to the Commandos and act the part of CTs to crew the junk when it reaches the river. They will also be responsible for taking the smaller vessels upriver when the junk encounters shallow waters.'

'Consider it done,' said a jubilant Police Commissioner.

The Field Marshal turned his fiery gaze towards the Air force Commander. 'I want a closer watch than ever kept on the *Sea Pearl's* progress.'

The Air Marshal smiled patiently. 'I'll see to it,' he promised.

Petherington concluded the session, 'Harry, get on to the SAS, I want that 10th Regiment man tracked right up to the enemy's bloody doorstep or I'll have that man Calligula's head!'

Nobody bothered to correct him this time.

★

The *Sea Pearl* had enjoyed an uneventful voyage until she had reached a position 260 miles south-east of the southernmost tip of Vietnam. Up until then the weather had been normal for that area and seasonal with the summer monsoon blowing from between south and east, and the surface currents setting north-eastwards, putting both wind and sea against her. The captain had made adjustments to his course in order to counteract the currents and the wind that was trying to force the vessel onto the Vietnam coastline. In order to maintain reasonable headway, he had resorted to using the *Sea Pearl's* powerful engines three times a day. Despite the hard battle against the elements, the heavily laden junk had made good a distance of 1,680 miles in fifteen days. With 360 miles still to go, the captain was steering a course south-westwards that would get the vessel to her destination on time.

The captain was worried. He had thought at first that it was his concern over Fantail's lacklustre sexual performance of the previous night. In fact, he had noticed of late that she had taken to prostrating herself on his cot to be serviced showing about as much emotion and enthusiasm as a dead fish; it was as if she was burned out. He dismissed the subject from his mind as he suddenly realised what was actually bothering him; it was the ship's motion as she ploughed her way though the water. It had changed from the lively bucking and prancing of a vessel happily playing with the sea to that slow, uneasy, gut churning roll that gave the toughest of seamen a sinking feeling in the pit of the stomach and induced sea sickness.

The uncomfortable movement was caused by a long swell that was running fast from the north-east catching the *Sea Pearl* beam onto the trough on her port side.

This swell, thought the captain, *is bloody bad news.* If the feeling in his bones was anything to go by he was about to do battle with a cyclone, a tropical revolving storm that in the China Seas is better know as a typhoon. He had noticed the lurid sky colouring at sunrise but due to his sexual exertions of the night he had failed to heed the obvious warning. He glanced at the barometer and found it to be unsteady, reading both higher and lower pressures than was normal; another indication of what was yet to come. By ten that morning, thick bands of cirrus cloud in a 'V' formation were converging towards the eye of the now clearly visible storm. The direction of the wind had changed too, whereas before they had been heading into it, the wind was now chasing the *Sea Pearl's* stern and there were frequent shifts in it to contend with.

Still undecided, the captain let things ride until midday. By then the sky had taken on an ugly, threatening appearance, the wind had increased to Force 6 and was gusting up to Gale Force 8 from the north-east. The glass had fallen to five millibars below normal and the captain was kicking himself for his earlier indecision. According to all the signs, he estimated the centre of the storm to be about a hundred miles away. It was advancing towards him at a rate 10 to 12 knots and it would take roughly ten hours for it to reach the *Sea Pearl*; there was actually no way of escaping from the storm itself, but the captain could try and avoid the centre.

The typhoon had a front probably hundreds of miles in diameter with the wind circulating around the centre, or eye, of the storm. Because of this circular passage the wind blew in a different direction for every one of the four quadrants of the compass, and there was a separate drill to be adopted for each quadrant. The experienced captain judged that the *Sea Pearl* was not directly in the path of the eye but to the left of it, putting him in what is termed as the left-hand semicircle. To ascertain this he brought in all sails and hove to with engines running. With the vessel stopped he observed the wind shifts to be on his left-hand side, confirming his assumptions. Not only was he correct but he was also positioned in the dangerous quadrant of the left-hand semicircle.

To better understand all of this it would be wise for one to stand in the captain's shoes as he looks out over the starboard beam of the *Sea Pearl* at the oncoming typhoon. Remember that you are not directly in the path of the eye that is still a hundred miles away from you, but some distance to the left of it, your left. Another hundred miles on the other side of the storm, out of sight beyond the earth's curvature, the wind will be blowing to the left and away from its path. A quarter of a circle later it will be blowing in the same direction as the typhoon is travelling but another hundred miles out from the centre. By the time the wind has completed a semicircle it will have reversed its direction blowing straight across your front from the left. And that is the dangerous part because you are being blown back into the path of the typhoon to be engulfed by the eye. The drill for this dangerous quadrant is simple, head into the wind with all possible speed to keep the vessel out of the path of the advancing eye at all costs.

And so the fight for survival commenced. The *Sea Pearl* was already a bit ungainly from the water she had shipped when the captain had brought the vessel about, now she was being tossed around like a cork by the hurricane-force winds. Huge seas engulfed her, cascading into the vessel and drenching her very soul so that the valiant lady shuddered with the impact. Her timbers creaked and groaned in torment and she took water into every part of her; but with the help of her courageous skipper she shook off the raging green menace that threatened to take them all to the bottom. The vessel held its own in the battle between twin diesel engines and ferocious winds, just maintaining a position on the north-west periphery of the swirling typhoon.

The captain and his crew pitted their strength and wits against the tumultuous seas that threatened to batter the *Sea Pearl* into submission, and that good lady responded to their commands; both ship and crew spurred on by the ever-present fear of being sucked into the seething maelstrom.

Night turned into day and still they battled on well past the point that is beyond the call of duty, grown men cried but held on with courage, tenacity and grim determination to survive against all odds. The captain shouted and screamed defiance into the

155

wind, he took the pounding seas on the chin and he fought for control with all his heart and soul. He willed his lovely amazon of a vessel through the turbulent waters, this phenomena of destruction. He prayed to his god, pleading for understanding. Looking to the heavens he cried out, 'Why, oh why God do you test me so?'

He begged for guidance and he went on pleading for inspiration as yet another day passed by, and the very act of remaining upright required a Herculean effort. On the third day, the captain prepared himself for the worst, he could hardly stand and it took four men to handle the ship's wheel, and only then with the aid of ropes. He was suffering an inner torment in that he had foreknowledge of worst things yet to come; if that was humanly possible in this hellish predicament. He carried within himself a point of fact concerning the behaviour of typhoons, a fact that he was reluctant to impart to his fellow seamen, better for them to be unaware of the fate that lurked in the deep should his worst fears be realised. The point in question was that most typhoons, after an indeterminate period of time, veered off to the north-west. That dangerous shift to the right of the storm's path would put the murderous eye on the same course as the *Sea Pearl*. She would be chased, overtaken and swamped; and that would be the end for them all. But he pinned his hopes on another fact, in latitudes this far south, typhoons sometimes failed to turn, and he prayed and sobbed for that to be so.

The fight went on. Men were scalded in the galley, bones were broken and rope burns, cuts and bruises were the trademark of suffering. Men seemed to have no eyes anymore, just red, sore sockets that reflected the opaque stare of the doomed. And all the time, relentlessly and without pause, the wind blew its howling, shrieking song that numbed the brain and laid bare the raw nerve-ends; so that the seamen, mere mortals, cringed in fear at the awesome might of mother nature.

By noon on the fourth day, the captain knew that his prayers had been answered, the typhoon had not veered, it had carried straight on. The storm, six hundred miles in diameter, had taken four days to pass over the tiny, battered but valiant *Sea Pearl* and her superhuman crew. At 13.00 hrs the typhoon had drawn away from the vessel sufficiently enough for the crew to observe an actual horizon instead of the solid green wall of water that they had become accustomed to throughout their terrible ordeal. Gone were the towering, heaving, soaking monstrous waves generated by the storm-force winds that whipped the seas into a cauldron of hell. Now the suffering men could see the changing grey shapes of a more ordered form of ocean behaviour, an abatement from storm to gale force winds, still a threat to life and limb but a welcome relief nonetheless.

By three in the afternoon they were out of it and the gigantic, swirling demon went on to blow itself out on the land mass of Vietnam, Cambodia and Thailand. Had they been caught up in the storm for another hour, the ship and her crew would have perished, smashed to pieces on the shores of an island that confronted the dazed and bewildered eyes of all aboard. An island looking as battered as themselves but sitting there in the ocean like a jewel in the sunlight for all to behold and wonder at, appeared not more than a mile away on the port bow. The captain, too tired even to work out where they were, ordered the crew to drop anchor and both vessel and seamen slept. They slept the sleep of the dead until the next morning, these men of extreme mettle. There being no orders to the contrary they did not stir their stumps then but laid on as if in a stupor.

As for Fantail, well, she had been as terrified as the rest but had taken no part in the horrendous struggle. Instead, she had stowed herself away in the captain's cabin for the entire four days; and the captain had not joined her there once. Fantail was grateful for that, and when he did eventually collapse onto his cot beside her, she was overjoyed when he immediately fell asleep.

In Hong Kong Fantail had entered into the spirit of the enterprise, giving her body freely to most members of the crew before favouring the captain in particular. Once signed on as a regular member of the crew and assigned to the duties of a cook, she was under no illusions as to what her primary function was. Simply put, she was to lay with the captain whenever that good man wished her to do so. That arrangement was fine by her, she was close to authority and privy to his most intimate thoughts. The captain was totally unaware of her true association with Kim

Bok and would soon unwittingly reveal any ulterior plans for the disposal of the cargo, especially if he discovered that some of it was gold bullion. She had thought that her sexual favours were now the exclusive privilege of the captain and he alone. On the short voyage from Hong Kong to Macau it did indeed seem to be that way but on departing from Macau on 6 August she came to realise that her assumption had been awfully wrong. The captain had a sexual appetite equal to hers and had things gone differently she might honestly have enjoyed the voyage with him. But this was not to be and for some time she was not sure whether the captain was turning the proverbial blind eye or was simply ignorant of the situation. The first indication that things were not going to go her way came on the first day out of Macau.

It was early evening and she had been taking gash from the galley to ditch overboard from the poop deck that was situated at the stern end of vessel. Fantail was about to return to her place of work when she was accosted by three members of the crew and propositioned. She rejected their advances, but remembering how readily she had let them taste the fruit before, they became forceful. Fantail tried to fight them off but was no match for the burly trio and in the end they all had their way with her. When she threatened to tell the captain they laughed like hell and gyrated their hips suggestively shouting, 'He next, he next lady.'

That night she had difficulty in matching the captain's vigorous lovemaking, but if he noticed it, he did not complain. The ordeal continued the next day with five men taking advantage of the one and only female on board the ship; and once again she found it hard to keep up with her seemingly inexhaustible companion of the night. The days wore on and she feared to walk out of the captain's cabin each morning. The only work she did now was on her back or in other positions as the mood took them. These men did not want passion and that was lucky for her for she had none left to give, they were happy enough just to use her as a receptacle for their seed. Although she had to endure much rough handling, Fantail did not suffer any malicious physical abuse.

She was lucky in another sense too because the two men that she dreaded the most amongst the crew preferred boys to woman, they were the chief cook and the sail maker. Great brutes of men, they got their pleasure out of abusing three young boys who were supposed to be apprentice deckhands. The youths were called chickens by the two sodomites who chased their little arses around all day long.

'Come here chicken,' they would shout, or, 'Get that done chicken.' At night the chickens really suffered; and long after the captain had exhausted his passion Fantail could hear the boys squealing with fright and screaming in pain as they were mercilessly buggered, and afterwards, her heart went out to them as the poor lads received repeated beatings. It took the edge off her own suffering and for both Fantail and the chickens the typhoon was a brief but welcome respite.

It was two days after the storm had abated before any semblance of order was restored aboard the *Sea Pearl*. The captain's first task was to assess the damage to his ship and effect repairs. He soon had work parties swarming all over the vessel to get her ready for sailing, giving them a two-day deadline to meet; he planned to depart from the island and resume the voyage to Malaya on 22 August. First though he had to establish where the hell he was departing from and to that end he took a sighting of the sun at noon with his sextant. Then after consulting his tables he fixed his position as being off the island of Con San fifty miles south-east of the nearest mainland point of Vietnam; they had been blown back and to the west a good two hundred miles. The captain plotted a new course to his destination and reckoned that he had not a hope in heaven of arriving there until the fifth of September. He was behind time by a long measure, but that was the sea for you.

Had Crazy Harry Blunt been able to glance over the captain's shoulder he would have chortled with glee, the destination marked on the chart was Palau Tioman, the largest island off Mersing situated on the East Coast of Malaya.

★

The tiger had travelled far, well away from his normal hunting grounds in the highland forest many miles behind him. What had started him out on this particular journey was a river; the tiger was not a stranger to rivers, of course, but this one was larger than any other that he had seen before and carried a peculiar scent that he liked, together with the refreshing sound of fast-flowing water. The pleasing smell was strongest from the direction that the water was flowing towards and the tiger followed his nose along the northern bank in anticipation of finding the source of this new-found mystery. First travelling north, then west and finally north-west the beautifully striped undisputed lord of the jungle stalked the strange aroma.

He passed other animals on the way and fed on opportune prey when and where he could take it. Lesser creatures in the order of things tried to keep clear of the tiger, some in deference to his superiority, others in fear. When the smell had become so strong that it was sending the tiger into a feline swoon he came upon another phenomenon that made him sit back on his haunches in wonder, it was yet another river, so wide that he could not see to the other side. The scent that he had taken a liking to was strongest here. He was in fact looking at the South China Sea and the smell was that of salt. But the big cat did not know this; such trivial matters were beneath his magnificence. He stretched out full-length on the shore, all nine feet of himself, to study this wondrous sight. He took an instant liking to the place, especially the sound of the sea lapping the beach that caressed his sensitive ears. It was his ears that picked up the foreign sound that invaded them and shattered his peace. He moved his glorious head in the direction of the noise and beheld a sight that saddened his heart. A funny shaped log was floating by with bubbles coming from one end that seemed to be causing the irritating sounds, but what made the tiger stiffen into alertness was the sight of the creatures riding on top of the log, they were the ones that walked on two hind legs and killed with smoking sticks. The beast of prey sniffed the air and tensed, his hackles rising; one of those loathsome apparitions was a predator like himself. The creature in question sensed the tiger's scrutiny and looked towards the shore, and for a second their eyes locked. The tiger sighed with resignation and great sadness; this was no place for him after all, because the Upright Ones were here too. The great jungle beast rose majestically to his feet and started back to where he had come from, to the natural highland rainforest and an honourable life. With one contemptuous glance behind him the regally coated prince of the forest stalked off. After all, was he not one of the famous Tigers of Trengannu!

★

Kim Bok was feeling uneasy and perhaps a little jumpy and he was damned if he knew why. It was nothing that he could put his finger on. His flights from Macau and Hong Kong had been uneventful and his rendezvous with the two couriers in Bangkok had gone without a hitch. It was not until he had boarded the train for the return journey that he had begun to get the jitters. Armed Thai Police guarded the trains making the crossing into Malaya, and from the very start Kim Bok was of the opinion that the police escorts were taking more than a cursory interest in him and his two companions. The feeling that he was being watched grew and the tension within him mounted, making the simple trip one of the worst journeys that he had ever undertaken.

No matter whenever he moved his arse off of his seat, whether it was to get food and drink, stretch his legs or even go to the toilet, the bloody Thai policemen were there; smiling and friendly, but still there. Kim had originally intended to terminate this particular leg of the journey at the railway station one stop from the Thai side of the border and then cross over into Malaya on foot. But due to his anxiety that was bordering on paranoia, he deemed it necessary for them all to jump the train at Tanjong Mat, the starting point of their outward trip.

The minute that he was free of the infernal overcrowded train the bad vibes within Kim Bok ceased their strumming on his nervous system and he felt almost liberated. He led the two guerrilla couriers north-east from the railway line, trekking fifteen miles down along the meandering Sungei Tanjong Mas to the sea and the fishing village of Bung Nara; although this diversion was hard work and a bloody nuisance he felt all the better for it. Kim Bok knew that he was safe amongst these simple fisher folk, simple in the fact that they were uncomplicated and they were motivated by only one thing, money.

Kim sought an audience with the village headman who owned four fishing vessels, and they being the main subject under discussion, the two men soon struck a deal. It was not such a difficult task for Kim because hard cash transcends such things as international boundaries, law and politics, with the wad of Kim's Thai bank notes being no exception. *A bunch of pirates if I ever saw one,* thought Kim when the business had been done.

The next day the fleet of fishing vessels put to sea. The boats were crudely designed and consisted of solid wood planks lashed together with ropes, the vessels had a pronounced raised prow to assist with launching through the surf and had centre boards to stop them capsizing when the lanteen sails were hoisted. The boats worked in pairs using trammel nets, drifting to and fro on the tidal streams and currents about two miles off the coast, well out of range of prying eyes. With less than two feet of freeboard, Kim was mighty glad that he did not have to stand up and haul in the nets.

The plan was simple, the fishermen would do all the work whilst the terrorists sat still on their precarious floating platforms. The fleet would drift southwards on the tide for about five hours, and then the passengers would be landed at the next fishing village to be introduced to another headman. Whilst the first fleet drifted back home on the reverse tide, negotiations would begin all over again, but with references from the happily paid up band of cut-throats. It was a time consuming process, not to mention a strain on the purse but it got them safely across a hostile border and well beyond it.

The time spent at sea was peaceful, almost idyllic, and Kim for one felt a little sad when after eleven days of travelling in such a manner the final landing place came into sight, Kuala Trengannu. They were running close inshore and were approaching the point where the state river called the Sungei Trengannu meets the sea. Quite suddenly Kim Bok shivered in fearful expectation as he felt eyes upon him, the ice-cold gaze of a hunter like himself. Fully expecting to be riddled with bullets within seconds Kim glanced quickly towards the shore and found those eyes, those cold, cold and contemptuous eyes. Kim Bok could not for certain identify the cause of his fright, but in a flash of russet colouring the menacing threat withdrew into the jungle. The bullets did not come but the jitters had returned, this time never to leave him in peace again.

From Kuala Trengannu they made better progress along a combination of cart tracks and roughly surfaced ways that constituted the coastal road between Kuala Trengannu and their next destination, the town of Kuantan that lay 110 miles further to the south. It was a perilous and painful journey fraught with danger at every step of the way, gone were the welcome and peaceful interludes at sea.

It was perilous because they now faced the constant possibility of encountering British Army or Federation Police Field Force patrols, checkpoints or ambushes. In addition there was the ever-present threat of treachery from the people that they had coerced into helping them. It was painful on the feet during the frequent periods when they were required to march over the baking hot and uneven road surfaces that blistered their feet mercilessly. They could have taken to the shady and comparatively cool jungle but it would have slowed them down; better to dive for cover whenever they heard military vehicles approaching than attempt to break though the thick, almost impenetrable jungle edge to take advantage of a possible lift from civilian traffic. To attempt the latter would have taxed the terrorists' physical and mental abilities to the limit. It was painful too when they were travelling in commandeered or hired transport. They often had to hide amongst food and other products destined for the coastal fishing villages, and as well as having to endure the bone-shaking rides, there was the added torture of running the gauntlet of prodding bayonets at army and police road blocks.

They suffered, as always, the terrible tension that is the constant companion of the hunted. When marching they prayed for wheels, when on them they wished to hell that that they had not bothered, they were in a no-win situation. But they survived yet another stage in their quest to help liberate the people of the Malay Races, arriving in Kuantan after three days of supreme effort. There Kim Bok made contact with a representative of the

10th Regiment, at long last he was back with the Guerrilla Army. The 10th was the CT's largest regiment and was renowned for its rapid deployment in emergencies, administrative efficiency and tactical ingenuity; for the plan that Kim Bok had in mind they would have to pull all those attributes out of the bag and more besides.

It took but a day for Kim to set things in motion. He appointed the two couriers as beach masters for the landing point at Mersing. First, though with the assistance of the 10th Regiment's Quartermaster, they had to assemble the transport needed to haul the gold through the jungle, namely, elephants and mules. To do this the two couriers were dispatched to a secret animal compound near a village called Maran, the place was known jokingly throughout the regiment as the motor pool.

Organising the animals, their mahouts and muleteers was one thing, getting them to Mersing secretly was another, in fact, it was damned near impossible so it had to be done openly, but how? With a lot of planning and scheming a plot was hatched, an enterprise so audacious that its execution beggared belief.

In tandem with that part of the operation, Kim Bok travelled by road to the village of Kampong Pahang Tua situated on the north bank of the mighty Pahang River. There he procured and organised a flotilla of small vessels into which he would transfer the gold from the *Sea Pearl* when she arrived off Palau Tioman. The terrorist fleet consisted of a thirty-foot twin-diesel trawler and six eighteen-foot sampans equipped with powerful outboard engines. The crews, all armed and vicious terrorists from the 10th Regiment, made up this task force of determined men.

On 2 September all was ready and two events took place indicating that morale within the ranks of the Guerrilla Army had received a boost; and even Crazy Harry Blunt's unorthodox approach to military tactics took a knock.

The convoy of eighteen vehicles looked impressive to say the least. It consisted of six five-tonne trucks that had been modified with bamboo cages in order that they could transport a Malay elephant each. And ten three-tonne vehicles similarly equipped on which were travelling an assortment of animals that would have done any zoo proud. There were also two vintage jeeps, one to lead the way and the other bringing up the rear. Canopies had been removed from the vehicles so that all cargo could be plainly seen and as is the custom in the Far East, the trucks had been painted in gaudy coloured designs. Huge silver horns adorned the bonnets and transistor radios blared away blasting the countryside with a selection of Chinese, Malay and Indian music.

The 10th Regiment Quartermaster had dipped deep into his mysterious bag of supplies, as only quartermasters can, and had produced a first class menagerie to cloak the true cargo of elephants and mules. The elephants, of course, had to travel alone in their respective trucks and these were dispersed evenly throughout the convoy. But as companions to the twelve mules were buffalo, wild boar, a horse, birds, monkeys, baboons, iguanas, a crocodile and two alligators; pride of place went to an ancient tiger that was so tired that it could not even swat a fly. The convoy left Maran in the early hours of the morning and at first did not attract much attention. Heading west they made good time, but as the sun came up they had to slow down to accommodate the crowds of people that were beginning to gather, after all, that was the aim of the exercise. By the time that the convoy had reached Temerloh the population had turned out in force to stare in amazement at the animal fair in the gaily-coloured trucks.

It was a lovely sight with the sun glinting off the highly polished metal and the jolly music enhanced the festive atmosphere, the people cheered, adding their voices to the calls of the birds and beasts. In a European country it would have generated some interest, but in a trouble-torn Malaya only eleven years after a World War it was a bloody good circus and brought light into darkness. As the circus took a marked turn to the left at Temerloh to head south along a nightmare of winding minor roads that more or less followed the railway line, crossing it here and touching it there, the word went out. The bush telegraph and the telephone both came into play; and the police and army radio networks also told the villages ahead of the great coming. And so with a confidence that defied comprehension, the guerrillas moved forever southwards towards their goal. Where the passage of the circus coincided with that of a train, passengers leaned out of windows, climbed onto the roof and crowded the old Wild West type platforms at the end of each carriage. And even the unsuspecting armed guards aboard the train waved their hats and joined in the fun; it was a time of jubilation. Elephants trumpeted past the police barracks in Rompin, mules brayed and buffaloes bellowed their way through Gemas. Children screamed along with the monkeys and baboons as the circus negotiated Segamat and onwards past the concealed Commonwealth troops along the Kluang road. The convoy turned east at Ayer Hitam towards Kluang where, because of the time of day the watching pundits of the security forces thought it would stop for the night. The crowds went crazy and jumped for joy as the circus approached the crossroads at Kluang, and it was not until it continued straight on towards Mersing that the penny dropped.

'They're heading for Mersing, it's them!' exclaimed an incredulous Brigade Commander. 'Get the Field Marshal on the line.'

'Good heavens, of course sir,' blurted out the Brigadier's aide.

'Strewth,' remarked the Australian duty signaller.

It was a jubilant Field Marshal who broke the news to Harry Blunt, and then had to laugh at the old soldier's look of utter astonishment. But the crazy one soon said with admiration, 'Well that's one up to them. What say you to "Who Dares Wins" now?'

'It's beyond me!' roared the near hysterical Army Chief.

The slightly amused Gurkha Riflemen smiled wryly from their concealed ambush positions along the Mersing-kluang road. At 16.30 hrs in the fading light of day on 2 September, the Gurkhas reported that the convoy had stopped near Kampong Jemalung, ten miles south of Mersing. The elephants and mules had been led off into the jungle, the vehicles were being driven into the swampy ground and camouflaged from view. The reptiles, birds and primates were being released into the wild, all other animals, including the worn out tiger, had been shot for food.

The second happening was not so spectacular but daring nonetheless. At precisely 14.00 hrs on the same day, a police constable manning an observation post at Pekan reported a strange sight. It was a trawler towing six sampans in a line astern heading for Kuala Pahang and the open sea. The constable, and quite reasonably so, thought that as odd as it seemed to be, anything that was done so openly must be above suspicion. His superior officer at police headquarters in Pekan thought otherwise and sent a coded message to the Security Services at Flag House in Kuala Lumpur.

By 01.00 hrs on 3 September, the suspect vessels had been picked up on radar sets aboard one of the naval frigates, she reported the targets to be off the island of Palau Berhala. The Navy was ordered to track the fishing boats that had altered course, the new heading should take them directly towards Palau Tioman.

Commandos who were becoming lethargic due to waiting around in cramped conditions throughout the necklace of islands were put on full alert. Ten hours later at 09.00 hrs commandos manning the OP on Palau Tulai three miles short of Palau Tioman reported that the vessels were anchored off the island. Every commando OP had been issued with the most recent photographs taken of Kim Bok and Fantail, those obtained by the Special Branch men in Hong Kong. A commando sniper looking through his X20 magnification telescope nudged his Corporal's arm, 'Here, take a look, that's Kim Bok on the deck of that trawler.'

The NCO studied the face of the man indicated to him by the sniper; he put down the telescope and looked at the photographs. 'Yep, that's him all right. Well done Hawkeye,' he said to the sniper with a grin. Then grabbing the radio handset he got on to his Troop HQ, 'Hello Zero this is...'

Back at Flag House Crazy Harry was positively preening himself at the news. And to justify him paying for drinks all round in the mess; a Gurkha platoon had tracked the elephants and mules, now dubbed the Gold Train, to a tiny inlet with a sandy beach only two miles south of Mersing.

Kim Bok had every reason to feel satisfied with the way things had gone. It had not been easy, the availability of vessels had posed no problem, getting the reluctant owners to hand them over had been another matter. It had required threats to their well-being before some level of co-operation could be generated, and to discourage any desire to inform the authorities, he had left a small but vicious force of the 10th Regiment behind in Kampong Pahang Tua. Out of sight but forever present they ensured security.

Kim had managed to procure only enough fuel for the sampans to make one journey, and that would be from Palau Tioman to Mersing, hence the towing operation. He had felt bloody proud as he had sailed his mini-fleet past Pekan despite the fact that he knew that they were being watched, it was a feeling that was well nigh constant these past few days. Coming out of the estuary had been a lively and exhilarating experience with the cross-currents and wind creating a very choppy sea. The trawler was being tossed about so violently that the towing line threatened to pull out the entire bow section of the leading sampan. The remaining sampans were not coping with the sea as well as they might due to the constraints of their towing lines, everyone was soaked to the skin and had to hold on for dear life. Weapons and equipment hidden out of sight were drenched, and it was a blessed relief when the trawler towed her six charges into deeper water and settled down to the voyage.

When they eventually arrived at the staging point off Palau Tulai, Kim was praying that the bloody junk would not keep him waiting on the god-awful trawler for too long. The vessel was now at anchor with the six sampans forming a trot alongside her; they rocked gently in the swell, protected in the lee of the island.

Kim Bok was in the middle of congratulating his men on a job well done when the words froze in his mouth as an icy shiver ran down his spine, and he knew instinctively that he was under observation. The men watched in puzzlement as Kim turned to face the shore only a hundred yards away, he looked long and hard but to no avail. There was no flash of russet this time; no, it was another kind of hunter that was out there.

Chapter Seven

Whilst these two extraordinary events were taking place in Pahang things were beginning to move on the Tong front too.

Following the meeting at Flag house, Jeremy Fairburne-Snape had returned to his residence in Gemas to find Fiona still in bed looking completely at peace with the world. She was in a drowsy mood but became fully awake and expectant when he walked into the bedroom.

'Jeremy darling,' she invited in a dulcet tone, 'do get into bed, I need you so badly.' Fiona was already panting with anticipation as she remembered the tempestuous coupling of the night before. Although Jeremy was angry with her and feeling a bit ashamed of himself, he needed little encouragement. Leaving a trail of clothing from the doorway to the bed he jumped in beside her and they soon became entwined in a passionate and vigorous display of lovemaking that far surpassed any sexual excesses that had gone on before; the couple simply threw all inhibitions to the four winds.

When at last they lay side by side utterly exhausted, their heaving, sweating bodies being cooled down by the overhead fan, Jeremy actually found the vanity to congratulate himself on his sexual prowess and seemingly new-found vitality. So engrossed had he become in this pleasurable indulgence of inner preening that he almost forgot the true purpose of the exercise. It was Fiona's incessant post-coital chatter that brought him back to reality; he judged the moment when he could get a word in edgeways and squeezed Fiona's right breast to stop the flow of verbal nonsense.

'Fiona dear,' he murmured, 'when will you be seeing Cynthia again?'

There was a marked pause before she answered. 'Oh, tomorrow perhaps, why do you ask?' she continued with obvious panic.

'Nothing really, just something I overheard at work that ties in nicely with what she told you.'

'Jeremy darling,' she chided now relaxed once more. 'You and your work, and while we're in bed too,' teased Fiona whilst she stroked his inner thigh. Fast losing control as he visibly responded to her ministrations, he just managed to plant the seed of misinformation before he once more rose to the occasion and made love to Fiona with such intense ardour that their gyrations were quite audible in the kitchen below. The cook and the maid smiled as they exchanged winks.

At the same time as Jeremy Fairburne-Snape had being doing his bit, so to speak, Tom Nobles returned to Rompin. In a separate office to that of Simon Belchard's he interviewed the two constables who together with their Commanding Officer had interrogated and killed the late guerrilla fighter. It was a long process with very detailed notes being taken that were later framed into a condemning statement, which both men signed. Tom now had them by the short and curlies and they knew it, the two policemen were very aware of the fact that they faced death by hanging. As they sat in front of him, Tom let them stew for a while, in fact, he got up and left the office leaving the two worried men to sweat it out for a couple of hours before returning to give them an ultimatum.

'This,' he stated grimly tapping the statements with a forefinger, 'is your ticket to the gallows.' He paused for effect. 'But,' he added, 'there is a way out of this mess that will absolve you of all blame.' The two Malay policemen looked at Tom with hope in their eyes. 'Do what I ask,' continued the Special Branch man, 'but do it well and I'll guarantee that you'll walk free.'

And so it came to pass that Simon Belchard, sitting only two offices away from Tom Nobles at the time, came under surveillance from within his own headquarters by the two people who were supposed to be his allies. It would have been impossible for Tom to infiltrate someone from his own department into the police barracks; surveillance from without, however, was no problem. From that moment on the Police Inspector would not be able to wipe his arse without Tom knowing about it.

Simon Belchard has spent a miserable night at his bungalow. He had finished late because that Special Branch fellow Nobles had been conducting an investigation into the behaviour of the two constables involved in this thing with him. They would receive comparatively light sentences, he thought, especially as he had shouldered the blame; after all, they had only been following orders. He was not worried about the situation; he was confidant that he had been successful in fobbing off the Police Commissioner and the Special Branch. He would use the valuable time afforded to him by the Commissioner's desire to keep things hush-hush for the time being to feather his nest and make good his escape with, he fervently hoped, the help of the Tongs.

No, the thing that was bothering him now was of a more personal nature, namely, his failure to satisfy Fiona on the last occasion that they had met. On that day he had received a terrific blow to his male ego and only a successful union with Fiona would alleviate the problem, besides, he needed more out of her that just sex: Simon desperately wanted information. The only way that he could get her to spew forth the insufferable garbage from her delightful mouth that he was required to sift through was to bring her to a climax and the more intense it was the bigger the harvest reaped. He was now in the mood for sex and that fact was pretty obvious as he admired his athletic figure in the full length bedroom mirror, the same bedroom in which he had seduced Fiona on innumerable occasions, although he often wondered at times who was seducing who. Thinking of it caused his imagination to run amok and his frustration to mount, later in bed he tossed and turned his mind in a turmoil of emotions. In a desperate attempt to relieve the tension and induce sleep he found respite in self-release.

Simon woke up with a headache, he was still suffering from it when he arrived at his headquarters later on that morning and it put him in a filthy, spiteful mood. Man management went completely out of the window, he did not cope with minor problems gladly and suffered fools even less. He for one was glad to get out of the place by midday; everyone else in the barracks was mighty pleased to see the back of him. Still in a bad temper as he drove out to his bungalow, Simon nearly crashed his car at the shock of seeing Fiona's Morris parked outside his home.

As if a great weight had been lifted from his shoulders, he fairly jumped for joy and rushed inside to embrace his beautiful lover in a huge bear hug. Then almost crying with yearning and wild with animal lust he carried her over the threshold of his bedroom, there, he literally tore the clothes from her luscious body and took her violently thinking only of his own want. Although Fiona responded to this sexual onslaught with equal vigour, Simon was so caught up in his own terrific orgasm that he failed to notice that his partner did not reach a climax.

He indulged himself in her innermost parts all afternoon hell-bent on proving something or other to her, Fiona was striving to match his endeavours and was not holding back in any way. She was using all her skills and feminine wiles to encourage him back to life after every bout of passion, but Fiona was simply not getting there herself; it was a one-sided encounter so far with the usual roles reversed for a change. Whereas before it had been her that normally displayed an insatiable sexual hunger that could reduce Simon to an exhausted, quivering heap, it was now him that was dominating their lovemaking with manly aggression. Then at long last during Simon's fifth Herculean performance, Fiona experienced that first tingling feeling in her loins that heralded the point of no return and she quickly ascended the heights of sexual bliss and ecstasy with him, convulsing helplessly until she was utterly spent.

Fiona drove back to the Gemas residence with mixed feelings and was puzzled by her strange mood. At about the halfway mark she suddenly stopped the car and burst into tears as the fact came home to her that she had been blind to all else except the desire to attain sexual satisfaction. But now at this very instant in time, call it belated women's intuition if you will, she fully comprehended everything and understood the folly of her ways. With hindsight Fiona now knew that Simon was using her to gain information appertaining to her husband's job. She had nothing concrete to go on mind you, it was just the way he had perked up when she had prattled on about that absurd gold story, and again at the mention of that strange lake up that funny sounding river. Now she realised that it was all serious stuff and she had probably dropped poor old Jeremy in the soup with her utter selfishness and stupidity. With that came the shocking suspicion that her own husband might be using her too. She cast her mind back to the question he had asked her.

'Fiona dear,' he had said, 'when will you be seeing Cynthia again?' Then he had gone on to tell her all about the gold shipment. Fiona accepted all these suppositions calmly enough and could not bring herself to blame Jeremy even if he was using her; she deserved it after the way she had treated him. But what was shocking her system to the core and making her tremble with emotion was her feelings for Jeremy himself, the realisation that he had completely recaptured her heart was overwhelming. Fiona remembered wistfully the previous night of passion with her husband that had overshadowed Simon's sexual blitz of the afternoon. With a feeling of self-disgust and pangs of remorse and guilt, Fiona continued her journey home resolved to go to any lengths in order to help her Jeremy, her dear sweet Jeremy. *What a fool I've been,* she thought sadly. But she smiled to herself and whispered, 'I'm coming home to you Jeremy my love, we'll fight this thing together.'

Immediately on arriving back at the Gemas residence Fiona ordered a maid to run a hot bath. Feeling like a woman scorned she immersed herself in the tub of soapy bubbles and cleansed her body of the day's lovemaking with the now detestable Simon Belchard. Afterwards she paced up and down the lounge rehearsing what she was going to say to Jeremy when he got home, but it was no good, she could not get her act together. In the event it mattered not because when Jeremy arrived home she was in his arms sobbing uncontrollably before he could set foot in the door. He gently led her inside and listened with tears in his own eyes as Fiona unburdened herself of all her infidelities, especially the one concerning Simon Belchard. She held nothing back and when it had all come out into the open Fiona stood trembling in front of him like a little girl full of guilt. Jeremy's heart went out to this beautiful woman, and he loved her more than ever because she had found the courage to confess to her sins; what kind of man could not forgive her now? They talked the problem through until the early hours of the morning then made love with a tenderness that neither of them thought they were capable of; now they were indeed a team.

It was a much-changed Jeremy Fairburne-Snape who faced the Field Marshal the next day. He too held nothing back and such was the strength of his argument regarding the employment of Fiona in an official capacity that he won the old soldier over in minutes.

'After all,' had been one of his points, 'we were quite prepared to use her before, now she can target documents, phone numbers and the like.'

Crazy Harry Blunt was brought up to date on the situation and being the old romantic that he was, the ploy appealed to him greatly. 'Well Jeremy lad,' concluded the Field Marshal, 'let's put some stick about the place.'

Simon saw Fiona off and then immediately telephoned Abdul to give him the news that they had all been waiting for. Within minutes the information had been passed on to Mr Tan, who in turn communicated with the Tong boss in Kuala Lumpur. Mr Tan was called to the Tong headquarters and by midnight all were pouring over poor quality maps of the Pahang River area. Mr Tan, who normally kept his station when attending these meetings of the bastion of organised crime in Malaya took his life into his hands by breaking in.

'I know somebody who lives there,' he ventured, pointing to a spot on the map of Central Pahang, 'he's a bit of a mercenary but will do anything for a drink.' Mr Tan paused and faced the steely-eyed stares of the Tong men.

'Go on,' ordered the boss.

'Well, he is a military man and is good in the jungle. He's fought against the guerrillas and knows how they think.'

'Take me there, I will talk to this mercenary,' commanded the top man.

'Certainly,' answered Mr Tan feeling highly honoured by this dubious compliment.

The place on the map indicated by Mr Tan was called Temerloh. The decision by the criminal elite to choose this avenue of opportunity was to provide Crazy Harry Blunt with an extraordinary stroke of luck. One of those chances of a lifetime, a golden opportunity that if acted upon with great tact would precipitate a course of action that would lead to the deaths of many criminals.

The surveillance operation mounted on Simon Belchard was well underway and Fiona's visit to his bungalow duly noted, but otherwise, the security services were no closer to discovering for whom the bent policeman was working.

Temerloh is a small town situated in the State of Pahang, a quiet place split more or less in half by the Sungei Pahang. A bridge that spans the 200 yards of water that flows from north to south at that point, connects the two halves. Temerloh is served by a B-Class road that follows the river and another minor road, both meeting to form a crossroads at the western end of the bridge.

At precisely 09.00 on 3 September the Englishman stood up from the milestone he had been using for a seat. The man had been sitting there at the crossroads for exactly ten minutes, as he did every morning like clockwork. He was five feet nine inches tall in his socks. Of a stocky build, he carried his shoulders squared back and held his stomach in. His hair was a silvery grey colour and was cut short, he sported a huge handlebar moustache and his skin was burned a permanent dark brown from years of living in the Far East; a military man if there ever was one. Clad only in khaki drill shorts and shod in a pair of army issue sandals he was obviously enjoying the sun as he started to walk across to the eastern side of the bridge. He stopped half way over to lean on the bridge parapet to watch the river flow gently by on its journey to the sea many miles away; by early evening after the rain it would be a raging torrent. Dennis Emanual Pothlethwait-Markham gazed into the water below and pondered over his past; another daily routine.

Dennis had not exactly been born with a silver spoon in his mouth but the Pothlethwait-Markham's were wealthy landowners with vast estates in the West Ridings. His parents' plans for his future had dominated his childhood and early youth but the only characteristic that Dennis had inherited from them was stubbornness.

His parents were absolutely appalled when he had announced his intention of going down the pits. 'A bloody coal miner,' his father had screamed, 'over my dead body, lad.' Then after weeks of bitter fighting between the parents and their recalcitrant offspring, Dennis had done the unthinkable, he marched off to Pontefract Barracks and volunteered for twenty-two years' service with the colours of the Light Infantry Regiment that was based there. When he had ventured home during his embarkation leave prior to sailing for India he was turned away. 'Never darken this doorstep again,' his angry father had roared, 'you're a bloody disgrace to the family name.'

Although Dennis had joined the army out of pure frustration and spite he actually fell in love with the tough and strange way of life, especially his service in India. Like Crazy Harry Blunt, Dennis had served his apprenticeship and experienced his baptism of fire on the North-West Frontier. He too fought the Japanese on the India-Burma border during the Second World War and whilst serving with the Chindits he helped push them back across Burma, through Thailand and Malaya to Singapore.

In the latter stages of the Fourteenth Army's campaign he volunteered for duties of a hazardous nature and was consequently parachuted into Thailand at a place called Ubon. There the special force that he was serving with liberated some prisoners of war that the Japanese had marked down for execution; they were the men who had built the bridge over the River Kwai. After the war he had returned to the ranks of his beloved Light Infantry Regiment now serving in Malaya. They were on hand from the onset to resist the armed insurrection by the Chinese Communist Terrorists in 1948 and Dennis once more found himself in the thick of the action. In 1949 an ex-Fourteenth Army officer was tasked to form a special unit of volunteers and Dennis jumped at the chance to put his name down. He had been bitten by the bug that is special forces work and in a very short space of time found himself soldiering in the ranks of the newly formed Malayan Scouts. A Lieutenant Colonel Harry Blunt better known to his men as Crazy Harry commanded that unit; the Malayan Scouts were later to become the Special Air Service Regiment. Dennis did a two-year stint with them carrying out deep penetration jungle patrols of three months duration or longer, not a job for the faint-hearted. The end of his tour of duty coincided with the return to the UK of his parent unit and his demob date, Dennis declined to return to England with the Light Infantry Battalion that had been his home for so long and took his discharge in Malaya.

After a brief but hectic binge he tried to settle down but found himself at loose ends and was soon craving for action. Together with two other men who had also served in the Malayan Scouts, and were also former French Foreign Legionnaires, he made his way to Indo-China and enlisted into one of the Legion's Parachute Battalions. A wrong move on his part because the unit was soon embroiled in the no-hope situation that was the Battle of Dien Bien Phu. Dennis managed to escape from the carnage, deserted from the now decimated Legion and returned to Malaya to seek his fortune there. But in a fit of remorse induced by hitting the bottle too hard and often Dennis wrote home to his family begging for reconciliation. The reply when it came was as abrupt as it was generous; the answer was an emphatic no, and the incentive to keep him off the doorstep of the baronial hall was a cheque for ten thousand pounds with the promise of four hundred pounds per month for life.

And so Dennis Emanual Pothlethwait-Markham became one of those quaintly named British Colonial characters known the world over as remittance men.

'And that's the story of my life,' said Dennis to any fish that might be lurking in the depths.

He straightened up and continued with his walk and when he had arrived at what could loosely be termed as the main drag he patted his stomach and announced to anyone who was interested, 'Time for breakfast.'

A minute later he stepped out of the bright sunlight into the gloomy, smoke-filled atmosphere of a shop that sold everything under the sun. It was an Aladdin's Cave-like place lit by an assortment of Tilly and Hurricane lamps, candles and coloured lanterns; and the smell of joss sticks, cooking food and dried fish permeated the air. Dennis had arrived home.

Halfway down the long narrow room was set a table and four chairs, this hallowed place was jokingly referred to by the inhabitants of Temerloh as 'his lordship's dining table', for Dennis was generous with his money. Dennis Emanuel Pothlethwait-Markham, better known to his friends and enemies alike as Dennis the Bloody Menace, sat down amongst the sacks of sugar, flour and beans, to name but a few things to await his breakfast.

He had already partaken of a livener, of course; that came with his early morning routine at reveille. He actually slept in an enclosed backyard on a charpoy that was positioned against the wall of a stone-built shower cubicle. At 06.00 hrs he would put his feet on the cold stone floor, pour himself a tumbler of arrack and swig half of it straight down. Then whilst the fiery liquid was warming up his insides he would jump into the freezing cold shower and scrub his outside. To complete his ablutions he had merely to clean his teeth whilst still standing in the shower, after spitting out most of the watery toothpaste and blood from his gums, Dennis would gargle with the remainder of the arrack and gulp down the residue. There being no curtain or door to the shower cubicle Dennis was in full view of all the children that lived in the shop and the immediate adjoining dwellings. They, with wide-eyed curiosity and more than a few giggles would gather around the shower every morning to watch the man with brown skin but a white bottom perform his strange cleansing ritual. Still watched by half the child population of Temerloh he would don a clean pair of shorts, the shop also served as a laundry, and set forth on his morning constitutional starting out dead on 06.30 hrs. He always terminated this mental and physical exercise at 09.30 hrs sharp at the table where he was now sat.

Breakfast consisted of a cold chicken breast, a bowl of monkey nuts and a pint bottle of Guinness, the vintage of which was uncertain. He was served by a thirty-year-old Malay woman wearing a green chiffon blouse with nothing on underneath to hide her firm and ample breasts, and a matching miniskirt that seemed to have no middle part, just a waist band and a hem. Thinking of his blood pressure, Dennis was relieved that she was wearing something under that. 'Thank you Petal,' he smiled.

'Not too much of that,' she replied pointing at the Guinness, 'or you won't be any good to me later,' concluded the strikingly pretty lady. She was referring to the afternoon siesta that they enjoyed most days, doing everything but rest because they loved each other very much. Petal had two children, who because of his early morning pantomime in the shower, knew Dennis's body almost as well as their mother's. Dennis provided for their every need and cared for and loved them dearly; and they loved him too. It could truthfully be said that at long last Dennis had happily settled down. The only thing that slightly marred his relationship with Petal was that by nightfall he was so far gone with drink that she refused to have him in her bed, so Dennis had been consigned to the charpoy.

Breakfast over, Petal brought Dennis another bottle of Guinness, on her way back to the counter she bent down to pick up some nutshells, it was her way of reminding him of what he would be missing if he went over the top.

Dennis really did like to sit there and watch the day's business unfold. On that particular morning alone the proprietor, Petal's father, sold an outboard engine, six bolts of cloth, several miles of rope, fishing nets and enough food supplies to feed a battalion. The shop was also a popular meeting place and positioned here and there amongst the piles of produce were stools, chairs and benches. It was a café, bar and mah-jong parlour, the food was good and Petal's skirts often encouraged the younger clientele to order second helpings. Two chickens had started to peck away at the nutshells and Dennis amused himself by throwing whole nuts around to make them chase about and fight over the titbits.

An hour before noon his look of amusement turned to one of speculation, he called Petal over to the table and ordered a chicken curry. The look of eager anticipation in the chicken's eyes vanished to be replaced by one of pure hatred. *You rotten bastard,* was the message received by Dennis before the endangered fowl scampered for their lives. The remittance man enjoyed the hot, spicy succulent dish; the two chickens were never seen again. Petal was pleased that her man had eaten, it was a good sign and an indication that he was thinking straight, she was looking forward to enjoying him soon.

Dennis looked at, or rather through Petal's blouse at her sharply pointed profile and felt a stirring in his loins; Petal glanced over towards him and smiled. Time to go, he said with his eyes. Dennis was about to get up from the table when the sound of excited children came to him from just outside the shop doorway. He slumped back into his chair as Petal's eldest little girl approached him dancing with glee and holding out a handful of sweets for him to see. 'It's Mr Tan, Mr Tan,' she shrieked for all to hear, 'Mr Tan, he come.'

'The bastard couldn't have timed it better,' muttered a now very frustrated Dennis under his breath. Petal sighed with disappointment because she would now have to wait until tomorrow for her sexual satisfaction.

Mr Tan's grand entrance was literally dwarfed by his companion, a man of colossal proportions and of good Chinese stock. *But one turned sour,* thought Dennis as he invited them to take a seat. The two men did not appear eager to sit down, indeed, Mr Tan seemed to be ill at ease; whilst the huge Chinese fellow gave the impression that the place was well beneath his status.

Mr Tan did not really know Dennis, it was more a case of knowing of him through his now dead brother who had helped the French Foreign Legionnaire deserter on his return to Malaya from Indo-China. Since the first introduction to Dennis by his brother, Mr Tan had struck up a distant sort of friendship with the man who he referred to as a mercenary. On Dennis's part, Mr Tan was an amusing casual acquaintance who would need watching; whilst Mr Tan regarded Dennis with undisguised awe. But all the time since his brother's murder he had in the back of his mind thought to use the mercenary's military expertise to avenge his kin's death; now with the added power of the Tongs, that time had come.

Mr Tan would have preferred to handle this particular meeting alone acting as a middleman. Now, being overshadowed by the ominous presence of the Tong boss who exuded menace in his every move, he felt decidedly on edge. That nervousness communicated itself to Dennis and immediately put the old soldier on his guard, his right hand moved slowly to a spot beneath the tabletop.

Dennis looked up at the pair from his comparatively lowly position. 'Do sit down gentlemen, and join me in a drink?'

They did not respond. The chatter inside the shop died down until it was so silent and tense that you could hear a pin drop. From outside, the sound of the children could still be heard, the wondrous gasps of delight suggesting that more than one car was parked out there. Mr Tan always drove his own car so he guessed that the other one was chauffeur driven and that the driver was entertaining the kids by showing them all the gadgets. *Three men at least,* he thought as he persevered. 'Come on, the beer is good here.'

'I'd rather we all sat in my car', answered the Tong boss before Mr Tan could find any words.

'No,' was the curt reply from Dennis.

'But I insist,' said the big Tong man with an air of imperial authority.

Dennis's reaction to this was simple and to the point, he drew a Browning 9mm pistol from its hidden holster beneath the tabletop and pointed it at the Chinaman. 'And I decline. You can bloody well sit down or you can bugger off, the choice is yours.' Mr Tan went as white as a sheet and he started to tremble like a jelly. The Chinaman met Dennis's cool look with a steely gaze but with a hint of admiration; he motioned for Mr Tan to sit down and pulled out a chair for himself, well away from the table because he could not get his legs underneath it. The proprietor put away the axe that he was holding and the cooks did likewise with their meat cleavers.

'If you don't want to be overheard,' grinned Dennis, 'then for Christ's sake whisper,' he concluded putting away the pistol. Dennis ordered the drinks and they were duly served up by Petal who gave her man a lewd wink full of eastern promise.

Mr Tan spoke for the first time. 'Dennis my dear fellow,' his hands were shaking so much that he spilt some of his drink whilst trying to clear his throat, 'my friend here has a proposition that he wishes to put to you.'

And then the three men went into a huddle for two hours that eventually ended in handshakes. Dennis looked grimly interested,

Mr Tan had regained his composure and the Tong boss seemed pleased. 'I'm impressed,' he said to Mr Tan before the two crooks got into their respective cars.

As soon as they had gone, and to Petal's utter astonishment Dennis dragged her off to bed where he excelled himself staying there with her all night for the first time in months.

The next morning Dennis did not disappoint the children and put on his show as if nothing untoward had happened the previous day. Although only one child had actually witnessed his gun toting performance, Petal's eldest daughter, she had soon spread the word and now there was an added wonder in the children's eyes as they beheld their very own brave warrior.

Dennis did not go for his walk that morning, instead, he commandeered the proprietor's cubby-hole of an office to study some maps that he had kept as souvenirs from his army days. He pondered hard, he plotted courses on the maps and then digging deep into his memory of the area he made some calculations. Dennis came to the conclusion that if those crazy communist bastards were even thinking of bringing a shipment of gold up the Sungei Pahang, they ought to have their bloody heads read. *But,* thought Dennis, *this is not like them at all, they're not that stupid.* He tapped thoughtfully on a map with his pencil. 'Unless,' he whispered with a wry grin, 'someone is feeding these criminals a load of old hogwash'. The remittance man thought long and hard, there was a lot at stake here. Mr Tan and that Tong giant, Dennis had guessed who the Chinaman was, had made two major mistakes where he was concerned. Firstly they had wrongly assumed that he was a down-and-out who would set fire to his own grandmother for a couple of cents. They obviously had no idea that he enjoyed a legitimate and secure source of income, Dennis had noticed the condescending way in which Mr Tan had picked up the tab yesterday. It was not that Dennis had any qualms about relieving the CTs of the gold, no, there was something not quite right and the whole thing stank to high heaven. The second mistake was all to do with Dennis's long-standing love affair with the British Army; they, like the guerrillas, were not stupid either. If the likes of the Tongs and their gangland lackeys had become privy to such valuable intelligence, then you could bet your life that the British knew too. If that were the case and the CTs were indeed bringing in funds to bolster their flagging liberation campaign they would have to chance their arm against a very formidable British Army, as would the criminal faction that had enlisted Dennis as an advisor. And that is where the old soldier drew the line, for no matter what the circumstances, he would never fire a shot in anger at a British soldier.

Dennis tossed the probabilities around in his head once more. Given the likelihood of the CTs smuggling gold bullion into Malaya was a distinct possibility, the theory that they would route it in through the Pahang River was utter rubbish. Dennis smiled and picked up the ancient-looking telephone thinking as he did so, *I know of only two men who would have the gall to put a story like that about the place.* He dialled a number that put him through to the Army Headquarters at Flag House in Kuala Lumpur.

'Hello,' he announced, 'I am an informer, I'd like to speak to Colonel Harry Blunt of Staff Intelligence please.' There was a brief pause while the line was connected. 'Hello Harry, this is Dennis, how are you, my good man? Look, I've just been told a cock and bull story about some mythical gold bullion. What the hell are you and old Petherington up to, eh lad?' Dennis laughed at the spluttering sounds coming out of the receiver and waited for a reply.

Crazy Harry Blunt was not often caught by surprise but the revelations disclosed by his old comrade in arms caused his jaw to gape open so wide that his pipe fell out of his mouth knocking ash and tobacco all over his desktop. Barely able to contain himself Harry listened until Dennis had run out of steam. 'Needless to say,' concluded Dennis, 'I'm on your side in all this and as such I offer you my honourable and loyal services sir.'

'Accepted, of course,' blurted out Harry, 'I'll have a word with the Field Marshal first and then get back to you. Don't go away.'

The Colonel burst into Petherington's office without so much as a polite knock. 'Sir!' he exclaimed, 'we've just received the most incredible stroke of good luck!'

Dennis really got dressed up for his meeting with Harry Blunt. In addition to his usual khaki drill shorts with their enormously baggy legs that were known as 'Empire Builders', he wore a pair of bright green socks, a gaily coloured printed shirt depicting various species of parrots and an Australian bush hat complete with hanging corks. Thus suitably attired, he kissed Petal a fond cheerio and boarded his transport, a multicoloured Chevrolet pickup truck that he had borrowed off Petal's father. With half the population waving and cheering he drove off towards the main road and all points south to Gemas, accompanied by the rattling and clanging of an assortment of gardening tools and implements in the back of the truck.

He had been given an address to go to on the previous day by Harry over the telephone and he arrived there at 12.30 hrs on 4 September.

He drove onto a spacious hard standing surrounded by well-kept lawns and parked up between an official-looking Mercedes and a clapped-out old Morris Minor. On approaching the main entrance, he was accosted by a female member of the household staff who in no uncertain terms was advising him to use the tradesmen's door when the gentleman of the house made a prudent appearance. 'That's all right my dear,' said Jeremy Fairburne-Snape, dismissing the good lady. 'You must be Dennis. Come inside and meet the others, we are all agog!' invited Jeremy ushering his guest in for a welcome cool drink. 'What will be your pleasure my good man?' asked the host.

'I'll have a long Barcardi and bitter lemon,' answered Dennis stepping into the lounge to be met by a deathly hush. 'Strewth!' he exclaimed in keeping with his Aussie headgear, 'this place reminds me of my Baronial Hall back home in the Yorkshire coal fields.' He looked about the palatial room with its marble floor; tiger skin rugs and other lavish trappings of Empire and felt quite at home in his shorts. 'Quite a tip you have here,' was his final comment.

After what seemed to be an age of stunned silence in which the formally dressed gathering stood gaping at the outlandish looking remittance man with a mixture of expressions on their faces, the Field Marshal came to the rescue and broke the ice. 'I like your disguise, Dennis,' he said with a grin, 'do you think that anyone spotted you on the way here?'

'Disguise?' protested Dennis with a deadpan expression. 'I'll have you know that this in my best suit.'

With that everyone burst out laughing and Jeremy introduced the star figure to Claude Rysdale, Tom Nobles and Fiona. He had already made the acquaintance of the Field Marshal and Harry Blunt but firm handshakes were in order. A waitress brought Dennis his schooner of ice cold drink and with no more ado they all got down to the business at hand.

The Field Marshal took the chair and for the benefit of the eccentrically dressed Dennis he went through the entire situation and concluded by thanking the old soldier for saving them perhaps weeks of surveillance work on Simon Belchard.

'Whether or not,' said Petherington, 'these Chinese Tong people in league with the Malacca underworld are actually Belchard's employers is pure conjecture at the moment, but into their hands his information is surely falling. My guess is that the Inspector is being blackmailed by someone in the middle, maybe even another policeman? If that is indeed the case, then it is only a matter of time before he or she slips up and reveals themselves to Tom and his surveillance team.' The Field Marshal paused for a drink. 'We have an ace up our sleeve,' he resumed nodding at Fiona, 'and Dennis here is the joker in the pack. We will continue to play this game of deception using Fiona to feed that blighter Belchard with a load of old rubbish and Dennis delaying the Tongs with some bogus strategy that has yet to be decided upon.'

Fiona had the good grace to blush; Dennis could not help but feel sorry for her. 'At the risk of sounding more stupid than I look,' he asked, 'why can't you arrest them now, they couldn't very well compromise your operation if they were locked up now, could they?'

'No Dennis, they couldn't,' answered Petherington, 'it's an option that I've considered but it's too risky.'

'You see,' broke in Claude, 'with an organisation as big as the Tongs, the shockwave that would be generated by arresting one of their top dogs would be felt as far away as Peking.'

'And,' added Crazy Harry, 'that same shockwave would send out warning signals throughout the terrorists' intelligence system, we would be spitting into the wind.'

'Point taken,' conceded Dennis.

'Besides,' said Claude, 'I'd like a few more of them in the bag before I draw the strings.'

'Don't forget this mysterious middleman,' reminded Tom Nobles, 'let's complete the round up here and not leave a bad apple in the barrel'. The discussion continued for another half hour, then the Field Marshal once again took the reins. 'Time is running out, the latest ETA I have of the *Sea Pearl* arriving off Palau Tioman is midday tomorrow. The earliest that Fiona can get to work doing her stuff with Belchard is also tomorrow if she is to stick to her normal routine.' Fiona went as red as a beetroot. 'The Tongs should hear about the vessel's arrival by tomorrow night if Belchard is quick off the mark. Dennis, I want you to advise the Tongs if and when it is necessary to mount lookouts at the Pahang River estuary, and at suitable points up the river.' Dennis nodded in agreement. 'Now, to give credence to our misinformation and to promote the Tong's confidence in Dennis and his obvious expertise in strategy,' he coughed, 'the SBS will take the junk up the Sungei Pahang having boarded her after the guerrillas have set off for Mersing with the gold. Once the vessel has passed Kuala Pahang and the Tongs have witnessed the fact, no movement connected with this deception plan is to take place south of the river. The river line is the key to our success; the Tongs' activities in regard to stealing the gold must be contained within that boundary. How do you see it Harry?'

'I see it the same way, but an additional snippet of information needs to be leaked out.'

'And that is?' prompted Petherington.

'How far upriver is the gold going to be taken? The Tongs can't really plan to intercept and steal the bullion without knowing a target destination.'

'Good point Harry,' agreed the Field Marshal, 'I suggest that as Dennis is going to be the Tongs' military advisor in this matter, he chooses the most suitable place. Dennis?'

'Off the top of my head I'd say Kampong Lubok Paku would be the favourite. It's situated on the north bank of the river at the end of the road that runs south from Maran.'

'The road might pose a problem,' butted in Tom Nobles, 'the Tongs might want to use it, and if they persist, bang goes any excuse to delay them.'

'Yes,' added Harry, 'don't forget that Maran was the forming-up point for the CT's convoy extraordinary, there's got to be a CT camp around there somewhere. Any unusual activity other than police or military might throw a spanner in the works.'

'In that case,' stated Petherington, 'we'll do something to discourage them from using that road.' He made a note. 'As soon as we're finished here I'll order an Infantry Battalion to mount a cordon and search operation in and around Maran. They'll seal it off so tight that the Tongs won't be able to get an ant in there. And the CTs will see it only as a normal routine operation.'

'Checkmate,' chortled Harry.

'More for you to handle,' said the Field Marshal looking directly at Fiona who had started to blush again.

'So we are back to the river and Kampong Lubok Paku,' put in Dennis.

'Right,' confirmed the Military Chief, 'I agree to that location but the Tongs won't reach it, the commandos and Claude's field force lads will see to that.'

'Ah,' sighed Harry with a gleam in his eye.

'Tell me more,' challenged Claude.

'Down boys, down!' joked Petherington with a smile. 'Now the best way to delay the Tong people is to get them onto that bloody river from the onset, any ideas gentlemen?' He looked around the room expectantly.

'Yes,' answered Harry, 'as you are well aware the Sungei Pahang is patrolled by Claude's chaps at frequent but irregular intervals. A large body of men and I presume they will be Chinese men at that, roaring downriver in a fleet of boats is going to attract attention. To ask the Field Force lads not to intervene would be too much, conversely, if they don't the Tongs might smell a rat.'

'Better not to tempt fate,' commented Dennis. 'But?'

'But the answer to that lies in a policy that we have been pursuing from the beginning of this vicious little war. I'm talking about the Hearts and Minds campaign. It covers a whole spectrum of subjects and activities but we want one that will accommodate the age group of the Tongs.'

'Adventurous training!' exclaimed Dennis nearly spilling his drink with excitement. 'Bloody rafts is the answer, I'll persuade the silly buggers to mount a rafting expedition!'

'That suggestion will have to come from Dennis himself, of course,' said Harry, 'Fiona can have a rest.'

'You really are a beast,' she flashed back.

'I'll need some back-up if I'm to promise them such things as permits, and even funds,' pushed Dennis.

'We'll make sure that you can do that,' reassured Petherington.

'Everything they'll need to get an expedition going can be obtained from the shop where I live,' advised a now thoroughly warmed-up Dennis. 'I can even get them a safety boat and they'll bloody well need one too. It's sixty-eight miles from Temerloh to Kampong Lubok Paku and I'll make sure that the bastards hit every damned obstacle on the way downriver.' He finished off his sixth Barcardi and bitter lemon in one gulp, the hanging corks swinging madly. 'Do you know folks,' he said, rubbing his hands together, 'I'm going to enjoy all this.'

'Right,' said the Field Marshal, 'I'll go along with the idea, but get those Tong people on that damned river and out of my way as of yesterday. Now for some details…'

★

Caesar had moved his base camp, advancing thirteen miles north-west from Bukit Chermingat to Bukit Bertangga. He was keeping pace with his squadron who had completed a total of 23,000 yards of gruelling and painstaking patrolling since the day after the contact at the old tree. Spurs, re-entrants, knolls, saddles, hills, streams and rivers: all were being systematically cancelled out by the seemingly tireless SAS soldiers. Caesar may not have known the whereabouts of the enemy camp but by the process of elimination he knew damned well where it was not.

By the same evening that Dennis the Bloody Menace had conceived his rafting expedition; all Caesar's patrols were positioned in an east-west line level with summit of Bukit Bertangga. All that is except one, that particular patrol had been tasked to proceed ahead of Caesar and backtrack the enemy force involved in the contact. They had already probed from Bukit Chermingat through Bukit Berangga and were now infiltrating well to the north of that. Their last communication to Squadron HQ was to inform Caesar that the four-man team was following the enemy tracks along the banks of the Sungei Kertau towards the Pahang River and the village of Kampong Kertau. That had been yesterday and the Squadron Commander would not know more until 17.00 hrs when all the daily situation reports came in from the patrols.

Chalky had led his patrol on the return march from the ambush position to Bukit Chermingat. It was a hard slog, not a heads down and arse up affair like the first 2,000 yards, but a slow, grinding ordeal at patrol pace with the full weight of the Bergen rucksacks pulling down cruelly on the men's collar bones and neck muscles. As many an old soldier has said, 'The Bergen is a bloody good pack but the trouble is that you can put too much gear in the buggers.' When carrying weights in excess of 80 lbs, a normal load for SAS men, balance is a huge problem when negotiating the many obstacles that are the bane of the jungle fighter's life. The crossing of logs over rivers and dry gullies is particularly hazardous, instant castration followed by a dunking or painful fall being a constant fear of the heavily laden soldiers. But to compensate for their suffering on the march, Chalky ensured that the patrol stopped in time to make a decent camp each evening, and to give everyone the chance to cook a hot meal and get into something dry for the night.

Fred enjoyed a good curry. In his first trip abroad to Kenya on board a troopship he had been given some advice by an old soldier who had served in Burma and Korea with the Durham Light Infantry. 'Bonnie lad,' said the man whose name was Abercrombie, 'if you curry every damned thing that you scoff the bloody mossies will steer well clear of you.' Fred had taken good heed of the veteran Geordie and had indeed curried all his food, he even went so far as to carry an Oxo tin full of curry powder that he used in lieu of pepper and on social occasions in the beer bar, as snuff.

As he looked into the flames of the heximine fuel tablet

burning under his mess tin he thought, *Well Geordie your theory didn't quite work out but thanks for introducing me to a delightful dish, but we'll say that half of the buggers that didn't get to me the other night were down to you and the curry.* As for sleeping, well, he simply took all his clothes off and wrapped himself up in some black silk airdrop parachute panels. The same material served as a mosquito net that he should not need according to his friend Geordie. But although they might not bite, the bloody things still got close enough to try and the improvised net kept them away from his ears thereby saving his nervous system one hell of a lot of punishment.

On arriving back at Bukit Chermingat they were greeted by Caesar and ordered to take a whole day off for a rest in his base camp. They were glad of the break that included a briefing for their redeployment further north. The task that Caesar gave them was to backtrack the enemy signs to establish whether or not a fifth man had dropped out of the small column somewhere in the Kampong Kertau area. They were to commence the patrol the very next day.

At 14.00 hrs on 5 September Chalky, who was up front doing a stint at tracking, called a halt only 1,000 yards from the south bank of Sungei Pahang. On the opposite side of the river lay Kampong Kertau. The SAS patrol had reached its current limit of exploitation northwards. But that was not the reason why Chalky had stopped, he could have gone on right up to the river. No, it was the realisation that he was now backtracking the sign of five men instead of four. The time had come to cast about and find the exact point of the split, to look for a single set of tracks that would hopefully lead the patrol eastwards towards the Chini Lake area. He looked down at the men's tracks, three of them were dead and a fourth was out of the game. If Caesar was correct this fifth bloke was an Intelligence Officer of the renowned 10th Regiment, and as such he would be no mug; Chalky made a tactical decision and moved Fred up front to take over as scout, a fresh set of eyes were needed here. Chalky whispered into Fred's shell-like ear, 'Listen, this could be the most important stint at tracking in your entire worthless career, so get your nose to the ground Fido. Go, get them boy!' he grinned.

Chalky signalled for Bob and Worm to follow his example and

break track to the left, leaving the right, or east side of the enemy trail clear for Fred's initial scrutiny of the ground.

Tracking the four men from Bukit Chermingat had not been easy. By the time the patrol had completed the follow up and the return march, plus the day of rest, the enemy tracks were already nine days old and had been overprinted by other initial SAS movements in the area. Fred now faced a situation similar to a safety play phase of a game of snooker, where whichever player makes the first mistake gives his opponent a golden opportunity to capitalise on it and go on to win the frame. He knew that his quarry would not have just walked off, there was a procedure to be adhered to called breaking track, the same drill that his three colleagues had just carried out. The man would have taken a huge step or even a jump to one side of his line of advance, making a clean break from any possible tracks that he might have made. It had been proven that some enemy groups fleeing from British Army follow-ups had actually gone aloft into the branches of the trees for a short distance to make the break more difficult to find.

After fifteen minutes of absolute concentration during which Fred was beginning to wish that he had a Sherlock Holmes magic magnifying glass, he spotted the 10th Regiment man's first mistake. He almost missed it so natural was the sight: he found himself looking at what appeared to be a centipede resting along the edge of a grey, mottled rotting leaf, but something did not quite gel. The leaf was in a place where no leaf ought to be, it was lying under the much larger leaves of a low-level ground palm where the jungle floor would normally be free of the daily fall of dead foliage. And then there was the reddish coloured, corrugated form of the worm-shaped insect, if it was indeed a centipede then it was the shortest one Fred had ever seen. *I suppose there are baby ones,* he thought as he poked at it with his fighting knife. As soon as the point of the blade touched the three-inch long object it became obvious that it was not an insect dead or alive, it was man-made and Fred knew for certain that he was on to something. He prodded gently and noticed immediately that it was actually attached to the leaf, which on closer inspection was too damned symmetrical to be anything of the kind. Fred lifted the object up and it broke away from the grey, rotting matter, the red coloured coating that was rust fell apart to reveal some spiralled wiring. What Fred had found was the grey cardboard backing and ring binding of a small notebook.

Thinking back to Caesar's briefing prior to setting out on his present task, Fred remembered the mention of a note found on the prisoner he had taken. *Bloody hell,* he thought, *it must have been the last page in this book.* Fred signalled for Chalky to come and have a look at his find; the Patrol Commander was elated and showed his pleasure by whispering to the scout, 'There's a biscuit in it for you if you find another, good boy.' He patted Fred on the head.

Thus encouraged and having been successful in finding the point of departure, it was not long before Fred found the second clue, an inconsistency in the leafy texture of the jungle floor, nothing more than a faint smudge really. He knelt down and leaned his body first to the right and then to the left in an attempt to see the spot from different angles and various shades of light, convinced that the slight mark on the ground would prove worthy of further investigation he moved forward until he was standing directly over it. He could now plainly see that a weight of some sort had made a depression in the soft ground. Kneeling again he began to peel away the leaves one layer at a time counting them as he progressed, each layer representing one day's fall of foliage. Eleven layers down the leaves had been crushed and the edges cut cleanly by the shape of a boot, one more layer gave him positive proof for outlined as if in plaster of Paris was the unmistakable imprint of a hockey boot with the toe end pointing eastwards. Fred faced that way on all fours as if praying to Mecca and sure enough he detected several more of the blemishes in the natural pattern of the leafy carpet, and soon he was well on the trail of the guerrilla fighter.

There was no need, of course, to uncover every smudge because the sign was now so obvious to him and the scout was able to follow in the man's footsteps, so to speak; and by so doing Fred quickly determined that the CT was a much shorter man than himself. Periodically he did clear the leaves away from the indentations to check points, discovering that the man's footprints were fairly even and slightly deeper at the toe indicating that he was travelling light at a rapid rate of knots. This theory was supported by the evidence that when he was required to step over fallen trees his leading footprint was well clear of the obstacle, had he been carrying a heavy pack the sign would have been closer to the logs, and even at right angles to them. Neither could Fred find any scuffmarks on the bark that might be made by the trailing foot of a heavily laden man. No, this bloke had a spring in his step and his selection of routes through the difficult terrain suggested a wealth of jungle warfare experience and smacked of a high degree of professional field craft. Yet he was rushing as if there was no tomorrow and because of it was making errors of judgement; Fred did not follow suit in a hasty pursuit but plodded along at patrol pace, observing, assessing, planning his next move and above all, learning from the bandit's mistakes.

After ninety minutes, Fred came across the terrorist's first resting place by a small trickling stream. He carried out a thorough search of the area and found that the CT had eaten there burying an empty tin afterwards, he had also smoked the last of twenty cigarettes, hiding the packet too. But wild boar had been on the rummage unearthing all the rubbish and the man's careful attempts to cover his trail had been in vain. Another hour's march later Fred located a second resting place, this time finding a live round of .38-inch ammunition and a small strip of cloth. The discovery of the short, snub-nosed bullet coincided with that time of day when the patrol normally stopped for the night.

Chalky ordered the men to proceed with their well rehearsed bivouac routine whilst he plotted the mean course taken by enemy soldier. His masterpiece completed, he made out his situation report and handed it to Bob who soon got busy with the Morse key.

The Squadron Headquarters' signaller tapped Caesar on the shoulder, 'This just came in from the Sungei Kertau patrol,' he whispered handing his boss the message. The SAS Major read it through twice just to make sure that he was not seeing things. 'They've done it!' he almost shouted. 'It's the breakthrough, they're on the trail of the 10th Regiment man!'

'Steady on sir,' reproached Lofty the Squadron Sergeant Major, 'you'll upset the leeches in my curry.'

Crazy Harry Blunt received the same signal directly from Caesar's deep jungle camp in Pahang. Hardly able to suppress a grin, he placed it before the Field Marshal, the message read:

> Located exact spot where 10th Regiment Officer split from main body 1,000 yards due south of junction – Sungei Kertau and Sungei Pahang. Man is five feet nine inches tall. Wears size eight hockey boots that are pretty well down at the heel. He is an experienced jungle hand who knows this neck of the woods well but is acting overconfident. Not carrying a backpack but has provisions. Last meal fish, tinned produce of Bangkok. Smokes Players cigarettes but probably out of them now. Armed with .38 Smith and Wesson Revolving Pistol, probably only five rounds of ammunition in the chamber. He cleans weapon with British Army flannelette, traces of rust but no rifle oil, looks like he is out of that too. Mean compass bearing of 95° suggests that he is heading for Kampong Bintang, distance 33,000 yards. Tracks found put him twelve days ahead of us. He is already at Kampong Bintang or has moved on from there.

Petherington looked up at Harry and smiled. 'You'd think they'd tell us how many wives the bloody man's got, wouldn't you?'

'Yes, damned remiss of them,' replied Harry and they both roared with laughter.

Chapter Eight

The long voyage from the island of Con San was almost at an end. After the terrors of the mighty storm, the *Sea Pearl* and her hard-pressed crew had enjoyed fair winds and weather, and as far as the male crew members on board were concerned, good sport as well. With only two more hours of sailing to go before the vessel was due to drop anchor off the island of Palau Tioman the men were in high spirits and happy with their lot. But the same could not be said of the only female to grace the ship's company, Fantail. She presented an appalling sight. A mere shadow of her old exuberant self, Fantail was hollow-eyed, gaunt and could only just manage to shuffle about listlessly as if in a dream; or more aptly, a nightmare. Her once beautiful breasts were bruised and hideously discoloured and it was difficult to distinguish the nipples on her misshapen mounds. Lips, eyes and inner thighs had suffered similar abuse and rope burns around her wrists and ankles were testimony to the fact that she had been tied down to endure the will of lustful men who had lost all sense of reason. Fantail had been subjected to the vilest of sexual excesses imaginable and then some more that defied description.

Fantail had made a fateful mistake on the day that the *Sea Pearl* had departed from Con San bound for Mersing, she had told the captain about the previous sexual abuse that she had suffered at the hands of the crew. The moment that she had made this disclosure Fantail knew that the captain had been completely unaware of the situation, and that he was very angry. Not with the crew as it turned out, but with her because she had not confided in him sooner. Now it was too late to remedy the situation and the captain was damned if he was going to share soiled merchandise with his men. To Fantail's surprise and horror the captain threw her to the wolves; and they took their prize with wanton abandon and perverse pleasure. But within the shell of her former self seethed an anger, no, a hatred so powerful that it gave her the will to suffer with hope; and deep inside her burned a fire that fuelled a love and passion that until now had been alien to her. For if her tormentors had taught her one thing, it was that she truly loved Kim Bok. Fantail now lived through every sordid moment of her present existence in the hope that she would survive to see him again, and to declare that love to him; and if and when that day came, she would exact a painful revenge from every soul aboard the accursed vessel. Oh yes, sweet, sweet revenge and she prayed for it now with all her heart.

Thirty minutes later a cry came from the duty lookout, 'Land! Land ahoy! Fine on the starboard bow!' Fantail broke down and sobbed uncontrollably.

Just before dusk on 5 September 1957, the captain gave the order to drop anchor. The junk *Sea Pearl* had arrived at her destination, Palau Tioman.

Kim Bok was not enjoying himself on board the motor fishing vessel as it trawled to and fro in the choppy sea about half way between Palau Tulai and Palau Tioman. He took no part in the fishing activities but kept a weather eye open towards the north-east, and a suspicious eye on the two islands. He still had the feeling that he and his men were not alone, there was a kind of menace in the air. At 15.00 hrs, Kim Bok caught the first glimpse of a sail, half an hour later with the aid of the skipper's powerful binoculars he knew without a shadow of doubt that the approaching vessel was indeed the *Sea Pearl*. He ordered the skipper to haul in his trawl and take the vessel back to Palau Tulai and the six awaiting sampans. Kim forgot his fears as a feeling of elation came over him. 'It's working!' he exclaimed in wonder. 'Now we can really get going!'

The commandos ashore on the seaward side of Palau Tioman who had been patiently awaiting this stupendous happening for weeks on end swore in disbelief, and then prayed to Allah for his forgiveness. The shock over, a marine radio operator grabbed his handset. 'Hello Zero this is Oscar Papa One Two One. Target vessel now at…'

Another commando observation point sited on the opposite

side of the island reported the movement of the trawler back to Palau Tulai.

Kim Bok had been correct to feel a menace in the air but he had no idea that the menace in question wore the coveted Green Beret.

Everyone in Kim Bok's flotilla was once again soaked to the skin. The rain came lashing down just as the trawler arrived back at Palau Tulai to pick up the six smaller vessels that were to transfer the gold ingots to Mersing. The rainfall was so fierce that it stirred the surface of the sea into a broiling cauldron and stung the seamen's bodies without mercy. With the rain came the wind that whipped up the swell making the task of securing the towrope from the trawler to the leading sampan and the rest to each other in line astern a damned difficult and hairy job. The brave little craft were nearly swamped as they pranced about doing battle with a cantankerous sea that was hell-bent on making life a bloody misery. Outboard engines were started up for the first time in an effort to make manoeuvring more manageable and to add dignity to the proceedings. Perseverance prevailed in the end and the trawler got under way towing her six charges towards the *Sea Pearl*. As Sod's Law will have it, within five minutes the rain stopped, the wind abated and the sea became as smooth as a sheet of glass.

The Commando Corporal in charge of observation post One Two One watched as the fluorescent-like wakes closed in on the *Sea Pearl*. He put down his binoculars and grinned at his radio operator. 'I suppose we'd better tell those lunatic SBS blokes to stand by?'

Eight miles south-southeast of the *Sea Pearl's* position and hidden from view in a bay on the east coast of Palau Tioman lay the spare Chinese junk bearing the same name. It was commanded by Lieutenant Clancy Deane of the SBS, crewed by ten naval personnel and was manned by thirty SBS Commandos of his troop. Before arriving at the present anchorage the matelots had taken much pleasure in putting the pissed off bootnecks through their paces in order that they could sail the *Sea Pearl* to

Kuala Pahang in some sort of approved Naval fashion. Clancy had ordered that the bogus *Sea Pearl* be camouflaged up to the eyeballs just in case the original vessel should make a pass close inshore. Clancy Deane who was nicknamed Nancy by his marines, but it must be pointed out that he was anything but one, was in the wheelhouse when the message came in from the observation post further up the coast. It simply read, Cargo now being transferred.

The six sampans formed a trot alongside the trawler that in turn was tied up to the *Sea Pearl* and was acting as a fender. Whilst the crew of the junk prepared derricks for the transfer; the guerrillas produced weapons from waterproof bundles and got them ready for action, Kim was taking no chances at this crucial stage of the game. He scrambled up the short rope ladder and vaulted over the gunwale onto the *Sea Pearl's* deck fully expecting to see Fantail's face amongst the assembled crew, but she was nowhere to be seen. Although disappointed and somewhat puzzled he could not allow his feelings to show as he shook hands with the captain.

'There is no need for them,' said the seaman pointing down at Kim's armed men.

'That's our trade,' answered Kim, 'you must know that?'

'Okay, point taken,' conceded the captain unable to do much about it. But the warmth had gone out of his voice as he suggested that they get things moving. 'I'll get the awkward cargo on deck first,' he announced curtly.

'That's a good idea,' replied Kim, an edge now creeping into his voice too. *Where the bloody hell is Fantail,* he thought as all sorts of possibilities buzzed around inside his head adding to the already uneasy feeling that all was not well. The fact that she was not on deck was a sure pointer that something was really amiss. Maybe Fantail had overplayed her hand at being the guardian of the gold and the captain, his suspicions aroused, had opened one of the crates to reveal the true contents? Was he holding Fantail captive as a hostage to secure some of the gold? Had the seafarer killed Fantail and was planning to seize the entire cargo of gold and murder Kim and his men? Kim dismissed the latter theory as being ludicrous given the terrorists' open display of armed might. Besides, the captain could have avoided contact with Kim by simply taking the vessel to any port of his choice, and with Fantail out of the way Kim would never get to know what had happened to the precious gold shipment. Whatever the reasons for her absence, he had to assume that she was still alive, he had to tread very carefully so as not to jeopardise her chances of survival. With that in mind, Kim turned his attention to the captain who was engaged in a heated discussion with his bosun regarding the movement of the twelve extremely heavy crates. As Kim stepped forward to intervene he thought, *If that man has got treachery in mind then he's a pretty cool customer.* 'Gentlemen,' he offered in his best arbitrator's voice, 'the answer to your problem is simple.' The two sailors looked at him expectantly. 'Open the crates where they are, within each one are eight smaller boxes. They'll still be heavy but much easier to manhandle down to the hoisting point here,' he concluded, pointing at the deck. He could tell by the captain's reaction and the expression on his face that he had not tampered with the cargo, for suddenly he and the bosun were all smiles and they soon had the crew working at the task with a will. And Kim Bok almost forgot about Fantail as the boxes of gold bullion began to heap up in front of him. He had one of them moved to one side then watched as the derricks commenced hoisting the cargo over the side with arc lamps lighting up the trawler and the sampans; and also providing the watching commandos with a perfect picture of events.

The sea was like a mirror and the transfer went just as smooth as one, as each sampan took on its quota of sixteen boxes it slipped from the inside of the trot to the outside until all of them were fully laden and ready to proceed. The captain had already been paid for his services but he would shortly be wondering when and where the rest of the cargo was going to be discharged? Also, if the old sea dog had something up his sleeve regarding Fantail he would have to make a move fairly soon. In order to create a brief distraction that would enable him to get his men aboard the junk to afford himself an element of surprise later on, Kim pointed at the box of three gold ingots that he had placed to one side earlier. Kim addressed the captain, 'Sir,' he smiled, hardly able to disguise a hint of sarcasm, 'this is for you and all these good men, a sort of bonus you might say.' The captain completely taken in beckoned to the bosun for him to open the box.

The burly individual soon prized off the lid to reveal three oblong shaped items wrapped in greaseproof paper and packed in wood shavings. He tore away the packaging from one of the items and held it aloft for all to see and this action brought a gasp of wonder from the watching crew, for there glinting dully in the artificial light was the unmistakable sight of a solid gold bar. It was worth more money than the entire ship's company had ever earned in their lives. It was a cruel trick that Kim Bok was playing, but a necessary one. The excited seamen rushed forward to touch and marvel at the gold, all with separate thoughts of what their share of it would do for them. What lifelong fantasies could now be fulfilled beyond their wildest dreams.

Caught up in a fever of hope and excitement they failed to notice Kim's armed bandits climbing aboard to surround them with evil intent reflected in their eyes. So overwhelmed and utterly blind were they to what was going on around them that it was little wonder that they were duped into a false sense of well-being, by this evil, Judas-like touch.

But not so the captain, the moment that he recognised the gold for what it was he knew that his fate was sealed. He knew for certain that nobody with knowledge of this gold's existence would be allowed to live, they were all doomed. The most that he and his crew could hope for now was a quick death; but even that hope was dashed by the appearance on deck of Fantail. The captain's fear was contagious and it broke through the crew's brief spell of euphoria as they suddenly realised that they were staring death right in the face.

In a silence broken only by the sound of lapping water and the creaking of rigging lines Kim looked aghast at the pitiful figure of Fantail. Her suffering communicated itself to him and the blood within his veins seemed to freeze, but his heart went out to her full of warmth and love, a really true love at long last realised. There was no need for words as she came to him and sobbed, and sobbed, and sobbed, great frame-shaking gasps of suffering and relief all rolled into one.

When at long last she calmed down Kim held her at arm's length, he looked at the captain grim-faced from over her shoulder, but it was not he that spoke; 'That man,' said a trembling Fantail seething with hatred, 'is for me to deal with.'

The captain knew then that his death would be a slow and painful experience. The now frightened seamen looked about them fearfully and for good cause, everywhere was to be seen gun barrels, and behind each one the cold gimlet eyes of a trained killer; but not for these men the luxury of a bullet in the brain. Kim Bok instructed his guerrilla fighters to escort the crew to their respective parts of the ship, and once there, to dispose of them in a manner that could be attributed to the notorious South China Sea pirates.

In front of the captain Kim Bok explained to Fantail that their original plan to blow up and sink the *Sea Pearl* was no longer on. 'I've been advised that it is virtually impossible to sink one of these things without trace. So we are going to leave it looted and drifting with the dead crew still on board to make it look for all the world like they have been the victims of a pirate raid.'

'Take him to the wheelhouse,' was Fantail's only comment.

Commandos observing from the hilltop overlooking the anchorage watched as merchandise from the holds was thrown overboard and the decks strewn with packaging and useless trash, rigging and equipment damaged, and finally the arc lamps smashed, plunging the stage of destruction into darkness. But not completely so, because by the gloomy illumination thrown out by the ship's normal deck lighting the commandos witnessed the crew being herded to their dreadful fate below decks; shortly after that, the screaming began. It went on for two nerve-racking hours, fuelling the imagination of the watchers and sickening even the tough marines to the core. The CTs finally abandoned the junk first having cast her adrift to float at will surrounded by jettisoned loot, gash and flotsam. The trawler, her task completed, headed back to the Pahang River and although they were all staunch members of the Min Yuen, the skipper and his trawler-men were under the pain of death should they be stupid enough to blab about their little venture. The sampans now under their own power and with Kim Bok and Fantail travelling aboard the leading vessel, set a course for the necklace of tiny islands that lay off Mersing. Also on board some of the vessels were the three chickens who had been mercifully spared at Fantail's request.

The ever-watchful commandos signalled news of their passage ahead of them.

As the six sampans angled down the west coast of Palau Tioman, Clancy Deane steered his junk up the east coast in the opposite direction, heading for the *Sea Pearl*. Intelligence reports from the commando lookouts suggested that there were no longer any crewmembers left on board the hapless vessel – alive that is. On the strength of those reports Clancy decided to go for plan 'B' of the three options afforded to him by the Admiral.

Plan 'A' was out because that entailed taking the vessel by armed force with stealth from a possibly hostile crew. Plan 'C' would have been simplicity itself. If the *Sea Pearl* had been sunk by the terrorists, Clancy was to have sailed directly for Kuala Pahang in his bogus junk. There, well off shore, he was to take on board a contingent of police jungle wallahs. Then in true Hornblower style, he was meant to proceed up a dirty great river pretending to be Chinese Communist Terrorists. This, mind you, with thirty hairy-arsed marines and a boatload of Malay coppers, none of whom looked the slightest bit Chinese. *Nothing to it really,* he thought, *now, of course, I'll have two ships; I could pretend that I'm the bloody Spanish Armada.* Clancy grinned at the idea then as the *Sea Pearl* came into view through the early morning mist he turned to the Naval coxswain and his own troop sergeant and commanded, 'Prepare to go alongside for Plan "B".'

'Aye Aye sir,' acknowledged the coxswain. 'Plan "B" it is sir,' repeated the sergeant, that bastion of the British military system. Young officers are two a penny. Seasoned platoon or troop sergeants are a priceless War Office controlled phenomenon. Plan 'B' was simple too. Clancy was to board the *Sea Pearl* and crew it with his commandos leaving the Navy lads in command of the bogus junk. They would then follow Clancy until he had picked up his police unit and at that point they would drop anchor and stand by in reserve.

In the cold and wet conditions of the first light of day, the commandos went about the business of boarding and taking over the *Sea Pearl*. They had been warned of what might have happened to the crew but the sights that the highly conditioned SBS men were confronted with made even them vomit and wretch in horror and disgust.

Clancy led his men from the front and was the first man in the assault team to board the junk, he was followed by two of his men who then covered him to the first objective, the ship's wheelhouse. Clancy kicked open the door that was slightly ajar and made his grand entrance, well, it would have been grand if he had not slipped on the wet slimy deck. He fell onto all fours and found himself staring at the castrated groin region of a naked man who had been tied spreadeagled to the ship's four-foot diameter wheel. Clancy now white-faced with shock let his eyes roam higher up the man's torso. It was obvious to him that whilst the poor wretch had been bleeding to death from the ghastly wound great strips of flesh had been cut and torn from his body: the man had been skinned alive. Clancy barely had time to stand up before the marine behind him rushed in; he took one look at the macabre sight and puked up.

In all parts of the *Sea Pearl* the rest of the assault team was encountering similar scenes of savagery. The sail maker and the chief cook had each been bent over a barrel, their hands and feet secured to the deck by nails. Lips had been sewn up and belaying pins had been hammered into their rectums right up the hilts. So excruciating must have been the pain that the stitches in their mouths had torn open to allow the victims to scream. Everywhere the marines found butchered and disfigured remains; the ship resembled an abattoir with the decks swimming in blood, cluttered with entrails and littered with parts of limbs and organs. Only the bosun had died in a seaman-like manner, he had been lashed to death. Clancy Deane, commander of a unit that was often considered to be a law unto themselves completely disregarded the rules and regulations that required him to keep the remains for evidence, he buried the unknown sailors at sea; and be damned to the bloody book.

The sampans proceeded in line astern for twenty-five miles at an average speed of six knots. The flotilla could have roared along much faster with their powerful Evenrude outboard engines, but to Kim Bok's way of thinking he would get all of the gold through to Mersing by being 'better safe than sorry'. He would keep that power in reserve to get them out of trouble if needs be. He could have brought the gold in by trawler but that would have been too great a risk; all his eggs in one basket lost through capture or by some natural disaster was unthinkable. No, the six sampans were the answer, even if they were to run slap bang into a British warship some of them would succeed in running the gauntlet and would make it to the beach; that would be the time to use his reserve of power.

In Kim's opinion they had just completed the most hazardous leg of the trip, the vulnerable twenty-five-mile run as a pack. Now being this close to home he was not prepared to take any more chances than were absolutely necessary. The 10th Regiment men chosen to crew the sampans knew this coastline well and it was time to put that local knowledge to good use. Kim faced aft and flashed his torch five times; back came the three-flash acknowledgements from each sampan in turn. The six little vessels fanned out and headed for their pre-arranged individual pearl-like island in the necklace. Once there they would hole up for the day before making a final run for the beach during the hours of darkness. Kim's masterstroke of strategy in dispersing his vessels over an eight-mile-wide front was nothing less than commendable.

But the vessels although safe, were not hidden. For every pimple-like piece of land that was not subject to tidal flooding was either occupied or could be seen by marine observation posts. As each sampan approached its haven for the day, the military airwaves got busy again.

Give or take half a mile, the sampans were positioned an equal distance apart in a north-south line with Kim's being the southernmost vessel, only seven miles due east of Mersing. At 18.00 hrs on 6 September, Kim set off on his ninety-minute dash to the beach; the other sampans also started to move but all of them headed south. The plan was that each sampan would not turn westwards towards the beach until it had reached a position immediately off Kim's departure point. In theory each individual vessel would arrive at the destination at fifteen-minute intervals, that being the minimum amount of time required for the cargo to be discharged, the vessel to be relaunched and the beach cleared ready for the next boat. Again in theory, the whole operation should be completed in one and a half hours.

Kim had spent an awful day in a makeshift palm-leaf shelter watching Fantail toss and turn in a fitful sleep. It's not surprising, he had thought, given the ordeal that she had endured. That and her own grisly performance with the captain's screaming body was enough to give anyone nightmares. He vowed over her heaving, tormented form that they would never be apart again, come hell or high water he would stick by her side forever.

Kim had woken Fantail up just before last light and he saw immediately that some of the old fire had returned to her eyes, although they had embraced passionately enough he knew that it would be some time yet before she would be able to make love again.

He looked at her now as they sped through the choppy, rain-splattered sea, she was soaked to the skin, wild looking and alive to the danger ahead, and she smiled for the first time since they had been reunited. Kim smiled back and they both faced the beach that was fast looming up out of the gloom; they were ready to take on the world.

The minute that the situation reports came in from his commando observation posts, it became obvious to their Commanding Officer what the enemy's next plan of action was. 'Well I'll be damned, I think this is it,' he said to his Adjutant, 'and well thought out it is too.' From his headquarters on Palau Sribuat he relayed the facts and his appreciation of the situation to the Commonwealth Brigade Commander who in turn alerted his own battalions and the Gurkha Rifles. The information filtered down from battalions to companies, then through platoons to rifle sections. From lip to ear the long-awaited news passed down the line, 'The gold is coming in, the Brass have got it right for a bloody change.'

It would seem that everyone was in the know about the impending landing except for the men who ought to be, the beach landing party themselves. Ah Fat and Kwong Yew, the two couriers appointed as beach masters by Kim Bok, knew that the operation hinged on the arrival of the *Sea Pearl* off Palau Tioman. And they, like Kim, could not put a time and date to that event. So from night one they had been required to wait in readiness to receive the shipment, load it onto the animals and take it up the Mersing-Kluang road to the courier route proper. The two men were sitting on a log under an attap palm lean-to shelter waiting full of hope and not without a considerable amount of frustration.

Could this be the night, Ah Fat thought as he looked at the luminous dial of his watch, it was 19.15 hrs. 'Come on,' he whispered in prayer. It was still raining but there was hardly any wind nor the horrendous racket that normally accompanied it, for that reason they could still hear the odd snort and snuffle from the tethered animals picketed 500 yards behind them in the jungle.

Grouped around the animals to keep them fed, happy and quiet were the six mahouts and twelve muleteers. When the gold train had first arrived at the Mersing beach location it had consisted of only the animal handlers and a force of guerrillas from the 10th Regiment. But since then the mysterious medium of the bush telegraph had been busy and men of the 3rd North Johore and Malacca Regiment, Fantail's first unit, had begun to trickle in to offer their services; these men now formed a protective cordon around the terrorist encampment.

Formed up in an assembly area just behind Ah Fat was the 10th Regiment beach party equipped with improvised wooden sledges that they would use to haul the gold up the soft, sandy beach. Ah Fat was tinkering with a large industrial torch and wondering if he was ever going to use the bloody thing when Kwong Yew said, 'Listen.'

Both men tensed up and concentrated all their powers of hearing towards the sea. Then slowly but surely and increasing in volume all the time came the banshee-like scream of an outboard engine giving it some stick.

'It's them!' laughed Ah Fat as he switched on the powerful torch that was both a recognition signal and a homing beacon for the incoming helmsmen. Back came the reply signal of repeated flashes, and to the accompaniment of snarling throttles and crashing surf, the triumphant sampan dug its prow into the sand, the gold had arrived. The camp erupted into action, two men rushed down the beach to hold the vessel steady and bow-on to the shore. The sledge teams followed and with great difficulty and much cursing, the heavy boxes were discharged from the pitching sampan and dragged up to the tree line. Kim and Fantail bent ·their backs with the rest, there being no time for the niceties of a reunion.

Within ten minutes the sampan was backing off the beach and the sound of splintering wood came from the direction of the assembly area as the gold ingots were broken out of the boxes. Individual gold bars were heaved onto shoulders and carried to the picket line where mahouts and muleteers barely had time to commence loading before the second boat arrived.

And so it went on for one and a half hours, the gold was actually landed well within the target time of ninety minutes but the camp remained a hive of feverish activity for a good hour after the vessels had departed back to their own fishing Kampongs. Fishing vessels are subject to registration laws and too long an absence from their usual moorings might provoke some sort of enquiry.

Speed was now of the essence, the landing itself had been a noisy affair but it was doubtful if anyone would be stupid enough to venture forth in the darkness to investigate. Come daylight, however, you could bet your shirt on the fact that the place would be swarming with Police and Home Guard units. So it was of paramount importance that the gold train be clear of the Mersing-Kluang road by first light. What had once been a simple track from the jungle edge to the picket line now became as a main highway with the traffic resembling a column of ants speeding to and fro, the load carrying being in one direction. The task seemed to be never ending, the ingots, although small, weighed twenty-six pounds and were awkward to handle with wet, slippery hands. The men sweated gallons that night, but by 22.00 hrs all was finished including the destruction of the sledges and boxes, which were burned. Kim Bok gave the order to move off and the gold train took to the road as bold as brass.

It was a galling sight for the tough little Gurkha soldiers to behold, and it was testimony to their high standard of self-discipline that they did not leap out of hiding and take a few ears that night. Some of these soldiers from Nepal were coming to the end of a three-year tour of duty in Malaya, three years of endless jungle patrols in search of an elusive enemy, in most cases to no avail. But suddenly right there in front of them as if on some weird ceremonial parade were dozens of the bastards marching down the bloody road. With bated breaths, commanders at all levels prayed and hoped that their men would hold steady, that no itchy finger would let loose a shot and start a full-scale battle, but they need not have worried. Because the soldiers, those damned magnificent Gurkhas who had served the British Army so proudly in the past did not let the side down now. They complied with a very unpopular and frustrating order and the enemy passed by unmolested; there would be another time and place in the not too distant future.

First to pass as a vanguard was half the men from the 3rd Regiment volunteers. The gold train itself with the mahouts and muleteers marching alongside their charges followed them. On the flanks and with some men deployed in the gaps between the pack animals, came the main body of the terrorists from the 10th Regiment. The remainder of the 3rd Regiment formed the rearguard. On they marched, this heavily laden column; in addition to the gold the sturdy animals were carrying supplies brought from Maran in the transport. Southwards they trekked first to the village of Jemaluang and then west along the winding road through Lenggor towards Kahang. Only half a mile east of that place at 05.45 hrs on 7 September the gold train turned north off the Mersing-Kluang road and entered the jungle at a point where the old wartime courier route bisected it; a line of communication that by now should have been reactivated.

Crazy Harry Blunt's hunch had been right on the button.

That particular gentleman had just handed the Field Marshal a full report from the Commonwealth Brigade Commander. Petherington studied the information and then made some notes, when finished he looked up at Harry. 'I really could do with these blokes being on our side,' he said peevishly, 'if you think their performance with the circus was incredulous, what about this?'

'Do tell sir,' encouraged Harry Blunt.

'In one night these half-starved sods transport a cargo of gold from a ship over a distance of about twelve miles in six separate vessels. They land the stuff from sampans on a beach pounded by surf and then reload all 288 gold bars onto the backs of eighteen pack animals before marching twenty-six miles in seven and three-quarter hours. And that along a road that is flooded in many places and resembles nothing more than a cart track in others. Having maintained a speed of three and a half miles an hour they then take to the jungle like will-o'-the-wisps. And all this, mind you, performed in the dark of the night.'

'And don't forget,' reminded Crazy Harry, "if it hadn't have been for a police constable on a cushy posting to Hong Kong, the buggers would have got away with it!'

'How bloody right you are,' conceded the Field Marshal, wiping beads of perspiration from his brow.

Whilst the two military men were singing the enemy's praises; Kim Bok was facing a few grim home truths. During both the beach landing and the march he had been impressed with the urgency and tactical awareness of the guerrillas from the two regiments. With the 10th being busy giving close protection and the 3rd always that little bit out of reach either too far forward or to the rear, Kim had not the opportunity to talk with any of the men, but he did have plenty of time to think. It had occurred to him that his old friends Shen and Liew must have moved bloody fast to get things this organised so far down the line.

When at last the gruelling march was over and the column was resting for a while in the jungle, Kim Bok took the opportunity to assert his authority as a leader and take command of the hodgepodge unit, introducing himself to each and every man at the soonest possible instance. He was mingling with some of the men from the 3rd Regiment and telling them how pleased he was that their Commanding Officer had seen fit to send him reinforcements in his hour of need. He was on the point of asking them if they had seen or heard from his two bodyguards when he noticed the look of puzzlement on their tired faces. This prompted him to enquire, 'You were sent here by your leaders surely?'

They shook their heads emphatically and one of them piped up to explain, 'The only order we've been given for ages is to lie low and await further instructions. But we were all bored stiff and when we heard about the circus it was obvious that something was going on, bloody circus indeed,' he laughed.

Kim laughed too but felt more like crying as his earlier feeling of doom returned. 'You don't know then,' he pressed, 'that we're reopening the old wartime trail?'

'No,' answered another man.

'Nothing has come through the grapevine,' added a third guerrilla, 'our bosses would have told us by now.' Kim wandered off thoroughly dejected to find some men of the 10th Regiment.

When Kim had arrived back from his trip abroad he had not been surprised at the high level of co-operation he had received. Indeed, he had expected nothing else because he was under the impression that the 10th Regiment had received their sealed orders from the great Guerrilla Leader himself; orders that Kim had personally handed over to the 10th Regiment's Intelligence Officer. Kim was about to experience yet another blow to his confidence; when asked if they had heard about or actually seen their Intelligence Officer, the 10th Regiment men were unanimous in their answer, it was no. Nor had they received any special instructions regarding Kim's mission. And no, like their friends in the 3rd, the men of the 10th had no idea that the courier route was to be reactivated. The simple truth of the matter was that they had all accepted Kim Bok's, Ah Fat's and Kwong Yew's authority as gospel. 'After all,' one of the men pointed out, 'you can't very well doubt one so high as a Paymaster General!'

Kim sat down as if in a state of shock. He thought back to the train journey from Bangkok to Malaya and his concern about the Thai Police escorts, and of how it had panicked him into jumping the train. Then there had been the eyes that he felt sure were watching him as he had approached Kuala Trengannu from the sea; and again whilst the trawler was anchored off Palau Tulai. He should have trusted in his instincts then, but what could he have done that would have made much difference? The *Sea Pearl* was commissioned to bring the gold to Palau Tioman and no action by Kim could have stopped it. Whatever his fears, no matter what trap he might be walking into there was one thing he knew of for sure. He had got the gold to within ninety-two miles of its destination without any apparent hitches and that must count for something.

He tried to think straight in order to make a positive commitment, to clear his mind and conscience before making a decision as to whether he should go on or not. The missing links as far as he knew were Shen and Liew, and the Intelligence Officers from the 3rd, 9th and 10th Regiments. The regimental areas of the former two men did not really affect the movement of the gold train itself. It had never been part of the plan to involve the men of the 3rd in the transportation of the gold, only to open up that part of the courier route within their regimental boundaries. The same went for the 9th that had not become involved at all. The current participation by the 3rd, although welcome under the present circumstances, had only been an opportunity for action seized upon by men anxious to do their bit. Shen and Liew would have been out of the picture too, they being required to map the courier route all the way down through Johore.

The absence or disappearance of the 10th Regiment man, however, was a bitter blow. It was he that had been tasked to alert the all-important 10th Regiment, the men who were charged with the responsibility to protect the Central Military Committee, the hub of the communist guerrilla movement in Malaya. Kim Bok asked himself, *What was the situation up there in the north, had the man got there, were they expecting him or was he walking into a trap?* If it was into a trap and deep down Kim felt sure that was the case, then he was already ensnared and evasive action would be useless. But every step that he took would be a bonus, every mile gained would bring him nearer to friends that might even be marching south to meet him. Each minute of freedom brought hope and every hour of effort was time well spent in their quest for liberation. But those steps and precious periods of time had to be devoted to travelling as far as possible in the right direction;

northwards towards the high jungle ramparts of a mountain called Gunong Chini. Kim made his decision; and Crazy Harry Blunt was proven to be right once again.

His mind made up, Kim Bok did not dwell on possible disasters but concentrated on success and ordered the gold train to move out. He was anxious to put some considerable distance between the column and that bloody Mersing-Kluang road. The men had been slightly spooked by all of Kim's questions but despite the fact that they suspected something might be wrong, they marched forwards with stout hearts and grim determination.

That night in his jungle camp lying beside his beloved Fantail he thought about the missing Intelligence Officer. 'Where are you my friend?' he whispered to himself. And when he finally dozed off it was he, not Fantail, who suffered a fitful sleep that night.

Kim Bok had good reason to have nightmares concerning his situation because had he deviated from his northerly course by any obvious degree and his pursuers were of the opinion that they had been detected, the end would have come well before he could have got his head down. But the Gurkhas were happy to let him live a little longer.

★

The snake with the orange coloured underside and shiny black top was tired. He had just spent an exhausting hour swallowing three eggs that he had taken from the nest of a brown, speckled feathered provider. These strange creatures with comical bobbing heads served only one purpose in life, and that was to ensure that the snake's larder was never empty. The cunning reptile, forever thoughtful, helped in this matter by never taking all of the eggs thereby ensuring that future generations of his feathered friends would produce even more eggs; and so life went on.

Feeling quite sleepy, the snake slithered down a bank to the edge of a muddy pool with huge leaves floating upon the surface. It found a solitary ray of sunlight that had somehow penetrated the jungle canopy and decided to rest there. The reptile's gastric juices were now working on the three-course meal causing him to become more and more drowsy. Looking forward to a peaceful slumber that would last a fair few hours, he became alarmed and a little annoyed by some vibrations that he felt coming up through the ground underneath his belly. The snake sighed, vexed at the thought of the impending intrusion by those that walked on their hind legs only, for only the dreaded Upright Ones could tread the earth so heavily that it trembled. It sensed that there was but one of them approaching, he did not move, the awkward moving beast posed no threat to his reptilian kind. At the very sight of a snake the lumbering upright beasts normally sent out vibes of pure panic and fear, the snake lay still and watched with heavily lidded eyes.

The Upright One came into sight, it was swaying from side to side because of an injured leg. The monstrosity with its skin hanging in great folds from an otherwise smooth body paused at the top of the steep slippery bank and looked down at the pond; for a split second the snake's eyes locked on to those of the Upright One. Panic emanated from the beast causing it to slip down the bank into the pond where it wallowed and thrashed about like a buffalo. The snake looked on as the loathsome thing struggled to get out of the water, then fear was reflected in the eyes of the Upright One as the realisation came that it was stuck in quicksand and was sinking fast.

Growing out from the bank at an angle and within easy reach of the creature was an old gnarled branch. It tried to grasp hold of the lifeline with its forearms but the frantic beast's paws were too slippery with slime and it cried out in frustrated anger as its repeated attempts failed. It plunged a paw into the now heaving morass dragging from beneath the surface a bent stick that was attached to a vine. It threw the bent stick in an arc around the branch so that it spun around twice on the vine and was held fast. The vine was attached to some part of the Upright One somewhere beneath the water and for a while it arrested the steady downward movement of its body.

The stricken creature's eyes were now level with those of the snake's and its lower jaw was almost submerged in the glutinous, sucking pond of death. For a whole minute whilst the bent stick held firm, the two sets of eyes studied each other's souls, both damning the other to hell. Then slowly the suction pulled the

Upright One down into the sand and the bent stick dragged its skin up the doomed one's body and over its head, the pond had claimed another victim and had won the tug-of-war of life. All that remained for the snake to see was a few bubbles that rose to the surface and the bent stick with its taught vine straining at the near-snapping branch. The snake slithered away in disgust, these upright-walking monsters soiled everything that they touched, even simple little things like ponds full of mud and sand.

Had the Upright One named Kim Bok been on the same plane of communication as the now thoroughly fed up snake his question would have been answered. But then the Upright Ones were far too inferior for that.

★

At 22.00 hrs on 6 September, precisely the same time that the gold train had commenced the twenty-six-mile march from Mersing to Kahang; Clancy Deane arrived off Kuala Pahang with the *Sea Pearl* to rendezvous with a sleek, grey frigate.

Clancy and his SBS Commandos had been extremely busy during the ten-hour voyage from Palau Tioman. In addition to burying the murdered seamen they had taken on plenty of fuel from the second junk, Clancy had decreed that sail was out and power was in from that moment onwards. The bloody mess below decks and the chaotic jumble of damaged equipment and cargo on the upper decks had to be cleaned up, and so as Clancy had set a course for the Pahang River at a steady six knots, his men had put their backs into the gruesome task. But true to the traditions of the Navy they had the *Sea Pearl* all ship shape and Bristol fashion by the time they met up with the warship.

The transfer of the Field Force men from the frigate to the junk went smoothly and soon the warship sailed off southwards to assist with the task of moving the commandos from the islands to the east-coast mainland. There in the filthy mangrove swamps they would deny the terrorists access to the sea should they decide to abandon their present operation or were forced to do so by some unplanned action.

It was obvious from the start that the grinning excited men of the Police Field Force were thrilled to bits with the honour of taking part in a Combined Operations Task. And they were especially proud of the chance to serve alongside the men who wore the coveted Green Beret of the British Commandos.

Clancy's men took to the Malays immediately, proof of this came to him every time that one of the Field Force men approached him or passed close by. 'Good day Mr Nancy sir!' or 'Pleased to meet you Mr Nancy sir!' they would exclaim with great gusto. For anyone outside the SBS to use his nickname was to court certain danger from some sadistic ritual that his commando heathens would dream up on the spot. In that regard, the SBS were almost as insane as their SAS counterparts. The fact that Clancy's men had given the Malay policemen their commander's nickname so quickly and readily was an indication of how highly the commandos rated them.

By the time that the *Sea Pearl* had reached the two-mile-wide estuary all the commandos had been consigned to the lower decks so as to be out of sight. Armed with .303-inch No. 5 Jungle rifles, Lanchester 9mm sub-machine guns and Browning 9mm pistols they were put on immediate standby for action.

Topsides, the cheerful Malay policemen had taken over the duties of ship's crew suitably attired as Chinese seamen. They would pass muster at a distance, which at this particular stage of the game was all that Clancy expected of them. And that august person was hidden from view in the wheelhouse from where he could give instructions to the Malay Police helmsman. So far so good, thought the SBS troop commander.

The lookouts watching from the Kuantan side of Kuala Pahang were not manning a camouflaged observation post in the approved military fashion. That was because the men were not of the military but were merely Chinese Tong thugs who did not want to be there in the first place. They were in fact sitting in a clapped-out American jeep of World War II vintage that had been stripped of its canvas canopy so that the occupants were completely exposed to the elements. They were not happy with their lot, these two men that had just driven twenty-seven miles along a deeply rutted cart track from Kuantan. The unhappy pair had been told to do this on the say so of some half-baked British mercenary, whom the big Tong boss thought was an authority on all things military. 'What the hell has a civilian Chinese junk got to do with the bloody military?' had been the favourite gripe during the bone-shaking, hellish journey that to cap it all had been made in the middle of the night.

Now at the uncivil hour of seven in the morning on 7 September the two Tong thugs lost some of their ill humour when they actually spotted a junk rounding an island that lay in the eastern approaches of the estuary. The vessel navigated its way through the northern channel that brought it to within half a mile of the observers. From that distance they were able to see the native crew scurrying about the decks. The junk passed by their position and in doing so presented her stern to the two Tong henchmen, using a pair of powerful binoculars one of them read out the name, '*Sea Pearl*,' he said. Both men immediately changed their opinions of all Tong bosses and mad mercenaries, and there being no form of communication available to them other than wheels, they turned the jeep around and drove madly northwards heading for Kuantan with their news.

As the jeep clattered its way northwards another jeep, this one sporting the livery of the Police Force and leading a Bedford three-ton truck, headed south out of Mersing. In the jeep rode the Mersing Police Sergeant and two constables; following them in the lorry was another Sergeant and ten men of the Mersing Home Guard. These local defence forces were off to investigate the noisy activity of the previous night, reported as sounding like a seaborne invasion. The wily old Police Sergeant had surmised that anything seaborne would have to come into a tiny inlet some two miles south of the town just off the Mersing-Kluang road. So standing up in the front of his jeep like a general at the head of an advancing column, he kept a sharp lookout on the seaward side of the road.

When he did spot his first clue he could hardly believe his own eyes, for there, slap bang in the middle of the road, was a trail of elephant droppings. Well, he did not need to be an expert big game hunter to be able to backtrack the now long gone enemy invaders to their campsite and landing point on the small beach. The sergeant knew better than to let his men trample all over the place so he ordered the Home Guard sergeant to deploy his men at strategic points around the area as sentries and guides; then he got on the radio to inform his superiors about the situation. What he did do immediately after that was to take into protective custody three boys that had been found huddled together shaking with cold, fear and shock. Each boy was clutching a waterproof package; unknown to them and the policeman, of course, they were the very same packages that Fantail had handed over to Kim Bok back at Gunong Ulu Merah. A kindly man, the seasoned police veteran talked soothingly to the frightened lads until one of them reluctantly handed over his parcel. Upon opening it he found that it contained a huge amount of paper currency, so, whilst he awaited the arrival of reinforcements the bewildered sergeant counted the money; the boy had been carrying 100,000 Malay dollars. He repacked the notes and handed the bundle back to the equally bewildered youth, the other two seeing what their friend had got frantically tore open their own parcels to reveal a similar pile of money. They watched dumfounded as the policeman counted their fortune for them too, all three boys had exactly the same amount. Also unknown to them was the fact that Kim Bok had paid the ill-fated skipper of the *Sea Pearl* precisely 300,000 dollars for the hire of his vessel. The big-hearted Police Sergeant looked at the boys who had obviously suffered much physical and sexual abuse. *You've earned every cent of that money,* he thought. But aloud and with tears in his eyes he said for all to hear, 'I'll see that nobody takes that money away from you, on my life I will!'

The small force from Mersing did not see the stealthy Gurkhas slip silently away to be redeployed elsewhere, hot on the heels of the gold train.

Wang Chong the huge Tong boss who had been so impressed with Dennis at Temerloh put down the telephone, it was the third call that he had received that morning. The first had been from his Kuantan-based people at 08.00 hrs to inform him that the *Sea Pearl* had entered the estuary only an hour earlier; that was another plus for Dennis. The second call had not been good news. Another surveillance team that had been sent out from Kuantan to reconnoitre Kampong Lubok Paku had found it necessary to drive through Maran in order to get there. This proved to be impossible to do because the place was swarming with Australian troops. The stubborn Tong men tried to bluff their way through the cordon but they pushed their argument too far and antagonised the Aussies to such an extent that they forced the Tong men back at bayonet point.

Although it was discouraging news it served to back up the English mercenary's theory that they should favour the river itself as a highway, and Temerloh would be an ideal point from which to embark upon the operation to seize the gold. So now Dennis had earned more points for his suggestion that that they mount a rafting expedition that would be quite legal and above board; the Tong boss could see the logic in it all now. Yes, it was obvious that he must give this guerrilla warfare expert his head, he would lead the Tong men downriver to intercept the gold, or rather, ambush the bandits from the bank somewhere in the region of Kampong Lubok Paku. Wang Chong was prepared to trust the mad mercenary who had second-guessed everybody so far. The third telephone call had been from a man that was on lookout duty at Pekan, he had reported the *Sea Pearl's* arrival there at 10.00 hrs. And according to him the vessel was boarded fifteen minutes later by customs, police and military personnel. Wang Chong winced at the thought of all that wealth being seized by the authorities, now completely duped the arch-criminal could only await the outcome.

The Police Field Force men on board the *Sea Pearl* were putting on a grand show of hoodwinking the watching Tong man, and all the ordinary onlookers that were lining the shore. The boarding party of civilian and military officials who to a man had been hand picked by Claude Rysdale and the Admiral ably assisted them. The combination of Customs, Police, Naval and Marine uniforms with contrasting colours and shining brass-work together with gold braid and striking insignia was an impressive sight. The Tong observer could be excused for viewing the pompous spectacle with some trepidation.

After being formally invited on board by the bogus captain, the party split up to perform their duties in various parts of the ship. A marine captain, who just happened to be the adjutant of the commando now deployed along the coast from Mersing to Kuala Pahang, stepped into the wheelhouse. He nearly tripped over Clancy Deane's feet that were sticking out from beneath the chart table where he was hiding from view. The captain who was charged with the duties of Liaison Officer between his own commanding officer and the SBS Lieutenant did not look down when he said straight faced, 'I've heard of undercover work old boy, but this is bloody ridiculous!' With that he dropped a package of sealed orders into Clancy's lap. Then trying very hard not to piss himself with laughter he left the bridge tossing the SBS man a final remark, 'I never thought I'd see the day when one of you lot would be drunk under the table by a bloody police wallah!'

As the adjutant stepped out of the wheelhouse the Malay police officer who was pretending to be the *Sea Pearl's* captain came in, but he did laugh; after all, it was all part of the game.

The commandos hiding below decks were sweltering in the heat and feeling a bit left out of things but soon perked up when the adjutant produced some all-important, moral-boosting mail. So whilst the tough marines read letters from home and the exuberant Field Force men revelled in their role as seamen, the Tong man watched convinced that the junk was being searched from stem to stern. The officials kept up the charade for an hour after which they all went ashore in the Pekan Harbourmaster's launch, their once smart uniforms looking suitably soiled from the supposed rummage. All that is except one man that went under the name of plain Mr Ipp; from somewhere under the carpet the admiral had found a genuine Pahang river pilot and a Chinaman to boot who knew everything that there was to know about Chinese junks. Mr Ipp's loyalty was guaranteed because the Admiral had threatened him with a drying-out clinic should he waver so much as an inch from his line of duty. Having made his point the Navy Chief had instructed the customs officers to carry two crates of VAT 69 on board for Mr Ipp's personal consumption. Now that the officials had gone and the *Sea Pearl* had been given a clean bill of health she was free to proceed.

The pilot glanced out of the after-window of the wheelhouse, which was facing the sea. Using his right hand as a shade he looked at the sparkling waters of the estuary and asked, 'To what island do you wish to sail?'

'Well that's a bloody good start,' answered a worried looking Clancy still sitting under the chart table. 'We're going that way, upriver!' he spluttered pointing past the huge ship's wheel. The policeman manning that antique contraption grinned.

The pilot, his face impassive remarked, 'Ah! I am therefore somewhat at a loss, something is very amiss here!' Mr Ipp dug deep into his capacious tunic pocket and produced some plastic beakers; he filled three of them full to the brim with VAT 69 from a bottle that he had seemingly conjured up from out of thin air. He passed one of them to the Malay helmsman, then picking up the other two he addressed Clancy.

'How,' he said soberly looking down at the SBS man, 'if you'll excuse the question, do I socialise with a person in such a lowly position?' Clancy just looked up at him helplessly. The pilot suddenly sat down cross-legged on the deck in one effortless movement without spilling a single drop of whisky. Facing the astounded commando he answered his own question, 'By sinking to your level of course.' Then with an impish grin, his eyes twinkling and full of humour and more than a little mischief he announced, 'Mr Ipp at your service, sir! I know this unreasonable river like the back of my hand, just tell me where you want to go, I don't need a chart,' he emphasised pointing upwards. He handed Clancy a beaker and held up his own. 'To us,' he toasted and downed the fiery liquid in one gulp.

Christ, thought Clancy, *and he only brought two crates with him?* But he was wrong, before the SBS man could finish his whisky a sampan came alongside the *Sea Pearl* with enough booze on board to get the entire special force pissed for a month. Included in the consignment was a plentiful supply of Woods Navy Rum and the pilot made a gift of it to Clancy and his marines.

'After all,' he said, 'you are part of the Navy and should get the Tot.'

Clancy could not argue with that perfectly good reasoning and gladly accepted the rum. As the sampan cast off and headed for Pekan, the *Sea Pearl* weighed anchor, 'First stop Kampong Pahang Tua!' instructed Clancy looking up from the deck.

'Kampong Pahang Tua it is!' acknowledged Mr Ipp now at the helm.

Petal's father Lin had never had it so good, trade-wise that is. He was reaping the benefit from some shady deal between Dennis, Mr Tan and that enormous Chinaman. A couple of days after the initial meeting when Dennis had demonstrated his true grit, twenty men of Chinese origin had invaded the shop. They had arrived in an assortment of pickup trucks and vans, two men to a vehicle. Parked as they were directly outside of the shop, they attracted scores of children who climbed all over them screaming with delight. Lin first did a roaring trade in food and drink and had the spending spree ended there Lin would still have been better off by the equivalent of a month's worth of business, but there was more trade yet to come. Because after consulting with Dennis at his Lordship's table the Tong man appointed as leader of the rafting expedition, Shu Ling, placed a large order for goods in front of Lin. Whilst Petal was kept busy waiting at the tables and dodging the odd grope, her father prepared the goods on the list. Petal had nothing to fear from these men; the word had been put about that she was the mad pistolero's woman.

After four hours the party was adjourned and Lin, Petal and Dennis watched as practically the whole store was taken outside and loaded onto the fleet of trucks. Included in the purchase was Lin's entire stock of outboard engines and rope.

Looking over at the proprietor Dennis said with a wink, 'Order some more,' then in a whisper added, 'I'll make bloody sure they'll need it.' Dennis joined the group outside and spoke again with Shu Ling, 'I think we should take the children down to the river with us. It'll add to the air of excitement and adventurous spirit a caper like this should have, don't you think?'

'Brilliant,' agreed the Tong man wisely, but smiled scornfully at Dennis's cork-adorned bush hat.

Supercilious sod, thought Dennis before answering, 'Splendid.' Then he shouted at the children, 'All aboard!'

The vehicles, piled high with provisions and equipment, were soon crammed full of children too. Dennis standing up in the front of the leading truck like some victorious, if not eccentric general, pointed forwards and commanded, 'Piggi Jalan!' To the roaring of throttles and delighted squeals of the youngsters the cavalcade proceeded towards the Temerloh Bridge.

Situated on the western side of the bridge and 500 yards south of Dennis's milestone seat lay a beach. It was only about 300 yards long and 100 yards wide but nevertheless a beach with a flat surface and it was an ideal place to site a camp and construction area to build the rafts.

Some people would say that Dennis was nothing more than a drunken sot but he did know how to organise things. He conducted the operation in a truly military fashion, delegating responsibilities and giving instructions and advice when necessary. Soon the area resounded to the hollow clunking noise of wooden mallets impacting tent poles and the cheers of the little ones whenever a tent was successfully erected.

In no time at all Dennis had transformed the beach into a neat campsite with orderly lines of tents, ten two-man bivouacs for personnel and three larger shelters for provisions, equipment and fuel, the latter being sited well away from the rest. Urinals consisting of large funnels that had been sunk into the ground stood like weird plants at one end of the camp, British soldiers the world over had christened them 'desert roses'. There were crude latrines too, simple affairs in the form of buckets with wooden seats. The licentious soldiery had a name for them too, it was 'thunder boxes'. These two essential areas of the camp were screened off with hessian to provide privacy within and decency from without, all this, mind you, purchased from Lin's shop. The camp was finished by nightfall, leaving the vehicles parked in organised rows and two men posted as sentries to guard the place, the expedition, followed by the kids, returned to Lin's shop for some well-earned sustenance.

The next morning with everyone feeling very much the worst for wear, work started on the rafts. Whilst the *Sea Pearl* commenced her journey up the mighty Pahang River the Tong men bent their backs in preparation for a trip down it.

The rafts were to be constructed from bamboo poles, an extremely buoyant timber. On the opposite bank to the camp, about 100 yards across the river, was a large clump of the stuff. Fifty yards to the left of it and almost under the bridge was a small muddy slipway that had been cut out of the riverbank. Dennis had already made arrangements with the Temerloh town administrators regarding the purchase of the bamboo at ten cents a pole, now it was time to carry out the laborious task of cutting the bamboo down and gathering it in.

The plan was to split the workforce into three groups, one to fell the timber, trim the ends and drag the poles down to the slipway. The second group was responsible for floating and lashing the poles together into manageable loads, and then to tow them across the river using a small boat that was powered by one of Lin's outboard engines. The remaining party was to commence building the first raft under the expert tuition of Dennis and local boatmen. In theory, by the time that all the cutting and carrying had been completed the first raft should be finished and the men who had constructed it would then be spread amongst the others as advisors. They would oversee the building of the other three rafts using their new-found knowledge. Dennis had set a target for completion of five days. 'If all goes well,' Dennis had told Mr Tan over the telephone at the end of that first day, 'the estimated time of departure allowing for a night's rest before we cast off, is 08.00 hrs on the twelfth of September.'

Chapter Nine

The scorpion was not happy. He had been enjoying a snooze under a rotting log when suddenly his temporary home was shattered into little pieces by some totally inconsiderate beast. He found himself fully exposed to the fading light of day for all his would-be enemies to see, in a blind panic and quivering with rage he scurried under some freshly fallen leaves to take stock of the situation. Peering out from the shadowy gloom of his new-found cover he quickly identified the culprits, as he might well have guessed; they were the Upright Ones, never satisfied with the perfectly adequate jungle environment they just had to trample everything down. The scorpion flexed its deadly sting itching to go on to the offensive, but on his first foray into battle he was forced to retreat from the poisonous dust that the creatures had scattered all about them. The lobster-shaped arachnid decided to back off and go socialising with some of its own kind for the night, there would be time enough with the return of light to exact his revenge.

Many other scorpions gathered around as he related his story. They squealed in disbelief as he told of how the Upright Ones had torn off their skin as the light had faded, they gasped in horror when he explained that they had detachable hooves that were kept on small poles whilst they slept.

By the time the light had once again blessed the world with its company, the scorpion was back watching the herd of Upright Ones, there appeared to be two sets of mates. He observed the fact that the monsters had acquired new skins and had shod themselves in smaller hooves, their old skins were still hanging from the branches of trees and the hooves remained on the poles. Perhaps the beasts were stopping for the day and the old skin and hooves would be used when the light next came.

Looking at the spare hooves hanging upside down on the sticks he had a brilliant idea, if he could attack the soft underside of an abhorrent creature's foot he might be able to inflict a death-dealing blow with his sting. His plan entailed getting inside one of the hanging hooves to attack from within. He swooned with pleasure at the thought of an Upright One screaming in agony, and then of how he would make good his escape when the beast dropped his hoof onto the ground. The scorpion considered his main problem, which was ascending the pole to get inside the hoof and that was something he had never attempted before. He crawled away from the distasteful presence of those that walked on their hind legs only and found a small sapling that was about the same size as the hoof poles. The scorpion set about perfecting a method of climbing up the wet, slippery obstacle, he did not have the capability to pull himself up the pole with his large front claws but he could push with them. All during the light hours he practised hard for his forthcoming challenge – to engage in mortal combat with the hated foe. Half way through the night he began his assault by making a stealthy approach to the battlefield. He was relieved to see that the Upright Ones were asleep and their hooves were still positioned on the poles, so far, so good. The intrepid scorpion approached one of the poles and guided his upwardly curved and jointed tail against the base. He pushed with his powerful front claws until his body was fully stretched; this forced his tail with its sting up the pole. At the limit of this movement he hooked the sting around the pole as kind of anchor to hold himself fast, then he pushed again with his front end until his body was bent almost double. At that point he exerted pressure with his claws and at the same time relaxed his sting muscles slightly to allow his tail to spring up the pole. And so he progressed, push-relax-spring-hold, push-relax-spring-hold. It did not always work, and for every two evolutions upward he took one downwards but his thirst for revenge gave him the determination to succeed, and succeed he did. By the time it was light again, he had reached the top of the pole where he was dislodged by the heel part of the hoof, luckily for the scorpion he fell not back to the ground but into the cavernous pit that was the toe. There, the tiny warrior waited for the enemy, sting at the ready. Vibrations being telegraphed up the pole served to warn the scorpion that the disgusting upright creatures were stirring; soon he would experience the sweet taste of revenge. But the brave scorpion was in for a shock, his world was literally turned upside down as if by an earthquake, then spinning and completely out of control he was flung unceremoniously back down to earth. Dazed and shocked, he looked up to see a shod hoof descending towards him and then all was darkness and oblivion.

Fred looked down at the crushed remains of the three-inch long scorpion and thought, *I take the trouble to put my boots on a bloody stake to stop the sods from crawling inside them and what do they do?* Fred put on the boot and laced it up. *Totally take the piss that's what, whoever heard of a tree-climbing scorpion for Christ's sake!* He gave the unfortunate creature a final stamping and whispered, 'But you didn't think I'd shake the bloody boot before I put it on, did you old son. Didn't get your act together, did you?' Quite naturally the scorpion was unable to answer the crazy SAS man. Donning his freezing cold, wet bush jacket that he had retrieved from a convenient branch, Fred remembered seeing a scorpion scuttling away when he had sprinkled some foot powder around the edges of his poncho to keep such creatures away. The patrol was preparing to continue with the pursuit of the 10th Regiment Intelligence Officer after having enjoyed a complete day's rest. If the man was indeed heading for the camp in the Gunong Chini area then, to quote Chalky's own words, 'He's bound to be there by now and even if we break into a bloody gallop we won't catch up with the sod.' So going along with the old adage less speed more haste Chalky had declared a day off. 'The thing is to get it right, not to race and get it done,' had been his convincing argument.

Since picking up his trail at Kampong Kertau on 5 September, the patrol had followed the man for 33,000 yards with Chalky or Fred doing most of the tracking. It had been a physically exacting trek but not too difficult in regard to following the trail of mistakes made by their quarry. In fact, by the third day it had become obvious that the man had developed a limp, he now had a gammy left leg or foot. On the rare occasion that Fred did find a clear footprint, he still had to remove layers of leaves especially in the soft ground either side of rivers and streams, it was evident that the right imprint was much deeper than was normal and the left one shallow in the extreme; this was because the man had to put most of his weight onto the right side of his body.

In a whispered conversation with Chalky, Fred formed and opinion. 'I think this bloke has busted his left foot or ankle,' he said with confidence.

'What makes you think that?' prompted Chalky.

'Well, from what I've seen of his tracks he's not dragging his foot. The man is picking it up and placing it down albeit gingerly, he's all top and no bottom.' Fred pointed at one print with the muzzle of his shotgun.

'Tell me more little white hunter?' encouraged the Patrol Commander.

'Look, he's keeping it well clear of the ground, if he has damaged his hip, thigh or kneecap he would be dragging his foot but he isn't. I think the bloke is pussy footing around because of the pain coming from his ankle or his bloody useless plate of meat!'

'Tarzan, bloody good man, you're getting there son.' A compliment indeed from one of the regiment's finest.

Not all signs, of course, came from the footprints alone. Because of whatever injuries he had sustained to one of his lower limbs the terrorist was finding it necessary to grab hold of saplings and branches for purchase when ascending hills and for support to stop himself falling when descending them. He was stumbling about all over the place snapping flimsy undergrowth and tearing handfuls of leaves from the foliage that he was being forced to use. Normal soldiers would be hard put to spot the signs of the bandit's passing, but to men of Chalky's calibre and with Fred's natural aptitude for tracking it was a piece of cake.

It had been in the afternoon of 9 September after four days of intense tracking that Chalky had burst forth with his pearls of wisdom that had resulted in a day of rest and recuperation. Now fully revitalised with hot food and drink, kit checked and repaired and weapons thoroughly cleaned and oiled; Chalky, Fred, Bob and Worm were ready once again to take up the chase with vigour. They had now been operating in deep jungle for twenty-eight days.

Fred took the lead; Chalky had warned him that they were approaching a village called Kampong Bintang. It was situated 3,500 yards south of the Sungei Pahang that was to the left of Fred's axis of advance, and 7,000 yards north of Gunong Chini that lay to his right; the nearest point of the Chini Lake was a mere two miles ahead of him. If Crazy Harry Blunt had got it right, and he usually did, the tiny SAS patrol was only about a seven-hour march away from the largest concentration of CTs ever thought to be in existence in Malaya.

As if the mental strain that particular thought generated was not enough to contend with, Fred's task was getting more difficult in other respects with every step that he took. The now days-old trail that he was following led him through some very unpleasant secondary jungle, just stalking along was tiresome, trying to follow the faint tracks left by the hunted man was pure bloody hell. Fred pondered over the reasons why the jungle ahead of him that was difficult enough to move through at the best of times was now fast becoming a filthy, almost impenetrable tangled mass that was threatening to block his way completely; as far as he could make out there were three.

The first was that vegetation growth was vigorous and plentiful due to the low-lying ground and the close proximity of the mighty Pahang River. The second cause was the village, or rather its inhabitants, who over the years had made enormous demands on the rainforest for timber to build and maintain their Kampong, but what is cut down grows back again twice as thick. Fred was looking down at the third factor contributing to the abundance of secondary growth. Bisecting his line of advance at right angles in both directions were many signs of wildlife especially wild boar that dug up and ate almost anything. The heavy concentration of animal tracks was due to the fact that the wise creatures were bypassing the human population of Kampong Bintang and in the process were doing their damnedest to obliterate the human spoor that Fred was trying very hard not to lose.

With so much evidence of wildlife on the move, one would have thought that Fred might have caught just a glimpse of some animal or other, but he did not, except for ants, mosquitoes and leeches. The latter were out in force in search of blood, the scent of which was being carried on the airwaves to the loathsome, gluttonous creatures. There were thousands of them, so many that the jungle floor resembled a weaving, pulsating, Gorgon-like carpet of snakes. Despite the fact that many of them were already feeding off of Fred's ankles, waist, arms and neck, he was not particularly bothered about them; it was all in a days work for a soldier to remove as many as forty-five of the things from his body each evening. When he did have to perform the unpleasant chore he often thought of his old Geordie friend Abercrombie of curry powder fame. 'I wish the bloody stuff would work on leeches,' was his oft-repeated prayer.

Fred smiled as the bloodsuckers went out of focus and he studied the ground five yards in front of him, over the past few days Fred had learned to second guess the terrorist and he knew instinctively where to look, and what for. Right at the present moment he was positive that his quarry had not taken another step towards Kampong Bintang, directly anyway; probably motivated by the same reasoning as the canny animals, he was steering clear of the village. But which way had he turned? In his shoes Fred would have made off to the right and the high ground of Gunong Chini so he cast about in that direction and by dint of much hard work and sensible guesswork he proved himself to be correct.

Having made up his mind on which way to look, Fred could not at first pick out any sign made by the enemy soldier amidst the confusing mass of animal tracks. The ground was pockmarked with elephant tracks, pigs too had left their mark by digging and snuffling about in the filthy mire. Rainwater and animal waste had filled the deep depressions, attracting clouds of mosquitoes; leeches lay around them in wait along this lucrative highway of blood-carrying creatures. All Fred could do at this point was go along with the main stream of traffic, so to speak, and hope for the best. The trail took a curved course around to the south side of Kampong Bintang getting more defined as the spoor left by the animals converged and the wide diversion became narrower until it merged with a much-trampled crossroads where the wildlife had split from the main track.

The left-hand way led into the village; the right would lead him up to the summit of Gunong Chini. Fred stuck to his guns and turned right again, or southwards. The animal tracks were thinning out now with only the elephants sticking to the main drag, they were lazy sods, not for them the steep-sided valleys because the great beasts would take the easiest route every time. They were frequent users of the main spurs and ridgelines; the leeches knew this and waited patiently, the bigger the prey the more blood there was to suck. Fred reckoned that the 10th Regiment man would have only followed this well-worn way through the jungle for a short distance to a convenient place from where he could transfer to a secret approach route, a marked track that the guerrillas would have established to control entry and exit from their camp, and it would be sited well off the beaten track. Fred knew, as would anyone else with a modicum of tactical sense, that the CTs would not site their main position on the actual feature, the peak was too obvious and was a well-defined target for aerial bombardment. The camp purported to house the all-important Central Military Committee would be well hidden and skilfully defended amidst the natural fortress with its maze of spurs, re-entrants, saddles, ridges, ravines, gullies and waterfalls. Although Bukit Chermingat and Bertangga were separate features in their own right they were still only part of the huge Chini Mountain complex.

With luck he would be able to follow this man in but first, as had been necessary back at Kampong Kertau in the opening stages of this particular chase, the patrol needed to find the spot where the terrorist had broken track. Fred signalled for Chalky to come up front, he did not have to confer with him because the old timer knew exactly what the lad had in mind. The patrol quickly redeployed and advanced along the main track in a diamond formation, Bob took over as leading scout complete with the shotgun that he had taken over from Fred, and Worm kept station as tail-end Charlie but much closer into the pack. Chalky and Fred broke track to the left and right respectively and so began the painstaking business of searching for the elusive enemy soldier.

Thirty minutes into the chore and Fred knew that he had cracked it. The main track had begun to rise into the foothills of

Gunong Chini and a spur was gradually forming with the ground sloping away steeply on each side of it. Fred could see Bob's feet ahead of him and slightly to his left at eye level; he could not see Chalky who was out of sight on the other side of the developing feature and would also be using Bob's feet as a guide. Worm was invisible to them all; but they knew that he could see them. What had caught Fred's eye was an almost ruler-straight gouge in the sodden earth that ran parallel to an exposed tree root. Because of the umbrella-like leaves of the flourishing palms, the ground was free from fallen foliage and the marks were clear to see. Fred could picture in his mind's eye what had probably occurred at this spot. The terrorist must have decided to break away from the spur, and very unwisely in his lame condition, had taken a giant leap down the slope. One of his rubber-soled hockey boots had made contact with the treacherous root and he had slipped, digging in his heels to stop his unplanned descent and to prevent himself from making any further sign, it was as simple as that. It was time to alert the patrol and show Chalky his find. He tapped the magazine of his Owen gun once with his index finger, it was an alien sound in the natural jungle environment and the other three soldiers immediately froze in their tracks, they remained so for a full two minutes listening for a reaction. There was a risk that any enemy troops lurking in the vicinity might have heard the signal too. They would also listen out for a repeat but if nothing was forthcoming they would in all probability discount the noise as a one off phenomena or a figment of their imaginations. Fred did not repeat the signal; indeed, he would not use that method of communication again for days.

Whilst waiting for Chalky to arrive on the scene, Fred sifted through the skid marks at the bottom end of the scooped out earth and found a short length of brown coloured cord that was frayed at both ends, it was a piece of broken bootlace, the metal threads long since gone. Chalky came down the slope in a more controlled manner than the terrorist must have done, keeping well clear of the sign but not missing a thing. He was cock-a-hoop and his nostrils were flaring with excitement, but not all of his obvious exuberance stemmed from Fred's success, he had enjoyed some too. Fred explained the evidence as he saw it and presented

Chalky with the telltale bootlace. 'Bloody good work son,' whispered Chalky, then making a circular motion with his left hand he continued, 'I've found a signpost, come and have a look.'

Fred followed his leader up the short but steep incline onto the main track where Chalky pointed at a young willowy sapling. There is nothing strange about a sapling growing in the jungle one would have thought, but this one was different. From a distance it appeared to be tangled up with other kinds of vegetation but on closer inspection it became obvious that the sapling had been arranged to form a loop in a loosely tied knot if you will, with the whole thing held in place by the spring-like tension of the young plant. The loose end of this ingenious form of communication was sticking out to one side like a car indicator or arrow, in this case it was pointing back towards Kampong Bintang; this was the signpost that Chalky had found. Man-made, the signals were widely used by the aboriginal tribes of Malaya and less extensively by the CTs. But as Fred was fast learning from Chalky, you must never put your trust in the obvious, there were a few tricks of the trade to be hauled in before going haring off into the jungle in entirely the wrong direction. The signpost was presented parallel to the main track and for all intents and purposes was telling the traveller to go in the direction of the village, when in fact, the opposite was the case; the first trick was to reverse the signal. That would draw the observer's attention towards the south and the summit of Gunong Chini, it was but a ploy to deceive the unwary. Now in the mind's eye a 90° turn in an anticlockwise direction had to be imagined, this would bring the pointer around to the right and this time the signal did not have to be reversed and the pointer was indicating the true bearing to be taken; the terrorist had complied with the signal and then had come a cropper on the tree root. Bob was signalled back from the point position, he was not rebuked for marching straight past the signpost; Chalky admitted that he too would have missed it but for the fact that he had approached the thing from a side-on angle. The patrol reformed into single file and commenced to follow the new-found trail. Fred, having retrieved the shotgun off Bob, led as leading scout to track the man. Chalky acted as a second scout and was looking for more signposts. Worm took over the heavy radio set from Bob and that worthy being did a spell as tail-end Charlie.

It soon became obvious that the 10th Regiment man was in dire straights and in no condition to tackle the difficult terrain of the high country that lay ahead of him. But Fred knew better than to write the bloke off just yet, the man would suffer hell on earth knowing that he was so close to home. The terrorist was still trying hard to cover his tracks but trying was not good enough and the young SAS scout was able to track the man without too much effort. By the end of a very hard day of soldiering, Chalky had found three signposts; Fred had missed only one of them, but then, he still had his man. As exhausted as they were, the patrol was in tremendously high spirits and were well aware that the approach route was their biggest find yet, a path that could lead them into the very heart of the enemy defences.

The next day, 10 September, with supreme confidence showing in their every move, the patrol continued with the chase. The going was getting harder and despite being lighter by two tins of food a day their backpacks seemed to be getting heavier and more awkward to carry. Although the ground was ascending generally all the time, it was undulating in great uneven steps formed by some violent volcanic upheaval, each wave-like fold in the terrain rising higher than it dipped.

By noon, the patrol was stalking through a stinking area full of evil smelling ponds that had huge mottled leaves covering the murky surfaces. Those leaves were a warning to them fortunate enough to be in the know. 'Quicksand', they spelt out. 'Step in and die', they invited. These treacherous obstacles were situated in a belt of low-lying land confined in a massive dip that contained trapped water; it marked the beginning of the mountain range proper. From that point onwards, the SAS men knew that there would be no more standing water, just gushing torrents at night and dry gullies during the day.

Christ, thought Fred regarding one of the crater-like ponds, *there can't be many more of these things, they give me the bloody creeps.* But there was one more even filthier hole and it lay at the bottom of the final dip before the ground started to rise sharply up the mountainside. *This is probably an old stream bed,* guessed Fred as he looked down the slope at the pond. Then he froze in his tracks with a horrified expression on his face, shocked to the core he felt that his whole being, including his faith, was trying to escape through the soles of his feet. Fred was utterly devastated; all those days of marching at a painfully slow patrol pace with the added strain of humping excessive loads. Carrying also the burden of responsibility that goes with the duties of a leading scout, where the slightest mistake could spell disaster for the patrol and might jeopardise the entire squadron's operation. The Herculean effort put in by him and his three comrades in arms since they had left the squadron base camp at Bukit Chermingat, had it all been for nothing? The high that Fred had experienced yesterday and again at the start of the day had gone, removed together with the bottom of his world that had just dropped out. He felt physically drained, mentally shattered and sick in the stomach. Fred was battling with mixed emotions of self-pity, an inner condemnation and a feeling of guilt because he thought that he had failed his three SAS colleagues. He was crying without shedding tears but his body was being wracked by uncontrollable muscular convulsions that threatened to reduce his otherwise tough character to near collapse. But help was at hand, and it was the same gentle hand that always seemed to come to his rescue. And it was the same soothing voice that brought him back from the abyss that was threatening his sanity, that bottomless pit of despair.

'Come on Fred lad,' encouraged Chalky, 'remember the will. That man's a goner but we still have the bloody signposts that he was following. Call in the will boy, dig deep for your own bloody will.'

Fred took a deep breath and dug even deeper into his reserves of resilience and found the will to rise supreme above the feeling of doom and defeat, he had cracked it but only with Chalky's help. Now calm and eagle-eyed once more, Fred took in the sight that confronted both Chalky and himself. There was not much to see really, just some skid marks similar to the ones that they had found the day before. The boot marks commenced at the top of the slope and ended at the pond's edge. It was pretty clear that whoever had made them had now disappeared into the quicksand forever. Proof of this was staring them in the face, for growing out over the pond from the bank was a branch; attached to it by a lanyard was a .38 Smith & Wesson revolver. The lanyard hung down to the surface but was not taut; floating on the slimy water amongst the large leaves was something that looked like the discarded skin of some reptilian creature.

Using a toggle rope as a kind of lasso, Fred and Chalky managed to snap off the branch and haul in the pistol, lanyard and the evil looking mess on the end of it. This proved to be some of the man's clothing and equipment that was covered in green, gooey slime and mud, the items recovered were a khaki drill bush jacket, a waist belt complete with pistol holster and water bottle, and a khaki cap sporting a Red Star cap badge. It was easy to imagine the man's last moments as the sand had sucked him forever deeper into the murky depths, the lanyard pulling his kit up over his arms and head thus allowing the glutinous morass to fully claim its victim. Chalky looked at Fred and shook his head; mirroring the scout's very own thoughts that there was not a hope in hell of recovering the remains of the dead terrorist.

Whilst Chalky and Fred had been busy at the pond, Bob had dumped his kit to move forward as a sentry. On his way into position he had located yet another signpost; the patrol was still in with a chance. Bob and Worm did not regard Fred's brief breakdown as a sign of weakness. It was something that all men who perform duties of a hazardous nature go through. Weeks of patrolling behind enemy lines takes its toll; they knew that because both of them had been there, as had Chalky in his earlier years of service.

If that august person was worried about the latest setback he did not show it, the old stalwart was more concerned about the welfare of his scout. He could see that Fred was recovering but he wanted his protégé completely back on the road so the wily Corporal chose the new man's sense of humour as the key to getting him back into the right frame of mind. Looking at Fred but pointing down at the pond he said softly, 'I'll get on the radio in a minute.'

'Normal situation report I suppose?' queried Fred.

'No son,' replied Chalky completely straight faced, 'I'm going to ask them to drop in some SBS divers, they can go down and take his fingerprints!'

'Ah,' grinned Fred, 'perhaps then I'll find out what was wrong with the bastard's leg after all?' And both men doubled up in silent mirth. *That's my boy,* thought a very relieved Patrol Commander.

As the four men set out once more on their mission to locate the enemy camp Chalky gave the thumbs-up sign to Bob and Worm. They acknowledged, Bob with a grin, and Worm with a nod of understanding.

Whoever had laid down the secret trail must have had only one thing in mind, to deter the most intrepid of hunters, for they had indeed thrown down the gauntlet. The task that lay ahead of the patrol was formidable and daunting enough to break the staunchest of hearts but if the wills of these four SAS men were anything to go by, they would succeed with distinction.

★

Temerloh had taken on a festive atmosphere; a rare luxury indeed in troubled times. What had begun as gleeful excitement on the children's part, and mild curiosity by most of the adults had, with the building of the rafts, escalated into a truly carnival spirit. The Tong men themselves ably encouraged this air of merriment, for despite being hardened criminals, they possessed the natural Chinese love for theatrical and spectacular celebrations. That maestro of deception, Dennis the Menace, was expertly promoting this national trait himself. Dennis was ever mindful of some advice given to him by Crazy Harry Blunt. 'Be very wary of those Tong fellows,' he had said, 'the inscrutable faced bastards can smile at you one second and slit your throat in the next.' But Dennis knew full well that if the Tongs were to ever smell a rat his end would not be that easy, so with subtle hints and suggestions he went to work on Shu Ling.

After a period of time in which to simmer away in his brain the ideas put there by the mad mercenary came back from the young thug as inspired thoughts and grand ambitions. Then as if the enterprise had been born of him, Shu Ling announced his brilliant plan. He expressed his fervent desire to give the expedition an explosive send off, explosive being the operative word. Dennis congratulated Shu Ling on his ingenuity and thoughtfulness. 'The celebrations,' Dennis had said, 'will certainly boost the morale of the participants and will be an excellent public relations exercise.' Shu Ling who had not even thought of either consideration beamed with pleasure at the compliment. Dennis made a point of emphasising that because of the emergency one had to obtain permission from the Security Forces and the local Government before fireworks could be used. To even get hold of these comparatively harmless explosives required an applicant to plough through miles of red tape. 'But,' Dennis had explained to the hopeful Tong man, 'it's not what you know, it's who.'

Promising to use his influence in high military circles Dennis had retired to Lin's shop and the antique telephone therein, not to mention a bottle of Guinness, a chicken chow mein and a large glass of arrack. He spoke to Crazy Harry and the well-oiled wheels of the old boy network turned smoothly.

The very next day a large box was delivered to Lin's shop by an unmarked police car; Dennis received it at His Lordship's table and his cries of mischievous enjoyment as he unpacked the box were genuine. He rummaged through the assortment of firecrackers, Catherine wheels, sparklers and rockets with childlike enthusiasm. Right at the bottom of the box he found a tin full of military pyrotechnics, they were in the form of giant bangers that were used by the army to simulate hand grenades and were called thunderflashes. Dennis recognised them for what they were and smiled wryly as he remembered a day long ago on the India-Burma border.

His battalion had been taking part in Brigade training exercises at the time prior to the British advance into Burma. During a rest period in which his platoon were being fed and watered, Dennis had decided to play a trick on one of his mates. He lit a thunderflash and placed it under the soldier's steel helmet that was lying on the ground next to his kit. The mock grenade went off with a huge bang, flinging the tin hat forty feet or more into the air and making everyone in the vicinity jump like hell. Had things stopped there he might have got away with a rough-humoured admonishment and an extra guard duty or so, but the gods were not smiling down on Dennis that day. The helmet plummeted back to earth and landed slap bang on top of the Platoon Sergeant's mess tin, splattering that indignant personage with good old army all-in stew; the writing was on the wall.

For his stupidity Dennis received seven days' Field Punishment. So when the battalion duty bugler sounded 'No more parades today' in the late afternoons and the rest of the lads fell out to rest in their tents, Dennis did not join them. Instead he was required to report to the Provost Sergeant. Under him he did pack drill, carried out heart breaking and meaningless tasks before being put to work filling sandbags until he dropped. Dennis learned his lesson the hard way, and for the remainder of his service he never copped for another charge.

The rafts were completed on schedule by the late afternoon on 11 September. Dennis had to admit that the murderous Tong bastards had come up with the goods, they had worked bloody hard and all four of the cumbersome craft were magnificent examples of man's ability to improvise and make do with natural resources. There was not a nail, rivet or nut and bolt to be found anywhere in the assembled fleet of rafts. The only concessions allowed were the outboard engines that had been shipped for use in dire emergencies only, and if required even they would be lashed in place by ropes and held steady by wooden wedges. The rafts were simple enough in design, being four layers of bamboo deep. The first or bottom layer consisted of thick poles fifteen feet long that determined the beam of the vessel. They were laid down on the beach like rollers facing the water and positioned two feet apart. The second layer of thinner poles was then laid stem to stern on top of the first, this time with only a twelve-inch gap between poles. Both layers were lashed together with miles of quarter-inch sisal rope to fashion the keel that was twenty-four feet in length. The keel now had to be partially floated because of the weight, being very heavy by now, it would be impossible to move later. Next the third layer, thicker poles once more positioned beam to beam but closed right up. After more lashings of sisal the raft had to be pushed and dragged even further into the water. Finally the top layer of poles was secured along the length of the hull as the deck, and the whole massive bulk was then completely launched into the river.

As each raft reached that stage of construction great cheers of joy had rung out from the builders, watchers and children-alike. It was a heart-warming experience and a time to show pride and human emotion at its best and even Dennis, who knew the true deadly purpose of the venture, could not help but get caught up in the high spirits of the moment. All further work on the rafts was carried out afloat with the children splashing around in the water with the ever-watchful safety boat standing by. Masts were stepped, not to carry sails but to act as tent poles for light canvas awnings. Dennis had made arrangements with a nearby sawmill to purchase some extremely thin cuts of unwanted waste timber, like gigantic shavings they provided for a flat deck surface; a sort of wooden carpet really, but it made life easier.

In the fading light of day Dennis had gathered everyone together to give them a pat on the back. Cutting and handling bamboo is a dangerous game and every man jack of the expedition was cut and bandaged in several places to prove it. They looked a motley crew, and evil cut-throats or not, Dennis actually felt proud of them. *Silly sod,* he thought wiping away some tears, then shouted, 'Let's have a party for tomorrow we sail!' And with great rejoicing the whole of Temerloh made merry.

★

The crocodile had been watching the great herd of Upright Ones for five days now. They had interrupted his daily habit of pretending to be a log whilst drifting downriver to swallow up the unwary. His anger at this intrusion into his normal daily routine had given way to curiosity, for the ancient old reptile sensed that there were rich pickings to be had here. He was not worried about food because he had an ample supply of rotting carcasses stowed away deep in a riverside mud hole. It had been a simple matter to dive down to his lucrative larder during the hours of darkness when the Upright Ones slept. This stretch of the river was his territory and he had reigned supreme over it for many battle-weary years. During that time he had taken no less than five young Upright Ones from the shallow water by the beach. He lay still, camouflaged in a mud bank just downriver from a large clump of bamboo and waited. He had been tempted once or twice to go in for the kill, especially when the loathsome creatures had been floating logs across the water. But each time he had been thwarted by a lone beast in a hollow log that made terrifying buzzing noises under the surface.

The crocodile decided to concentrate on the young ones who were venturing ever further into the water, it was high time that he tasted the rare delicacy again and he drooled in anticipation at the prospect as with unblinking eyes he watched the young upright morsels. At long last, his instincts told him that the time had come but he was not quite prepared for the way in which it did.

There were now more of the disgusting creatures crowding the beach than he had ever seen before. Some of them were standing on huge flat logs that were beginning to float down the river with the strange beasts poking about under the water with long poles. Loud noises just like the sound of splitting trees startled the crocodile. Many of the Upright Ones were holding small sticks that belched fire and coloured smoke that added to his confusion. Thunder in the sky and small balls of lightning falling to earth made the reptile's muscles quiver, and all the while the Upright Ones jumped up and down roaring to some kind of bestial ritual. Then the lone beast in the hollow log swam past throwing smoking sticks into the river. The deafening claps of thunder reverberated through the air and huge shock waves caused havoc underwater. Great fountains of it shot skywards to cascade back down again in a sparkling shower. The flat logs were now in midstream and the young beasts on the shore had surged forward so that they were almost waist deep in the water. The crocodile slipped unseen into the river and dived resurfacing, also in midstream, where he prepared himself for the kill.

With his cold merciless eyes fixed on a small creature that was slightly apart from the others, he dived into the attack like a torpedo. At that precise moment hundreds of stunned fish rose to the surface distracting the crocodile. Never in his entire existence had he been confronted with such an abundance of food. He had been handed at least a week's worth of goodly fare on a plate, and

240

that was an offer not even a crocodile could refuse. With his lethal tail thrashing about madly and with gaping jaws he went on a frenzied trawl that alerted the Upright Ones on the beach to his presence. The adults dragged their young from the water to the safety of higher ground, and those afloat on the flat logs became wary. Later in the cool darkness of the night with a full stomach and his mud hole larder full to overflowing, he pondered over the strange behaviour of the rambling Upright Ones. But he gave up, he knew that he would never understand the ways of these primitive and abhorrent monsters, they were fathomless.

★

The smoke had cleared and the excitement abated as the rafts disappeared from view around the first bend. The children continued to wave and shout goodbye until they too realised that the fun was over; reluctantly, parents took their offspring home. Other Tong men came to pack up the camp and took away the trucks, but before leaving Temerloh, and surprisingly for men of their ilk, they returned all the unused kit purchased from Lin's shop and made a present of it to him. The beach was clear and soon the log that everyone knew to be a crocodile would be up to his crafty tricks again. Temerloh settled down to its normal slow pace of life but something was missing. It took time for the good people of Temerloh to put their fingers on what it was, an important part of their lives was conspicuous by its absence, nay, it would be more correct to say him, for they were missing Dennis. Without realising it they had become dependant on the eccentric old soldier for his fearlessness and the sense of stability that his presence generated. They could laugh at his antics one minute and then look at him with respect and pride the next. He was a born leader and had guided them through troubled times when the town had been threatened by terrorism. Dennis was an inspiration, he was a drunken sot but a kind, gentle and loveable one; and the entire population of Temerloh loved him. Until he returned to the town, until the mad English pistolero came home to his beloved Petal and her little children, nobody would be allowed to sit at His Lordship's table.

★

Whoomph, whoomph, whoomp, whoomph beat out the erotic and rhythmic sound of the overhead fan that was turned on at full speed. But it was not in cadence with the frantic, uncontrollable bucking and thrusting of the couple making love on the bed beneath it as Simon Belchard exploded into his third orgasm of the afternoon.

As he lay fully deflated and spent beside Fiona he looked at her heaving breasts with their still-erect nipples and at the rivulets of sweat that was trickling between her cleavage to roll down her sides and thought, *When am I ever going to satisfy this bitch?*

Things had changed between them, at least as far as he was concerned anyway. It was not anything that Fiona had done; it was the bloody awful mess he had got himself into that was sidetracking his thoughts and emotions. Whereas before, their relationship had brought him closer to love than he was ever likely to be again. He was now motivated only by the pure animal lust for release. And, of course, his quest for information to feed his blackmailer Abdul. Fiona was breathing easier now and her lovely shaped mounds were moving gently, the downdraught from the fan had dried her exposed torso and Simon longed to take her enticing body again. With her legs akimbo as wanton as you please and the throbbing machine overhead playing havoc with his imagination Simon strove to rekindle his desire, but it was no use, he knew for sure that his lovemaking was over for this fine day.

Well, he thought, *who can complain about a hat-trick?* Having admitted defeat, Simon began to doze off but was shaken out of his drowsiness by Fiona uttering the word 'junk'. He nearly jumped out of bed with the shock of it, causing Fiona's breasts to tremble seductively.

'Junk,' he almost shouted. Then realising that he may have overplayed his hand he added in a much softer tone, 'Junk dear, I have no rubbish here!'

'Oh Simon darling, I don't mean that kind of junk you silly old thing. I meant a boat, one of those quaint Chinese junk things that look like Spanish Galleons.'

'I see,' he laughed in relief. 'What about this boat, Fiona dear?' And the good lady went on to tell Simon all that he wished to know about the *Sea Pearl* terminating her long voyage from Hong Kong at a small fishing village named Kampong Kinchur. An hour later, having failed to revive Simon's flagging ardour Fiona left the bungalow for her home in Gemas.

Fiona lay on her bed in the master bedroom waiting for Jeremy to finish his shower. She was excited by the prospect of making love to her husband and her loins were aching with want. She was not sprawled out with naked abandon but attired in a sheer pink negligée that left nothing to the imagination. Fiona was reclining in a coy position, she felt warm, feminine, happy and wanted, indeed, she felt at long last that she was a whole woman. Whilst waiting eagerly, Fiona thought briefly about the afternoon's work, for that is how she now regarded her assignations with Simon, nothing more, nothing less and she was quite pleased with her performance. In regard to the lovemaking, she was now doing it as if by rote with no feeling at all. Fiona had become quite adept at faking orgasms and had not climaxed once, she was saving it all for Jeremy. Her gymnastic and vigorous sexual gyrations had been convincing enough to fool Simon, and by the time that she had drained him of his seed he had been too far gone to notice that Fiona was not with him in paradise. Gone were the insatiable cravings for sex just for the sake of it, now there had to be a meaning to it. As for passing on the information, well, she had been hard put to stop herself laughing at his astonishment when she had mentioned the word junk, but Fiona had merely smiled into her pillow.

Jeremy entered the room in his birthday suit obviously toned up for action. Husband and wife were soon lost in their own private world of passionate embraces, entwined in the unbridled lovemaking that they had so enjoyed in their earlier years together.

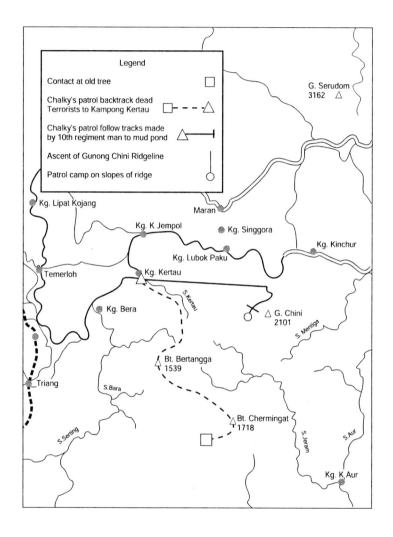

Legend

Contact at old tree ☐

Chalky's patrol backtrack dead Terrorists to Kampong Kertau ☐ - - - △

Chalky's patrol follow tracks made by 10th regiment man to mud pond △ ———⊢

Ascent of Gunong Chini Ridgeline

Patrol camp on slopes of ridge ⦿

G. Serudom 3162 △

Kg. Lipat Kojang

Maran

Kg. K Jempol

Kg. Singgora

Kg. Lubok Paku

Kg. Kinchur

Temerloh

Kg. Kertau

Kg. Bera

S.Kertau

G. Chini 2101 △

S. Mentiga

Triang

Bt. Bertangga 1539

S.Bara

Bt. Chermingat 1718

S.Jeram

S.Aur

S. Serting

☐

Kg. K Aur

244

Chapter Ten

Caesar was studying his map whilst scoffing a mess tin full of curried corned beef and baked beans. All the daily situation reports were in and he was able to plot the positions of all his patrols, in his mind that is, because marked maps were taboo in the regiment. His headquarters patrol was still located on Bukit Berangga which was situated at the western end of the Gunong Chini ridgeline. Forward and to the east of him were the two remaining patrols of Chalky's troop that were working their way along each side of the ridge slowly inching forever closer to the mountain. Another troop of three patrols were searching a bowl-like depression fifteen miles to the east of Bukit Berangga and ten miles south of the ridge, they were systematically patrolling northwards. The third troop had consolidated at Kampong Batu Balic on the south bank of the Pahang River sixteen miles east of the Chini Lake. On the morrow they would begin to clear the Sungei Mentiga, a river that ran mainly off the eastern side of Gunong Chini.

So far, except for Chalky's patrol, nobody had found so much as a fag end. With the ground slowly being cleared to the east, south and west of the feature, it looked very much like the camp was situated pretty close to the mountain itself. Caesar was pinning all his hopes on Chalky coming up with the goods, his patrol at least were following up a definite lead. If Chalky did manage to ferret out the enemy without being detected Caesar would have to move his squadron into the immediate area of the find very bloody fast and that posed a slight problem regarding logistics. The squadron had already received one airdrop of rations that would soon be running out, Caesar knew that the next resupply would have to take place before he ordered his patrols in for a close reconnaissance mission where stealth and secrecy would be the order of the day. *It would just not do to have the bloody Air force clattering about above our heads,* he thought with a grin.

Another problem associated with the resupply was the distance that his three troops were spread apart, normally they took a squadron airdrop and the troops came into the base camp to collect their grub and kit replacements but that was out of the question in this instance. Caesar looked up at Lofty.

'It'll have to be three separate drops,' whispered the Sergeant Major reading his Commander's mind.

The Major was pleased with the suggestion, *Where would the army be without Sergeant Majors,* he thought. He tapped his map with a twig in the area where Chalky's patrol was now located.

'But you're worried about them aren't you?' murmured the tall mind-reader.

'Yes,' answered Caesar, 'if they're as close to the enemy camp as I think they are then it'll be impossible to resupply them without giving the game away.'

'Win some, lose some,' commented Lofty, 'we'll all just have to pitch in and carry their rations until we meet up with them again.'

The next day the SAS Squadron continued with the arduous task of closing in on the enemy.

★

Dennis sat at the helm of the safety boat watching the rafts ahead of him with some amusement. *I wonder,* he thought, *what they'd do if they knew that my sole aim in this caper is to ensure that they waste as much time as possible until they can all be killed off.*

Actually, they were doing remarkably well and Dennis was hard put to think of a way to bugger things up, the fleet had just negotiated a long curving left-hand bend when the Tong men managed to do the job admirably for him.

The leading raft had encountered an island in the form of a sandbank and the intrepid crew tried to steer around the left-hand side of it. It was a mistake and they paid for it by running aground, no amount of pushing with their long poles or pulling by hand from the water could free the heavy raft. The situation got worse as two of the rafts following in line astern could not steer clear of the stricken vessel and piled into it, the three rafts were now in a hopeless tangle and panic reined supreme amongst the crews. But although Dennis was as pleased as punch he had to show some willing in the name of credibility so he went alongside the fourth raft and steered it into the right-hand channel and instructed the crew to moor it from some huge overhanging branches. It then took all the rest of that day to extricate the other rafts from their unfortunate predicament making it necessary for the expedition to moor up for the night where they were. Dennis supervised that particular drill and soon had all the rafts secured to stout branches.

The rain came, the river rose and flowed faster, flooding the decks and drenching the crews and their equipment. And so it came to pass that after the explosively spectacular send-off, the great rafting expedition spent the first miserable night afloat, freezing cold and soaked to the skin only four miles downriver from the beach at Temerloh.

Late into the night, Dennis who was swigging arrack from a one-gallon plastic container could be heard cackling with glee. The Tong men who thought the man was merely drunk ignored him. 'Oh Admiral,' whispered Dennis looking up to the dark heavens, 'I wish you could've been here this fine day.'

The next morning enthusiasm for the maritime enterprise was on the wane, the rafters were a sorry sight to behold being both disgruntled and bedraggled. But as the sun came up and they dried out a bit, the Tong men pulled themselves together and made a start. They cast off and broke free of their primitive moorings and the fleet of rafts set off once again. The day went well and the crews got better at poling the cumbersome craft in the right direction, good also at reading the surface of the water for good passages and signs of obstacles. Twice that day, Dennis had to rescue crew members that had been knocked overboard into the crocodile infested river by overhanging foliage. That afternoon they were able to run the rafts aground in a controlled manner onto a gently-shelving bank on the inside shore of a bend. The fast flowing flood that came with the rain later raced around the long outside channel giving the tired Tong men a restful night.

Dennis had no problem motivating the expedition members

on the third morning; encouraged by their success of the previous day, they went at it with great zest and vigour. Dennis could not help but notice that a competitive spirit was developing and each crew was keen to show off their raft as the best.

Mid afternoon found them passing Kampong Kertau, the place where the courier route crossed the river and Fred had found the 10th Regiment man's tracks. They had rafted well, making good distance but the river had run a straighter course than it had done for the first two days, now at Kampong Kertau they had to take on an acute left-hand bend. The water was being forced around the outside lane, so to speak, giving the expedition an exhilarating ride, ducking under overhanging trees and warding off the threatening riverbank with the poles. But they made it to the accompaniment of much cheering from the now transformed Tong men.

Their joy, however, was short-lived because as the leading raft surged out of the bend it swung beam onto the flow. The crew tried their hardest to correct the sideways movement of the craft but to no avail and the raft went crashing into another sandbank island, pure mayhem followed. The second raft successfully steered past the first but ran aground on yet another island some 200 yards further on. The third and fourth rafts also avoided a collision with the first then went on to spin out of control into the left-hand bank of the river to become jammed fast amongst the exposed tree roots. Dennis almost clapped his hands with joy at the welcome hold up; the expedition was proceeding far too well for his liking. He looked at the scenes of utter chaos before him. 'Right,' he said to himself, 'where the bloody hell do I start?'

As Denis went to the aid of the fourth raft hoping that if he freed it the bloody thing might go crashing into the others, he noticed a Malay fisherman paddling his prau downriver away from the carnage. He hoped that the man was heading for his native village, if that were to be the case then more delays were in the offing that would be a pleasure to behold.

Dennis was inventing a fault with his outboard engine when a voice shouted in Cantonese, 'Help coming!' Sure enough, a fleet of small boats could be seen advancing upriver towards the scene of the nautical disaster, the entire village must have turned out on this mission of mercy. Most of them were in praus under paddle power but there were eight sampans driven by outboard engines.

The Malay villagers engulfed the four bamboo vessels and took over the situation completely. Dennis could do nothing but split his sides laughing as for a whole hour the happy people laughed and shrieked at the Tong men's misfortunes and did absolutely sod all about it. Then with much gesticulating and delegation of responsibility, the rafts were suddenly floating free once more and the villagers herded them downriver in their smaller vessels to the sounds of hilarious jubilation. After about two miles the procession was safely beached on the left bank of the river, the rafting expedition had arrived at Kampong Chenor. The villagers took the Tong men in tow farming them out amongst various homes as guests, they were to be fed, watered and there was a plentiful supply of Tuak on hand, some of the more luckier men would be serviced too.

Before being captured by the village headman and taken away to be stuffed full of food and drink, raped and maybe buggered, Dennis got his head together with Shu Ling. They unpacked from its waterproof container a radio set that had been supplied by the Tong boss. It was a Chinese military model that was more than powerful enough to communicate with the Tong HQ at Kuantan. Whilst Dennis erected the antenna Shu Ling tuned in the set and in no time at all he was gabbling away in Cantonese to his chief on the east coast. When he had finished, Shu Ling said to Dennis, 'Some news has come in from the Malacca grapevine.'

'Sounds promising,' acknowledged Dennis.

'Yes, the junk will stop at Kampong Kinchur. Cargo will be unloaded there,' stated Shu Ling. Then with a wicked grin he added, 'we kill them there, no?'

'No,' answered the mercenary, 'we must watch points before we strike.' Dennis did some rapid mental calculations. 'She should be there by now or bloody close anyway.' They packed the radio away before being dragged off to more important things by the impatient Malay elders.

★

The Valetta aircraft took off from the British Air force base in Kuala Lumpur and headed east. It flew across the State of Negri Sembilan and over Central Pahang passing high over Bukit Chermingat; the Pig turned north before reaching the coast and started to descend. When the pilot saw the river glinting in the early morning sunlight he turned the aircraft west and followed the meandering Sungei Pahang flying at the dangerous height of 200 feet. A short while later, he identified the fishing village of Kampong Batu Balic that was situated at the junction of the mighty river itself and a smaller one called the Sungei Mentiga. He banked there and took the Valetta into a tight left-hand circle whilst his observer looked out for the target that was somewhere below. 'There they are!' exclaimed a voice over the intercom, 'in that clearing marked with a letter T!'

'Got it,' replied the pilot. He operated the warning light switch to alert the crew that were standing by in the Pig's belly, then began the approach run towards the dropping zone that was marked by a bright orange marker panel that had been pegged out on the ground by the waiting SAS men.

'Christ, an easy one for a change!' screamed the skipper to his co-pilot. 'They must be on bloody leave or something!'

The red light came on in the aircraft fuselage and the service corps men of the Army Air Dispatch Company made ready to drop the first load of supplies to the SAS troop on the ground. The staff sergeant dispatcher looked out of the open doorway and screamed above the terrific din, 'Will you take a look at that, the lazy sods are not even in the jungle!' He grinned at his sweating men and added, 'I suppose even those crazy SAS bastards get soft!' The green light blinked on and the airdrop lads did their stuff, manhandling the supplies out of the aircraft door. They watched as the small, silk airdrop parachutes developed and began the rapid descent to the DZ then they got on with the job of preparing for the next drop.

The aircraft climbed again as the pilot coaxed the old sow southwards at first, then he took her into a great right-hand circle that kept the towering peak of Gunong Chini on his starboard side until the plane was heading north, at which point he straightened her out. It was the pilot himself who spotted the target area first, it was marked by a solitary bright orange marker balloon that was floating just above the trees and about 200 feet above the ground. He flew the Pig down as low as he dared into a depression that put the high ground on three sides of it well above the plane. The lights turned from red to green once more and the parachutes took the vital supplies into the jungle canopy and hopefully from there to the ground and into the grateful hands of the SAS soldiers. The pilot quickly sought higher altitudes to escape the terrible turbulence that threatened to shake the old Valetta apart, and to clear the main ridgeline that was fast looming up ominously. Once safely over it he manoeuvred the Pig into another long lazy turn, this time to the left until he had her thundering along on a southerly course. The crew was now on the lookout for another marker balloon that should become visible somewhere on the western slopes of the lesser-defined feature of Bukit Bertangga.

Lofty looked up at the trees, not a difficult thing to do seeing as he was standing amongst millions of the bloody things. But these trees were different because one of them, an old gnarled monster, had come to the end of its days and had collapsed taking many more down with it. This action had created a huge scar in the jungle canopy, the sunlight still did not quite penetrate through the trees but it was a sort of hole none the less. And that was precisely what Lofty had spent the past hour searching for, a hole in the jungle roof where the parachutes of the forthcoming airdrop would not get hung up in the trees. When this invariably happened it was the devil's own job to retrieve them. *This is it,* thought the lanky Sergeant Major as he sat down on his pack to work out the map reference of his position. He nodded at the man carrying the radio set and the signaller acknowledged the unspoken order with the thumbs up sign and prepared the set and established communications with Squadron HQ.

Lofty had brought five men with him for the task of receiving the airdrop, the fourth member of the headquarters patrol and a complete four-man patrol from Chalky's troop that had been called down from the Gunong Chini ridgeline; it was their radio that Lofty was about to use. He sent the location of the DZ to Caesar who was positioned back on Bukit Bertangga some 2,000 yards away. Leaving the radio net open just in case he needed to communicate with the aircraft in the event of a problem, Lofty got on with the next stage in the proceedings, that of marking the DZ.

This was a job that Lofty particularly hated doing, the fearless six-footer who had fought in the Korean War and had served in the SAS for three years in Malaya was bloody uncomfortable and wary of inflating a marker balloon. With trepidation Lofty laid the dreaded contraption out on the ground before him in the centre of the tree-fall area. It consisted of a combination of a water bag that was shaped like an upside down funnel and a deflated marker balloon. With this ancient do-it-yourself kit came a packet of crystals that had to be fed into a small opening in the topside of the water bag. Next water had to be added to the crystals, the chemical reaction was instant and in many cases bloody alarming. The mixture formed a pungent smelling gas that rose upwards through the funnel and into the balloon so inflating it, nearly choking the hairy-arsed Sergeant Major in the process. The balloon also came equipped with a 300 foot length of light cord with which to tether it down, otherwise the bloody thing would have gone soaring off up into the heavens.

Seeing Lofty tying the balloon down the signaller thought, *I'm glad he did that, knowing the Air force they'd have chased the bloody thing all over the globe and we'd never have got our sodding grub!*

Lofty had got to the stage where he was ready to launch the balloon and was standing up with tears streaming down his face holding the four-foot diameter orb in his hand by its string looking for all the world like a sad-faced circus clown.

'Work for Bertram Mills, do you?' murmured the signaller with a grin.

If looks could kill he would have been a goner there and then. Lofty let the cord run through his fingers until he judged that the balloon had ascended to 200 feet then he anchored it down. Now all they had to do was wait. The thin cover above their heads allowed in more light and direct heat than was normal, being hotter the men's feet dried out and the rubber-soled jungle boots began to draw them. This caused intense itching and everyone was getting irritable so that nerves were becoming frayed. The light also accentuated the soldier's sallow complexions; they looked gaunt, hollow eyed and bone weary.

At 11.00 hrs when the sun was approaching its zenith, Lofty cocked his ears to a faint droning noise that soon developed into the unmistakable sound of a Valetta aircraft, the airdrop had arrived. The SAS men peered nervously up at the trees, they were not looking forward to recovering supplies from the lofty branches but you cannot have things all your own way. Opting for this type of DZ they had reduced the chances of parachutes hanging up in the trees but the things could land on top of you because it was impossible to see them coming. It the event they did not have time to worry about it for the bloody drop was suddenly amongst them anyway. The aircraft had not made a preliminary pass over the DZ, instead, the pilot gave the green light on the first run-in and the drop took place immediately. The plane was so low that it darkened the DZ momentarily as it passed overhead and the SAS men could hear the dispatcher shouting commands to his airdrop crew. The parachutes had barely time to open before the wooden boxes slung underneath them crashed through the trees to impact the ground with great velocity. Boxes splintered and burst open to scatter cardboard containers full of tinned rations in all directions like so much shrapnel. It was a terrifying experience but all over within seconds. The awesome roar of the flying Pig diminished into the distance and the animal kingdom gave vent to their feelings, howling and screeching in defiance and indignation; but they too soon quietened down and order returned to the jungle.

Only one parachute had got hung up leaving its load dangling about ten feet out of reach from the ground. It was but a simple task to get it down that entailed joining all the men's toggle ropes together. Then the signaller threw a weighted bobbin that was attached to some thin cord up and through the parachute harness. The weight brought down the cord, and the toggle ropes attached to it and in turn pulled through the harness. With something substantial to pull on, the lads heaved until to the sound of ripping silk and the snapping of branches the parachute and rations came to earth much to the relief of all concerned. Now began the task of packing it all away. The six men quickly loaded their own Bergen rucksacks first, then they packed the remaining supplies into sandbags that had also been dropped in for that very purpose, one sandbag for each of the absent SAS men. The six men of the DZ party had the unenviable task of carrying the ten sandbags between them up to the squadron HQ on Bukit Bertangga.

Once there, Caesar and his four-man patrol would conceal their own gear and hump the rations destined for Chalky's patrol up onto the ridge and dump it there. Caesar would then return to Bukit Bertangga. The four-man patrol still on the ridgeline would be resupplied by the men carrying the other four sandbags. Given the tremendous weights involved, it was a daunting task even for the tough SAS soldiers. Eager now to get away from the scene of so much noise that made the area vulnerable, they commenced the first leg of the march looking like six green-clad replicas of Father Christmas.

The Valetta headed west towards Kuala Lumpur after dropping the third and final load. The staff sergeant dispatcher was thinking that they normally only dropped fourteen days' rations at a time to SAS troops, but this time it had been twenty-eight days' worth. Something big is going on down there, he guessed, but shouted to his men, 'I like my grub, but I wouldn't accept an invitation for dinner from those blokes!'

★

The *Sea Pearl* was indeed at Kampong Kinchur, or to be more precise, anchored off it; Dennis had been correct in his thinking. The river was still almost a mile wide at the anchorage and that suited Clancy's strategy down to the ground. By positioning the vessel half a mile off the village it could be observed and activities noted by any Tong watchers, but close scrutiny of the crew that might jeopardise the operation was not possible from the shore. It was doubtful if the Tongs had accessed the village at all, and hoodwinking the inhabitants of the Kampong would be easy, Clancy was extremely optimistic about his success. All that was required from him and his men was that they wait patiently for darkness to fall when they could get started with the really interesting tasks.

The passage from Pekan to Kampong Kinchur had been a challenge for the Malay crew but bloody murder for the marines and the rest of the field force men that were cooped up below decks in the stifling heat and cramped conditions; their ordeal would soon be over. The vessel could have made better progress but the pilot had insisted on putting the crew through countless revolution's every time they had got something wrong, and the ever-cheerful Malay's loved every minute of it. One such spate of seamanship drills took place whilst the *Sea Pearl* was passing Kampong Pahang Tua, the home port of the trawler and six sampans that had taken the real gold from the junk at Palau Tioman. From a concealed position, Clancy observed the village through a powerful sniper's telescope; there was no untoward reaction to the ancient old girl's passing, just friendly waves and shouts of goodwill from the onlookers lining the shore.

The terrorists that had crewed the boats, Clancy guessed, had long since made themselves scarce and had gone back into hiding.

Despite the fact that the pilot had drunk so much booze that his belly would probably have displaced more water than the *Sea Pearl*, he was bloody good at his job. Even more surprising was that the old man had achieved wonders with his amateur crew, who, although bursting with enthusiasm, were ever mindful of their true vocation and the more serious purpose for them being on board the vessel. As it was, the lively old lady of the sea came to rest at anchor having arrived at Kampong Kinchur on 12 September.

When darkness came, the *Sea Pearl* weighed anchor and the pilot took her closer inshore; the marines and the field force lads were tooled up for action. Clancy said goodbye to the pilot with a feeling of genuine sadness. To the Malay Police Officer he said cheerio for they would meet up again. Clancy glanced at his watch, 19.55 hrs, in five minutes it would be time for his group to make a move. At 20.00 hrs the Malay Police Officer would continue with the deception plan, and the drunken old pilot would receive the biggest surprise of his life.

★

On the tenth, two days previous to the *Sea Pearl's* arrival off
Kampong Kinchur, the gold train crossed the Johore-Pahang State
border. It had taken the column four days to make the thirty-mile
trek from Kahang, a tough march but hardly gruelling because the
pack animals, especially the elephants, had done most of the
ground breaking. Kim Bok had every reason to be pleased with
the excellent progress made, and he was, but he couldn't help
feeling more than a little uneasy. The trouble was that by
travelling with a pack train in this manner, stealth went
completely out of the window.

On the rare occasions that the British Army used mules, the
animals were placed well to the rear of a column. This allowed
the infantry to advance stealthily in order to conceal their
presence from the enemy. In jungle warfare most approach
marches are made in a single-file formation, and in a brigade-
strong column the banging and crashing of ammunition boxes
and suchlike being carried by mules cannot be heard by the first
man of a point battalion of 800 men.

Kim Bok did not have the manpower for such textbook tactics
and just had to forge ahead regardless of the risks. He had called a
halt for the day and was supervising the bedding down of the
animals. Their loads were removed each night and they were fed
some of the fodder that the elephants had carried on their backs.
The nights are long in the jungle and both men and beasts rested
for longer periods than they actually marched. But every night,
just to be bloody awkward, the elephants always insisted on
foraging about and wolfing down vast amounts of succulent attap
palm, much to the consternation of the mahouts who tried their
hardest to restrict the movements of the huge beasts. Watching
the elephants munching the attap with explosive-like snapping
sounds Kim Bok could not help but smile. He knew all too well
that the elephants were quite capable of burrowing through miles
of brittle attap without making a sound, leaving in their wake a
perfectly formed tunnel as you would expect to find in an
underground railway system. But these six cantankerous sods, no
doubt because they were heavily laden with difficult loads,

seemed to derive some animalistic and perverse pleasure from banging against every sizeable piece of solid wood that their mean little eyes could spot. *And I thought mules were supposed to be the stubborn ones,* mused Kim.

If the elephants were being contrary then it was nothing compared with the massive dose of the sulks emanating from the mahouts. They would not actually say what was wrong and Kim could only suppose it was because they could not ride atop of their charges. To do so, of course, would be foolhardy in the extreme and they would run the risk of being cut to ribbons by the razor-sharp leaves of various palms, or at the very worst, lose their heads. Needless to say they were feeling dejected because they had been required to march all the way together with lesser beings. 'Poor little bastards,' murmured Kim in disdain, 'I'll never complain about my band of cut-throats again.'

Kim Bok moved on to the mules that had performed admirably from the very start. Oh there had been the odd occasion when they had dug their heels in but only in the form of statements such as, 'I'm a bloody mule, don't you think that I know the best way through here?' They were right; given their heads, the mules often found an easier route around an obstacle than the one that they were being urged to follow. They also seemed pleased that they were not being asked to carry such ungainly loads as the elephants. In fact, the cream of pack animals had been selected to carry nothing else but the gold; and even that had been packed into comfortable, hand-made canvas saddlebags especially designed for the purpose. Each gold bar weighed 26 lbs and every mule was carrying sixteen of them, a total pack load of 416 lbs; very heavy but a cinch to carry for the tough, stout-hearted beasts of burden. The twelve mules were carrying 196 gold bars between them; and the elephants were making light work of the remaining 96 ingots together with everything else that the column needed in the way of supplies.

The light was fading fast, the mahouts had the elephants well under control and the muleteers were holding whispered conversations with their charges as if they were fellow human beings. Kim had sited his defences, designated stand-to positions and posted sentries. Moral amongst the terrorists was high, and as tired as they were, they were bright-eyed with purpose and determination; Kim knew that they would fight to the last man to protect the gold. He made his way to the shelter that Fantail had built whilst he had been busy, she had also prepared a meal of boiled rice and tinned fish, with a brew of tea to swill it down with. When they had eaten their fill and it was completely dark, the two lovers stripped off and stood naked in the pouring rain letting the cold water wash away the filth and grime of the day's march. As they settled down for the night together, cuddling in for warmth and moral support, Kim thought about their daily routine.

Kim had gone for broke deciding that because he could not proceed in the customary silent manner there was no point having anyone scouting ahead. Therefore, leading the column was an elephant that was controlled by his mahout walking beside the animal. Each elephant would be required to carry out this groundbreaking duty for a whole day at a time. Following the leading elephant came a navigator, for this task Kim, Ah Fat and Chong Yew took it in turns to keep the gold train on course. It was a full time job on any march but doubly so on this one because the elephants tried on numerous occasions to go their own way. This annoyed the mahouts who in turn stressed the navigators with their constant moaning. Accompanying the navigator were two men to provide flank protection covering an arc of fire each side of the track. This defensive measure was repeated between each animal right down the line. Kim was not able to deploy a tactical flank protection force because, in order for the men to keep up with the tireless forest giants, they had to tread the same path as them. Men trying to pick their way through the jungle on each side of the column would be left trailing miles behind. As it was, everyone was finding it difficult to match the pace.

Letting the elephants blaze the trail had its advantages especially in the initial push through the tangled mass of vegetation, but as each animal in turn followed in its predecessor's footsteps, so to speak, the damp, soft jungle floor was churned up into a heartbreaking quagmire of slippery mud and blood from crushed leeches, not to mention those bloodsucking creatures that were still alive and thirsting for more. On top of this, or rather mixed in with it, were enormous dollops of jumbo droppings and mule crap. All that together with splintered bamboo, shredded attap, tendrils of barbed thorns and angry red ants that had been dislodged from damaged foliage, went a long way towards making life pure bloody hell on the march. Those men who suffered most were the tail-end Charlies, they had to march faster in order to keep in touch with the column, and in their honest endeavour to do well, often tripped up on the newly formed treacherous highway to end up flat on their faces in the stinking, heaving morass. And, of course, when they had extracted themselves from the clogging mire they had to double their efforts to make up for lost ground.

Like most soldiers, Kim had a terrific sense of humour, a little warped maybe, but it helped to get him through some pretty tough situations when he was able to see the funny side of things. It was his own chuckles that now brought him out of his reverie.

'What are you laughing at?' whispered Fantail into his ear, the lobes of which she was nibbling with her beautiful lips.

'It's the men, you'd think that after all they've been through they'd be as sick as dogs but here they are as happy as pigs in shit!'

'Perhaps they are sick, but with bloody gold fever,' she giggled and moved suggestively against his body in the dark. And so in the wild place that is the jungle they resorted to more natural things and were soon lost in the world of intimacy and loving bliss.

★

Chalky was knackered to say the least, bone weary from the sheer physical effort required to climb up the Gunong Chini ridgeline. An ascent that could normally be accomplished in one and a half days had taken the patrol four days to complete because of the necessity to track the elusive foe. Now with 200 feet to go, only the fact that they were still in touch with the jungle signposts kept them going, so exhausting was the present task that even the legendary SAS will was on the wane. Chalky felt that his arms were being pulled out of their sockets from the strain of hauling himself up by tree roots and rocks. His legs were numb and leaden from the leverage that had to be applied in order to heave his body and the heavy Bergen forever bloody upwards. *Fred must be going through hell,* he mused, thinking of the tall lad's skinny legs, *they must be the thinnest pair of pins in the army, I've never seen such a long thigh bone on a bloke.* Both factors put Fred at a disadvantage when marching uphill or climbing.

Had Fred been able to read Chalky's mind, he would have agreed, in more ways than one his legs had been the bane of his life and the subject of much derision and ribaldry from all and sundry. That together with his fleshless buttocks had earned him the dubious honour of being addressed as, Oh arseless one that walks on stilts! But Fred was coping all right, an inner strength overcoming his lack of muscular development in his lower regions. His performance on assault courses and his endurance on long marches had never ceased to amaze his fellow soldiers. On halts when most men would sit down on their packs to rest he would remain standing, chatting to his mates up and down the line, he was born to lead from the front and by example. His legs were there to stay and his prowess on stilts was fast becoming a thing to wonder at, after all, had they not got him into the SAS?

'One hundred and fifty feet to go,' gasped Chalky looking back at Fred trying not to lose his balance on the wet and slippery incline, 'Take over from me for this last leg.' Fred worked his way around the Patrol Commander and took up the lead for the third time that day, it was only 12.30 hrs. All four men had agreed that when the ascent had been completed the patrol would call it a day and make camp for the night.

The slope had now become a steep incline of between seventy or eighty degrees; normally it would be taboo to use trees as a means of pulling oneself up. But that unwritten law had to be tempered with the demands of the moment, and the present situation demanded that it was necessary to use trees as an aid to climbing. Fred did not proceed straight up the mountain but took a forty-five degree angle to the left of his axis of advance. He pulled himself up with his right hand whilst holding his weapon in the left, jamming his feet between the steep ground and tree roots to stop himself from slipping back down again. And so began the final, soul-destroying leg of the ascent.

Fred had selected his route for the first five paces for that was the limit of visibility, the jungle being very thick at that point. It was boiling hot and sweat was stinging his eyes and his hands were slippery making it difficult to grasp hold of his chosen hand holds, control of his shotgun was proving to be a problem too and only with an iron tight grip was he able to stop it slipping from his grasp.

One: step up, search the ground for tracks. Two: look further afield for enemy signposts. Three: freeze to listen; have the jungle noises changed? Four: look behind; are you still in contact with the man behind you? Five: select the route for the next five paces.

Progress is not simply a matter of forging your way upward and forward. Fred's way was barred by fallen branches and in some cases by whole trees, there were palms and great ferns cluttering his route and hanging vines threatened him with strangulation. Trailing attap thorns plucked his jungle hat from his head and caught up in his hair when he decided not to wear it. The thorns also snared his ears, eyebrows, lips, hands and clothing.

Holding on to a tree sounds easy enough but many of them are covered with marching columns of ants, more thorns and razor-sharp leaves. Bamboo is often splintered and the surface of the poles covered in a powdery substance with the properties of ground glass, it itches like hell inviting the unwary to rub it off, an action not recommended if one wants to keep a whole skin.

Ten paces completed and time to change tack onto another bearing, this time to the right. Five paces later Fred glanced down at his feet to observe Worm's head just behind his heels; he was still on the left-hand tack. The pace was painfully slow and strength sapping. *Life gets tedious isn't the expression,* thought Fred, *bloody unbearable is more like it.*

On he went using his left hand for purchase, the shotgun having been transferred to the right one when he had changed tack. It takes longer to climb in this crab-like manner but it was safer and easier albeit only achieving six feet in height for every tack. Fred's confidence grew when he found sure evidence that whoever had used the trail before him had adopted the same technique as him but had been more careless. Snapped branches, trampled palms, damaged bark, turned leaves and boot scuff marks on moss-covered rocks were all there plain to see. And just to prove that athletic, muscular legs are not everything, Fred had found no less than five signposts.

It was now 13.30 hrs, the patrol had been climbing steadily for two hours since the last swap-over, they had not stopped because there was nowhere to rest and it was easier to just keep going. The gradient was now an acute ninety degrees and the entire patrol were aware that they were in a hopelessly vulnerable tactical position, the strain was showing on all their faces, the heat was oppressive and the tension was terrible to bear. The mosquitoes dive-bombed and stung, the leeches drank their full and the ants bit. With nerves stretched to breaking point, and wide-eyed with fearful apprehension the SAS men inched their way up the side of the mountain. Fred hauled his body up the final step of a starboard tack and glanced to his left already beginning to select his next line of advance.

Visibility at that point was down to a mere three yards and the patrol had closed up almost head to toe, suddenly Fred froze in his tracks and his whole body stiffened in alarm. Chalky, close behind him but with his head somewhat lower, picked up the vibes that told him something was amiss. The feeling was contagious and all four men became tense expecting the worst, with pounding hearts they awaited a hail of bullets and perhaps thrown grenades. But none came because Fred had not encountered the enemy, he had reached the top of the ridgeline, they had bloody well done it. What had brought Fred up with a start was a sudden change in visibility, one second and he could barely see a yard in front of him and then, bingo, he was looking across the ridgeline track at eye level, all fifteen feet of it. And as an added bonus there standing out like a Belisha beacon was another signpost. With eyes streaming with pent up emotion and more than a little pride Fred heaved his long carcass up onto the ridge, then he assisted the others in completing the climb so that they too could enjoy their triumph.

Chapter Eleven

The time was 20.00 hrs on 12 September, in military parlance the expression used to describe this particular moment in time was H-Hour. It was the time Clancy had decreed that his ambush party should commence their covert departure from the close confines of the *Sea Pearl*, to Clancy it was time to go; to his men it was time that he took his bloody finger out. To the exact second he gave the order to proceed and thus justified the previous two hours of hard preparation work that the sweating 101-man force had been required to endure.

It had been 18.00 hrs before Clancy had been able to give the go-ahead for the work to begin, it had taken until then to convince local boatmen that were carrying traders and visiting village elders to the junk, that the vessel was a no-go area. Eventually the message had got across and the boatmen had returned to Kampong Kinchur with exactly the right impression, and so the preparation work had begun.

The force had first to prepare their vessels for sea, the craft that they were going to embark in were twenty inflatable rubber assault boats that had been taken on board at Palau Tioman from the second junk. Stowed as they had been since then they had taken up surprisingly little room, now all that had changed. The boats had to be positioned in places from where they could be launched when inflated without the bloody things jamming in companionways, stairwells and the many other awkward places to be found aboard a junk. It was a nightmare of organisation but in the end the twenty crews were allotted a working place in which to inflate their respective assault boats. The chore had to be done with a hand pump and was very time consuming; soon the ambush party was busy at the task with every man taking a turn at pumping. Every available space in the upper part of the *Sea Pearl* was jammed packed with the black rubber boats and their sweating crews, the vessels slowly took shape like some weird

Quatermass type experiment; and all the while the Malay police officer and his cheerful crew kept vigilant watch topsides. Whilst Clancy pitched in to help inflate his command boat he thought about an incident that had occurred earlier on in the day.

Clancy had spent the morning writing out his ambush orders and had come to the paragraph regarding the fighting strength of his force. The assault boats had been designed to carry five men and he had twenty such craft at his disposal. Five men to a boat added up to one hundred men, but for this task he had a nominal roll of one hundred and one men, that was one man too many. This odd number jumped out at him from his notebook and reminded him of his father who loved to rant on about his pet military mystery, the fighting strength of an infantry battalion. His father had been a Pongo, the naval term for a soldier, and in his day battalions were fielded with 1,001 men. 'Nobody,' Clancy senior used to fume, 'could ever tell me who the odd bod was. Was it the CO himself? Perhaps it was the MO or even the bloody Padre? Cross my heart.' He would then drown his sorrows in gin cursing army rules and regulations for being so damned uninformative. In Clancy's position it was not a question of whom the odd man was, but of which poor sod he was going to reject. Of one thing he was sure, it was not going to be one of his commandos. At lunch he informed the senior Malay officer on the ambush party that one of his men should be stood down, and that the man concerned ought to be informed immediately, then he dismissed the matter from his mind and got stuck into his grub.

Later in the day he took a turn below decks to chat with his men and walked straight into a macabre situation. A Malay policeman was actually sobbing his heart out and getting the normal callous response from his SBS blokes.

'Why can't I go,' he wailed, 'why have I been taken off the job?' Clancy deduced that this must be his 'one too many' policeman. 'I'll kill myself, I mean it,' threatened the now almost deranged man frothing at the mouth.

It was dark and hot in the hold where the men were berthed amongst wooden crates, statues and ornate brass-work. Hurricane lamps cast shadows that added a gloomy touch to an atmosphere already charged with apprehension, a mixture of excitement and fear that all men who are about to go into action experience. Up until now, they had been mere decoys, now the commandos and their Malay friends were going in for the kill. The lamps swung to the ship's motion as she rolled to the sound of lapping and gurgling water in the slight swell; conflicting emotions showed in the men's faces as they sweated out the hours of waiting. A marine was sharpening a parang, the oiled stone rasping against raw nerves as well as the blade. The Malay policeman was still bemoaning his fate much to the annoyance of everyone within earshot.

After enduring this mournful tirade for another five minutes, one of Clancy's commandos held out his hand to the distraught man. 'Here, use this lad,' he said, offering him his fighting knife, 'go on, use it. It only takes four inches of blade to puncture your ticker.' Nobody had yet noticed Clancy's presence in the hold.

The SBS man with the parang butted in, 'Hang on mate,' he called as he whirled the parang around his head forgetting for a moment about his cramped surroundings. As men ducked frantically out of the way he continued, 'Use this it's sharper, go for the throat.' With that the Malay cutlass impacted a beam and stuck fast. The now blubbering wretch of a policeman looked at the quivering blade in horror, he was obviously terrified.

Meanwhile another commando had fashioned a noose out of some gash rope, he looped it over a beam and announced gravely, 'This bloke hasn't got the bottle to do it himself, let's give him a hand!' Two more marines stood up with the intention of hauling the man to his feet, and whilst the rest chanted 'For he's a jolly good fellow' someone advised the cringing lawman, 'Come on Copper, you'll soon get the hang of it!' The rest of the Malay policemen could only look on uneasily as the intended victim of the lynch mob showed everyone the whites of his eyes and fainted. At which point Clancy jumped in and declared, 'That's enough, leave him be!'

'We only wanted to shut him up.'

'Then you've bloody well achieved your aim.' Clancy looked around the dimly lit hold. 'Sergeant,' he commanded, 'bring this man around now!' That worthy being ordered two marines to hold the unconscious man's head back and his jaws open, then from a height of two feet the sergeant poured neat Navy Rum straight into the policeman's mouth. When that capacious orifice was full to the lips, he gave the word of command, 'Close trap!' And his able helpers forced the brimming gob together and pinched the man's nostrils; there was no need to plug his ears. This drastic action forced at least ten tots of Navy neaters down his gullet and the response was immediate. Coughing and spluttering with his eyes nearly bulging out of his head, the victim of the rough SBS humour and of his own remorse returned to the land of the living. He looked stupidly up at Clancy, then his eyes took on a crazed, fierce look as he presented his two fingers up in that time honoured gesture of insolence.

'Mr Nancy,' he burbled, 'that to you and your bloody ambush!' Then he passed out again. In any military unit other than the SAS or the SBS the constable would have been clapped in irons to await trail by court martial. But on board the *Sea Pearl* in dangerous times and in such rough company he earned the admiration of the tough commandos and won the heart of Lieutenant Clancy Deane. That august member of the Marine Corps immediately reinstated the prostrate policeman back onto the ambush party. 'Tell him when he wakes up,' Clancy instructed the grinning sergeant, 'and splice the mainbrace!' he added thus authorising a double issue of the tot. 'He's had his share, and what's good for the goose is good for the gander!'

'I'll bet he'll never drink the foul stuff again,' laughed one of the marines, who just managed to duck out of the way of a belaying pin thrown by Clancy. The troop commander no longer had the problem of having one man too many, it was now a question of where to put this gutsy little man in his order of battle.

Clancy had commandeered the butcher's chopping block in the galley for his office, perched on a stool putting the finishing touches to his orders he was suddenly interrupted by his troop sergeant and the senior police officer; another problem had cropped up. 'What's the matter?' Clancy asked his vexed looking sergeant.

'It's camouflage cream, sir.'

'What about it, haven't we got enough?'

'That's not the problem, I've got bloody tonnes of the stuff.' The sergeant took a deep breath looking decidedly uncomfortable, 'When I told the men to cam-up I didn't issue any cam-cream to the Malay blokes. You see sir it's their colour and now there's bloody hell to pay.'

Clancy coughed, 'I see, you didn't think they needed to blacken their faces?' he prompted with a wicked grin on his face.

'Well no, they're pretty swarthy as it is,' countered the sergeant, which was damned diplomatic coming from him. The Malay officer, who was having no trouble seeing the funny side of the situation, came to the rescue.

'The way out of this,' he said pointedly to the SBS Sergeant, 'is for you to come up with a theory. Tell them that although you consider their faces to be dark enough their cheekbones might shine in the moonlight owing to the unusual humidity that we are experiencing at the moment.' The old marine smiled broadly as he saw the light. Clancy added, 'That'll let you off the hook, and they'll all get to look like our lads.'

And now after all the planning, the logistics of it all and the fuss and bother it was time to go, it was H-Hour. The time of 20.00 hrs had not been chosen at random. It had, on the advice of the pilot, been determined by the tide that still influenced this part of the river. Prior to H-Hour the river had been on the ebb and was now in the process of turning into a flood tide. There is a period of time between the ebb and flood when the water is still, this is known as the slack. Slack water as it affected the *Sea Pearl* on that dark night commenced at 20.00 hrs and would last for fifteen minutes. That was the time available to Clancy for him to launch his fleet of assault boats and get underway in favourable sea conditions, that is to say, no tidal streams or currents. In theory by the time that the crews were ready to paddle the flood would have commenced thus aiding the ambush force in their efforts to proceed upriver.

It had stopped raining but the clouds still formed a thick blanket over the land making it hot, humid and pitch-black. The boats were to be lowered over the side one at a time from the lowest deck on the port side. The *Sea Pearl* was not at anchor but

267

was being held steady facing upriver, the ambush party was disembarking on the opposite side of the vessel from Kampong Kinchur.

Clancy's boat was launched first and he and one of his men quickly followed it, whilst he held the boat steady against the side of the junk, packs and weapons were handed down to the other man. When that task was completed the assault boat took on its full compliment of five men and the jaunty little craft was paddled away, all this done in complete silence. This procedure was repeated until the remaining nineteen boats had been successfully launched and the entire force was on its way upriver, led by Clancy. To say that conditions aboard the tiny vessels were cramped would be an understatement. In Clancy's boat two men were posted forward to man a Bren gun, on either side were the men who had been detailed off to take the first stint at paddling and they were armed with Lanchester sub-machine guns. Clancy himself was at the helm; he carried two weapons, a Browning 9mm pistol and a mark-5 Sten gun with a pistol grip. Kit and equipment occupied the entire centre part of the boat, fixed to a wooden transom was an Evenrude outboard engine that would be used when the fleet was well out of earshot of Kampong Kinchur.

The second boat was crewed by five more SBS men armed with a mixture of Lanchester and a new weapon called the Patchet sub-machine gun. The next seventeen assault craft were manned by one marine and four field force men each. Starting with the first, every other boat was armed with a Bren gun sited to fire out to a flank, one to the left, the next to the right and so on down the line. In addition to the Brens, the commandos were armed with Lanchesters and the policemen with the No. 5 Lee Enfield rifle. Sergeants and corporals carried Sten guns and the officers sported the .38 Smith & Wesson revolver. Last but not least came the troop sergeant's boat, he had a crew of four commandos and an extra man; the Malay constable of Navy Rum fame. Now completely sobered up by some highly secret and questionable SBS technique, he had been assigned to watch the commando sergeant's back with his life, and he was bloody proud of it.

Although the river did not actually flow backwards during the flood, the titanic struggle between the downward movement of the mighty river and the awesome force of the tides made life easier for the men paddling the assault boats as they all followed their leader into the pitch black of the night.

Breakdowns were inevitable and would produce stragglers; it was the troop sergeant's job to keep a weather eye open for such eventualities. That old campaigner turned and whispered to his newly appointed bodyguard, 'Keep a good lookout for anyone dropping out,' he said to the shadowy form beside him, 'you made a good job of camouflaging your face, lad.'

'Yes, fine, innit. No shine anymore!'

The ambush force paddled for two hours before pausing for a while in order to await the opportune moment to start up the outboard engines.

Captain Nassar Surdar of the police field force, now in command of the *Sea Pearl*, waited one hour for the ambush party to get well clear of Kampong Kinchur then he summoned forth his own particular force of eighteen men for a final briefing, phase two of the Kampong Kinchur operation was about to commence. For this task he had selected the very best swimmers out of the entire company of 100 men. In a nutshell, their mission was to steal six sampans from the Kampong, return to the *Sea Pearl*, load the vessels with wooden boxes that hopefully any watchers would think contained gold bars, and then disappear upriver with their cargo. The small task force was split into six teams of three men each, one team per sampan. Police sources ashore had informed Nassar by radio of the exact location of the moored-up fishing vessels and he carefully briefed each team regarding their specific target and wished them good luck. The pilot took the *Sea Pearl* closer inshore her keel almost scraping the bottom, then the Malay swimmers slipped silently into the murky river. These men were now in their element, like fish they sped through the water towards the lights of the Kampong knowing that being natives of this very riverbank they would succeed. No commando could have done better and in less than fifteen minutes they had accomplished their mission, purloining the six sampans in complete silence. There was only one slight disappointment to mar the success of the heist; one of the boats was not equipped with an outboard engine, in the actual taking of the vessels the engines could not be used anyway; but once clear of the beach by a good 100 yards and in undisputed possession of the boats they threw caution to the wind and started up the engines and roared towards the junk under full power towing the one without a motor behind them.

Lights blinked on aboard the *Sea Pearl* as the smaller vessels went alongside and in full view of the now fully alerted inhabitants of Kampong Kinchur the stolen sampans were piled high with wooden boxes, that actually contained the field force men's weapons, equipment and supplies. To the watchers ashore, including the local police force there could be no doubting where the thieves had come from and it was blatantly obvious that whatever cargo the junk had brought upriver was now being transferred to the stolen property for further shipment upriver by them. Had the powers that be been able to listen to the rumblings of discontent they would have been pleased to note that blame for this audacious act against the well-being of the fishing village was being laid fairly and squarely across the shoulders of the Chinese Communist Terrorists.

The Kampong Kinchur police department boasted four policemen good and true. They had been warned about a possible 'happening' a couple of days beforehand, sworn to secrecy they had fairly wallowed in the mysterious cloak and dagger atmosphere and being confided in at all was the biggest event so far in their entire lives. When asked by their superior officers in Kuantan to provide them with the exact location of the Kampong fishing fleet their enthusiasm knew no bounds and they took on the mantle of overt surveillance agents with great alacrity. Flitting amongst the fishing boats, hanging nets and tackle stores or slinking about the beach keeping to the shadows, they wrote pages of notes and made many sketch maps, and all the while they looked furtively over their shoulders. They were completely oblivious to the strange looks that their curious antics were inviting. The good citizens of the Kampong could not but wonder what was affecting the uniformed ambassadors of law and order. 'Perhaps they'd found an illicit rice-wine still' was the consensus of opinion.

After the great 'happening' the diligent policemen made a

great play of informing the upper echelons of power, and then announced that very big guns indeed were on their way to the rescue. Only the river served Kampong Kinchur and the entire village fishing fleet had been stolen, they could do nothing more than wait for the help that must come by using the great waterway; but assistance was closer to hand than even the privileged policemen realised.

Claude Rysdale did not believe in letting the grass grow under his feet and had been busy organising what he termed as, The Relief of Kampong Kinchur. Long before the SBS had set forth on their way to the ambush position with some of Claude's men. Hours even before some of his men had actually stolen the precious sampans belonging to the hapless citizens of Kampong Kinchur; another of his jungle squads had taken to the waters of the Sungei Pahang and were closing in on the *Sea Pearl* pretty damned fast, Claude was hell-bent on pleasing the Field Marshal. The Commissioner had based himself at Kuantan in order to run the police side of the operation that would involve only action that could take place on the north side of the river or actually on its waters. His Special Branch men were in an excellent position to watch the Tong headquarters and the thugs could not move a muscle without Claude knowing about it.

For the 'Relief' operation, as everyone was now jokingly calling it, Claude had withdrawn a fifty-man jungle squad from coastal patrolling to the north of Kuantan. Equipped with assault boats similar to the ones being used by Clancy's commandos they were quickly briefed and redeployed by road. Taking the Kuantan-Maran road at first they branched off southwards at Gambang and headed for the river, a very torturous and bumpy ride indeed. Once there and in the fading light of day the jungle squad went through a final co-ordinating conference before launching and boarding their vessels for the great 'Relief' operation.

The policemen and all other inhabitants of Kampong Kinchur heard the approaching task force a good five minutes before it arrived, even so, nothing could have prepared them for the ensuing spectacle. Although there was no mistaking the fact that many boats equipped with outboard engines were getting ever closer by the second, nobody could see a damned thing in the inky darkness of the night. Then into the ambient glow cast by the odd beach lantern appeared four assault boats each an equal distance of ten yards apart. The helmsmen did not slow down and nudge the shore in the normal seaman-like manner, instead, they drove the bloody things right up onto the beach at full speed scattering people and domestic animals alike. When the assault boats finally came to rest amongst all the fishing paraphernalia the men aboard them sprang into action. Each boatload of men consisted of a Bren gunner, a No. 2 on the gun and a third policeman that was in charge of the team. Spread out on the ground behind the assault boats facing the river they soon had the light machine guns operating with deadly precision, the deep staccato signature reverberating from shore to shore waking up the sleeping jungle wildlife. Each fifth bullet speeding through the air was a tracer round and the four guns hose piped a wicked stream of red death towards the junk, the muzzle flashes illuminating the gunners' faces in rapid exposures and extending outwards for twenty yards lighting up the surrounding area in a bizarre fashion. For the villagers who had never before experienced gunfire of this magnitude, it was a frightening and mind-numbing ordeal. Just above the din they could hear frantic words of command being shouted out by the Malay team leaders. 'Hit the deck! Keep your heads down!' But the locals were slow to respond so mesmerised were they by it all. At that point four more streams of tracer spumed across the front of the bewildered folk, this time from more Bren guns that were being fired from assault boats positioned downriver from the *Sea Pearl*. Shots and muzzle flashes accompanied by screams of agony coming from the direction of the junk added to the confusion. At long last the villagers took the hint and dived for cover, terrified cats, dogs, chickens and even pigs snuggled into the sides of human beings; all hugging the ground for dear life. Their plight was not made any easier by the furious clamour of the tree dwellers crashing around in their lofty domain shrieking, howling and hooting their displeasure. The winged ones joined in too and screeched in protest at this untimely intrusion by mankind.

Back out on the water searchlights from the jungle squad

vessels had lit up the *Sea Pearl* and a ceasefire was being called. Gradually the tremendous pounding of machine-gun fire stopped and people wondered if their eardrums would ever be the same again. In the spectacular display of small arms fire nobody except the 'Relief' force noticed that all shots fired at the junk went above or to either side of the ancient vessel. Nor could the dazed onlookers have been aware that gunfire coming from the decks of the *Sea Pearl* was actually being aimed straight up into the air; at no time were the good people of Kampong Kinchur or their pets in any danger.

Now that the firing had stopped those confused beings watched as armed policemen stormed the *Sea Pearl*, and amidst the battle cries and some sporadic shooting they took the vessel, the end being signalled by a great cheer. Soon after, the inhabitants of the village, proud of the bravery shown by their Malay brethren, cheered too. It was a moment that they would forever remember; the 'Relief of Kampong Kinchur' was over.

At first light a Navy general purpose launch appeared and tied up alongside the *Sea Pearl*. The still excited citizens witnessed the transfer of the murderous terrorists from the junk to the launch. Not as they thought under arrest, but to receive a pat on the back from Claude Rysdale for their part in the operation.

There was one more chapter in the 'Relief' operation to be enacted before the book could be closed. At 10.00 hrs two assault boats brought the Admiral and the police commissioner ashore, both attired in jungle greens but resplendent in their respective gold and silver-braided caps. Accompanying them dressed in Navy Whites and wearing a row of World War II medal ribbons but carrying his hat, was the pilot. He could not wear his hat because his head was bandaged, to fit the picture that individual had been required to undergo some voluntary rough treatment. When this had been suggested to him the pilot had entered into the spirit of the ploy immediately. 'Go ahead,' he had urged pointing at his scull.

'Do you wish to be anaesthetised first?' asked a Navy medical orderly.

The pilot just laughed and then proceeded to drink a full bottle of Woods Navy Rum in about ten minutes. 'Go ahead,' he repeated, 'use this,' he slurred handing the empty bottle to the medic before collapsing in a heap onto the deck. The medical orderly, a tough native of Liverpool, took the old man at his word and cracked him over the head twice, smashing the bottle on the second swipe. That and the drink were the reason why the Admiral's little ceremony was two hours late.

The pilot stood facing the Admiral on the beach surrounded by the population of Kampong Kinchur. The Navy Chief addressed the crowd. 'I have gathered you here today,' he commenced in the time-honoured manner. Then went on to explain how the pilot had been kidnapped by the terrorists, taken aboard the *Sea Pearl* and forced to pilot the vessel upriver very much against his will. They were told that he bravely resisted at first but physical torture and threats to his family's safety finally forced him to succumb to the terrorists' demands. But the valiant seamen of many years loyal service to the Crown had managed to get a radio message out to the authorities, hence the seemingly rapid response to the emergency that threatened the well-being of the villagers. 'We will get your boats back and that will be your day,' announced the Admiral bringing the ceremony to a climax. 'But this day belongs to this man,' he said stepping forward to present the puzzled pilot with a sheaf of official looking documents.

'What's the old windbag on about,' wondered the pilot as he accepted the proffered papers.

The Admiral continued, 'My Government and that of this great country have seized the junk *Sea Pearl* under articles of war. In recognition of your sterling service the heads of both governments present you with the vessel. The package contains the ship's papers. Sir, the *Sea Pearl* is yours, may God bless you and her together, and all who sail in her.'

The seventy-year-old seaman who had spent his entire life serving other masters could hardly comprehend that he now owned his very own ocean-going vessel. He was at a loss for words and tears were streaming down his lined and seamed face. He looked down at the papers and then out towards the *Sea Pearl*, his lively little lady that looked as pretty as a picture lying proudly at anchor with the ebb flow creating a small bow wave and wake.

Alas, he thought, *we're both too old to sail the seas anymore!* His thoughts were interrupted.

'What will you do with her?' asked the Police Commissioner.

'Oh, I'll keep the old girl afloat at Pecan and if I can raise the money I'll turn her into a bar and eating place, the Sea Pearl Oyster Bar would be a good name for it, don't you think?'

'Very fitting,' remarked the Admiral, 'I'll make sure that every man in the fleet spends money there.'

'Add coppers to that,' said Claude getting his penny's worth in.

'May I ask you all aboard my ship for a drink?' invited the new master of the *Sea Pearl,* 'the bloody sun is over the yardarm already!'

'Try and stop us,' chorused the top brass. Then to the echoing cheers from the villagers the official party returned to the *Sea Pearl.*

To hasten up the bush telegraph a bit, Claude sent boats downriver to spread the gossip, he also deployed patrols upriver as far as Kampong Bintang so that they would attract attention away from Kampong Lubok Paku. It was important that nothing was done to compromise the ambush, or the bogus gold shipment that was going to lure the Tongs into it.

The great ploy at Kampong Kinchur had worked. If the Tongs had harboured any doubts that the gold shipment was coming in via the Sungei Pahang they had been dispelled and their trust in Dennis was well and truly cemented; they would follow his every suggestion from now on without question.

As far as the Chinese Communist Terrorists were concerned, those in the know were puzzled, of course. But anything that kept the British chasing some unknown idiots around north of the river was all right by them. After all, it kept them away from the real action further south.

★

Fiona was almost ready to drop her latest snippet of information to her supposed lover, the double-dealing bastard Simon Belchard, but first she had to have her fun. Probably for the first

275

time in her life she was in complete control of herself, albeit others were controlling her, but they had given Fiona a sense of trust and purpose. And oh boy, was she ever going to make that Casanova suffer for his sins.

At that particular moment she was really holding the reins and was totally on top of the job. Quite literally on top because she was straddling Simon's sweating, heaving body, clenching and controlling him with her pulsating loins and torturing the hell out of him. This bout of lovemaking had been going on for hours and she had not allowed him to climax once; it was driving him mad. It had started out in the customary manner with Fiona adopting the submissive missionary position. As was usual in their previous amorous engagements the sight of her naked body had excited him to fever pitch and he was blind to anything except a successful release. Until he had achieved that goal at least twice he was completely oblivious to the true purpose of his assignation, the milking of Fiona for information. But today had been different, on his first attempt she had sensed his approach to the point of no return and had contrived to disengage, and slipping out from beneath him she had slapped his bottom and said, 'Let's try something different.'

Red in the face with frustration Simon had gone along with her whim but she had put him through the same ordeal again, pulling away before he could be satisfied. And so it had gone on all afternoon with her exhausting nearly all of the positions in the book, and Simon to boot; and if the truth were to be known, Fiona found the whole thing rather kinky.

Poor old Simon lost his temper with her a couple of times and with it went the urge, he could not win but he let her revive his flagging ardour each time only to be let down again. *Some men would pay me for this,* was one of the thoughts that ran through her mind. *I hope you get bloody blisters,* was a more relevant one; but now it was time to bring the little session to a close. From her position above Simon she was able to control the pace of their lovemaking, although he did try on occasions to take over from beneath her Fiona was having none of it and thwarted such attempts with sheer dead weight to overcome his physical movements. Now her breasts were trembling and jumping wildly about as she decided to bring him close to a release, she felt his need within her and he clutched at her bouncing mounds hurting her with the intensity of his grasp as the moment of explosion approached. With perfect timing she heaved herself upwards and was suddenly free of him, the shock of the parting making him cry out in pain and anger. As she ran into the bathroom Fiona could hear him thumping the bed and shouting, 'Bitch, bitch, bitch.'

She laughed seductively and he came running after her. 'Bitch!' he shouted again, 'I haven't finished with you yet.'

His face was bloated with pure animal lust and frustration as he looked at her still fully rampant for all to see; she caught hold of him, pulling the trembling man into the shower against her naked body. As the freezing water cascaded down his warm torso she felt him go limp in her hands.

'You bloody rotten cow,' he sobbed and collapsed onto the floor in a quivering heap. It was over and still naked and dripping wet Fiona made coffee whilst Simon sulked and got dressed. When she too was fully clothed and ready to go he looked at her expectantly. Knowing full well what he wanted she said, 'Before I tell you anymore about this gold business I want you to promise me something.'

'What is it Fiona?'

'Promise me that we'll get something out of this. Promise me that you'll take me away from that horrid husband of mine?'

'Oh Fiona, is that all. Of course I'll do all that for you, I promise.' Fiona told him that the gold was being taken to a place called Kampong Lubok Paku but it was only a staging point, the boats would eventually take it much further upriver. Assuring Simon that she would keep him informed Fiona took her leave, as she pulled away in her old Morris Fiona said in passing, 'Don't forget your promise!'

'Bitch!' he said to the dwindling number plate.

★

It was that time of day when the young baboons and other primates of that ilk got restless and resorted to crashing around in the high treetops of Gunong Chini, howling, hooting and screaming out their frustrations like demented souls. It was that uneasy period just before the wind and the rain came. The two eldest baboons of the family had outgrown this habit of cavorting about, it was undignified and they preferred more genteel distractions. They left the bedlam of the loftier perches and descended through the tangled jungle to their favourite spot, a huge branch that overlooked the main spur that led to the summit of the mountain. They could see down to the well-used track below but they were quite invisible against the dark jungle backdrop from any inquisitive creature looking up from the ground. The two friends settled down to their most pleasing pastime; picking fleas out of each other's coats. Having caught the annoying, irritating creatures the baboons would inspect the minute vermin for a while before gnashing them into oblivion with their razor-sharp teeth. They chatted away in squeaking baboonese so fast that it sounded like the clicking of Morse code, only twenty times faster than a very good eighteen words a minute. Forever aware of lurking predators their little eyes darted here, there and everywhere.

It was this high degree of alertness that brought a slight movement at the edge of the track below to the attention of the male baboon. 'I think something is about down there,' he clicked.

'A snake perhaps?' hissed his female companion. The creature in question was now inching its way over the steep edge of the ridgeline and up onto the track.

'It's got a big head,' observed the gentleman of the trees.

'Maybe its one of those striped ones that knock you out with their jaws before crushing and swallowing you?' suggested the lady with a shiver. They lapsed into silence watching the abhorrent-looking beast down on the track, it had been joined by others and they were all smoothing their skins that hung in great folds from tall frames, and their detachable humps were sagging with weight.

'Their humps are bigger,' he pointed out.

'It could be a sign of development?' she answered hopefully.

'You might be right there, and look, they have hair on their faces just like us!' exclaimed the male excitedly nearly tumbling out of the trees with shock.

'Steady dear,' admonished the female, 'they're not that far advanced yet and you'd look a right fool falling out of your natural habitat in front of them, whatever would they think?' Thus chastised, the old man of the jungle continued to look on in amazement as the four loathsome creatures declined to huddle together as had been their want in the past, instead, they spread out many paces apart and detached their humps. The two tree dwellers did not feel threatened by this particular group of Upright Ones because they seemed to fit in with the wild surroundings. The strange beasts with the large humps and hairy faces were trying hard not to damage the jungle or make a noise; they had not spoken or moved too quickly and these Upright Ones had the agility of monkeys, were as stealthy as the big jungle cats and only the birds could better them in alertness.

'Oh,' came the feminine sigh, 'they're getting so close to nature, please let it be soon.' They held hands but the male baboon did not answer, he looked intently at the upright beast immediately below their perch. It had taken something strange and shiny out of its hump and was filling it with water. The creature next made some flames and placed the object over them, it was hollow like a square-shaped nutshell and soon steam rose up from it. But unseen the acrid fumes emanating from the fire itself rose up into the air to assail the sensitive nostrils of the two primates who visibly recoiled in discomfort. This angered the pair of hopeful baboons and the female plucked a nut from a nearby branch and threw it to the ground in temper, the nut landed in the water that was now bubbling over the flames. The Upright One was startled at first, and then it looked up and gave the baboons a knowing smile.

The female baboon pointed upwards towards the infernal racket that was still coming from aloft and said, 'Come on my dear, they're not ready yet and we'll be better off with them up there.'

'How long do you think it'll be?' asked the gentleman as he led his lady back to her own kind.

'Oh, I think a few generations must pass before we can accept them into our kingdom in the trees!' she answered sweetly.

★

The patrol was mentally and physically exhausted after climbing up onto the Gunong Chini ridgeline but Chalky could not afford to let his men flop out all over the track in order to recuperate, a short rest they would get but an organised one. They were not as vulnerable on top of the feature as they had been when they were climbing it but to dawdle about on the track in a group would be asking for trouble. Whispering to each man in turn starting with Fred he commanded, 'Spread out twenty yards apart.' Then emphasising the point with a stabbing gesture that broached no argument he added, 'and brew up!' He was not giving them an option; it was a direct order for the old Far Eastern hand knew the true recuperative value of a simple mug of tea.

British, or what, thought Fred with a tired grin. When men were as exhausted as they were, it was a bloody effort just to take off a pack let alone delve into it for a mess tin, Tommy cooker, fuel and the makings of a brew-up. But the end product was that it got tired men going and in a disciplined manner at that, it brought men back to the real world of lurking menace and that is precisely what Chalky had in mind. Yes, thought that wily fellow, the revitalising properties of a good old cup of char never failed.

Fred took out the cooker first, a flat compact affair about six inches square and two inches deep. The sides were hinged so that when opened up the bottom part of the sides formed legs and the top a resting surface for a mess tin. Nestling in the central platform of the cooker was a packet of heximine fuel tablets. Fred removed the packet, lit one of the tablets and placed it back on the perforated platform. Then he half-filled his mess tin with water and positioned it squarely over the flames and sat cross-legged on the jungle floor to wait for it to boil. Tea, he thought was so much part of army life.

Fred let his mind wander back to the first time that he had noticed the importance of tea, it had been on his first posting abroad to Kenya. There, his platoon had spent countless hours marching all over the bloody place in the blazing heat chasing some Kikuyu Tribesmen, the dreaded Mau Mau terrorists. Whenever a halt of over ten minutes had been called and water could be used, woe betide those men who drank it without permission, the impulse was to gulp the precious liquid down as if there was no tomorrow. Indeed, most of the younger soldiers did just that, and stupidly so. But the older and much wiser veterans waited patiently for their water to boil first, then relaxed with a nice mug of tea. Afterwards on the march again it was them that put their best foot forward with a zip in their step and they had regained their good nature. A picture is worth a thousand words, the saying goes, and Fred watched and learned a lot from those old sweats.

The water was boiling now so he flung in some tea leaves from a small tin, the tea bag had not yet arrived. Letting it stand for a while he recalled how the County light infantry regiment that he had been serving in at the time had been influenced by years of service in India. One of the customs that had evolved from the sub-continent was a routine known as gunfire. It was quite simply an early morning cup of tea that you could stand a spoon up in. Having drunk this elixir of army fare at four thirty in the morning the troops were required to perform various exacting physical jerks whilst doubling around the camp perimeter weighted down with full packs for forty odd minutes. By then everyone would be busting for a piss, and it is recorded in Regimental Journals, that clouds of steam could be seen for miles around as thousands of men relieved themselves, and not always in the desert roses either. From another tin, Fred added some sugar to his brew, and from a small toothpaste-like tube he squeezed in some condensed milk. Then with a wooden spoon fashioned from some bamboo he stirred it all up until he was satisfied with the colour of his culinary masterpiece. To make the tea leaves drop to the bottom he tapped the side of his mess tin with the home-made spoon, had he tried that little trick with the metal army-issue type it would have made a hell of a racket and woken up the dead or, even worse, he might have received uninvited guests in the form of CTs, for tea.

Fred let the brew cool down for a minute and thought with some amusement about all the various wallahs that had come marching out of India. Gunga Din the water carrier was an Ayer wallah; the lads that cooled people down with huge feather type fans were punka wallahs. Dhobi wallahs did the laundry; boot boys for some obscure reason were never promoted to the rank of wallah. But without a doubt the wallah that will forever be remembered by the common as muck front line soldiery will be the man who made the tea and wads, the char wallah; bless his black-enamelled soul. The leaves had descended to the bottom of the mess tin and Fred was reaching for the handle intent on taking a swig when, splash, a bloody great nut landed slap in the middle of his precious brew spraying the hot liquid over his hand. He nearly dropped the lot but somehow managed to save his drink and saw the funny side of the situation, looking up he could not actually see anything other than green and russet foliage but he knew, he was positive that he was being scrutinised by unseen eyes.

'You little bastard,' he murmured up at the trees, 'so you don't like my bloody tea!'

The four men had enjoyed fifteen minutes' rest and had cooled down, hot tea actually helps this process along, but it was time to get going again. It would not be for long because it was already 16.00 hrs and it would be dark in half an hour but they could not bivouac on the track. Chalky took the lead and the patrol was soon descending over the other side of the ridge following the last signpost that Fred had found. In a surprisingly short space of time, in a distance of only about 100 yards, Chalky found another signpost this one directing him to turn at right angles to the right. In other words, away from the summit and parallel to the ridgeline.

It was now almost dark so Chalky called a halt for the night. Kipping on a steep slope is bloody uncomfortable and decidedly dangerous. To sleep on the deck, poles would have to be cut or pulled out of the ground to be used as props that would stop one rolling down. But that was a lengthy job and there was always the chance that they might be heard, with the best will in the world, messing about with trees would inevitably result in some noise being made. It would also alarm the jungle creatures that would first become silent, then excited and angry, both warnings to those men well versed in jungle lore that someone was about. Chalky took the soft option and decreed that hammocks should be slung between trees taking the patrol off the ground completely, not a particularly tactical position to be caught in, but then, who would be crashing around this treacherous terrain in the middle of the night to find them? Nobody, thought Chalky; they would be quite safe in suspended animation, so to speak, until first light.

A new day dawned and apart from stiff muscles, the patrol had recovered from the ascent of the ridgeline. Hammocks and ponchos were quickly packed away and the SAS men prepared themselves for the day's patrolling by drinking a mug of gunfire. A tin of baked beans and sausages put Fred on top of the world and by 07.00 hrs he was raring to go; and a signal from Chalky indicated that he should do just that. Fred advanced due west along the side of the steep ridge that fell away sharply on his left-hand side. Roughly ahead of him, some thirteen miles distant along the same ridgeline, the other two patrols of his troop were advancing towards him, one patrol each side of the feature. Also ahead and over the next major spur, down in a low-lying depression but much closer at eight miles was another troop of three patrols working northwards up to the ridge. In the low ground to his left where streams formed the headwaters of the Sungei Mentiga the third troop was patrolling up each side of that waterway directly towards him looking for signs of enemy activity to the south, they were a mere six miles away. It was Chalky's theory that before they reached the next spur, only two and a half miles away, the signposts would lead them down off the high ground and southwards. He was adamant that this particular leg of the approach route was a last attempt at discouraging any would-be trackers, it was simply an embuggerance factor, to put it in his own language.

Well that it surely is, thought Fred as he battled his way through the thick green mass of vegetation, his every step was a nightmare. The going was extremely slow and the normal patrol pace was halved reducing the rate of advance to 500 yards an hour at the best. Direction was difficult to keep too, this was mainly because of man's natural tendency to take the easy route along the side of a steep gradient; a personal bias was causing Fred's left foot to seek a lower path than his mind had intended it to. Any height lost had to be regained at great physical cost. The ungainly Bergen rucksacks did not help matters either, the awkward load was continually trying to pull Fred off balance almost as if it was in cahoots with his left leg; both attempting to force him downhill. Traversing the side of any feature is always a difficult task but cross-graining these permanently wet and slippery gradients was pure bloody hell, there was one consolation though, whoever had laid down the trail must have been in the same boat. This was all too evident to Fred as he noted the damage caused to the undergrowth by men clawing and scrambling their way back on course every twenty yards or so. The frantic efforts had left marks, literally so because mistakes had been made and extra sign left for Fred to follow, making his task easier. There was a pattern emerging too and as time and yards passed by the scout was able to anticipate the habits of the trailblazers. Signposts were being used more frequently; it was almost as if the terrorists were frightened that their comrades would not be able to follow the track. Then at the end of a hard day's patrolling, a day in which it had taken the patrol seven long hours to cover one and a half miles and Fred had located twenty-six signposts, they discovered the biggest breakthrough yet. Fred had come across fresh tracks that bisected his line of advance at right angles. The sign was only one day old and the man who had made them was heading south, a new signpost pointed that way too, it looked as if Chalky's theory was correct.

★

The rafts were still at Kampong Chenor and the expedition members were firmly entrenched within several family homes. Dennis being no exception was lodged with the headman and his forty-year-old sister of who shall be said no more. The Tong men needed little encouragement in order to take advantage of the kind hospitality; they were enjoying the break and, indeed, seemed to be almost near-normal human beings. Dennis was pleased with the delay too and knew that the SBS would need a little more time yet before they could lay the ambush. But he would be pushing his luck if he allowed things to go on as they were for longer than two more days. He was glad, therefore, when Shu Ling came to him with the news that the gold shipment was staging for an unknown period of time at Kampong Lubok Paku.

'But,' said the Tong man, 'they're coming upriver a few more miles yet, maybe this far?'

Dennis smiled his appreciation at Shu Ling but thought, *Well done Fiona my girl.* To the Tong man he said, 'I don't think so, this village is too lively for what they have in mind and there's too many anti-terrorists here. Their final destination has got to be in one of two places, Kampong Pesagi the next village downriver, or Kampong Jempol, the second one.'

'We kill them and take the gold where then?' asked Shu Ling.

'I'd opt for Kampong Jempol myself,' answered Dennis, 'you see it's got to be there where we know that they have to pass if they are coming any further upriver. If they stop there all is well because we'll be waiting for them. But if we sit at Kampong Pesagi on our fat arses and they terminate the journey at Kampong Jempol we'll miss them and all our heads will roll.'

'Too damned right they would,' grinned Shu Ling, passing his forefinger across his throat. 'So what do you think we should do now?'

'We must get away from this distraction and move to Kampong Pesagi and work out an ambush plan. Your lads will need some training for that and I'll feel better doing it well away from prying eyes. We'll stop a fair distance from the village, you see.'

'What about Kampong Jempol, do we wait for them to land there before we hit them?' asked the Tong man excitedly.

'No Shu Ling, we leave the rafts there and march downriver a couple of miles and site the ambush on the bank. We'll kill them with rifle shots and recover the sampans full of gold intact. I have a plan, of course, but we'll have to clear it with your bosses in Kuantan first.'

'I'll get on the radio now,' said Shu Ling heading for the rafts.

★

Up until the time that the gold train had crossed the Johore-

Pahang State border the Gurkhas had been following behind in a huge crocodile-like column of eight hundred men spaced out five yards apart. Only the first platoon felt that they were contributing towards the effort, everyone else seemed to be plodding along behind regardless. But the fact that the SAS had made contact with the enemy further north put the situation in a different context and tactics had changed accordingly. The platoon doing the tracking now had flank protection that was being provided by the two other platoons of their company. So now three separate platoon-strength columns like Neptune's trident were dogging the gold train. Gradually the second and third companies of the battalion were overtaking the first, one company each side of it at about a mile distant, leapfrogging from one tactical position to another ready to react to any unforeseen eventuality. The Australian infantry was keeping pace with the Gurkhas further to the west along the railway line, as were the commandos along the east coast. If something was to go wrong and the enemy decided to flee they would first have to deal with the two forward flanking platoons. If by some miracle the terrorists managed to get through them they would then encounter the two flank companies long before reaching the Australian cut off groups in the west, or the commando infested mangrove swamps in the east. Well, has it ever been said that the Gurkha Rifles need help?

For the leading section of the tracking Gurkha platoon the task was proving to be an absolute piece of cake. The plucky little soldiers from Nepal who were renowned for their high standard of stealth and jungle craft could afford to take it easy on this particular chore because they found those natural attributes to be quite unnecessary. As for the skills needed for the actual tracking of the gold train, well, with elephants leading the way, the ground had been pounded into a soft spongy substance, then it had been stirred up by the passing mules and human beings to become a trail of mud, a sticky, slippery morass about four feet wide; who needed trackers?

The Gurkhas, of course, did not march up this dubious highway through the wilderness, instead, they advanced along each side of it to keep their boots clean and retain some sanity for even the poor bloody infantry were entitled to some measure of decorum. And then there was the noise factor, although not excessive to lesser beings, to the finely tuned shell-like ears of the Gurkha riflemen the enemy might just as well have sounded foghorns. The trackers could have sat down for long periods at a time and taken compass bearings on the sounds, then followed up at their leisure. They could have followed the smell with their eyes closed but that would have been taking the piss, and that was not the way of the Gurkhas. They kept themselves amused by making close reconnaissance patrols of the enemy flanks, getting to know the faces of every terrorist in the column, the mahouts and muleteers came under close scrutiny too; the Gurkhas had even put names to some of the animals. Their patrols established that the enemy fighting strength had not altered since the gold train had joined the courier route at Kahang. The Gurkhas were impressed by the enemy's discipline on the march, their tactical deployment and the fact that they took effective defensive measures at night. With reluctance, the Gurkhas had to admit that had they been lumbered with a bloody great baggage train, they would not have fared much better.

★

After crossing the state border the gold train had proceeded northwest into Pahang passing close to the 2,752 foot-high Gunong Bereman that lay to the east, or right of the column. Kim Bok adhered to that course keeping the Sungei Jehatih on the same side and the Sungei Pukin to his left. At the point where those two rivers met and became the Sungei Keratong the courier route followed that river until it reached its westernmost point passing Bukit Perloh, the first SAS base camp, that lay six miles distant to the west of the route. At the western extreme of the Sungei Keratong's course the courier route took a turn away from the river and would have led the gold train west-northwest in an arrow-like bearing straight for the Tasek Bera Swamp. The original navigators had deliberately plotted that part of the route in an attempt to throw the Japanese Army off the scent. Kim Bok did not intend to follow the courier route in this instance, being only eighteen miles due south of Bukit Chermingat where he could once more join up with the courier route he chose to ignore the Tasek Bera Swamp completely and head due north for the hill. Taking an easier route had been one factor that had influenced his judgement but the elephants, or rather their love of wallowing in water, was the biggest consideration that had brought him to his final decision. To take them through such an abundance of waterholes and mud pools would be to invite disaster on a grand scale. The elephants were acting up now, as were the mules to a lesser degree, and that was only because they could smell the sheer volume of the water in the swamp from five miles away. Skirting around the swamp would be bad enough but to expect an elephant to dutifully plough through all that water without playfully cavorting about spraying everything in sight with his trunk was asking too much, not to mention tonnes of bodyweight rolling all over the place, breaking the load carrying harnesses and maybe dumping some of the precious gold into the unknown depths of the green, slimy mud pools. Kim Bok could see himself ending up with six grey-haired mahouts and some pretty distraught muleteers. He had to smile at the picture that his thoughts had conjured up but his mood sobered when he envisaged the firing squad he would have to face if he lost the gold.

The journey north from the Sungei Keratong was a steady plod for the pack animals but not so good for the men who had to suffer the consequences of following in their path. To make matters worse it was September and the monsoon was starting to blow a little early, and of course, with the wind came the torrential rain that thundered down mercilessly turning even the smallest stream into a raging torrent. Although this made life a bloody misery for the hapless terrorists, mahouts and muleteers it actually helped combat the elephants' constant yearning to go galloping off towards the swamp; it cooled them down and took the edge off the situation. The great beasts were co-operating, the mahouts were pleased about that; and the mules sensing that all was well up front did as the muleteers bade them to. They were all working as a team and that was all one could ask of them really.

The first four days of the northerly course towards Bukit Chermingat was fairly flat, well, as flat as you can get in the jungles of Malaya; perhaps a better term would be ruggedly undulating, anyway, there were no bloody great hills to climb. But after that the terrain changed as the gold train reached the foothills that would develop firstly into Bukit Chermingat and then Bukit Bertangga to eventually become the Gunong Chini mountain complex. This was country where the elephants really excelled, they liked spurs and ridges and instinctively knew the easiest way up or down a feature or through a labyrinth of knolls, rockfalls and gullies that sometimes form a sort of pass. It would be a very stupid mahout indeed that tried to stop an elephant going his own way through the high ground lush with his beloved attap palms. So as happy as the proverbial pig in shit they forgot all about the swamp that lay stinking and festering not too far away to the west of them. Then at long last on the seventeenth of September the gold train began to ascend the southern spur of Bukit Chermingat; they had completed the short cut and rejoined the courier route on the very slopes where the SAS had clashed with Kim Bok's colleagues nearly a month earlier. Counting the overnight march from the Mersing beach to Kahang the gold train had trekked one hundred and nine miles in twelve days through some of the toughest terrain imaginable, a tremendous feat of endurance and derring-do.

It's no wonder we've taken seven long years to get only this far, thought the watching Gurkha Riflemen.

The going was steep at first but the elephants took it in their stride zigzagging in a series of forty-five degree angle tacks until they reached the main track that would take them to the summit. During that hair-raising experience Kim Bok could not help but hope that the leading elephant would not slip down the slope; it would take the bloody lot of us down with it, was his main fear. But nothing as drastic as that happened and Kim had the mahout's coax their charges to turn right at the top to head northeast and continue up the hill, an easy task really because that is exactly the way the elephants wanted to go. Kim Bok had dropped back to see how Fantail was faring; she had fallen in love with one of the mules known as Ulu. Ulu, correct or otherwise, is the popular term used by soldiers to describe the jungle. This particular mule was not entirely happy unless he was in the ulu or some other wild place. Coming from the CT motor pool in Maran, he was seldom out of the jungle and as a result was more or less a permanently agreeable creature. Ulu's handler was not very happy with his charge's relationship with Fantail, muleteers being a possessive breed of folk. And Kim suspected that he was probably jealous because Fantail's affections were not being directed towards him. Kim Bok had just reached Ulu's position of last in line of all the pack animals when a furious trumpeting sound came from the head of the column, this was followed by panic-ridden shouts from some of the men and even more trumpeting as the other elephants joined in the hullabaloo. Naturally the superior-minded mules stood aloof to this unbecoming display of emotion. Ulu nuzzled one of Fantail's breasts. The muleteer looked up and prayed to Allah for his forgiveness. Kim Bok smiled and took Fantail up front with him to investigate.

The problem was a tree, an old gnarled monster of a tree. But even a bigger problem was going to be how to convince the leading elephant that it was actually only a tree and not some unknown species hell-bent on attacking him. He stood firmly in front of the jungle giant with ears flapping and trunk raised bellowing in anger, trumpeting forth a challenge whilst gouging out great clumps of earth from the soft jungle floor with one enormous foot. *I suppose,* thought Kim, *that with a little imagination one could see a face in the ancient tree trunk.* The elephant suddenly stopped its bellowing and stood with trunk swinging from side to side swiping leeches as a distraction; it was almost as if he knew that he had just made a bloody fool of himself. Kim Bok gave a sigh of relief and ordered that all pack animals be unloaded, it was the only way that he was going to be able to get the buggers around the tree that straddled the entire track. And so the great task began with the mahouts performing wonders with their mysterious powers of persuasion. It took all the rest of that day but in the end, the mission was accomplished with no loss of life or limb, just gallons of sweat. By the time they were finished it was too late for them to go on, so Kim called a halt for the night. The gold train would rest on the track where they were.

Kim Bok and Fantail put up their basha in sight of the old tree;

in fact, Kim had chosen one of the buttresses as a sentry post. He could not stop himself looking at the tree and it was putting Fantail on edge. 'What's up?' she asked.

'I don't know,' he answered with a shiver, 'I feel it's trying to tell me something.'

'Yes,' Fantail murmured, 'there is something strange about it.'

Kim had no way of knowing, of course, that his friend Liew had met his end there, nor that he was sitting in the very spot where Shen had been wounded. What he did know was that he felt very, very cold.

The gold train moved on the next morning followed by the Gurkhas. The terrorist column had obliterated all sign of the SAS fight on Bukit Chermingat, but the eagle eyes of the riflemen from Nepal did not miss the rotting remains of the two terrorists that had been killed there.

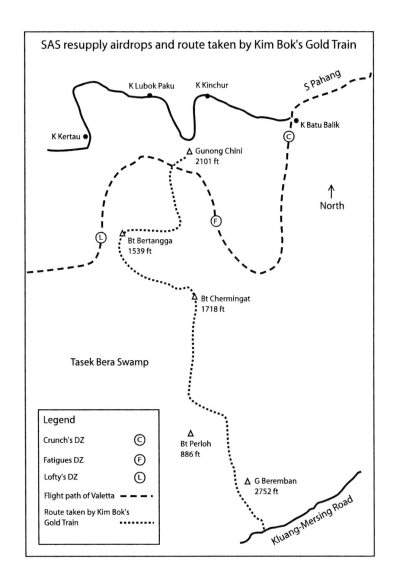

SAS resupply airdrops and route taken by Kim Bok's Gold Train

K Lubok Paku K Kinchur S Pahang

K Batu Balik

C

K Kertau

△ Gunong Chini
2101 ft

↑
North

F

L

△ Bt Bertangga
1539 ft

△ Bt Chermingat
1718 ft

Tasek Bera Swamp

Legend

Crunch's DZ   ©

Fatigues DZ   Ⓕ

Lofty's DZ   Ⓛ

Flight path of Valetta   ▬ ▬ ▪

Route taken by Kim Bok's
Gold Train   ••••••••••

△
Bt Perloh
886 ft

△ G Beremban
2752 ft

Kluang-Mersing Road

Chapter Twelve

On the very same day as Kim Bok's gold train was battling with the Bukit Chermingat tree, Fiona was taking a shower in Simon Belchard's bungalow, the same cubical where she had reduced him to tears during her previous visit. A meeting that had left him feeling as frustrated as hell and deeply humiliated. Today though Fiona had let him have his way and was now scrubbing off the afternoon's filth that he had left all over her beautiful body. It had taken little encouragement for him to take her four times with depraved lust and no finesse at all. She felt ravished but took great pride in the fact that he had not been able to promote even the tiniest spark of desire in her, she had not experienced a single orgasm. *If they were awarding Oscars for this,* she thought whilst soaping herself down, *I'd surely get one.*

Fiona looked down at her breasts now bitten and bruised, her buttocks too were sore from where he had clenched them so hard. But despite the afternoon's ordeal, Fiona still felt that she was winning, on the physical side she had given as good as she had got leaving Simon with a lacerated back that would be bloody painful later on. Mentally Fiona knew that her part in the intrigue was nearly over, perhaps one more meeting with Simon regarding the gold shipment, and there was some possible involvement in a plot that Tom Nobles was hatching to catch the middle man. *Yes, it will soon be over for me,* she thought. Fiona brought her mind back to the job at hand today; she was not quite finished yet. She had been tasked to leak out some information that would hopefully add credence to a theory that Dennis would be bandying about on those horrid rafts to the murderous Tong people. According to Crazy Harry, Dennis was doing fine without their help but the odd snippet from another source was always a bloody good clincher. She liked Crazy Harry and tended to regard him as a kind of uncle figure; as for Dennis, well, he was the most loveable rascal she had ever met.

Fiona had finished her shower and was getting dressed, she listened as Simon whistled 'Land of Hope and Glory' whilst he was making tea. 'That's bloody rich coming from a traitor,' she murmured as her mind turned back to an hour earlier. When Simon had collapsed beside her after his fourth bestial performance she knew that he had exhausted himself for the day. Fiona had resisted the impulse to rush away and cleanse herself; instead, she had endured another twenty minutes pretending to doze off at first, then fondling Simon under the pretence of wanting him again she let drop that the six little sampans full of lovely gold bars were going to terminate their journey at a little village called Kampong Jempol. 'It's on the north bank of the river only eight miles from that Paku town,' she had said, 'you know, the place where I told you that they'll be resting, remember?'

'Ah yes!' answered Simon scratching his head. Fiona gave up her attempts to get him aroused. 'You mean Kampong Lubok Paku?' he asked.

'Oh Simon dear, I knew you'd get it right.'

With that Simon lost all interest in her and ran off stark naked to his study. It was then that Fiona had been able to escape to the cold, but ever so refreshing shower. But she still had more misinformation to plant in the numbskull's minuscule brain, and this one was for Tom Nobles. He had asked Fiona to cast some doubt in Simon's mind regarding the mysterious man that he was reporting back to, to promote a feeling of distrust especially concerning any payment he thought was forthcoming. 'Don't overdo it,' Tom had said, 'just a subtle hint will do for a start.'

Fiona joined Simon in the lounge, he had stopped whistling thank God and she accepted a cup of tea from him and sat down. He was attired in only a sarong and a pair of flip-flops, still unwashed he smelt strongly of sex. The scent that before would have excited her now made her want to dash off to the shower again but she held herself in check and said sweetly, 'Thank you darling.'

'You were terrific Fiona dear,' he answered, flashing a hairy thigh and winking at her lewdly.

'I do try,' she laughed and drank some tea. They chattered away for a bit before Fiona plucked up enough courage to say,

'Simon my love, you are going to get some of these gold bars aren't you?'

'Fiona, what a preposterous idea, of course not, why do you ask?'

'Ask? You said we'd get rich. You promised to take me away from my horrid husband. Now you've changed your mind and have the bloody cheek to enquire why I'm asking!' She took a sip of tea with trembling hands. *My god,* she thought, *I ought to get another Oscar for this.* Simon looked positively aghast, he had not the slightest clue that he was now the one being used, he really felt genuine concern at her look of despair. Actually, he could not for the life of him remember the point in time when they had first started to talk openly about matters pertaining to the gold shipment, it just sort of happened. *Top secret information or not, so strong,* thought the vain fool, *was their love for one another that it transcended such mundane things as the Official Secrets Act.*

Looking to reassure her he cried, 'But Fiona! Of course we'll get some money, heaps of it. All I meant to say was that it wouldn't be in the form of actual gold ingots, can't you see that my love?'

Fiona breathed a sigh of relief. 'Oh Simon,' she said meekly.

'That's all right, stop worrying now, it'll all be over soon.'

Fiona smiled. 'Of course darling, it's just that I've put my mind on leaving that brute forever and I'd hate for anything to go wrong.'

'Nothing can go wrong Fiona, we've done our bit.'

'I know darling, but people do get greedy.' Fiona could see by the expression on Simon's face that the point had gotten home. She had planted the seed.

★

Fred followed the fresh tracks that must have been made by the very last man to walk this final approach route to the very well hidden terrorist HQ, a hideout that had remained secret for seven years despite intensive patrols by the British Army. Both the ground spoor and the signposts were leading him across the grain of the country, roller coasting him along with an acute left-handed slant. Fred was quite aware that he was no longer traversing the side of the main ridgeline but was slowly changing direction from his westerly course and gradually coming around to a southerly one to coincide with another spur running off the ridge. Now it was turning even more to bring his bearing more or less south-easterly.

On the map the top part of the spur was bow shaped and that was the contour that Fred was navigating to bring the patrol around in a left-handed curve. The spur naturally led down off the mountain and traversing the side of it did not alter that fact, but Fred began to notice that the enemy tracks were veering lower than the actual gradient of the feature, and it was not because of a lazy bias either. It was obvious to Fred that the tracks were taking them down into a ravine or gully, he stopped to check his bearing and look at his map. His present compass course made it quite clear that he was now heading dead southeast long before the spur line conformed to that bearing. He was tapping a spot on his map with a twig when Chalky whispered over his shoulder, 'That's the western headwater of the Sungei Mentiga, Fred my boy, if you don't find that bloody camp along there somewhere I'll curry my own crap and eat it!'

Encouraged by this unquestionable faith in his ability, Fred resumed the hunt sniffing his way through the undergrowth like a bloodhound. The headwater that Chalky had referred to was a thin blue line on the map that should materialise on the ground as a stream about 200 yards in front of him and to his left. The scout was finding it difficult to cope with the steep incline, balance being the biggest problem again.

Keeping weapons constantly in the ready position was well nigh impossible due to the fact that two pairs of hands seemed to be the minimum required to make any form of dignified progress. One of the lesser-known lores of the regiment was that rifle or sub-machine gun slings were taboo. SAS soldiers are required to carry their weapons with two hands in the alert position whenever humanly possible. Naturally it is acceptable to shift a weapon from one hand to another when negotiating obstacles and difficult terrain. On long non-tactical marches it is permissible to adopt a one-handed carrying hold, the trail arms of the light infantry and rifle regiments being one of the more popular. But the order 'Sling Arms' or 'March at Ease' is never given in the regiment.

The descent into the headwater of the Sungei Mentiga was now so treacherous that far from being at the ready, weapons were being used more like ski poles to keep the hard-pressed SAS men steady from one tree to another. Vegetation was lush with huge palm leaves and ferns blocking the way, some of them were as hard as iron with sharp leaves that could easily cut the unwary and bad tempered. They were noisy too when mishandled, passage through these beautiful dark green plants was a real test of patience. Giant water vines hung down to shoulder height threatening to throttle the slipping and sliding SAS men.

But water from this source is absolute nectar; the vines are soft and easily cut with one swipe of a parang. To obtain water from a vine it is necessary to cut out a complete section and then quickly hold it up over one's mouth or a container, once tasted it will never be forgotten but any dallying about after the two cuts have been made will result in all the water pouring out of the vine onto the ground.

Without immediately becoming aware of it, Fred found that he had high ground on either side of him; his compass indicated that he was now facing due south, he paused to take stock. The ground under his feet was rocky and covered in moss. The tree trunks up to head height were thick with an orange fungal type growth that resembled sideways growing toadstools. The place stank of rotting dampness and even the prolific palms were not growing where Fred now trod, instead, they flourished just above the fungus and hung down umbrella-like overhead. Although visibility straight ahead had improved since Fred had entered this obvious watercourse and it made for easier going, he knew that come the rain the gully would be a dangerous place to be caught in. He moved down the as of yet dry headwater of the Sungei Mentiga, as he knew that other SAS patrols miles to the south of him would be working their way up a very wet part of the river. The gully got wider and a definite waterline was now clearly visible. At one point Fred lost sight of the right-hand bank but after a few paces it reappeared, then he stopped suddenly as an ice-cold feeling came over him. He had only experienced this sensation twice before, once when the patrol had passed close by the CT water party back at Bukit Chermingat and again but to a greater degree immediately prior to the contact at the big tree. It was that same sixth sense that had made him bring his shotgun up into a firing position seconds before he had seen the terrorist, the warning that had given him the edge and kept him alive whilst his adversary had perished. He recognised that feeling for what it was now as it held him in its grip, a grip so strong and certain that it was impossible to ignore. Yet he also knew instinctively that there was no immediate threat to him or his mates; but onto something he surely knew he was. Chalky, forever the mind-reader, crept up to Fred's position as if walking on air. 'What have you found this time O Enlightened One?' he whispered.

'I don't know yet but it's in the air, I can smell it,' Fred replied looking up at the solid green jungle roof.

'Well, if you must go with Allah be bloody careful,' advised Chalky with a mischievous grin as he indicated that the all-seeing, all-knowing scout should set forth on his quest for deliverance.

Fred's heart was thumping like a drum and his temples were throbbing, the sounds within his chest and head threatened to cancel out even the constant symphony of the wildlife creatures, the jungle norm and his natural early warning system. His hands were tingling with anticipation as he strove to identify the sign that his inner being was telling him was there to find. *Come on,* he thought, *look, look, look.* Fred was almost crying with exasperation as he practically advanced on all fours in his eagerness to pick up a clue dreading that all this might be nothing but a false hope, another brick wall that is so much part of jungle warfare. His mind and body, not to mention his soul were numb with the effort of concentrating on his task and he was fast coming to the end of his tether. At his wits' end, he was about to seek help from that old wizard of the wilds Chalky when he had delivered unto him a sign. But it was not Fred's eyes that produced the goods – it was his ears. For amidst the background clatter of the jungle he could hear the soft musical sound of trickling water; he was puzzled, where could the sound be coming from? He studied the dry bank to no avail, he put his ear to the ground in order to ascertain if he was hearing an underground stream but came up with nothing. Fred looked up and cocked his head to one side listening intently, yes, the sound did seem to be coming from above.

But that's ridiculous, he thought looking down again. A slight movement caught his eye, a very minute flash of light near the jungle floor. He fixed his eyes on the spot and waited. 'Ah,' he whispered to himself, 'there it is again.' What Fred had seen was a drop of water landing on the edge of a leaf causing a springing movement that had reflected off the droplet. He moved forward and stood under the spot looking up knowing full well that the water could not possibly be from the last rainfall. For a fleeting moment he had a crazy vision of a baboon having a slash all over him. *This place in driving me nuts,* he thought as a drop of water hit him in his left eye. He cleared his eye with a finger and tasted the liquid, definitely not monkey water, he judged. 'But where the bloody hell is it coming from?' he asked himself once again. Fred reached up and moved aside some overhanging palm and fern leaves, in the gloom of the thick vegetation that covered the source of the Sungei Mentiga like a second jungle canopy he could see nothing untoward, not at first anyway. Then it dawned on him that the picture before his eyes was not quite right, there was a certain amount of symmetry about it and in this very unsymmetrical environment that spelt out interference by man. Something above Fred's head had been rearranged and he soon detected a dark shadow about eight inches wide that was spanning the gully diagonally as straight as a die. *Definitely man-made,* guessed the jubilant scout. He took off his pack and stood on it, then using his shotgun he poked at the shadow and was immediately rewarded by the sound of the muzzle making contact with solid wood. In addition to that he disturbed whatever it was to such an extent that water sloshed down all over his head.

'Well I'll be blowed,' he murmured nearly falling off his pack and discharging his shotgun, so excited was he. Disaster was averted by the steadying grip of Chalky's hand on Fred's shoulder, that man having performed another of his famous silent approaches. 'You'll blow yourself to kingdom come if you fire it in that condition,' he admonished pointing at Fred's weapon and the water pouring out of the barrel in particular.

'I've found water,' Fred almost blurted out in frustration.

'Well I'm not completely blind,' retorted Chalky with a deadpan expression, 'do tell me more O Illustrious Diviner.'

'It's an aqueduct,' insisted Fred, 'they're using a bloody aqueduct to get their water supply.'

Chalky tried to look suitably aghast but could not control his facial expression any longer, so following Fred's example he too looked up. Shaking with bubbling mirth he whispered, 'All right son, I promise I'll never take the piss out of Allah again.'

The feeling of elation emanating from the young scout and now the wily old patrol commander was contagious; Bob and Worm came forward of their own accord to share in the moment of triumph, for they sensed that the patrol had cracked it. For the second time on this operation Fred had located an enemy water point and if the carefully chosen site and high standard of camouflage was anything to go by, this one was being used by a very important enemy group indeed. The entire patrol were fully aware that they must be virtually sitting on the enemy's doorstep, but now Chalky needed confirmation so he asked Fred to indicate to him the configuration of the overhead water channel. Once Chalky's eyes had been pointed in the right direction he found no difficulty in following the dark outline of the aqueduct as it emerged out from the bank on his right-hand side to pass overhead at a sixty degree angle to disappear from view over the top of the left bank, a total span of about fifty yards. Water obviously flows downhill, so Chalky surmised that the source of this particular water supply must be from the high ground that lay behind the patrol somewhere over the right-hand bank.

He was about to announce his next plan of action when Fred had an inspiration. 'I've got it,' he stated.

'I know son, it happens to us all at first but it'll soon wear off, you'll see, besides, Allah is with you.'

Fred looked at him and thought, *Does nothing ever faze this man?* The scout pointed back towards the way they had come. 'Well, bloody Allah is telling me to backtrack to where I lost sight of the right bank, and if that's not another gully leading to the source of supply for this contraption,' he pointed upwards, 'then I'll forsake religion forever.'

Chalky winced and said, 'I'll pray to His Magnificence for your forgiveness O Arseless Blasphemer, but in the meantime this is what we'll do.'

Chalky had not lost sight of the fact that the gully was still the approach route to the suspected enemy camp, and as the fresh tracks indicated, was still in use. An enemy patrol might well be following them, or one could be on its way outward bound from the camp at this very moment. To base the patrol in the gully for the forthcoming reconnaissance would be to risk certain detection leading to another contact and whichever way the ensuing fight went it would compromise the entire operation. No, the SAS patrol must melt away into the jungle out of the gully, he knew that he could follow the enemy tracks down it until they turned off left to lead them to the camp but Chalky decided to go for the aqueduct, it was like an arrow pointing the way. First though, he would search for the source. He ordered the patrol to break track to the right and the four men picked their way out of the gully; any carelessness here and the patrol might well end up being the hunted. Once at ground level again, so to speak, the patrol turned right in the opposite direction to which they had been advancing down the gully, they had already reversed their order of march so that Fred was still in the lead as scout. He soon located the spot where the aqueduct commenced spanning the gully, and as he had suspected, it was made out of overlapping sections of bamboo that had been split down the middle to form channels. The sections had been covered in attap palm leaves to provide camouflage from above and to prevent falling jungle debris from clogging up the waterway. Fred continued with the honour of following the course of his discovery and found it to be a comparatively easy chore and after only forty yards or so the channel turned markedly to the left and the incline became steeper.

Fred considered the bend in the aqueduct. *That would have been on my right coming down the gully,* he thought, *about the same place that I lost sight of the bank, this must be another smaller gully.* The gradient became even steeper and rocks littered the ground, some of them were enormous and were covered in vines that resembled blood vessels lining a wizened, ageing face, it was dark, dank and bloody spooky as well. Here and there Fred spotted signs of enemy activity suggesting that the precious water supply route was being patrolled but not very frequently. They probably only come out in response to a breakdown in the system, he guessed, fallen trees and suchlike. Fred had reached an obstacle in the form of an almost vertical cliff face with one giant step in it at head height. Twenty yards before the cliff, the aqueduct had been elevated off the ground to rest on the step. The end section of the bamboo channel had been jammed into a crack in the rock from which spewed forth a continuous flow of water that in turn gushed along the wooden watercourse.

Fred took off his Bergen and climbed up to the step, he could not stand on it because it was in fact a rock pool some eight feet wide and at least six feet deep. Water was also being forced into the pool from an underground source and was bubbling away like a witch's cauldron. Fred looked at the pool and the cut bamboo arrangement with complete amazement and a considerable amount of admiration. *You've got to take your hat off to these bastards,* he thought, *it's nothing less than ingenious.* He thought about the gully where one would naturally search for a water point. He grinned wryly when he thought of how by night it would be a raging torrent and all sign of enemy activity made during the day would have been washed away, and no amount of reconnaissance would ever detect a water point on its banks. Why? Because the crafty sods had a twenty-four hour supply on tap running overhead and had no need to go anywhere near a river to collect it.

It was a million to one chance that anyone should stumble across that particular fifty yard span of camouflaged bamboo. But then, it was not every day that the guerrilla army came up against the SAS in the form of Fred; and Allah of course.

★

Dennis woke up on the morning of 18 September decidedly under the weather and definitely feeling the strain. Not because of his undercover work for the British, which the lord only knows was dangerous enough, but because of the disorientating effect of the local brew and the strength sapping activities of her that shall be nameless but was the headman's daughter of fourteen stones and was of a dubious vintage. It was now decision time; Dennis had made up his mind that the expedition would depart from Kampong Chenor that very morning. Extricating himself from the Michelin tyre-like folds of flesh he made a mad dash for the safety boat and his own private supply of arrack. Looking around furtively in case he was being spied upon he took a hefty swig from the one-gallon container and gasped with pleasure, 'A decent dram at last!' There was nothing wrong with the local brew normally; it was simply the fact that his band of Tong thugs liked the stuff so much that they had drunk the well dry. For the past day everyone had resorted to drinking unfermented Tuak that packed a kick like a mule, tasted bloody horrible and gave everybody the shits. 'Ah yes,' muttered Dennis taking another drop of the hard stuff, 'it's time to move on all right.' Dennis was also getting a guilt complex over Petal and thought to himself, *Well, at least none of these Tong bastards will live to tell the tale, the only way Petal will find out is if I take home a dose of the clap, an occupational hazard for soldiers the world over.*

Having imbibed his morning livener Dennis was once more ready to don the mantle of the ruthless mercenary hell-bent on his quest for fame, glory and money. It took over an hour to wrest the blissful Tong rafters from their various places of comfort and pleasure but by ten in the morning Shu Ling had assembled the crews and put them to work making the rafts ready for the next stage of the journey. Dennis gathered everyone around the beached safety boat to give them a speech, thanking the headman and his flock for their hospitality. Then especially for the benefit of the villagers he addressed the members of the expedition, reminding them that they still had a long way to go but he felt confident that they would all make it safely to Pecan. 'Bon Voyage!' he shouted, and with some assistance from the villagers launched the safety boat.

The rafts cast off at 11.00 hrs to the sound of cheers from those ashore, the good people of Kampong Chenor had done them proud and there were more than a few tears of sadness being shed amongst the throng of waving inhabitants. But soon the rafts were gone and the jolly Malay villagers settled back into their idyllic way of life.

The rafts did not go far. The fleet navigated its way around the first sandbank with commendable efficiency and drifted serenely downriver for three miles passing Kampong Pesagi at noon, one thousand yards further on they encountered another huge sandbank that took up half the width of the river. Dennis led the rafts through the right-hand channel and when they were all well out of sight of the village he directed them to beach onto the right bank, the rafts were pushed and pulled under the overhanging trees and other foliage, in no time at all the entire expedition were invisible from the river; the holiday was over for these still half-dazed Tong men.

Through Shu Ling, Dennis issued his first operational orders for the forthcoming ambush. The twenty-man force was to thoroughly clean all weapons and prepare their personal equipment for action. On the morrow they would begin intensive training in jungle ambush techniques and commence rehearsals. Most of the men had opted to sleep ashore and Dennis spent the afternoon teaching them how to erect shelters and generally live in the jungle. He was a mine of information and the tough Chinese cut-throats took to him greatly. They liked his philosophic outlook when he said to them, 'An amateur can survive here in the forest, but it takes a professional to do it in comfort. Work with the place, like it even, and you will be a winner.'

By last light the Tong men were as ready as they would ever be and were eager to start training. Dennis retired to his base aboard the safety boat to guard the radio and his precious, bottomless container of arrack.

Whilst enjoying a nightcap of at least a pint of the potent white spirit he thought about the other half of the deception plan, Clancy Deane. He and the real ambush party should be in position by now, or bloody close to it. They, Dennis realised, were only a mere eight miles away downriver and things were getting pretty damned close. Of course, the whole sodding thing was dependant on those mad SAS blokes finding the enemy camp, if the buggers did manage to pull that off then the top brass would be quids in. They would get their precious time in which they could plan, prepare and play chess with the Commonwealth Brigade; there would be Brits, Aussies, Kiwis and the Gurkhas. The lot of them would be on the move and by the time that Kim Bok's gold train was safely in the CT camp, and the Gurkha riflemen that were following him had closed the trap behind his column, most of the attacking force would be in position. Dennis knew that he was required to lead the Tong men into the SBS ambush at the precise moment that the attack was to commence, in other words he was to precipitate the action. But therein lay a problem. Dennis knew in his bones that the SAS would produce the goods, he was confident that the SBS would reach the ambush position on time. The big question was how were the commandos going to inform him of what time he should lead the doomed force of criminals to their deaths? He took a swig and did some mental arithmetic. Assuming that the SAS had found the camp today, the eighteenth, they would want at least a day to mount a close reconnaissance operation and another two in order to complete the job using other SAS patrols that by then would have arrived on the scene.

'That takes us up to the twenty-first,' he mused. He further deliberated that during the period when information from the SAS patrols would be pouring in over the radio time would be saved by moving the cordon and stop troops close to Gunong Chini into an assembly area. If Crazy Harry's theory was correct and the camp was indeed near the mountain, Dennis envisaged the Commonwealth Brigade being inserted via Bukit Bertangga and the main Gunong Chini ridgeline. To get there the three thousand troops would have to be ferried to various road heads before beginning the long march in.

'If they're already on the move,' he muttered to the container of arrack, 'they won't get up onto that bloody great hill until at least the twenty-third. Now add two or three days for the final stages of the deployment and I'm left with the twenty-sixth or twenty-seventh.' He gulped down a final mouthful of his gut-varnish and sighed, 'Providing that the bloody minded elephants and those stubborn mules co-operate and Kim Bok actually does get there then good old H-hour should be on one of those days'.

Dennis did not subject the Tong men to an early start mainly because it would have interfered with his early morning tipple, besides, the answer to his sums of the previous night equalled plenty of time. To start the working day off he had long poles cut that were then wedged between the forks of standing trees to form improvised benches for the men to sit on. A little uncomfortable maybe but it kept the Tong arses dry and gave Dennis their undivided attention. His makeshift lecture area occupied three sides of a square the centre of which had been scraped clear of leaves. Ferns, palms and saplings had been pulled up, the easiest way to remove such plants from the damp earth. Swiping at them with a Parang is a total waste of time and effort, it is noisy, merely bends the plants over in most cases, leaves sharp roots poking out of the ground in others and invariably frustrates the would be lumberjacks to the point of suicidal distraction. Using four thin saplings as legs and two more as side supports Dennis fashioned a five foot high table-like structure, topping it with a length of platted attap leaf the whole formed a reasonable lectern. He toyed with the idea of placing a square of bark on top of his head as a mortarboard but let the moment pass, he was not that academically minded.

Dennis faced his assembled pupils to commence his lecture on the subject of ambushes. Because of the expert advice he had given them during the building of the rafts, his natural ability to organise and his helpfulness when making camp the night before, he had found a place in the hearts of these hard men. His recent demonstration of constructing the lectern in just five minutes flat had simply amazed them. As they looked around at this classroom in the wilds their eyes said it all; without uttering a single word as yet in this his first lecture, Dennis knew that he had them eating out of his hand.

'I first became familiar with the word ambush,' he opened with, 'watching cowboy films when I was a little boy. I used to visit the local flea pit, cinema to you, every Saturday morning and every western film I ever saw had an ambush in it, sometimes even two or three.' He paused to let Shu Ling translate, wishing that he had his container of arrack to hand. 'In military life,' he continued, 'the word ambush crops up in whatever field of operations a soldier may find himself involved in. Whether it be in internal security duties, an emergency such as we have here in Malaya, a limited war or a full scale one; you can be bloody sure that an ambush will rear its ugly head to plague the lives of commanders and their men alike. If you are not actually involved in laying an ambush you might well be walking into one; the thought of an ambush in always there, ever present like the air all around you.' Dennis wiped his brow. Shu Ling rattled away in Cantonese and the other Tong men looked about uneasily. Dennis resumed, 'Ambushes can vary in size from a single sniper to thousands of men. Let me give you a couple of examples of the latter kind.

'During the first Afghan war a ten-thousand strong British Army column marched out of India to relieve the besieged garrison at Jelalabad, a fort in Afghanistan, only one man got through and he was a doctor. The rest were slaughtered by fierce Afghan tribesmen from a position of ambush sited on the high sides of the Khyber Pass.

'In more recent times and not too far from here in Indo-China another great ambush took place. A French Army mobile brigade known as a Force Mobile was ambushed by the Viet Min, the entire five-mile-long French convoy was annihilated. The Viet Min melted into the jungle and inflicted death and destruction on a three-mile-long convoy of French troops forty-eight hours later, nearly a hundred miles away from the first incident. It was a stupendous feat of organisation and endurance, especially by men that were existing on a handful of rice a day.

'In guerrilla warfare the ambush really comes into its own. Most of the Chinese Communists Terrorists that are fighting the British Army today once belonged to the Chinese 8th Route Army, and later the Malay Peoples Anti Japanese Army. The Japanese were a formidable foe and were regarded as unbeatable in jungle warfare; they were much feared by all those who came up against them. But you Chinese,' he pointed at his enthralled audience, 'ambushed them at every turn and gave the invincible Japanese a bloody nose.'

Once translated his last statement brought huge smiles to the Tong men's faces, and Dennis was aware then that they would follow his orders come what may. But he pressed home the point by saying, 'You might well ask why I am labouring the subject, why do I go on about the word ambush so? Because an ambush is the most complex military operation in the book, the written orders alone are the longest, so detailed and thorough must be the plans. It is a mind-boggling challenge and we are going to mount a perfect bloody example. Now the trap that we are going to set is only twenty men strong but the details involved will be the same as if it were to be hundreds. The only way to get it right is to live it, breath it, sleep with and bloody dream about it.' Dennis let them chatter away whilst he lay some bits of wood, string and other odd items of kit on the ground, the end result was a rough model of the ambush position. He got their attention once more and explained that until he had received news from Kuantan regarding how much further upriver the gold was going to be transported he could not tell them exactly where he was going to lay the ambush. But of one thing he was sure, the trap would be sprung from the north bank of the river, and no matter where the actual ambush was sited the plan would be the same. Dennis then explained that the normal aim of an ambush was to totally destroy anyone or anything caught in the killing ground. On this particular ambush, the mission was to kill the enemy but to capture the six sampans and the precious cargo intact. 'Because of that factor,' Dennis had said, 'the ambush will consist of two groups. A killer group of ten men and an equal force deployed downriver as a stop group, in addition to killing any escapees the stop group were to recover the unmanned sampans.'

A pause followed and Shu Ling did his bit. Then in answer to their unspoken question Dennis continued. 'I know, I know, the ten best rifle shots are to comprise the killer group.' He looked at Shu Ling. 'You pick them but don't include yourself as I want you to be in charge of the recovery party. Remember, the gold is the all important thing here.'

Shu Ling seemed disappointed but said, 'Okay by me, I pick now.' He soon selected the required marksmen and rearranged the seating plan so that the men sat in their respective groups; eagerly they waited for Dennis to enlighten them. 'Before we get bogged down with details I'll give you the general idea as I see things happening.

'First of all we'll move from here downriver to a point one mile this side of the chosen ambush position. We'll go on the rafts and dump them there, hopefully for good. From there the two groups, less Shu Ling and one man from the stop group who will crew the safety boat, will march to the ambush area. Once there the killer group commanded by myself will set up the actual ambush whilst the stop group proceed down the riverbank for a further five hundred yards. The safety boat that will have maintained visual contact with the stops will secure a rope to a tree on the opposite bank,' Dennis looked at Shu Ling. 'You'll then pay out the rope and pass the end to the stop group who are to secure it to another tree; it is important that the rope has plenty of slack in it. When that task is completed Shu Ling and the other man are to join the stop group having concealed the safety boat.'

Dennis paused to let Shu Ling explain in Cantonese. The Tong men were really interested now and leaned forward in eager anticipation.

The old soldier picked up a sapling and using it as a pointer tapped two lengths of rope that were laid out on the ground in parallel lines. 'These,' he announced, 'represent the river. The six bits of wood positioned between them are the sampans, the piece of string lying across the river is Shu Ling's rope that is anchored to each side of the riverbank. Now imagine that the sampans have crossed the slack rope spanning the river and are now in the killing ground. The ambush will be sprung by a single shot fired by me.' He looked at the designated riflemen, 'And you lot are to follow my example and kill all the enemy with well-aimed shots, trying your hardest not to sink the bloody boats.' Dennis rearranged the bits of wood so that they were no longer lying in line astern. 'Immediately that we open fire, the terrorist will begin to react, some will have been hit, others will attempt to return fire or jump overboard. Whatever they do,' he flicked the sticks with his pointer, 'the sampans will lose way, career out of control and drift downriver.' His pointer now moved to the string. 'But this rope that will have been pulled taught as soon as the ambush has been sprung will help to stop them. Half of the stop group are to hang on to this rope whilst the others look out for survivors and kill them. Also, Shu Ling will launch the safety boat and help with the recovery of the sampans. I will bring the killer group down to the rope and help out. Once we have the gold safely in our hands we'll board the vessels and make for Kampong Lubok Paku, where we hope your Tong masters will have us picked up. Well lads,' he concluded, 'that's the outline plan, the next stage is some individual training in camouflage and concealment techniques. But first we'll have a break.'

As Shu Ling accompanied Dennis to the safety boat he said, 'They like it boss.'

During the break Shu Ling spoke to his Kuantan HQ on the radio. As Dennis watched the criminal's eyes got wider and wider and he started to shake with excitement and could hardly wait to impart the news. Offering him the arrack the mercenary said, 'Here, take a swig for Christ's sake.' Shu Ling accepted the drink and in between all the coughing and spluttering it caused he managed to spit out that Kampong Jempol was to be the final destination of the six gold carrying sampans, and that Australian troops had been seen debussing from transport ten miles north of the village on the Maran road. 'But the sampans have not moved yet, they'll let us know when they do,' he finished.

Dennis thought, *that dear girl is really working overtime.* He gulped down a last mouthful of arrack and slapped Shu Ling on the back. 'Come on, let's lick your men into shape.' But under his breath he muttered, 'More like let's lead the lambs to the slaughter.'

Chapter Thirteen

Nothing on earth could have dampened the spirits of the SAS patrol that had unquestionably found a direct indicator that pointed the way to the very heart of Chinese Communist power in Malaya. All these men had to do now was follow the aqueduct straight to the enemy camp, on the face of it an easy enough task for SAS soldiers, in reality it was anything but. Not one to leave anything to chance, Chalky made an observation. 'As well camouflaged as this little gem is,' he'd expounded, 'nobody, not even a blind man could walk past that contraption without being aware of it. Why hasn't someone found this place before now?' He decided to check out the ground to the west, north and east of the rock pool and after one hour of patrolling he had his answer. The jungle immediately around this secret place was so thick that it would deter the most diligent of searchers, most would simply find a way around the obstacle and bypass the water source. The same conditions existed to the south, east and west of the gully to a point well past the aqueduct; the terrorists themselves must have found the rock pool by pure chance. Unless someone was sent into the area specifically to penetrate the obstacle no one in their right mind would attempt to navigate their way through the impenetrable wall of jungle that hid the whole ingenious affair. Fred had found it by luck; he had heard the water and saw it dripping because the aqueduct was sagging in mid-span causing the water to surge and overflow, even so, it was a brilliant example of an inquisitive mind and phenomenal use of the senses.

The patrol had finished up crossing the gully at the western end of the span, the time being 16.00 hrs Chalky judged that there was no safer place to spend the night so he called a halt. He reasoned that the enemy would not even consider that the British would have the audacity to camp right on top of their precious bloody aqueduct. Also, in the unlikely event that the CTs themselves might be stupid enough to go burrowing through the vegetation barrier this late in the day, then the SAS men would get ample warning of their approach from the racket that they were bound to kick up. 'In any case,' he had concluded gravely, 'what's the sodding use of having a motto like "Who Dares Wins" if you don't dare now and again?'

The next day, the eighteenth, at about the same time that Dennis had made his mad dash for the arrack pot, Fred began a thorough investigation of the thicket in the immediate area of the bamboo span across the gully. His eagle eyes had spotted a slight change of colour in the thick undergrowth at ground level, a lightening of the density about the width of a man's body. He got down on all fours and probed about in the area with his hand to find that after only a depth of six inches the foliage had been removed, he had found a secret entrance. Fred poked his head into the leafy screen and found himself peering along a cleared tunnel through the dense thicket running away at a forty-five degree angle for ten yards. He withdrew his head and looked up at Chalky, the old sweat had already guessed what Fred had found so he pointed at the scout and commanded, 'Begone mole, lead us through the bloody hole!'

Fred advanced on his hands and knees with his Bergen hanging over to one side making life a bloody misery. At the end of the ten yard stretch the maze-like way turned right for a similar distance and the tunnel came to an end. Fred probed again and sure enough six inches into the green wall he broke through the screen into near normal jungle. He stood up and moved to one side in order to let the others through, the patrol spread out and Chalky took stock of the situation. The rainwater that had literally gushed through the gully during the night's downpour had disappeared completely and not even the small trickle of water passing along the bamboo channel could be heard. Apart from the daily heaven-sent addition the volume of water coursing through the artificial water supply system was not greatly affected, it not being influenced by topographical contours such as the gully. The access tunnel that the patrol had just crawled through had not followed the course of the aqueduct, which ran parallel with the general line of the thicket and was now lost from view. Chalky had to locate the spot where the aqueduct emerged from the thick cover, it would be interesting to see how the bandits had coped with that particular problem. He whispered into Fred's ear, 'Find the end of this thicket O Master Plumber and tell us where the water goes.'

Fred prepared to advance; he was facing south in line with the path of the gully, visibility directly to his front, behind him and to the left was three yards but on his right-hand, or the gully side, it was like a solid green wall. He kept this unpleasant obstacle at one yard distant, probing any irregularity in it until he was forced back out again. In this manner he made slow progress for an hour with the ground falling away in front of him at a forty-five degree angle, then suddenly he came to the southern extremity of the thicket. Turning right to follow its edge he soon arrived at the gully that now lay fully exposed for all to see; but of the aqueduct there was no sign.

'I suppose,' suggested Chalky who had been summoned forth by the scout, 'that we ought to consult with Allah once more.' He went to work with his map and protractor. 'Firstly lad,' he said kindly to Fred, 'is that the bastards would not have gone to all that trouble for nothing, the conduit must be around here somewhere. Fact, we have been marching downhill for an hour. Fact, the conduit does not appear to be here. Fact, unless the CTs have taken to sapping and mining, the bloody thing must be above our heads once again. Answer, it's that Allah bloke again!' Chalky tapped his map thoughtfully with a finger. 'If they had taken the aqueduct aloft back there at the tunnel I estimate that it would be at least a hundred feet that way,' he pointed upwards.

'That's out of the question,' butted in Fred, 'they'd want to maintain it and at that height it would be a bloody joke.'

Chalky smiled and said, 'Right on lad. Now you being six feet two inches tall with a young man's spring in your step you should be able to jump up in the air and bang your bloody head on the thing.'

Fred began to probe the jungle canopy with his shotgun once more. 'Use the butt end this time,' advised Chalky, 'and mind you don't shoot yourself in the bloody swede.' After ten minutes he was rewarded by a hollow thunk and Fred knew that he had found his divine aqueduct again, now that it had been physically located and identified it would be fairly easy to keep it in sight.

'The thing is,' observed Chalky, 'they would avoid having any bends in the thing, it's my guess that the aqueduct will run as straight as an arrow towards the camp.' He did some more calculations on his map first orientating it with the overhead waterway, when finished he gathered the patrol in and gave them his findings. 'Working on the assumption that water flows only downhill and that the CTs would have laid the aqueduct in the straightest possible line I have worked out where it will terminate. If I'm right, the aqueduct will continue to carry water in a westerly direction until it meets the high ground forming the next spur running off Gunong Chini. There, not even with Allah's help will it be able to run uphill, and that point I'm guessing is the centre of the enemy camp.' He emphasised his theory by pointing to the spot on his map with a twig. Each man then consulted his own map and slowly they all formed the same opinion as their leader. Chalky had a very serious expression on his face now. 'My plotting puts the camp at no more that a thousand yards away from here, knowing the importance of the place, I reckon that they'll have at least 200 guerrillas defending it.' He paused and when he spoke again it was with emotional pride. 'We'll break track here and dump the Bergens. The pussyfooting about is over, let's go and find that bloody camp for Caesar!'

Whenever Fred removed his 80 lb Bergen rucksack from his back his shoulders seemed to spring forward of their own accord so light did they feel. Thus liberated and with their packs hidden behind them the patrol rejoined the axis of advance under the aqueduct and proceeded to stealthily probe forward in search of the foe.

The first thing that Fred found was a signpost; the aqueduct overhead was being marked on the ground, so to speak, in a similar manner to the approach route. One hundred yards further on he found signs of enemy activity at the base of a tree, it was obvious that someone had climbed up the lower branches probably to repair a damaged section of the bamboo channel. These occurrences seemed to have been repeated five times in the space of 300 yards. Then at an estimated distance of 400 yards from the end of the aqueduct Fred struck gold, it made life more difficult but gold it was.

What Fred had found were enemy tracks, dozens of them, probably made by daily clearing patrols coming out from the camp on a regular basis over a very long period of time, it was like a leafy path through an English wood. To follow this trail any further would result in a certain contact and that, to put it mildly, would drop everyone in the shit. Fred turned around and covered his face with one hand fingers outspread, and then he pointed to the left-hand side of the track. In a split second the entire patrol had broken track to the left and was ready to ambush any enemy patrol that might venture along it, or remain concealed until they had passed by.

The signal that Fred had given was 'Immediate Ambush' but Chalky had also noticed the ground spoor guessing that Fred was being cautious. Chalky moved up to the scout and gave him the thumbs up sign, the equivalent of a pat on the back. Next he made a walking motion with his hand and followed that by pointing both index fingers straight up in the air before flicking an outspread hand in front of Fred's face twice, finally he tapped his left breast pocket. The signals took but a second but the scout got the message, in the order that they were given Fred was to advance parallel to the track at a distance of ten yards. Chalky would navigate the scout; he had tapped his left breast pocket because that is where he kept his compass. Fred found no more sign as they crept forward at less than 200 yards an hour, then he heard a sound and froze. Very slowly he turned around and gave the silent field signal for extended line to Chalky who passed it back and so on. As if by magic Chalky arrived in line with Fred and to his right, with Bob and Worm to the right of him. They all sensed that they were now pretty close to the objective and bloody hairy was the only way to describe that feeling. Should they come under fire from the front they were in an excellent position to defend themselves putting Chalky in a good position for command and control. Single file was the ideal formation to adopt for moving through the jungle but it did have its drawbacks. In this instance being so close to an enemy position it was quite conceivable that they might run into a machine gun nest. The cone of fire from such a weapon would encompass the complete

315

depth of a four-man patrol advancing in single file; in other words, one bloody good burst would mean curtains for them all. But as they were now in an extended line, any machine gunners, or anyone else for that matter, would be engaging four separate targets requiring a positive change of aim to fire at each one. It was to Fred's credit that on being alerted by some sound or other he had seen fit to instigate the change in formation. Chalky looked at Fred, his eyes begging for inspiration because he had so far heard nothing. Fred covered his mouth with a hand, Chalky acknowledged that he understood that his scout had heard a cough. That sort of noise did not carry very far in the jungle so it was enough to set the old campaigner's nerves tingling. *Bloody hell,* he thought.

On moving up he had noticed that Fred had adopted the kneeling position so he had followed suit, as had Bob and Worm; he now thought carefully before ordering the advance. If he ordered the men to adopt the lying position every time that they stopped to take cover the bloody racket that they would make in the undergrowth when getting up and down would be a dead giveaway, dead being the operative word. No, he would not make them hit the deck unless he decided that the patrol should crawl forward. For the time being he opted to advance in a crouch taking up the silent and easy kneeling position after each very short leg. Everyone was looking inwards at Chalky, he did not speak a word but nodded at Fred who immediately moved forward; Bob seeing his buddy advance did likewise and so it began. Fred and Bob first for the limit of visibility, three yards here and maybe five or six there. Stop, kneel and observe in the aiming position. Then whilst being covered Chalky and Worm would move up into line and carry out the same drill. It was never a leapfrog and in no way hurried, it was stealth at its best. No one doubted that Fred had heard a cough, no one doubted that it was a man who had made it; and that bastard could be taking a bead on any one of them at this very moment.

It was a sobering thought and it made for an extremely hairy, nerve-racking hour that threatened to break the calm fortitude of these SAS soldiers. Then the four men reacted as one as they froze, all stopped by the unmistakable, heart stopping sound of metal on metal. Considered to be a heinous crime in the British Army, what they had heard was an eating iron clanging against a mess tin.

Ah! thought Fred, *unless the bloody baboons have been taught to use a knife, fork and spoon and are attending a mess dinner, I guess that we've found the enemy.*

Chalky, slowly, ever so slowly, moved out of his mid-stride, statue-like pose to take up the kneeling position cupping a hand to his ear as he did so. The others knelt equally slowly and listened as they had never listened before. Now totally committed to the task without having to watch every step and move least it be them that made the noise, they were able to concentrate their acute sense of hearing on detecting the slightest sound of enemy activity. With cocked ears and thumping hearts they listened out. Gradually the giveaway sounds came to the ears of the waiting patrol – the cocking of a bolt-action rifle after it had be cleaned probably. The sound of someone digging and a thud made by a cutting tool impacting wood.

To Chalky's way of thinking these were not the sounds of an enemy camp under threat of detection, a man using a mess tin is a soul relaxed. These people felt safe and had no idea that the SAS men were within spitting distance. A slight movement caught Chalky's eye; it was Bob swirling a finger upward in a spiralling motion and pinching his nostrils. He was telling his boss that he could smell smoke. Chalky indicated that the patrol should adopt the lying position, they would be crawling forward from this point on. Chalky could have ordered a withdrawal back to the place where they had dumped the packs, he had enough to go on to justify a report with a fairly accurate map reference of the enemy location but that was not his way; he wanted visual confirmation before he put everyone's hopes up and so the patrol bellied forward in search of it. They used a method of movement known as a leopard crawl, it was slow, stealthy but physically exacting. Fred had crawled fifty yards when he hit an obstacle, or rather, he stopped just short of one. It was in the form of a crude vine fence that had rusty tin cans hanging from it in bunches that served as an early warning system and had he walked into them it would have caused a hell of a racket and the enemy would have been alerted; Fred had arrived at the CT camp.

The fence did in fact run away from Fred at an angle, he had hit it at an apex that constituted a corner of the enemy defences. The jungle on the far side of the obstacle had not been cleared so he knew that this was not an actual perimeter fence; on inspecting Fred's latest find Chalky agreed. The sounds coming from the direction of the camp seemed to be louder now and more frequent. It was almost as if the fence was offering them credence to what had been up to that point pure supposition; in the jungle it is the norm to see and hear things that are not there but Chalky needed to actually see at least one enemy soldier before committing himself to a situation report. He had decided to recce forward on his own but changed his mind.

'Hang on,' he said to himself, 'I've had my day. Young Fred's riding a certainty here, let's give him the winning post.' He tapped the scout's arm and circled an eye with a forefinger and thumb. Fred acknowledged that he was to advance alone to carry out a close recce, should he come under attack he was to withdraw rapidly under covering fire from the others and join them in a bugging out tactical movement that was to become known as 'shoot and scoot'.

Fred eased himself under the low hanging tins and crawled forward in a line equidistant to the two angles forming the apex aiming to take the most direct route through the enemy defences. Twenty-five yards and a bucket of sweat later, he noticed that it seemed a little lighter, slightly puzzled he moved on a bit further and there directly in front of his eyes was a pangi. This was a short bamboo stake sharpened at both ends and positioned in the ground like a miniature spear pointing outwards to catch advancing troops in the legs, only there was not just one of these vicious booby traps, there were thousands of them. Fred moved back slightly and raised himself up until he could see over the top of the pangis and his eyes opened in amazement. A great swathe of undergrowth had been cut away hence the lighter hue to the surroundings caused by the lack of depth in the vegetation. A massive effort must have been required to clear the area from about knee height to at least seven feet from the ground. It was not a clearing as such because the jungle canopy was still intact, it was more of a defensive measure that afforded the CTs a panoramic field of view across, Fred judged it to be 100 yards, of cleared jungle. The effect was rather like looking at a wide screen film with that annoying black border top and bottom of the screen. *The manpower required to maintain the cleared area alone,* thought Fred with a shiver, *puts their fighting strength in the hundreds.*

Fred moved even further back and slowly adopted the kneeling position and bingo, he found himself staring at two men that appeared to be repairing a damaged earthwork. Propped up and pointing over the parapet of that defensive position was a machine gun. As far as Fred could see the cleared area continued and he surmised that it probably extended all around the enemy camp. Fred melted back into the jungle that was fast becoming his friend and ally and rejoined the patrol to make his report to Chalky, trying very hard not to scream out his success. Instead, he gave the old hand the thumbs down sign and whispered, 'I have sighted the enemy.' Then unable to resist the temptation he reversed the hand signal to the thumbs up position as if to say, 'Isn't that bloody clever of me?'

Chalky grinned and gave the scout a wink. He now had to make a choice, to stay where he was and make a more detailed reconnaissance of the enemy dispositions and send in a report at first light the next day; or withdraw to the packs and give Caesar a preliminary report immediately: he chose the latter. Chalky knew from the nightly reports that the gold train was barging its way northwards through the jungle at a fair rate of knots, and it was of paramount importance that he get news of this find through to his HQ quickly. This would enable Caesar to deploy his patrols up around Gunong Chini to reinforce Chalky's attempts at a close reconnaissance. Brigade HQ could also initiate some pre-emptive troop movements that would save time later. Chalky had to steel himself to proceed at snail's pace back to the hide, one mistake now would cancel out many days of hard work and jeopardise the lives of him and his men. Despite the slow pace the patrol managed to establish a base camp by 16.30 hrs just before the rain came. Half an hour later in the dark with the thunderous roar of the daily deluge battering his flimsy shelter, Chalky sent out his report to Caesar. It included details from a sketch map that Fred had drawn on a piece of bog roll showing the enemy defences as he had seen them, nothing more, nothing less. When the reply came back it was brief. 'Congratulations. Commence close recce at first light. Rest of us will join you post haste, but not at a gallop I fear. Out.'

★

Caesar sat down to drink some tea that Lofty had brewed up. 'That new man is doing well,' he said.

'Yes,' replied the sergeant major, 'but you wouldn't have thought it when I found him dangling from a tree only three inches from the ground, thought he was in heaven, poor sod.'

'Praying wasn't he?' queried Caesar with a grin.

'He sure was.'

'Well, he's heaven-sent, and that's for sure too.'

★

At exactly the same time as the field force Bren gunners had opened fire from the beach at Kampong Kinchur, Lieutenant Clancy Deane started up the outboard engine of his rubber assault boat. It was a signal for the other nineteen helmsmen in the water-borne force to do likewise and soon the twenty craft were underway at the best possible speed. Every man jack was sweating buckets from their efforts of paddling the light but ungainly vessels, and the transition from muscle to motor power was a welcome relief. But relax they could not, the war would not stop for this little caper and there was a real danger that the ambush force could become embroiled in a fight quite unconnected with their current operation. *And that,* thought Clancy, *would leave them right up the proverbial creek without a bloody paddle.* He winced at the thoughtless pun.

For the first two hours it had been pitch black and keeping the small fleet together had proven to be a difficult task made possible only because of the slow paddle speed, but they made the planned distance with time to spare. Clancy had waited fifteen minutes for the relief of Kampong Kinchur to commence, making just enough way to stop the boats from drifting back downriver. The sound of gunfire had been his cue and under cover of the noise he had got going. By then the cloud had lifted and the gap between the trees lining the river line that was silhouetted against the night sky made the job of navigating that much easier. But little else was visible and keeping his flock in a fair resemblance of 'line astern' was a nightmare. What became a valuable aid was the fluorescent wakes churned up by the outboard engines that gave each helmsman, except for Clancy, an aiming point to steer for. The best possible speed that could be maintained under these hostile conditions was three knots, the total distance between Kampong Kinchur and the objective was eighteen miles. But this was not going to be a straightforward, dead reckoning voyage of naval perfection.

'No indeed,' bemoaned Clancy, 'the only return I got from two hours of paddling was one lousy mile.' There were only two Kampongs along the way to the ambush position, Kampong Bintang and Kampong Lubok Paku. Bintang was four miles away and fortunately was situated a mile inland from the riverbank so their passing should not be heard from that distance. The gunfire had ceased now and Clancy became fully aware of the noise being made by the outboard engines. Probably because of the tension of the moment it seemed to be excessively loud, coupled with the fact that sound does travel further at night he knew that he would have to be bloody careful; nobody must see or hear this ambush party.

With his map and compass on his lap Clancy navigated the river checking his position at every bend. To plot his course he would disappear under his poncho and work with the aid of a pencil torch. Even these periodic exposures to the dim light were enough to ruin his night vision so that when he emerged from under the cover he was blinded and had spots before his eyes. It was trying his patience and during each period of adjustment he was glad to see that his eagle-eyed commandos had kept him on course. After forty-five minutes he estimated that they were within half a mile of the small landing stage and track that served the village from the river. Clancy reduced speed until the engine was making only low gurgling noises, when the boat behind him began to close up the helmsman got the message and slowed down too. This procedure was repeated right down the line and the hundred and one man force purred by Kampong Bintang without waking a soul; by midnight having paddled for two hours and motored for another two the fleet were half a mile beyond the village. Another one and half hours later at a speed of three knots saw the force positioned one mile from Kampong Lubok Paku, it was time to switch off the engines and take to the paddle once more.

Three long hours later placed them an equal distance the other side of that village. As they had passed by the commandos had not seen a single light but a few dogs had barked, sensing the silent menace in the night. Then it was back to engine power for the last leg of the journey, they did not make it before first light as planned but nobody was around to see the heavily armed force arrive at an extremely sharp bend at 07.00 hrs.

The boats were quickly beached and the commandos and field force men disembarked dragging the vessels ashore behind them, soon they were out of sight from prying eyes. The ambush party was now in a position two and half miles south-southeast of Kampong Jempol and only five miles as the crow flies from Dennis and the rafters at Kampong Pesagi.

The reserve battalion of the Commonwealth Brigade was ordered to withdraw from the Maran area immediately upon receiving Clancy's report that he had arrived in position. The Aussies were instructed to make a big play of pulling out and this they did with great gusto by marching past homesteads proclaiming their intention of living it up in the nearest bars and brothels. Boarding a convoy of trucks that had been assembled at Maran they roared away towards Kuantan shouting such endearments as, 'We'll leave you to stew in your own shit,' or, 'Farewell arsehole end of the world.'

In reality only half of the battalion departed leaving behind a secretly deployed force of two companies whose job it was to cordon off Kampong Lubok Paku. The tactics had changed from an overt presence to discourage the Tongs from approaching the village, to a covert operation to let them in but under observation, and to protect the bogus gold shipment from possible interference from the real guerrilla army.

The Malay Police Officer commanding that very same flotilla of sampans heard Clancy's message too; he ordered his signaller to acknowledge it so that both Clancy and the Australian CO would be aware that he knew the positions of each piece on this chessboard of deceit. It was now up to him to make the next move.

Kampong Lubok Paku lay on the north bank of the Sungei Pahang and was served by a road that branched south from Maran. The population was wholly Malay and one hundred per cent anti-communist and had always fiercely resisted intimidation by the terrorists at every turn. It was an ideal spot for the ploy and at first the top brass had considered taking the entire village into their confidence, but at Crazy Harry's objections decided otherwise. The local police though were let in on the act and it was their intelligence regarding the distribution of the local community that had given Harry an idea. The river at that point was 300 yards wide and living in splendid isolation on the opposite bank to the village was a drug-crazed spiritual doctor and his equally raving woman. Known as Bhomo's they were Malaya's equivalent to the more popular-named witch doctors and were accredited with some miracle cures but generally they were avoided like the plague. They were also persuaded, often violently, to live a leper-like existence well away from the village; in this case the community had pitched in to build a wooden house that jutted out from the far riverbank on stilts. Presented with a small boat the couple was allowed to cross the river to collect supplies but they were discouraged from lingering least they cast some evil spells.

Having received the brief message over the radio, the commander of the bogus gold shipment led the sampans closer to the shore hugging the south bank until he arrived at the Bhomo's house. He indicated that all six sampans should beach as close as possible to the precarious looking structure, then accompanied by two of his men he rushed into the dwelling to seize the good healer and his concubine. But their valiant efforts were in vain because both of those worthy beings were too far gone on drugs and booze to even acknowledge the presence of the three policemen. As for the villagers on the opposite bank, well, at 300 yards and dressed in the khaki drill uniform of the guerrilla army it was hard to distinguish between Malay and Chinese. But they did see the sampans arrive and witnessed three men dashing into the house in a hostile manner brandishing what looked like rifles. The irate villagers summoned the local duty policemen and voiced their concern. As if on cue, the policeman sought help from one of his colleagues and commandeered a fishing boat, in it they then proceeded towards the Bhomo's house and when closing in on the fleet of sampans one of the policeman held up a white flag. What the good inhabitants of Kampong Lubok Paku saw were the two emissaries of law and order being escorted very roughly and at gunpoint into the house and out of sight. What they did not see was the officer warmly shaking hands with the two men. 'What'll you have, Tuak or Tea?' he asked.

'Give us some of whatever those two had,' grinned the older of the two, a corporal.

Whilst they all had a good laugh at that the officer looked at the corporal's companion, a very young constable. Addressing him he said, 'I'm sorry about this my boy,' and then punched the unsuspecting lad full in the face. The muttering crowds ashore observed that the two policemen were being herded back to the boat, they waited patiently for the vessel to return to the home bank and helped the policemen ashore. The corporal was hopping mad and the constable seemed dazed and was nursing a bleeding nose and a cut lip.

'They're terrorists,' blurted out Corporal Tamsin Hassim, 'they've taken the Bhomo and his woman as hostages. And at the first sign of any trouble they'll kill them both and stick their heads on poles!'

'What do they want?' asked the village headman.

'Nothing, they're not making any demands other than that they wish to be left alone. I got the impression that they need some time.'

'We'll have to do something,' the headman replied, 'get onto your bosses in Kuantan for some advice. In the meantime we'll comply with the terrorists' wishes, we don't really want anything to happen to those two, do we?' The answer to his question was a simple no. The community was as one in their opinion that although the crazed couple were to be wondered at, perhaps even feared and in many cases regarded as kind of pets, they were part of the community and as such had the right to be protected.

Corporal Tamsin Hassim returned to his dwelling that also served as the village police station, there he went through the motions of reporting this outrageous intrusion to his superiors in Kuantan.

Dozens of children that had been disappointed when the Australian troops had departed had followed the uniformed man and were now gathered outside the open wooden shutters of the police station in the hope that they might hear news of the soldiers' return. Their open, honest and innocent wishes were granted and they pranced excitedly about when they heard a voice crackling over the ancient, hand-cranked radio to announce that the army would be sending help soon. Little did they realise that the rough but kindly Australian soldiers were already there, and that some of them were actually watching the police station and grinning at the children's antics.

It had taken but one short boat trip to elevate the young police constable to the position of village hero complete with the scars of battle inflicted upon him by the communist terrorist. After much back-slapping, hugging and kissing three dusky maidens took him in tow. They dragged him into a house where it must be presumed that he received medicinal ministrations from the buxom trio. He was not seen again for the rest of that day.

★

The Chinese Tong Boss held Dennis in high esteem for his military expertise and tactical perception; he had come to rely on the information passed down to him through Mr Tan and his mysterious source. To run a tight ship requires constant supervision and confirmation of intelligence was the name of the game in the Tong arena. The countless eyes and ears of his organisation reported the Australian troop withdrawal from

Maran. He knew that if and when the gold shipment made an appearance in Kampong Lubok Paku it would only be a matter of time before the troops returned, he saw a small window of opportunity and he took advantage of it.

The very same Chevrolet pickup truck driven by the same two men that had first spotted the *Sea Pearl* off Kuala Pahang now bumped and clattered its way to Kampong Lubok Paku. They had come from Kuantan via Maran and the village of Singgora. In many places along the way they had seen the clear tyre imprints of heavy vehicles, ample proof that the army had been and gone. The Tong men stopped and parked up outside the Lubok Paku general store-cum-bar. The two men went inside and ordered a drink then sat down to listen to the chatter of the exited clientele. It soon became apparent that a 'happening' had occurred and that extra police and the army were being rushed to the scene. The Tong thugs did not even have to make any enquiries so loud was the conversation and obvious the topic that centred around six sampans, some armed guerrillas and two hostages. The locals also sang the praises of the young constable who was conspicuous by his absence. The two crooks were quite happy with the information gleaned so far but under the pretence of turning their vehicle around they drove it down to the water's edge to have a quick look-see. Sure enough there were the six sampans in question tied up on the other side of the river and loaded down to the gunwales with wooden crates. It was proof in plenty and the criminals made themselves scarce before the window closed. Probably due to the excitement of the moment none of the villagers could actually remember seeing the strangers or their vehicle, not even the pretty waitress that had served them with their warm beer.

But seen they were by the men of the Commonwealth Brigade reserve battalion. As the pickup truck was driven out of Kampong Lubok Paku the Australian corporal commanding No. 1 Section, 4 Platoon of Bravo Company picked up his radio handset.

'Hello two this is two-four alpha. Suspect vehicle has departed, over…' The section Bren gunner who had the receding truck full in his sights wished fervently that he could squeeze off a burst right up their bloody arses, but instead, Shovel kept the change lever of the gun on S for safe.

In the combined naval and police operations room situated in Kuantan the news that the Tong men had probed, observed and withdrawn from Kampong Lubok Paku was met with jubilation. 'Well,' said Claude to the Admiral, 'that pretty well seals the fate of the raft Wallahs, not counting that Dennis fellow, of course.'

The old sea dog looked at the police commissioner. 'Oh! He'll come out of this smelling of roses is my bet. As for the rest Claude old chap, they're ready for gaffing, the chumps fell for it hook line and sinker.'

★

The twentieth of September was a busy day; it saw Clancy Deane's ambush party safely into position and the partial withdrawal of Australian troops from Maran. It witnessed the arrival of the bogus gold shipment at Kampong Lubok Paku and the subsequent Tong visit that clinched the fate of the rafting expedition. There were three more events of note that day, they were the withdrawal of Caesar's HQ from Bukit Bertangga, the redeployment of his squadron; and the arrival of elements of the gold train on the hill.

Caesar had been contemplating such a move for a couple of days motivated by the fact that he was becoming too far removed from his patrols, he wished to close up on them for reasons of command and control. Also, reports coming in from the Gurkha Rifles indicated that the gold train was moving like the clappers from Bukit Chermingat towards Caesar's position. There was a very real threat of Kim Bok's bloody elephants bowling him right off the top of the hill. But it had taken the success of Chalky's patrol to precipitate him into action and he had ordered the redeployment of the entire squadron.

All the other patrols would be well and truly on their way by now and by 08.00 hrs Caesar's HQ patrol was ready to move. Being at least one day's march behind his squadron, Caesar knew that the move to his new HQ would have to be done it two stages. The first leg would be over a distance of seven miles and because of the urgency of the situation and the fact that the journey would be along the well-defined tracks of the Gunong Chini ridgeline, he had decreed that the march would be a heads down, arse up affair of some speed. His target for the day's march was the area where the ridgeline took a very marked turn to the east and to make it before last light required the patrol to maintain a speed of one and a half thousand yards an hour.

'It's bloody marvellous,' remarked Lofty, 'we end up being chased off the bloody hill by the very bastards that we are supposed to be pursuing!'

'Those leeches in your curry are making you grumpy, Sergeant Major,' said Caesar with a grin, 'where's your sense of humour man?'

'If we hang about long enough we'll be able to catch a train!' dared the signaller.

'That's not likely,' responded Lofty, 'there's too many leaves on the track!' On that cheerful note Caesar led his patrol down off the feature from his command station to make way for the gold train that was approaching from the south-east.

About five miles north-east of Bukit Bertangga the two other patrols from Chalky's Troop that had been working the ridgeline were already one and a half hours into their particular march. Although they were well up in the highlands and navigating along a well-established route, they found the going was heavy; this was due to the fact that they were burdened with the extra rations destined for Chalky's patrol. They were to set up a troop base camp 1,000 yards south of the ridge and 200 yards north-east of the gully that Fred had found, that would place them 1,000 yards north, and above the enemy camp. The two patrols did not envisage having any difficulty in accomplishing this feat of endurance and hoped to link up with their boss by nightfall, for although Chalky was the leader of a patrol he also held the appointment of troop commander. In most other regiments that position would carry the rank of lieutenant but the seasoned old corporal did the job standing on his head.

The troop that had been patrolling the headwaters of the

Sungei Jeram in the bowl-like depression south of the ridgeline was also on the move. But not for them the luxury of a well-trodden way through the jungle. This troop that was actually commanded by a lieutenant out of the same regiment of fusiliers as Bob headed east to negotiate the massive, steep-sided spur that split the Jeram and Mentiga rivers. Their task was to establish a second base camp on the east side of the spur, but on the opposite side of the gully from Chalky's troop. It would take a hard taskmaster indeed to put a time on that horrendous slog but the lieutenant who could be pure bloody minded on occasions did. 'I want to be there by four,' he had said, 'just in time for tea.'

The third troop, this one under the wing of a sergeant who hailed from the airborne artillery, did not have it so good either. The troop were deep in the mire, so to speak, them having to flounder about on each side of the meandering and turbulent Sungei Mentiga; a far cry from the daily drying gully that their mates had encountered six miles to the north. Navigating was not a problem but in the lush undergrowth that flourishes in the wetlands progressing for more than two yards without getting hopelessly tangled up was. The tough gunner had declared the chore to be a piece of cake. 'Anyone who lags behind will be deemed surplus to requirement,' he had threatened, 'and I'll have their guts for garters.'

In the event Caesar made the first leg of his march in record time. Chalky's patrol got their rations, the lieutenant had his tea and the sergeant had to do without garters.

With no soldier of the squadron having to march more than seven miles the task that they had been presented with would seem on the face of it to be an easy one. But one has to consider the tropical climatic conditions, the inhospitable and heartbreaking terrain cloaked in its wet, steaming blanket of thick forest that is a nightmare of obstacles; a jungle in which every single plant seems to be intent on impeding man's progress. It is only then that one can begin to comprehend what these men were up against. Add to that the enormous weights that they were carrying, an 80 lb pack, another 20 lbs around their waists with the average weapon weighing about 10 lbs. They had to negotiate obstacles at every turn and contend with an insect population that was hell-bent on making life impossible.

The soldiers had to proceed at the quickest possible speed but with the utmost caution. They had to concentrate on navigating whilst maintaining a high degree of alertness. Above all, the SAS men had to keep going against all odds, and all this in close proximity of a vicious and ruthless foe; for they were treading the hallowed ground of the Guerrilla Army's 10th Regiment, the enemy's finest.

With a combination of guts, determination, endurance and the famous SAS will, all three troops had made it to their respective destinations by 16.30 hrs. The squadron had performed a stupendous feat of military expertise bordering on the impossible. If you were to have asked any one of those SAS lads how they had achieved their individual aims that day an honest or definite answer would not have been forthcoming simply because there is not one. From the professionals in that honourable trade a salute or the doffing of caps would be sufficient, for there are no words to describe due admiration for such a high calibre of soldiering.

Bukit Chermingat and Bukit Bertangga were linked more or less by a series of spurs and saddles that could, with a little imagination, be described as a ridge. It was blessed with a good track that meandered its way west-northwest from Bukit Chermingat and in places was six feet wide. In this close and difficult country such an opportune route constituted a major highway through the wilderness. The elephants loved it and their body language was telling the humankind, I told you so, just as if it had been their idea to come that way.

Kim Bok smiled and made a change to his tactics, for most of this particular stage of the journey the column would be preceded by scouts. Fantail volunteered for this duty and Kim Bok agreed sending her forward with two men.

At 09.00 hrs on the eighteenth the gold train continued its trek northwards. Kim Bok was still feeling spooked by the old tree on Bukit Chermingat so it came as no surprise to him when one of his scouts reported back to him with the news that some tracks had been spotted. Kim stopped the column and went forward himself to have a look. Fantail had already removed the leaves and other debris from the footprints of four men who had been marching south towards Bukit Chermingat, Kim guessed that Shen and his party had made them. But what was exciting Fantail to the point of distraction was the alarming discovery of some much fainter signs showing that an unknown number of men had marched in the opposite direction, northwards and away from the gold train. Fantail judged that there were two groups, one set of tracks being a few days older than the other, the most recent being a week to ten days old. Kim Bok stared at the evidence before his eyes not really wanting to believe it; a shiver ran down his spine as a montage of images flashed through his mind. Once more he relived those moments of suspicion that he had experienced on the train from Bangkok. The unseen eyes on the east coast, and again off Palau Tioman. Then closer to hand at that damned old tree. He cursed himself for not trusting his instincts, those feelings that he had never questioned before, the hunches that had got him through many a sticky situation. Kim found and looked into Fantail's eyes and deep down to her very soul, their shoulders slumped as one as the realisation dawned upon them that hope was eluding the cause and that they were about to tread the last fateful path. But they had come too far and suffered too much to give up now. He held Fantail close and whispered into her ear, 'We must keep going, when the time comes we'll fight like hell together.'

And so on they went, the elephants, the mules and the men who had hoped to liberate Malaya from the British, and with them went a woman who was determined to die alongside her lover in battle. Kim Bok did not impart his feelings of doom to his men, of course; but they had lived with danger too long to ignore the signs, Kim's men could smell trouble when it was around. They would, Kim knew, give a good account of themselves in the final showdown. For most of that day the gold train made good progress mainly downhill reaching the comparatively low lying areas half way between the two hills by nightfall, and there they made camp for the night.

At ten the next morning, and much to the elephant's disgust, they took a ninety-degree turn to the left and plunged down a steep slope for 500 yards before climbing up again for a similar distance. This 1,000-yard diversion placed them on a spur that led up to the main Gunong Chini ridgeline. Kim ordered another right-angled change of direction, this time to the right, which brought the column back onto its original axis. Following another huge track up a steep gradient, the gold train struggled on with the ground falling away sharply on either side of the spur. At the bottom of the right-hand slope flowed a tributary of the Sungei Jeram, down to the left a watercourse running off Bukit Bertangga fed the Sungei Bera and the Tasek Bera swamp. About 2,000 yards from the top of the spur, the column was brought to a halt by the scouts who had found the spot where Shen's group had joined the feature having marched due east from Bukit Bertangga to do so. It was another dog-leg designed to throw off enemy trackers. It had been Kim Bok's intention to follow the courier route to Kampong Kertau where he hoped to meet up with a force from the 10th Regiment who were to lead him to the camp. But he now knew that that plan would have to be abandoned in light of the new developments so he felt it prudent to call a halt for the day to revise his appreciation of the situation. Before making any further plans he needed confirmation of the enemy movements in the immediate area.

To do this he instructed Fantail and the two scouts to recce westwards as far as the summit of Bukit Bertangga. The scouting party departed immediately knowing full well that they would have to stage somewhere overnight as the day was nearly gone. Kim had advised, 'Try and get as far as the Sungei Bera before last light and then carry on in the morning. Be back here by midday.'

On her return, Fantail had given Kim some grim news. She had established beyond doubt that the enemy had backtracked Shen's party to the top of Bukit Bertangga, and that the tracks were, as the others had been, about ten days old. But she had found more recent signs suggesting that an enemy patrol had just vacated the summit. 'The tracks were no more than a couple of hours old,' she had stated concluding her report.

Bad news indeed, thought Kim as he looked at his map for inspiration. It was bloody obvious that the British were not following Shen, they were trying to find out where he had come from. They were ahead of the gold train, so who the hell were they after? If the enemy patrols continued to backtrack Shen's group they would reach Kampong Kertau and that would slam the door shut in Kim's face. *If they're probing ahead of me,* he thought hopefully, *perhaps they've no idea that I'm here.* But on second thoughts Kim, forever the pessimist, could not imagine that the British were ignorant of the gold train's existence or of its whereabouts. For the present though he was thankful that the British were concentrating their efforts to the north of him. It would give him some leeway, precious time in which he could make an all out effort to reach his goal. Kim went to work with his map and protractor plotting the most direct route from his present location to the main camp on Gunong Chini. It was not an ideal course to take but he had a burning desire to join up with the great guerrilla leader and warn him of the British menace.

His plotted course would take him across the grain of the country, it would be bloody hard going but by the time that the dawdling British Army turned around and found his massive tracks through the jungle he should be home and dry. And in a well defended position at that.

Of several things Kim Bok was completely unaware of. Whilst he had been plotting his route; a Gurkha Rifleman from a distance of ten yards and with some amusement had been watching the last man in the column picking his nose and eating the harvest with relish. Behind that soldier were thirty others formed up in single file.

When crossing the tributary of the Sungei Bera on her way to the summit of Bukit Bertangga the left flanking Gurkha platoon was monitoring Fantail's movements. Within fifteen minutes of her departure from the summit elements of the left flanking Gurkha company had occupied the hill.

When Kim Bok ordered the gold train to proceed little did he know that they would be passing through even more of the bloodthirsty warriors from Nepal because the right flanking Gurkha platoon were lining the western most tributary of the Sungei Jeram. Backing them up on top of the next spur were the right flanking Gurkha company. Meanwhile the second Gurkha Rifle battalion had been deployed east in a pre-emptive move to seal off all escape routes south of Gunong Chini.

By the time that Kim Bok had reached the Jeram tributary the SAS were grouped all around the great leader's camp, whilst he was boxed in by over six hundred Gurkha soldiers; the Paymaster General and his gold train were going nowhere fast: except to hell.

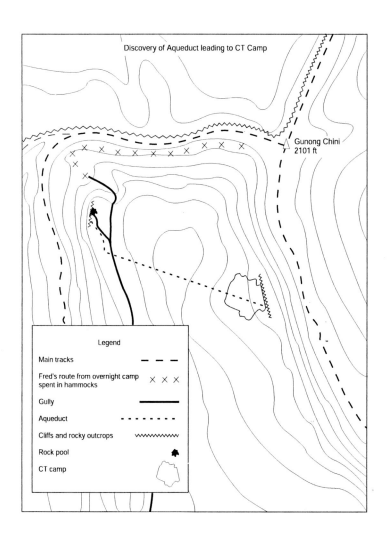

Discovery of Aqueduct leading to CT Camp

Gunong Chini
2101 ft

Legend

Main tracks

Fred's route from overnight camp
spent in hammocks

Gully

Aqueduct

Cliffs and rocky outcrops

Rock pool

CT camp

Chapter Fourteen

Tom Nobles had just returned to his office after a very successful meeting with the Field Marshal, Crazy Harry Blunt, Claude Rysdale and Jeremy Fairburne-Snape. The meeting had been convened at Tom's request and the outcome of it had been to his advantage. Feeling quite pleased with himself he doodled away in his notebook with an evil glint in his eyes.

The meeting had been all to do with the mysterious middleman in the Belchard and Tan set-up; who the bloody hell was he? Despite the constant surveillance of Simon Belchard by the two constables during working hours they had failed to come up with any clues as to who the inspector's confidant was. All telephone calls to and from his office had been via a switchboard, calls had been logged and recorded as official communications. Whoever Belchard was passing his information to it was not being done from his office telephone, that was for sure. The constables could not finger any special personal relationships between the inspector and his officers or other ranks. Simon Belchard seemed to keep himself in that splendid isolation reserved of those in high office, outwardly anyway.

Tom's own agents who were watching Belchard day and night whenever he set foot outside of the police barracks or his bungalow had so far sent in equally negative reports. The man was a complete loner, except that is, for Fiona; and it was her visits that provided the watchers with Belchard's method of communication to his contact. Tom had infiltrated one of his agents into the Belchard household as a relief gardener, the regular man having suddenly contracted an illness after being offered substantial remuneration. Tom's man had reported that whenever Fiona departed after a session of lovemaking, and sometimes at the latter part of her stay, Belchard would get busy on the telephone. It was not being tapped so there was no way of knowing at present who Belchard was calling. Mr Tan perhaps? No, Tom did not think so. Tom also had Mr Tan under surveillance and although the man had led the watchers to every Tong contact that he knew, the arch criminal never once made a move towards Rompin or Simon Belchard's bungalow. As a direct consequence of Mr Tan's agenda including meetings with the top Tong bosses; Claude Rysdale was able to locate and box in the Tong operation in Kuantan. The police commissioner was determined that when the time came to close the net it would not just be the rafting expedition that got caught up in it. Because he was absorbed with catching bigger fish Claude had neither the time nor inclination to bother with minnows like the middleman; but Tom Nobles did.

Tom let his mind wander back to when he had been looking at his desk piled high with files with more of the same scattered all over the floor of his office. Something had been niggling away at his memory then, amongst the reams of paperwork was a connection, if only he could find it. Tom had burned the midnight oil and was ready to give up when he found himself glancing through Belchard's service record and not without a certain amount of amusement. His eyes flicked over a tiny entry highlighted in brackets, he froze and his heart missed a beat. He read the paragraph again, what was there about it that was exciting him so? He read it for the third time:

> On posting to Malaya this officer was appointed Area Inspector of the Rompin District, but served for a short period of time at a provincial station (Masjid Tanet) before taking up his appointment.

The warning bells had clanged in Tom's head. *Masjid Tanet, Masjid Tanet,* he thought to himself, *where have I seen or heard that name before?* He sifted frantically through the Tan files and there it was, several of his agents had logged Mr Tan's frequent lunch appointments to a mah-jong parlour in the village of Masjid Tanet. Tom could remember reading the reports before but without the connection between Mr Tan and Belchard the name had meant nothing to him, now it did. Tom looked again at all the log sheets concerning Kampong Masjid Tanet and came up trumps, on every single visit by Mr Tan the local police sergeant had seen fit to visit the house of pleasure. But his men had not made a connection between Mr Tan and the policeman, the consensus of opinion being that even police sergeants were human and in need of some relaxation. But Tom had had a hunch that there was another bad apple in the barrel, however, bigger events had overshadowed his trifling snippet and the subject had been put on hold.

Now though things had changed and with Fiona's role in the plot all but at an end, Tom had requested the meeting. Fiona had one more vital piece of information to impart to Simon Belchard, and that was to inform him of the departure time and date of the bogus gold shipment from Kampong Lubok Paku for the final destination at Kampong Jempol. Fiona would have her work cut out because she was also to imply that the security forces planned to attack the terrorist at the landing point and seize the gold. She was to promote Belchard into leading the Tongs into believing that this was the last opportunity they would get to steal the gold bullion, and to stand a chance of outwitting the Police and Army they would have to make their move when the six sampans were somewhere between the two villages. Everyone present at the meeting was aware that Dennis would have been pushing that very point home to the Tongs on his front. Confirmation of his theory through the Belchard, middleman and Tan grapevine would help convince them.

Sometime back the Field Marshal had gone along with Tom's suggestion that Fiona should attempt to poison Belchard's mind against the mysterious middleman, the idea being to provoke Simon into inadvertently revealing who that person was; so far that ploy had netted in a miserable zero.

Now at this latest meeting Tom had volunteered his idea of how to expose and get rid of the middleman, the emphasis being on the words 'get rid'. In his opening argument he gave only the general idea and did not mention who his suspect was. The Field Marshal who had sent thousands of men to their deaths and many of them to hell looked aghast. Claude Rysdale who had not balked at bending the rules to suit himself in the Belchard affair appeared shocked that Tom could even contemplate such an extreme measure. The Navy and Air force chiefs wondered what had happened to the rules of cricket. Only Jeremy seemed to be in favour, well foul play was his stock-in-trade, what! Tom met the wall of objection, this solid front of rebuttal, coolly. Being the crafty copper that he was he had kept something up his sleeve and he used it now to turn the argument in his favour; he revealed to the horrified audience that his suspect was another policeman, 'Sergeant Abdul Hassan of Masjid Tanet is the man,' he announced gravely.

Claude had exploded. 'A sergeant blackmailing an officer? Ye Gods!' he had exclaimed thumping the table.

'What an absolute bounder,' added Petherington looking straight faced up at the overhead fan. 'He deserves Uncle Tom's treatment,' had been Crazy Harry's verdict. Jeremy had agreed with a knowing wink. Ships and Air looked aloof but said nothing. Having won the approval of these powerful men Tom planned the demise of the once courageous and model policeman, Sergeant Abdul Hassan. In a nutshell Tom would arrange that Belchard became aware of Mr Tan's true position in the game and suggest that Simon now deal direct with the gangland boss. Lack of communication between Belchard and Abdul might force the latter man to make an error of judgement, bringing himself out of the shadows and into the limelight thus providing proof positive of his involvement. If and when that happened Tom would have Abdul compromised in the eyes of Mr Tan. The special branch man aimed to feed the bent policeman to the wolves where he would come to a sticky end, but first things first.

★

In accordance with Caesar's orders, Chalky did not hang about in the area of his overnight camp to await the arrival of the rest of his troop, instead, he had the patrol hide their Bergens and marched off to commence the close reconnaissance of the enemy camp. Starting at 08.00 hrs the patrol retraced their steps back to the spot where Chalky had ordered Fred to proceed forward on his own to discover the pangi field; once there Chalky split the patrol in two. Fred and Bob were to plot the direction and extent of the camp perimeter starting at the apex and working left, they had three hours in which to complete the task but could terminate the job if the defences took a marked change in direction. Chalky and Worm would carry out a similar patrol to the right of the apex but with the added task of locating the actual point where the aqueduct entered the camp. Chalky's theory was that the aqueduct-crossing point would be heavily defended for he reasoned that that would be where the main gap in the pangi field would be sited. If he was correct they could expect to find sentries posted at all times at that crucial point. All four men had unpacked their army-issue binoculars, in an environment that normally afforded an observer with about five yards of visibility it might seem like an unnecessary item of equipment to carry. But because Fred had reported that a considerable field of fire had been cut out of the jungle directly in front of the enemy position, then an optical aid would be invaluable.

Fred arrived at the apex of the pangi field and was observing the cleared area of the defences with interest. As he had noted before the undergrowth up to knee height was still intact and concealed the needle pointed pangis. Even the cut strip up to just above Fred's head could not be considered a clearing in the true sense of the word because vision was still being obstructed by larger trees that had been left in place. Nevertheless, to jungle fighters that were normally restricted to close visibility the 100-yard strip was a rare sight and would save the SAS soldiers hours of painstaking work. The trouble was that the luxury was a two-edged weapon; the area had not been cleared for them to look in, it had been cut to afford the enemy a good field of fire.

The earthworks Fred had spotted were in the form of parapets, raised areas in front of machine gun pits that allowed the muzzles of the weapons to clear the pangi field. He studied the mounds of earth that although poorly camouflaged would be hard to spot if you did not know that they were there, but with his foreknowledge and the binoculars the machine gun position stuck out like a sore thumb. But this one was not manned, as it had been the day before, there was no sign of the machine gun either.

Fred knelt down and whispered into Bob's ear, 'See if you can spot any CTs or weapons over there.' Bob slowly stood up taking Fred's place as observer standing well back from the edge of the clearing. He scrutinised the area Fred had indicated and had no difficulty picking out the slit trench but could not see any sign of CT activity, Bob shook his head. Fred logged the location of the apex gun position and worked out the bearing of the cleared area. He could not just step out into the open and take a compass bearing, such a course of action would be suicidal. He laid the compass on his map and turned it until the pointer on the lid was orientated with the line of the clearing, then picking up the compass, making sure that it remained on line, he took a reading through the prism and noted down the bearing. And so began the compilation of a sketch map of the enemy camp. The two men carefully manoeuvred their way along the edge of the pangi field taking it in turns to observe and guard-cum-record.

The jungle creatures had long since accepted the presence of the guerrillas in the camp and any change in the tempo of wildlife sounds would alert the guerrillas who would guess that it was the British who were upsetting the sensitive inhabitants of the wilderness. The SAS soldiers were well aware of this and tackled their mission with extreme caution, stealth equal to that of the many predators who had so far condoned the human intrusion of their kingdom. One mistake would be enough to set off an explosion of indignation, objection and rage to the unwanted presence so warning the enemy and putting them on their guard.

At the end of the appointed time of three hours the perimeter had remained more or less constant on Fred's original bearing for 250 yards, an awful long way for such a fence to extend. Fred and Bob could only surmise that the camp was defended by hundreds not dozens of men. This theory was strengthened by the discovery of three more weapon pits, and judging by the size of the earthworks they had been constructed to accommodate medium or heavy machine guns. Four such emplacements sited along a 250-yard front suggested a platoon strength unit of about thirty men, and they would be stretched to the limit. To defend four sides of a square of that size a minimum of one hundred and ten men would be required. Add to that the staff of the Central Military Committee and the many administrative minions plus the expected gold train and a figure of over two hundred becomes a real possibility. Before Fred and Bob withdrew, they determined the bearing of the second leg of the perimeter that ran off at right angles to the right at the end of the 250 yard stretch, this was easy to do because they could look straight along the ninety-degree turn away from them. But because of the undulating configuration of the ground it was not possible to estimate the extent of it, Fred guessed that it must be in excess of 100 yards.

They got back to the hide at 13.00 hrs to find Chalky and Worm already there waiting for them. Over a brew-up Chalky joined the two maps together and it became apparent that an expert using a compass had laid out the camp, the two dog-legs at each end of Fred's aspect were at exact right angles. Fred noticed that Chalky had only reconnoitred 100 yards of his area of responsibility and the indicator he had drawn on the map signified that the perimeter continued on for an undetermined distance. Fred tapped on the map with a twig and looked at the older man expectantly. Worm glanced up at the heavens for inspiration whilst Chalky just grinned and told them all to make camp before the rest of the troop arrived. But Fred had a feeling that his commander had a tale to tell later.

As Fred and Bob had commenced their task of reconnoitring the left-hand apex, Chalky and Worm had begun to search for the entry point of the aqueduct having first, like their two colleagues, ascertained the compass bearing of their aspect. It was obvious from looking over the top of the concealed pangis that the aqueduct was either taking water through the pangi field or was still delivering the precious life giving liquid from just above the visible tree canopy. The latter being a more feasible answer Chalky estimated that he was at or very near to the axis of advance the patrol had been negotiating before he had given the order to break track on the previous day. If his calculations were correct the aqueduct should be positioned somewhere above his head. Looking up Chalky thought, *Well Allah, you gave young Fred a helping hand. What about me, am I not a worthy son of a bitch?* At that instant Worm who was five yards to the right of Chalky feeling his way along the edge of the pangi field stopped and cupped a hand to his ear because he had heard something. Both men listened out for sounds of enemy movement, then through all the natural jungle clatter came faint but unmistakable noise that trickling water makes, the two SAS men homed in on the sound and crept towards it on all fours. The trickling developed into splashing and long before they reached the source their hands and legs were soaking wet from trapped water. Water that was gushing out of a damaged section of bamboo, they had located the aqueduct yet again and the leakage was so quiet because the water was pouring out against the side of a tree and then cascading down the side of the trunk. Luck figures greatly in a soldier's life; he constantly hopes and prays for good luck but invariably as plans go wrong he is often the recipient of the bad kind. The Bukit Chermingat contact was a typical example of bad luck on both sides, bumping the enemy had nearly compromised the entire operation; for the enemy it had resulted in the deaths of four of their soldiers. Now bad luck had struck again for the CTs in the form of a broken-down water supply. Chalky and Worm would have found it eventually but valuable time could have been lost in a protracted search, and in that scenario the bad luck would have befallen the patrol. Because they were tensed up and alert to the fact that the CTs would not sit on their fat arses and let the vital supply of water drain away into the ground they were prepared for anything, so the snapping of a twig across the far side of the pangi field did not come as a complete surprise to them. Guessing that a maintenance party in the form of a patrol was coming out to investigate, the two SAS men withdrew until they could just see the broken end of the bamboo channel spouting water then slowly sank to the ground. With hearts in their mouths and weapons at the ready they waited prepared to sell their lives dearly if needs be.

The speed in which the enemy negotiated the pangi field was a sure indication to Chalky that the CTs had advanced through a gap in it. Soon they came into sight, there were six of them and one was carrying a spare length of bamboo channel proving that this was a frequent and well-rehearsed occurrence. They seemed a little surprised at the closeness of the emergency but soon got down to the business of repairing the aqueduct, one man sitting on another one's shoulders whilst two more kept close guard, and the remaining men went further afield along the approach route to act as a listening post.

The CTs had not uttered a word; nor were they aware that they were under observation from a distance of ten yards by two SAS men. Camouflage and concealment is a skill that infantrymen in particular have to excel in. A soldier can spend all day camouflaging himself and concealing his position so that he blends in with his surroundings. An expert will know when he is invisible to an observer, even to specialists such as snipers. In training, photographic proof is often presented to the doubtful to promote confidence in their own ability but it takes years for that attribute to come to the fore, that high degree of trust in one's own skill ensures positions are not given away by pure acts of nervousness. For many a man has made a fatal mistake simply because he thought he could be seen. Such was not the case in this instance because Chalky and Worm had long since acquired that confidence. But with perhaps two hundred-odd enemy soldiers encamped in the very near vicinity and six CTs staring them in the face, so to speak, the SAS men had to draw on all their reserves of patience and cunning. They were shallow breathing through open mouths so close were the foe, they dare not blink or attempt to wipe away the streams of sweat that were running into their eyes, stinging them and blurring their vision. Nor could the soldiers brush off the ants and other creepy-crawlies that chose to use their bodies as a thoroughfare, gritting their teeth the men endured the toe curling, spine chilling sensation of many little legs marching onwards. Mosquitoes could not be swatted, not even gently waved away; and the leeches were given licence to gorge freely of the men's blood. Heartbeats sounded like jungle drums from within, they feared to cough or sneeze and stomach rumbles seemed like great claps of thunder.

It seemed like years but in reality it took the terrorists fifteen minutes to affect the repair to the aqueduct. As the CTs prepared to withdraw to the safety of their now not so secret hideout Chalky thought grimly, *Lesser men might have crapped in their pants by now.* But nevertheless he clenched the cheeks of his buttocks to lock his sphincter least he give the game away with an involuntary fart.

'And then what?' asked Fred as Chalky brought his tale of woe to a close.

'Oh, nothing really,' Chalky replied, 'we waited ten minutes for the CTs to go home then toddled up behind them and located these two machine gun positions.' He paused and pointed them out on the sketch map, 'the guns cover the gap in the pangi field,' he said by way of explanation.

Worm got a word in. 'There's another one there,' he advised pointing at a cross marked on the map, 'then we ran out of time.'

The hide had been too close to the enemy camp for comfort and Chalky had led the patrol to within 500 yards of the Gunong Chini ridgeline for obvious reasons.

At 15.00 hrs a particularly spectacular monkey call echoed its way down from the direction of the ridge, the whole patrol cocked their heads to listen and again the call came but it was even more artistic the second time; finally the creature gave vent to a masterpiece of primeval gibberish that climaxed in something akin to maniacal laughter. Worm stood up and faced the ridge, then cupping his hands to his mouth he pierced the air with a similar call of the wild, he did it twice and sat down to await the results. A short time later eight men filed into the base camp looking for all the world as if they had just completed a Sunday afternoon's stroll, Chalky's troop was complete. The leading scout was a man named George, a native of Holland who had been killing Germans at the age of twelve whilst serving in his country's resistance force, he was also the monkey on the ridge. The troop had now been on constant deep jungle patrols for thirty-seven days.

Caesar, still high up on the Gunong Chini ridgeline and six miles departed from his squadron, handed the radio headset and Morse key back to his signaller. 'They all made it,' he informed his patrol. A good night's rest and they'll be ready for anything, he reflected as he went to work with his map and protractor to make some sense of the facts and figures that Chalky had bombarded him with. In the fading light of day he looked at Lofty who was busy de-leeching himself, first burning them off his skin with a cigarette before placing the bloated creatures into his mess tin, presumably to flavour his curry. 'It looks to me,' mused Caesar, 'that from the information we've got so far the camp is basically square-shaped.'

'Well blow me,' remarked Lofty adding some water to the leeches and lighting a fuel tablet.

'But now that I've orientated the map it looks more like a

diamond than a square, with the northern apex closest to the ridge.'

'I wondered how long it would take to get pear shaped,' grinned the Sergeant Major dumping a tin of baked beans and sausages into the brew of leeches. 'It fattens them up,' he explained in response to Caesar's raised eyebrow.

'If Chalky has got his sums right and knows where the bloody hell he is,' continued the Major, 'the northern perimeter of the diamond backs onto the main spur that runs south off the mountain.'

'The most dangerous combination known to man,' whispered Lofty to the heavens, 'is a British Army officer armed with a map and compass.' He left the bubbling, heaving mess that he was cooking long enough to glance at his own map. 'The contours are very close together there, it'll be almost like a cliff face.' He spooned some curry powder into his mess tin followed by a soggy Oxo and topped it all up with a tin of army issue spam that had the properties of latex.

'So,' said the bemused squadron commander, 'we should be able to box them in nicely?'

A short pause followed this hopeful wish. 'Or,' they both deduced in unison, 'they've got a secret means of escaping.' Caesar could not really give his troop commanders specific and detailed orders because he only had Chalky's partial plan of the enemy camp to go on. The area that he had filled in was pure guesswork tempered with topographical information gleaned from the map and his experience as an army engineer. But he had to get the show on the road so he once more picked up the radio gear and was soon tapping out his patrol programme for the morrow.

'Tell me,' asked Caesar later, 'why do you put leeches in your curry?'

'Well,' answered Lofty, 'there are two ingredients contained in this mess tin that are almost indestructible, the spam and the leeches. The spam will eventually succumb to the heat and break up but the leeches will still be alive and kicking for some time after.'

'And what am I suppose to deduce from that?'

346

'It's pretty obvious really, whilst the leeches are still alive and moving they save me the trouble of stirring the bloody stuff. When they stop moving they're dead, and the curry is done.'

At first light the next morning Caesar broke camp and moved fast along the ridge bound for Chalky's base camp. Compared with the previous day's almost continual uphill slog the bash was easy, a bit of a roller coaster maybe but with a good track to follow it was a doddle. As he forged ahead to join his squadron, Caesar prayed fervently that his lads would produce the goods.

Basically, all that he had asked them to do was define the camp perimeter in its entirety and glean as much other intelligence in the process just as Chalky's patrol had done. He had sent out over the radio a series of map references that when linked up by the troop commanders on their maps would give them Caesar's projection of the camp, being a sapper his opinions and theories on such matters were highly regarded. His projection did indeed resemble a diamond shape but with a misshapen northwest perimeter or side, this effect being due to the ground distortion caused by Lofty's cliff face that cut into the symmetry of the diamond. Caesar had named the four sections of his projection as the north, cliff, south-east and south-west aspects.

Chalky's troop was responsible for continuing with the reconnaissance of the north aspect until the pangi field reached the cliff face. One of his patrols was to link up with and guide in the troop that was to cover the south-west aspect.

That task fell to a lieutenant of fusiliers who was nicknamed Fatigue. A response from most people who discover that a friend or acquaintance is serving in the regiment is, 'Good Lord! Well I must say you don't look like an SAS bloke.' Which poses the question, what is an SAS bloke supposed to look like? Now the lieutenant was fanatically fit, as tough as nails and utterly ruthless and a sharper mind under adverse conditions you could not wish to find. But he did not look like any of those things; he appeared to be portly and seemed to move at a snail's pace. His facial expression suggested that he carried the whole world's problems on his shoulders and he looked permanently tired out. He really conveyed the impression that everything was too much for him so fatigued did he look, hence the nickname. At the southern end of his patch he was to link up with the third troop that were to take on the south-east aspect.

The sergeant of Airborne Artillery was known as Crunch. That was because he did not believe in placing wayward soldiers on a charge, instead, he would take the offender behind the back of the gym and give him crunch on the nose. He, like Chalky on the opposite side of the diamond, was to patrol as far as the cliff face.

Caesar had reserved the cliff aspect for his own worthy self but that was dependent on his men proving his theory correct by the end of the day. All being well he would begin that task on the morrow, 22 September.

The squadron went to work with a will resolved to capitalise on the magnificent achievements of Chalky's patrol. Not counting Caesar's group, thirty-six SAS soldiers working in teams of four and further split down into pairs at times, crept up to and around the biggest concentration of guerrillas ever encountered so far in the conflict. The mission of these SAS men was two-fold, their primary aim was that of close reconnaissance but they had the added responsibility of containing the terrorist in their present position should the operation become compromised. They were to stop the enemy breaking out at all costs. But that extreme measure was not necessary because compromised they were not and all day long the determined soldiers stalked, crawled and even slithered around the objective, except that is for Lofty's cliff that was actually there in all its glory. It was duly recorded on sketch maps as viewed from the limit of both Chalky's and Crunch's aspects. The men of the squadron watched, identified, recorded, plotted, sketched and, of course, lost buckets of sweat. They accomplished all this without alarming the jungle creatures in any way, the SAS soldiers performed feats of jungle navigation in close proximity to each other without clashing with or spooking adjacent patrols. They achieved this daring, hair-raising miracle of reconnaissance with stealth and efficiency, a level of expertise that when heard tell of brings the heart into the mouth and is the envy of armies throughout the world.

One does not join the SAS to do mundane jobs whilst a

chosen few grab the limelight, for the great leveller in this unique regiment is equality. Every man jack has earned his place in the elite unit after undergoing a rigorous selection process allowing them to wear the Winged Dagger cap badge and the distinctive SAS Parachutist Wings, the design of which was born of the desert scarab. The successful volunteer is free to enjoy the dubious honour of doing anything, including the impossible, anywhere and at anytime. SAS soldiers come from every regiment and corps in the British Army giving the unit a fount of knowledge that each individual can draw upon from another, this provides constant online enhancement of each individual soldier's skills thereby ensuring that no task given to him is insurmountable. No one in the regiment is indispensable and rank, as such, seldom means a damned thing. Which is why Chalky did not opt to continue with his task of the previous day, instead, he delegated that responsibility to the other two patrols knowing full well that they would carry out the reconnaissance to perfection. He would, however, guide them up to the apex to save time before leaving them to their own devices. The two patrols aimed to follow the directions given to them by Fred before leapfrogging their way along the uncharted part of Chalky's aspect. By 08.00 hrs on the twenty-first the troop had split at the apex, Chalky left Fred and Bob to watch points at the aqueduct whilst he and Worm went to rendezvous with Fatigue.

Before leaving the base camp that morning, the commanders of the two patrols in question had consulted with Fred who had talked them through the first 250 yards of the north aspect as well as giving them a sketch map. Leading the recce of the second leg was a distinguished looking gentleman who was a native of Glasgow. A butcher by trade he was hooked on knives and so adept had he become in their use that he was arrested one fine night for attempting to practise his occupational skills on a member of the public in the city's Sauchiehall Street. No actual bodily harm was done and no charges pressed, he was released with a caution on the condition that he sharpen up his act. Thoroughly shocked by this experience he resolved to follow the path of the righteous and use his talents for a more honourable purpose. To that end he swapped his meat cleaver for a scalpel by joining the army as a medic. Unfortunately for him and luckily for others, lowly private soldiers in the medical corps are not likely to be given Harley Street type assignments. Disappointed and driven to distraction at the prospect of spending his entire service in a military hospital emptying bedpans and listening to dozens of moaning bastards he took the bit between his teeth and volunteered for a real cut and thrust outfit, the SAS. He had passed with flying colours and was now on the final operation of his two-year tour of duty. His name was Alec James Gall, of which he had a lot of, but because he always went around armed to the teeth with fighting knives, a parang and a scalpel that he used for skinning animals, he was known as Jim Bowie, or more often than not, just plain Jimbo.

Jimbo followed the pangi field noting the weapon pits that Fred had located, he too observed with interest that they were not manned. When at last he reached the turn to commence his recce proper he checked Fred's bearing and found that his stretch of the pangi field ran southeast and more or less parallel with the spur line and Lofty's cliff. Being a loyal soul he hoped that the bloody thing would turn again soon or it would put pay to Caesar's projection. But Jimbo need not have feared so because instead of carrying on to miss the cliff face the pangi field took another turn after only 100 yards and headed right, straight for the high ground.

Onwards the SAS men crawled and stalked forever fearful of discovery and an almighty cock up. Then fifty yards into the new and third angle of the north aspect Jimbo hit a problem; the pangi field took yet another turn, this time to the left doubling back along the line of the spur in the opposite direction to where the camp was thought to be. It just did not make any bloody sense at all. He stopped to think about it for a bit, looking at the rows of sharpened pangis on his right with interest, he was lying at the corner of the turn and supposed that the ground immediately across the other side of the new clearing must rise sharply. It was madness to think that anyone would be so stupid enough to site a defensive position over there where the weapons would be pointing at comrades in arms sited fifty yards away behind Jimbo. *The silly sods would be firing at each other,* he thought, *but I know they're not that daft.* Just thinking about it made him feel around in the undergrowth directly to his front. 'Bingo,' he muttered to himself, 'no pangis, it's time for a new pair of eyes.'

Jimbo handed over the reins to the other patrol commander, a lanky individual who answered to the name of Pole, not because he looked like one but because he was born in Poland. Of Second World War vintage he had fought with the Polish Parachute Brigade in the Battle for Arnhem in 1944. Prior to that he had made a name for himself serving with the Polish Resistance Movement in which he was renowned for his prowess with a knife and had dispatched several German soldiers with his deadly blade. He had taken Jimbo under his wing during the early days of his tour of duty and taught the Scot the art of knife fighting; needless to say, the pair were inseparable friends.

Pole took store of the situation and whispered to Jimbo, 'I think this is a job for Feather.'

Jimbo nodded in agreement and answered, 'I thought you'd use that bloody will-o'-the-wisp.'

Feather was the smallest man in the regiment and by far the stealthiest; he had the instincts of a ferret and could be equally as ferocious as one. Being as light as the proverbial one he had been nicknamed Feather. It was 'he who walked on air' that was now sent forth to investigate the strange pangi-less field of no reason.

'Go Feather, seek for Pole?' grinned the patrol commander and suddenly he that was there had gone. He was, in fact, gone for an hour, and nobody could actually say for certain when it was that he returned so silent was he. Feather took his map case out of a pocket and laid it on the ground for Pole to see, inside was a sketch map that Feather had drawn showing that the pangi field to their right extended straight across the new clearing until it met with the high ground that could not be seen because of the trees. He had marked in that high ground as being a wall of rock with at least a ninety-degree gradient; it was Lofty's cliff face. The new clearing extended exactly fifty yards to the left and contained no obstacles. Feather had drawn in an arrow that indicated that the clearing was a cut field of fire for a weapon emplacement that he had located at the limit of the north aspect. Other arrows originating from the far side of the pangi field portrayed a perfect crossfire. It was clear to Pole that should anyone come down off the spur in an attempt to work their way around to a flank, or just end up there, they would be caught in a deadly trap.

At the point where the pangi field met the cliff face Feather had drawn in a question mark, he pointed at it and then passed his forefinger across his throat meaning that nothing more could be achieved by hanging around, let's bugger off home and discuss it there. Pole agreed and picking up Jimbo's patrol on the way, they marched back to the troop base camp arriving there by 16.00 hrs; it had been a long hard day.

Fatigue made the rendezvous with Chalky south of the aqueduct on the west side of the gully. He had brought all three patrols of his troop with him having first struck camp and then concealing their packs in a hide. He had to keep in mind that his troop was twelve men strong and this was still the enemy's main approach route to the camp. No matter how careful and skilful the SAS men could be it would be damned near impossible for a dozen of them to cross the gully in single file without leaving their mark. The troop did not need telling what to do and in no time at all had spread out along the bank of the gully with five yards between men. The twelve men crossed the gully singly, quickly and quietly but at the same time seeming as one. An enemy sentry sited to look along the gully might catch sight of some movement and come up into the aim expecting more, but their efforts would be in vain, for the SAS lads had regrouped and were long gone leaving nary a sign. Continuing in single file they followed Chalky to the apex that was the parting of the ways. Fatigue led his men along the first 100 yards of pangi field in his south-west aspect, leaving Chalky to monitor any enemy activity in the area of the apex. Like Jimbo, Fatigue familiarised himself with the positions already located the day before and that put him nicely into his stride. For this particular phase he had deployed two patrols as a protective screen to watch his back with the capability of extracting him from trouble should he encounter any. Thus secured he could better concentrate on the reconnaissance task at hand. The pangi field extended ever onwards with weapon pits sited at regular intervals, but again, they were unmanned. At 14.30 hrs he reached a bend in the defences, another almost perfect right angle that turned the pangi field in the direction of the high ground and marked the limit of Fatigue's area of responsibility. The surprising feature of his stretch was its length, according to the gentleman of fusilier's calculations it was all of 300 yards long and it would take sixty men spaced out five yards apart to defend it. And what's more, he thought, Caesar's projection although sound was proving to be a very odd-shaped diamond indeed. Fatigue deployed the troop into an all-round defensive position in the area of the corner of the turn and settled down to await the link up with Crunch.

After only five minutes a signal was passed down to him from a man sited just around the corner who could see quite a way back along the length of the aspect that they had just patrolled. The signal, outspread fingers placed on top of the head followed by a forefinger and thumb encircling an eye meant that Fatigue was required to close on the observer and take a look for himself. The lieutenant crawled up to the man and looked in the direction of his pointing finger. He slowly adopted the kneeling position in order to see over the pangis and because he was on the bend he was able to observe nearly half of the south-west aspect, but try as he might he could not spot anything untoward.

'Look to the right of the line of trenches, look at the trees, think of a spider's web with raindrops glinting on it,' prompted the trooper who had summoned him. Fatigue now having a clue as to what he was looking for did indeed notice a kind of sheen to the jungle edge that was only visible at the angle afforded him by the bend. He took another, much longer look using his binoculars and breathed a sigh of incredulity, for there almost invisible to the naked eye was revealed many strands of wire comparable in thickness to that of the cheese cutting type. *What a bloody obstacle*, he thought as he envisaged men being cut to ribbons on the vicious mesh of wire. At that point Crunch made contact with one of Fatigue's sentries.

Whereas Jimbo had completed his pangi field reconnaissance before encountering the cleared area that ran parallel with the cliff face, Crunch had come across a similar feature right at the onset of his mission, at first it had puzzled him and he did not know quite what to make of it.

The previous day he had brought his twelve men out of the Sungei Mentiga wetlands looking like drowned rats, now after a night's rest they were ready for anything. He had started his approach using the dry high ground of the steep-sided spur as a base line but when it became almost cliff like he deemed it prudent to descend and creep along the bottom edge of it. *If Caesar's thoughts on the matter are correct,* Crunch had pondered, *I'm bound to hit the camp.* He did, but not in the manner expected.

He had been thinking that they must be getting damned close by now when he was summoned forward by his scout. The man had been brought up short by what appeared to be firebreak that had been cut out of the forest but with the canopy still intact. About fifty yards wide it stretched away for at least 100 yards parallel with the base of the spur line, not a natural feature by any stretch of the imagination. He decided to send a patrol up each side of the clearing keeping his own patrol back to observe along its length. Crunch waited for an hour before his men returned and gave him their reports. The right-hand patrol had not found anything except a solid rock outcrop about seventy-five yards along the bottom of the slope. The other patrol though had come up with pay dirt, it was another clearing almost doubling back on the first one at an acute right angle to the left, furthermore it was full of bamboo pangis.

Crunch ordered the successful patrol to lead the way to the junction of the two clearings and once there the tough old gunner had a good scan about with his binoculars. He looked and looked and looked again, quartering his field of view in the approved figure of eight fashion. But for some unknown reason his attention was being drawn to an area where for want of a better term, the false clearing ended at the other side of the pangi field, in particular, the corner of it furthest away from him at the base of the rock outcrop that was now just visible through the thick undergrowth. He kept looking and was about to give up the ghost when he spotted something right at the top of the object lens of his binoculars. He elevated the glasses to centre the target for better clarity and then muttered, 'What the bloody hell is that?' He indicated the area to his scout who was a qualified sniper and therefore an expert in observation techniques. 'Tell me what you think that is?' he whispered. What Crunch had seen was a long, dark shadow, a symmetrical shape that looked out of place and seemed to be about six feet wide.

After five minutes of intense scrutiny the sniper said with absolute conviction, 'It's a rock shelf or ledge, and they can see the full length of that clearing from it; and us,' he added.

Crunch did not doubt his man; he just plotted the find on his map, something that artillerymen are very good at. He annotated his sketch map to suggest that the feature was elevated seven feet above and overlooked the part of the pangi field and all of the clearing that ran parallel with the cliff face.

Crunch continued with the task of plotting the course of the pangi field and sighed with relief when at long last he reached a spot that was out of sight of the bloody rock shelf and any weapons that the CTs may have sited up there. One hundred and fifty yards and four more raised machine gun platforms later, the defensive field of bamboo stakes took another turn, the final one because an hour later Crunch made contact with Fatigue's troop.

At the junction of the south-east and south-west aspects he handed over all the information he had gathered to Fatigue. That individual in turn entrusted both sets of intelligence to one of his patrols who were to act as couriers and deliver the day's handiwork to the apex and into the safe hands of Chalky. A bloody hard day's soldiering done, all three troops made their weary but alert way back to their respective hides for the night.

Chalky had barely set up his base camp when Caesar and his headquarters' patrol arrived. Soon he had in his possession the undisputed outer dispositions of the enemy camp defences, and he was mighty pleased with the splendid effort put in by everyone concerned with the hazardous reconnaissance mission.

★

Whilst Caesar's SAS squadron was settling down for a long night's rest in the jungle Mr Tan was looking forward to a pleasant night out with one of his favourite girls. Dressed to perfection in a light coloured tan suit with a cream shirt and yellow tie, he aimed to please the eye. To overcome the senses of his voluptuous companion for the night and send her into a submissive swoon he was heavily pomaded and reeked of Old Spice aftershave lotion. About to set forth on his amorous venture he was arrested at the doorway by the loud and distinctly unromantic jangling of his telephone.

Who could it be? he thought, none of his crooked underlings would dare to interrupt him at this time of the day, not happy hour. Mr Tan picked up the receiver, if the sound of the ringing telephone had been enough to dampen his ardour then the information imparted to him over the infernal machine really deflated the arch-criminal. All he managed to say in reply was, 'I see, I'll do that right away.' He put down the receiver, tore off his tie and threw it across the room. It was very uncharacteristic of Mr Tan, but then so was his next move, he opened an ornate drinks cabinet that hitherto had been merely a showpiece and took from it a bottle of Teacher's Whisky, grabbing a glass he sat down at his desk and poured himself a stiff measure of the amber fluid and tossed it back in one gulp. Refilling the glass he fairly screamed at the wall clock, 'Abdul! Bloody Abdul blackmailing a police officer!' Two large whiskies later his anger abated to be replaced by wonderment and not a little amusement. 'Well, I'd never have thought the spineless bastard had it in him.' He muttered into his malt.

What the mysterious caller had said was disturbing but he had assured Mr Tan that he, the caller, only had Mr Tan's best interest at heart. He went on to explain that he had been a close friend of his dear departed brother. To prove this the informant had quoted some pretty accurate details of his illegal business interests in Port Dickson; Mr Tan was convinced. The main snippet of information was the revelation that Mr Tan's good friend and confidant Abdul was receiving his information from a sex-starved Area Police Inspector who lorded over the minions of law and order at the Rompin police barracks. Amongst the criminal population that was not such a bad thing, but the suggestion that Abdul was suffering pangs of remorse was, in fact it was tantamount to disaster. It had also been hinted at by the mysterious voice that the situation could be saved and possible Tong wrath staved off if Mr Tan was to cut out the middleman

Abdul and deal directly with his source. In order to assist Mr Tan to come to a hasty decision the caller had given him a name together with a telephone number.

'Only contact him during the afternoons or evenings, preferably the latter,' had been the caller's last words before he had rung off. With a sigh of resignation Mr Tan picked up the receiver once again.

In a quiet restaurant on the outskirts of Malacca a lady belonging to the oldest profession in the world sat at a table for two and waited. An hour later she was still waiting and was beginning to look a bit embarrassed. The host who fully understood the situation knew that the woman was a guest of Mr Tan and for him to be late for an appointment such as this proved that something was amiss. The man was also aware that the woman's only visible means of support were her legs. He walked over to her table, sat down and smiled. 'Dear lady,' he said, 'may I have the pleasure of your company tonight?'

'Well thank you,' she replied, her honour restored.

★

Simon was trembling with emotion and exhaustion from having once more surpassed himself in an afternoon's lovemaking with the ever-resourceful and wickedly ingenious Fiona. She had matched his every challenge with masterful finesse here and fanatical, wanton abandonment there, turning the acts of love into a duel of sexual ascendancy. Now they lay flat on their backs on the bed with arms and legs akimbo, sweating profusely with chests heaving and eyes closed with drowsiness.

Fiona had no real information to pass on, only a subtle suggestion that he be wary of his source, and that he should start thinking of himself, and of course, her. So amongst the sheer volume of verbal diarrhoea that gushed forth from her petulant lips for his benefit, Fiona mentioned her fears concerning those matters a couple of times but staggered so as not to arouse his suspicions.

Simon, on his part, managed to extract the relevant information from the ceaseless stream of gibberish with great difficulty before Fiona finally fell asleep. Far from sleeping, Fiona had to steel herself to make her pretence seem natural and all the time her skin crawled and itched with disgust and loathing. But suffering in silence she succeeded and after an hour she was able to take a shower and drink the obligatory cup of tea before making a dignified, ladylike exit.

Simon's phone rang at five-thirty in the evening, he answered it and listened for a while before blurting out, 'Look here! You do know that your speaking to a police officer?' But whatever the reply to that was it changed Simon's attitude from indignation to wheedling co-operation. 'Did he by Jove!' said a much more agreeable police inspector. 'I see, then we'll just have to cut him out before he gets too dangerous.' Simon listened intently to more advice that was forthcoming from the caller, Mr Tan. 'Funnily enough,' Simon confided smoothly, 'I've been having thoughts about the chap for some time now.' The bent copper did not feel obliged to disclose that Fiona had warned him about a possible double-cross. After another pause he agreed, 'Absolutely, it wouldn't be a good thing for us to meet, we'll communicate by telephone only. It'll be best if I initiate the calls, me being on the receiving end of the business at hand.' Another pause then, 'I'll be in touch, Mr Tan. Oh dear! Silly me, no name no pack drill. Until next time then my dear fellow.'

★

Caesar had compiled a master plan of the CT camp copying the sketch maps drawn by his patrols, and was now studying it. The camp perimeter did resemble a diamond of sorts with a distorted eastern apex, a funnel effect leading into the centre of the cliff face. At the two points where the pangi field met the cliff face the extra strips of cleared jungle stuck out each side like a pair of wings, why?

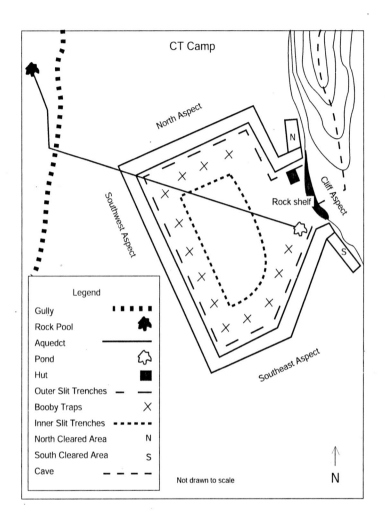

CT Camp

North Aspect

Southwest Aspect

Cliff Aspect

Rock shelf

Southeast Aspect

Legend	
Gully	■ ■ ■ ■ ■
Rock Pool	♣
Aquedct	——————
Pond	⌂
Hut	■
Outer Slit Trenches	— —
Booby Traps	✕
Inner Slit Trenches	■ ■ ■ ■ ■ ■
North Cleared Area	N
South Cleared Area	S
Cave	– – – –

Not drawn to scale

N

If, as he and Lofty had surmised, over the disgusting leech-flavoured curry, there was indeed an escape route then it would be heavily defended. Again the question arose, where and how? The answer Caesar knew lay in two areas marked on his plan, Feather's question mark, and the rock shelf spotted by Crunch and the hawk-eyed sniper.

On the twenty-second the squadron was deployed around the enemy camp yet again, this time with the specific aim of watching it in order to determine the enemy's routine, and to see if any activity might reveal more weapon pits and defensive obstacles. There were, however, two exceptions.

Feather breached the northern cleared area once again to take a closer look at his question mark and located a rock shelf that was six feet above the pangi field and six to eight feet wide in places. In a moment of madness following a hunch, Feather climbed onto the ledge and from that slight elevation he could actually hear subdued conversation coming from within the enemy camp below the rock shelf. Inching himself forward on his belly he looked down over the edge to see one sturdily constructed hut-type basha, in it and talking were two men. Feather backed off out of sight and examined the shelf finding two machine gun positions, one sited at the end of the ledge to fire out over the cleared area, the other one though was different. The gun platform had been raised to such an extent that it allowed the muzzle of the gun to be depressed at an acute angle thus enabling the gunner to pour fire down on his own camp. The intrepid Feather continued to chance his arm and advanced along the rock shelf past the second gun position to find two more similar emplacements. Another look over the edge revealed a well-worn track, a convergence of many others really that led directly to the base of the cliff and out of sight. Observers are not supposed to conjecture but the word 'cave' immediately sprang to Feather's mind. He looked long and hard at the unmanned gun positions and thought, *This is meant to be a last ditch stand if I ever saw one. The blokes that bring their guns up here to fire them aren't meant to leave.* Thinking of bringing up the guns up prompted him to inspect the edge of the shelf more closely and sure enough positioned in line with each gun emplacement and leaning against the wall of the rock shelf were wooden scaling ladders.

The second exception was a similar excursion into the unknown being carried out at the other end of the rock shelf. The sniper from Crunch's troop who was named Lamps for obvious reasons, well, obvious to the disturbed minds of SAS animals anyway, was coming to the same conclusions as Feather having found much the same evidence. As previously agreed by their respective troop commanders over the radio, the two men restricted their limits of infiltration to twenty-five yards to give each other leeway. It is worth noting that the leeway, the remaining distance that separated Feather and Lamps was only twenty yards. Such was the skill of these two SAS soldiers that despite working in close proximity of one another neither saw nor heard his colleague, one need say no more about such expertise. But Lamps had a real gem to report, from his vantage point he had spotted a huge pond that had been dug up out of the ground and lined with ponchos. Trickling into it was a steady stream of water that kept pace with the daily usage and inevitable leakage of such a contraption. Lamps had located the end of the aqueduct and the enemy was actually using the water point only twenty yards below his position on the rock shelf.

One of the CTs carried a container of water towards him and disappeared from view under the ledge a mere two feet from the observer. Like Feather, Lamps thought, cave, and got the bloody hell out of there.

It was always within the bounds of possibility that the SAS would find the camp, it was also thought highly likely that they would map out the shape of it. But for two of them to actually infiltrate the very hub of the place, and for one of them to come within two feet of an enemy soldier was beyond anyone's comprehension and expectation.

That night Caesar was able to add a few more details to his map, and they were duly sent out over the radio to the Regimental HQ in Kuala Lumpur.

★

Abdul was down in the dumps and sulking. He had not heard

from Simon Belchard for nearly twenty-four hours and although he had tried repeatedly to contact the police inspector by telephone he could not get an answer. Now, on the twenty-second of September he was biting his nails in frustration whilst he watched the clock go round until it was 13.00 hrs, a time that he knew full well Simon would be at home to service that toffee-nosed British cow of his. Almost to the second he telephoned the inspector's bungalow but to no avail. He tried again fifteen minutes later and kept on trying, fruitlessly, until the hour of two in the afternoon.

There followed a period of indecision as he toyed with the idea of trying to contact Simon through the Rompin police barracks, a course of action that he had agreed never to use. But curiosity got the better of him and he dialled the number only to be informed that the inspector had retired to his private residence for the day. Now very puzzled and somewhat angry, Abdul persevered and rang the bungalow again and that was the story all afternoon and well into the evening when he gave up, thoroughly pissed off and decidedly worried.

He could not sleep that night and as he tossed and turned in his bed sweating streams the word 'gold' kept cropping up in his mind. Was that bastard Simon trying to cut him out, was he attempting a crafty double-cross? If that were to be the case should he betray his superior to Mr Tan and the Tongs? On second thoughts, Abdul realised that to travel down that path might mean curtains for himself too. Totally at a loss as to what to do, he panicked and tempted fate by deciding to pay Simon a visit at his bungalow in Rompin. *Yes,* he thought, *I'll go tomorrow.* Abdul might well have remembered that curiosity was supposed to have killed the cat, well it certainly helped to bring about his own downfall.

★

On the twenty-third elements of the Commonwealth brigade began the ascent of the Gunong Chini ridgeline, eighteen hundred men from Britain, Australia and New Zealand were closing in for the kill whilst their Gurkha comrades continued to dog the heels of the gold train. And all the while the crazy SAS men kept unseen, silent vigil on the enemy's very doorstep.

Within the ranks of the Australian battalion was Shovel's platoon that had been relieved in the line from Kampong Lubok Paku by a contingent of the Police Field Force men.

The Field Marshal had ordered his Intelligence bods to produce a huge plan of the CT camp and it now adorned one complete wall of his office. Addressing Crazy Harry he tapped the plan in the area of the rock shelf. 'This,' he said, 'is the key to a successful assault. Assuming, of course, that this Bird fellow is on the right track.'

'Feather, sir, and the other man is called Lamps.'

'Feather and Lamps! Where the hell do these SAS chaps get their bloody names? I suppose if this Lamps trooper were in the artillery he'd be known as Battery?' Petherington roared with laughter at his own joke.

Crazy Harry looked up in search of the Magnificent One for inspiration. 'Well sir,' he offered, 'he's certainly helped to shed some light on the matter.'

The Field Marshal winced but remembering the gravity of the situation he got back to the point. 'This Lamps chap said he saw a CT carrying a container of water from here,' he pointed at the pond, 'and disappeared from view with it under the rock shelf. It's obvious to me that there's a cave there, but is it a dead end or does it extend right though the mountain?'

'Well it isn't mapped that's for sure,' stated Harry.

'Neither was half the bloody jungle a few years back,' answered Petherington alluding to days when great areas on the maps consisted of blank spaces marked only with the main waterways. Over the years troops using the ground had drawn in the contours and other topographical information for the map-makers. 'Harry,' resumed the Field Marshal, 'I'm going to assume that there is a cave and that the bloody thing provides the CTs with an escape route. Let me put you through what I think their drill will be in the event that they come under attack.'

He paused in case Harry had a point to raise but the crazy one just said, 'Fire away sir.'

'Their general plan will be to fight like hell until the Central Military Committee make good their escape, after which all the surviving CTs will attempt to get away too. They'll probably execute the plan in three stages.

'The first will be to occupy the outer defences and cover the pangi field with sustained machine gun fire with a view to inflicting heavy casualties in the early stages of the attack.

'Phase two will be a tactical withdrawal to secondary positions to cover the cheese cutting wire and any other obstacles that the SAS have yet to find. At the same time I see the enemy hauling more machine guns up onto the rock shelf in preparation for the final ploy.

'I can envisage there being an abandonment of the inner defences as the second escape party follow in the footsteps of the CMG. That withdrawal will be covered by the rock-shelf machine gunners pouring a withering defensive fire plan down onto their own camp irrespective of any wounded that might be there. In the main that last-ditch stand will be in the form of indirect fire because of the restricted visibility, but some of the foliage will have been cleared by the initial bombardment and the small arms fire from both sides.'

Petherington looked at Harry, his face grave. 'Harry, I can't send in the Gurkhas knowing that fact. It'll be pure bloody murder and I'll not do it. Somehow we've got to take that rock shelf at very the onset of the attack.'

'The men for that job are already there, two of them have actually stood on the rock shelf.'

'Yes, I knew you'd say that you old bugger.' Harry smiled; even Field Marshal's needed moral support.

Also on the twenty-third, Caesar ordered his squadron to probe the pangi field for signs of other defences such as booby traps. He felt justified in taking the risk because during the previous day's long watch not one single CT had approached the weapon pits, nor had any patrols ventured forth from the camp. Also, he felt in his bones that the enemy was not taking up stand-to positions at first and last light, or if they were, the deployment was being confined to some as yet unknown inner defences. Caesar's theory's regarding the enemy's defensive strategy was uncannily similar to Petherington's. He recognised the importance of taking out the rock shelf and denying the CTs the use of it. It would not come as a great surprise to him if he were tasked to carry out that mission.

The SAS men breached the pangi field in twelve separate places, in all cases the patrols reported that there were no hidden obstacles amongst the sharpened bamboo stakes. But behind the line of slit trenches were sited miles of cheese cutting wire strung from tree to tree at varying heights to form a vicious and almost impenetrable barrier. It was difficult to spot before one became ensnared in the spider-web-like trap that would inflict severe cuts to any unfortunate soldiers trying to extricate themselves from it.

That night Caesar withdrew half the squadron from the pangi field to spend the night in their respective base camps. The rest were to rough it out on the enemy's doorstep to establish whether or not the CTs carried out a stand to routine.

At 08.00 hrs on the twenty-fourth the patrols that had watched and listened all night long sent in their reports to Caesar, no stand-to had taken place at the outer gun positions. But at last and first light sounds of enemy activity that included the cocking of weapons had been heard coming from deeper within the bandit stronghold.

★

During his restless night Abdul had resolved to have it out with Simon Belchard or else. He was suspicious of the lack of communication and affronted by being snubbed, after all, it was supposed to be him that was calling the shots here. Realising now that Simon was deliberately ignoring him Abdul had planned to descend on the police inspector like the proverbial ton of bricks at about one in the afternoon. But the impetuous sergeant could not stand the strain and actually departed from Kampong Masjid Tanet at the unearthly hour of four in the morning having first left a message at the police station informing his minions that would be away all day.

He drove out of his home village in a rusty black Mercedes

that was a cast-off of Mr Tan's and sounded like a tank. It woke up half the population, hardly a discrete departure and not a difficult one to spot by two Chinese observers sitting in an unmarked Wolesly police car; they were two of Tom Nobles' special branch officers.

They followed Abdul first to Alor Gajah then Tampin and onto the road for Gemas. By the time that they had reached the town that housed the source of Simon Belchard's distraction, Fiona, it was daylight. The special branch men had merely to follow in the wake of thick black clouds of smoke that belched forth from Abdul's mechanical relic to keep tabs on their target. Soon they arrived at Rompin far too early and there followed a long wait in baking hot cars for Abdul and the watchers alike. The agents got in touch with Tom Nobles by radio to give him an update on the situation; and he came back with some emphatic orders. 'All I want is proof that he makes contact with Belchard well outside of his own patch. Get a photograph of him approaching Belchard and then break up the meeting, I do not want any dialogue to take place between them. Neither of them will have the slightest clue as to who you are, with any luck they might think that you are Tong men!' He laughed, 'It will add to Abdul's dilemma. But Mr Tan will put Belchard right on that score.' Their orders received and understood the two men settled back to wait.

At 13.10 hrs Simon Belchard arrived at his bungalow fully expecting to hear Fiona's Morris trundling up the road from Gemas. He did hear a car but it was not hers, the thing roared to a halt belching smoke and steam as well as stirring up clouds of dust from the roadside. Out of it struggled a near demented Abdul to confront the startled police inspector.

'Look here!' he shouted in an apoplectic rage but he got no further because another car made a grand entrance onto the scene by screeching to a halt and discharging two burly oriental gentlemen of Chinese origin. They just stood looking at Abdul with evil grins on their faces; it was enough to send Abdul packing and he made a standing start that would have thrilled motor racing enthusiasts the world over. Giving Belchard a long, hard look but saying not a word, the two men got back into their car and drove off too, leaving a very bewildered Simon Belchard to stew in his own uncertainty.

Tom Nobles had flushed the middleman out into the open and had secured all the evidence that he needed. What he had would not be conclusive enough to hold up in a court of law, but then, it would not be going that far, would it?

At 09.00 hrs the same day, the twenty-fourth, Caesar's men again infiltrated the pangi field. They probed past the line of trenches to reconnoitre the jungle fortress in depth. Through the cheese cutting wire they crawled and beyond it to find yet more obstacles placed to impede the progress of an attacking force. They were booby traps and there were four kinds in all, three made completely from natural resources and one partially so.

The simplest consisted of a sapling bent over with the end anchored at ground level to a tripping device constructed out of a short branch, a wooden toggle and some tough vines. The bowed sapling held down by the toggle had its upper facing edge shaped and sharpened like a blade and the cut area soiled and camouflaged. When activated by someone tripping the vine the toggle securing the bowed trap was released allowing the sapling to spring upward under the victim's chin or between his legs.

Pig traps had been sited at higher elevations than was normal to accommodate human targets. These traps were bow-shaped affairs with the bow being set in the horizontal plane and secured to two sturdy trees. The device fired a sharpened stake like an arrow and was triggered by the same vine and toggle trip system. It has been recorded that one such trap aimed too high had been triggered sending an arrow straight through a Bergen rucksack full of tinned rations being carried by an SAS soldier. In another more tragic case a trooper had been transfixed though both thighs.

The third kind of booby trap encountered by the SAS men were pangis again. But this time they were much smaller and had been set into pits that were camouflaged with vegetation trap doors.

Finally there was a combination of bamboo and the No. 36 hand grenade, or Mills bomb. To make this trap short lengths of bamboo had been cut the insides of which had to accommodate a grenade that was placed within the pin having first been pulled, rather like an egg into a cup. The bamboo cup would retain the lever of the grenade until the trap was sprung. This highly volatile assemblage had then to be carefully positioned onto the ground or placed atop more bamboo sections that had been secured to the trunks of small trees. A whole series of these traps could be sited along a common vine fence with a short length of vine attached to each of the grenade cups thus securing them to the fence. When advancing troops blundered into the fence, the short lengths of vine would pull the cups away from the grenades so releasing the lever and four seconds later the air would be buzzing with lethal shrapnel as the grenades exploded.

The squadron also located and mapped the inner circle of slit trenches. The area between the two sets of dugouts was so littered with booby traps that it was little wonder that the CTs were loath to venture through the maze of death every morning and evening to follow the ritual of a stand-to.

The SAS squadron had accomplished more than anyone could have expected but Caesar knew that he and his soldiers would be asked to do more. The Field Marshal would ask them to draw on their reserves of fortitude and resilience, to evoke that indomitable spirit that makes the parachute soldier in general, and the SAS in particular, such a formidable fighting machine.

Chapter Fifteen

Upon arriving at the ambush position on the twentieth, Clancy Deane had reorganised his force into two groups, the main ambush party itself, and what he termed as his boat extraction force.

The ambush party that was to be commanded by him consisted of twenty-five SBS Commandos, three officers and fifty-seven men of the field force company. For the initial stages of the operation they would be located in a jungle base camp positioned well back from, and to the west of the actual killing ground.

Clancy had placed the boat extraction force under the command of his troop sergeant and it consisted of the sergeant's Malay minder, four SBS Commandos plus ten more field force men.

The split had been necessary because of the boats; portage when negotiating stretches of river that were not navigable was one thing, carting twenty assault boats through the jungle was another. Clancy could not take them with him and he dare not leave the bloody things behind unguarded, so his trusty troop sergeant had copped for the job of protecting them. Many men would have jumped at the chance of getting such a cushy number but to the sergeant it was tantamount to an insult. However, that worthy being just shrugged it off by saying softly, 'Now don't you go getting yourself lost sir!'

The force remained together for the first day to allow the men to recover from the hair-raising overnight river journey. On the morning of the twenty-first as an afterthought Clancy had given the 'one too many Malay policeman' the option of going with the ambush party or remaining with the boats. He chose the latter and with pride written all over his face he had pointed at the sergeant, 'Me guard him, he most important. If bandits come, me kill for sure!' he exclaimed brandishing a wicked looking Malay dagger around the place. 'Well I can't argue with that,' Clancy had agreed grinning at a highly embarrassed grisly old Bootneck with three stripes.

By 09.00 hrs Clancy and his ambush party had taken their leave of the boat extraction force to head south and away from the river bank. He did not go far, just about 800 yards then he turned right, or west, for 500 yards before stopping to site his base camp. Then in accordance with instructions from on high he thoroughly briefed the three Malay Police Officers. Under their direction the ambush party moved forward to occupy the base camp with Clancy's commandos spread evenly amongst the field force men as advisors. By nightfall the combined force was able to stand-to in a well defended position complete with a perimeter fence, trip flares, booby traps and a well-dug shit-pit.

The Field Marshal had given Claude Rysdale the honour of disposing of the Tong thugs, and it was that gentleman who had deployed the field force company to the SBS and the *Sea Pearl*. Clancy's orders from the Admiral had been simple. 'Set things up, produce a plan and brief the entire force. Convince yourself that the execution of that plan can be carried out to perfection then stand off and let the police chaps get on with the job, it's their show.'

The plan had been made, the orders written and a lengthy briefing given on the twenty-second. Training and rehearsals had commenced the same day and proved to be a difficult task. This was because the force was on active service and armed to the teeth with weapons charged with live ammunition. There was a distinct possibility that whilst practising for the ambush, an actual CT might pop up and this made it hard to draw a line between make-believe and reality. But they persevered and by noon on the twenty-third it was obvious to Clancy and his SBS lads that the field force men were bloody well trained and did not need much advice from the marines. But when the commandos began to stand down from key roles in the ambush formation in favour of the more senior of the field force men, the proud Malays were unanimous and adamant in their objections, they would not countenance such a thing. To a man they wanted, nay, demanded that they be part of a Green Beret operation and not the other way around; so far from taking a back seat the commandos continued to be an integral part of the police operation and Mr Nancy was the revered and undisputed figurehead of the ambush force. The threats of refusal had been real, 'No Mr Nancy up front, no bloody ambush!' Deep in the wilderness surrounded by danger and coping with hard times, sentiments such as those shown by these loyal Malays can bring lumps into the toughest of men's throats.

Clancy did not doubt that the field force boys would do well in the ambush. He knew also that the Tong men on the rafts did not pose much of a problem. They would be vulnerable on their precarious floating platforms with only a crocodile infested river offering them an avenue of escape, neither were the criminal elite any match for the combined military and police force arrayed against them. He was though concerned with the possibility that some element of the ambush party might be bumped by the CTs, either from the local 10th Regiment or an independent group on the rampage as a killer squad. His force would be more than a match for both of those possibilities but a contact was bound to warn the rafters and frighten them off, and that would not please Claude Rysdale at all; Clancy dared not even think what the Admiral's reaction would be. With that particular problem weighing heavily on his mind he gave his final operational orders after the training session on the twenty-fourth, he concluded by giving all concerned a warning, 'If the enemy proper approach your position and it appears that they will pass by, let them do so, do not open fire! If it is obvious to you that they will breach the ambush perimeter, also do not open fire, let them in and kill them silently!' With that statement he looked pointedly at his commandos who were so well trained in the use of their famous fighting knives. They looked back fingering the hilts of the deadly weapons. The men settled down to the night routine knowing that they would be setting up the ambush the very next day.

At 07.30 hrs on the twenty-fifth the ambush party struck camp and Clancy led them off east-northeast for 600 yards to an assembly area that was only 200 yards from the killing ground. Backpacks were dropped there and a small force left to guard them, equipped with a radio they would also act as a listening post to warn Clancy of any CT activity to his rear. The rest moved on to a dispersal point from which they deployed into the five areas comprising the ambush position. They were the killer group, the left flank and rear protection group, the right flank and rear protection group and the left and right flank listening posts. A Malay police officer commanded each of the main sub-units with Clancy taking overall command from the killer group. By 14.30 hrs the ambush was set and fully operational and Clancy proudly reported it so to the Admiral's HQ.

★

The twenty-fifth was a busy day for Mr Tan. He had received dozens of telephone calls, some of them good but there were a few bad ones thrown in just to make life interesting and more of a challenge. He did though receive two calls that were important to say the least and were enough to promote his ever-present fear of losing money, and so panic stations prevailed. But he was also acutely aware that not only wealth was at stake here, his very life hung in the balance. He had no wish to die, especially in the manner that would be prescribed by the Tong Boss should he cock up this gold bullion operation. Both communications concerned his little friend Abdul who was fast becoming a nasty thorn in his side.

Belchard had been the first to ring and he had sounded as if he were in a blind panic and that had started off Mr Tan's bout of anxiety. Having related the goings on at his bungalow he confided that he had been frightened more by the two Chinese fellows that he thought might be Tong hit men, than he had been by Abdul's belligerent manner. 'Rest assured,' Mr Tan had informed Belchard, 'had they have been Tong men I'd have heard about it by now.' But Mr Tan had terminated the call not really assured of anything himself anymore.

The second call was more serious and required positive action to be taken on his part, the caller was the man who had warned him about Abdul and put him onto Belchard. The information was enough to make the hairs on the back of his neck stand on end. He cursed the sheer gall of the little upstart who he had financed all these years.

'I'm telling you Mr Tan,' the informant had said, 'our man has made arrangements to meet with a top police official, you know, the special branch?'

'Where's this meeting supposed to take place?' Mr Tan had fairly screeched in reply.

'At his house in Masjid Tanet, probably tomorrow sometime but it could be sooner.'

'Okay, thanks for the tip, I'll put a watch on him straight away.'

'I should if I were you. I'll be in touch!' Tom Nobles put down the receiver and smiled.

★

Whilst Clancy Deane was setting his trap and Mr Tan was battling with the jitters and posting a watch on Abdul's dwelling; Caesar's SAS squadron had been busy around the CT camp.

Their main task of the day was to reconnoitre and make themselves familiar with the most suitable approach routes to the camp so that they could guide in the advancing Gurkha assault troops speedily without undue hindrance. The brunt of this mission fell to Fatigue's troop who were responsible for the 300 yard long south-west aspect that was to be the start line for the final assault.

The Gurkhas following the gold train had been instructed to halt on the spur line that separated the Jeram and Mentiga waterways. The point where the gold train passed over the spur would become the assembly area that all troops participating in the attack would pass through. Initially, patrols from Fatigue's troop would meet the Gurkhas there and guide them down to the gully that had been designated as a dispersal point, from which the various formations comprising the attack force would be led off to their start lines.

Caesar had received some preliminary orders concerning the attack and knew that because of the close country, the configuration of the ground and the particular dispositions of the defences, the assault was not going to be along conventional lines.

Definitely not a gung-ho charge of screaming kukri-wielding Gurkha riflemen in wave upon wave of extending lines. No, it was going to be more like a series of fierce pinpricks that would probe and breach the obstacles in a leap-frogging fire and movement manoeuvre that would pave the way for the final assault troops. They would pass through the positions already taken and fight their way inch by inch through the objective, and even more riflemen would pass through them to chase the enemy beyond that into the fields of fire of the Commonwealth brigade who were lying in wait on the high ground to the north, east and west.

It would be Fatigue's job to co-ordinate the movement of the Gurkha sub-units from the dispersal point to the start line that was to be in his aspect. He was also to allot guides drawn from Chalky's and Crunch's troops to the Gurkhas that had been tasked to provide flank protective covering fire from the north and south-east aspects.

From the dispersal point that was very close indeed to the enemy camp an entire Gurkha battalion would be required to manoeuvre into position without making a sound or bumping into one another. The choice of routes was critical to the success of this tricky operation and the SAS patrols would have their work cut out to come up with the goods. As difficult as the task already was, it was further complicated by the fact that the assault troops would not be able to move up onto their actual start lines before the planned aerial bombardment. When they did move the enemy would be shocked and dazed but fully alerted none the less. The guides would have to lead their charges in like greased lightning and with pinpoint accuracy. The squadron worked hard at the problem all day and by 15.00 hrs they had it cracked. Soon the troop situation reports were pouring into Caesar's HQ.

Caesar's signaller had been working overtime taking down a stream of Morse code that had been sending him dotty for at least an hour. During a short pause he remarked to Lofty, 'Looks like the Field Marshal must have enough to go on, this really is the big one.'

'Well, I expect we'll manage it,' whispered the unflappable one. Caesar accepted the reams of army issue toilet paper on which the signaller had jotted down the entire plan of the forthcoming attack. 'This is from our friend Mercury, the God of Speech,' explained the Sergeant Major.

'At least he hasn't used it yet,' said Caesar inspecting the paper and sniffing it. 'One must be thankful for small mercies, let's hope he hasn't made an arse of decoding it.' Caesar studied the sheets of written orders for a while. 'I'm relieved to say that everything is okay.'

The communicator in question got in with a quip, 'You see, I'm not just a fart in a trance.'

Lofty looked at him and enquired, 'What do you wipe your arse on by the way?'

'My finger, of course, that's why you've always got to tell me to take the bloody thing out!'

'I surrender,' conceded the grinning Sergeant Major, and then went on a rummage patrol to gather in the ingredients for a curry. Caesar commenced making his extraction of orders that he would issue to his men later.

One of Caesar's favourite pastimes was that having made a plan he would put it to his wily old Sergeant Major as a kind of test, for the plan that is. So when Lofty returned and had laid out his harvest on a large leaf in preparation for the evening meal the Major said, 'Try this one on for size.'

'Don't tell me we've got to do the bloody job on our own because the Gurkhas won't work on Ramadan or something?'

'No, it's not quite as bad as that. The Gurkhas are still going to be there but as well as guiding them in we've been given three more little jobs to do; just to keep us on our toes, you understand?' He paused while Lofty started to make a curry sauce by launching six bloated leeches into a mess tin full of Oxo, chilli, and curry powder flavoured water.

'And what are these jobs that the Exalted One sees fit to punish us with?'

'Well first off he thinks that it will be too damned dangerous for the Gurkhas to go in for the kill immediately after the Air force have finished bombing the camp without some sort of covering fire going down.'

Lofty crushed some cherry red ants and dark grey beetles on a stone with the hilt of his bayonet. 'Go on.'

'So he wants the Gurkhas to lay down close supporting fire from their own 3-inch mortars. He realises that most of the bombs will explode well up in the trees but he thinks it will certainly distract the enemy.'

'But they can't fire them up through the bloody trees, right?'

'Right. Under cover of the Air force bombing run we are to blow a clearing for the Gurkha mortar base plate position using our own explosives.'

'That's no problem, surely? We can use Blaster in Fatigue's troop for that, it's just up his street,' recommended Lofty whilst cutting two centipedes into sections and dropping them into the now boiling water. Like Caesar, Blaster was a sapper, a gentleman of the Army Engineers and what he did not know about explosives and booby traps was not worth a cent.

Elated, Caesar ticked off Blaster's name that he had already written down. 'What are those pod-like things that you are cutting up?' he asked.

'Why pods of course, senna pods.'

'But don't they give you the shits?'

'Oh yes! But if you put some of these in too you'll be okay,' he assured chopping up a jungle onion, 'you see, the onion on its own will make you constipated. The senna pods will give you the runs, but taken together in equal parts they just keep you regular.' Lofty looked at the signaller. 'Mercury, what's that over there?' he asked pointing at nothing in particular. Whilst the unfortunate man was looking away Lofty popped a senna pod into his all-in stew. Caesar raised an eyebrow. 'That'll make him shit through the eye of a needle, it'll teach him not to out-ad-lib me won't it?'

'Yes it will, but make bloody sure he's regular for the attack!'

'And the second job?' prompted Lofty finishing off his culinary masterpiece with a tin of Irish stew and one of kippers.

'We are to take the rock shelf in the very early stages of the attack,' announced Caesar as if that sort of thing was an everyday occurrence.

'During the bombing raid no doubt?' guessed Lofty with absolute conviction.

'Correct, you're a bloody genius,' congratulated Caesar.

'And whilst the Gurkhas are raining mortar bombs down on us?'

'That is indeed so. To spearhead that little chore I thought I'd use—'

'Feather and Pole on the north side and Lamps and Cannibal to the south?' butted in Lofty.

Caesar ticked off the names as he thought, *How nice of him to agree with me.* Lofty smiled. Cannibal was from Fiji and a more fierce and loyal soldier you could not wish to meet, it was unlikely that any CT defending the rock shelf would survive a confrontation with him.

'I suppose this little group will be taking part in this rock shelf shindig too?' broke in the fourth member of the headquarters' patrol who was nicknamed Ball, as in ball and chain and he was an Australian. The story goes that he was actually deported from Botany Bay to England because he was too rough for even the Australian authorities to handle. Somewhat at a loss as to what to do with him the British Government had appointed him as a role model for the SAS selection system, but then, the SAS is full of legends like that!

It was Caesar's turn to smile as he addressed Lofty, 'You too can come a-waltzing Matilda up the rock shelf providing that you come through the third job alive. It's the most dangerous task on the Field Marshal's list.'

Lofty who knew damned well when Caesar was taking the piss groaned and said, 'Go on, do enlighten me?'

'It's balloons!' announced the Major with evil glee, 'he wants a ring of marker balloons around the camp perimeter to give the Air force a clear target to aim at rather than let them saturate a bloody great area of jungle with us being somewhere in it.'

'Strewth!' exclaimed Ball in a whisper, of course, 'don't send me with him for Christ's sake!'

'Yeah,' said Mercury, 'fancy being gassed to death by your own side on the eve of an attack?'

It was still only 16.00 hrs when Lofty held out his hand for Caesar's mess tin, to eat a hot meal at such an early hour was a rare luxury. He was about to pour in half of the curry when Caesar said, 'Well I'm not so sure I like centipedes.'

'Here, have some of mine then,' offered the god of Morse unaware of the questionable treat that was in store for him. 'On second thoughts,' smiled Caesar weakly at the Sergeant Major, 'just a little.'

During all this banter and cooking that went on within 1,000 yards of the enemy stronghold, Caesar had reversed the bog paper and written out his own set of orders, he handed them to Mercury who had just finished his stew. 'Send this out to Fatigue and Crunch.' To Lofty he said, 'I'll brief Chalky personally.' The signaller was quick off the mark and was soon tapping away in excess of eighteen words a minute.

'I hope he can run as fast as he can send Morse,' Lofty jested with a wink.

In tandem with the thoughts of Caesar session, Chalky decided to show off his prowess at living in the jungle selecting Fred as his audience. He first cut a section of bamboo eight inches in diameter and twelve inches long that he split down the middle to form two trough like receptacles. Sawing one trough in two he cut a 'V' shaped notch out of each half on the convex side. Placed on the ground with the notches uppermost they made a fine cradle on which to rest the remaining and intact trough. Bamboo contains water and from another section Chalky poured some into the trough. With the shavings from his previous handiwork he lit a fire under his wooden cooking pot, bamboo shavings will burn, solid components will not. He then added some bamboo shoots to the water and in no time at all he had produced a meal made completely from bamboo, but he chucked in some succulent young tree roots, the pith from certain palms and a handful of rice to make it wholesome. Fred had learned a little more and after that day he was never seen to use a mess tin in the jungle again.

Whilst the patrol was eating Caesar came over to their bivouac area and sat down. 'I'll give you a full troop briefing later,' he informed Chalky, 'but here's a warning order for a special task that I want your patrol to carry out.' The whole patrol swivelled their eyeballs upwards. 'Looking to Allah won't get you out of this one,' grinned the Major, 'I want you to take out the machine gun positions located at the apex. You are to capture the guns and turn them onto the enemy and create some havoc. Think about it.' He stood up to leave; stepping over Fred he looked down at the new man's mess tin. 'I see you haven't graduated to leeches?'

'No sir, I haven't been with you long enough to be that bloodthirsty yet,' chuckled Fred.

He'll do, thought Caesar.

Only 1,500 yards north of Caesar's camp the Commonwealth brigade were arriving atop of the Gunong Chini ridgeline. The Australian battalion was already working its way around the summit of Gunong Chini to take up positions on the spur immediately east of the enemy camp. The British battalion had established itself on the ridgeline to the north and the Kiwi's were peeling off south along the spur west of the gully. Further away to the south the second Gurkha Battalion was following in Crunch's footsteps and advancing up out of the filthy Sungei Mentiga wetlands to seal off escape routes to the south.

★

Fantail had, on the surface, seemed to have recovered from her ordeal aboard the *Sea Pearl* and looked for all the world as if she were thriving on the harsh existence of the long march. If she was at all concerned about her fate Fantail did not let it show in her outward demeanour. She did, however, communicate some of her fears in the urgency of the snatched moments of lovemaking with Kim in the early hours of the mornings when they thought that most of the others would be asleep. During the night that followed the day when the gold train had broken away from the courier route to head east for the main camp, they were both acutely aware that time was running out. She had come to him that night with her defences down suffering a craving for his love. They had coupled like wild animals and lost themselves in a night of passion that cemented forever the bond between them. Whatever their fate, they would share it, suffer the same pain and die for the cause as one.

The next morning as Kim had been checking the column

prior to giving the order to move off Ulu had taken a snap at him. Had the mule's teeth made contact with the intended target, Kim's thigh, they would have removed a sizeable lump of flesh. Kim had looked at Fantail and winked. He knows, had said his eyes.

'Love is a serious business,' Fantail had giggled as Kim had sprung out of the way of one hell of a mean mule.

The first leg of the new bearing that would eventually take the gold train over four spurs that barred the way like the razor-backed tails of some prehistoric dinosaur was relatively easy. They first crossed the western most tributary of the Sungei Jeram to climb up the side of the first and smallest of the spurs. The ascent was completed by noon and Kim was pleased with the progress, although the elephants did balk at having to cross straight over the top to plunge down the other side when their natural instinct was to turn up or down the spur line. The descent was not so easy; the going being steep and treacherous with the fear of falling uppermost in the minds of humans and animals alike. The skill of the mahouts and muleteers was tested to the extreme and the patience of all concerned tried to the limit, but by 16.00 hrs the column had reached the bottom safely and camped by yet another tributary of the Jeram River so ending the first day of the final approach. And whilst the guerrillas rested and two lost souls made love in the darkness; the Gurkhas waited, listened and sharpened their kukris.

Day two was the reverse of the first. The river crossing was no problem but the ascent to the top of the second spur was a nightmare. The hearts of hard men went out to the animals because both elephants and mules were magnificent, slipping and sliding the beasts of burden regained lost ground time and time again until they triumphantly broke through to the track that ran along the spur line. The mahouts who had put much effort into the climb were utterly exhausted, too tired to control their charges for just a minute or two; but it was enough for the leading elephant to take advantage of his master's momentary lapse of concentration and he went lumbering off down the main track for a short distance instead of carrying straight on as would have been requested. The normal jungle noises were completely out-staged as the liberated elephant broke forth into a deafening bout of trumpeting that was soon taken up by his five friends all of whom were milling about with the obvious intention of following the rogue. The mules that could not complete the ascent because the elephants were blocking the way, gave vent to their feelings and joined in the mad symphony of the gold train. Parrots screeched in protest whilst other birds provided a chorus, monkeys howled, hooted and crashed around in the treetops in crazy consternation; Kim Bok could do little else but double up in a fit of laughter, and be damned to the bloody British!

The mahout who was supposed to be in charge of the melodious one struggled through the line of enormous, cavorting beasts to investigate and could tell by the elephant's boastful demeanour that he wished to impart a suggestion. With feet planted firmly, trunk curled upward like some great horned musical instrument, albeit out of tune, and flapping ears he stood facing to the left. The mahout smiled in understanding and turned to Kim who had recovered his composure having fought his way forward through the column of exasperated, mud-splattered animals and men. Almost apologetically the mahout explained, 'He's trying to tell us that he's found an easy way down off this accursed hill, we'd be fools not to heed his advice!'

'Get him to stop that infernal noise! I can't think straight.'

One tap of the mahout's staff was enough to silence the elephant, well, reduce the noise to a contented growl anyway. 'That's his equivalent to a cat's purr,' said the mahout weakly, 'he's happy now.'

'Thank god for that.' Not willing to go charging off the hill at the say so of the forest giant, Kim looked at his map. Under the years of smudges and rubbed out pencil lines was a small feature jutting out from where he was standing, a mini spur if you like, a frog's leg shaped affair that led all the way down to a third tributary of the Jeram water complex. It would take them slightly south of his plotted course but, what the hell?

Kim Bok slapped the mahout on the back so hard that he nearly flattened the little Indian fellow. 'Give him his head,' he said, 'let's get things moving before the bloody mules go on strike!' The mahout did his thing and with a final triumphant bellow the elephant forged his way down the hill adopting a gait that could only be described as a swagger.

A day later they were progressing slowly through the depression that Fatigue's troop had been clearing prior to Fred discovering the CT camp. Depression by name it was certainly depressing by nature. It was low ground in comparison to the high ridgeline that lay north of them with its spurs running off southwards to form a rugged, uneven basin. Had there been no trees the area would have resembled a huge sugar bowl half-full of broken lumps and cracked open at one end. But there were trees in abundance and that made it all the more difficult, the place was one bloody great obstacle.

It took one and a half days for the gold train to cross the depression with the elephants slowly but surely deteriorating into an antisocial mood bordering on the cantankerous and bloody minded. Conversely, the mules remained aloof and tackled the difficult and filthy terrain with almost regal dignity. Ulu continued to pursue Fantail with affectionate zeal but bared his teeth at the very sight of Kim Bok.

The stalwart Gurkha riflemen followed, watched and wondered. Whatever else might happen during their army careers they would remember this mission for the rest of their lives.

On the twenty-sixth the column crossed over the last but one spur that lay in their path and arrived at the final tributary of the Sungei Jeram, the gold train had reached the base of the last obstacle. On the other side of it the camp was located, the weary guerrillas and their pack train had only three miles left to march.

At first light the next morning they set off to tackle the last leg of their journey. They had to dig deep into their reserves of human endeavour to overcome flagging resolves and diminishing determination, to combat exhaustion and sum up the will to conquer pessimism and that overriding feeling of, what's the use? But with great fortitude and indomitable spirits this bedraggled band of fellows and their female companion made it. By noon on the twenty-seventh Kim Bok and Fantail led the gold train into the headquarters camp of the renowned 10th Regiment and the

Central Military Committee. In the emotional feelings of the moment even the recalcitrant elephants were forgiven as marchers and defenders alike cried unashamedly.

Behind them on the spur, the Gurkhas closed the trap and linked up with the Kiwis on their left hand and sub-units of the second Gurkha battalion that had force-marched from the Mentiga River on their right. The CTs were now completely surrounded.

At the gully and the apex the SAS men watched as the gold train passed by. There was no hatred or animosity on their faces, only grudging admiration in recognition of a tremendous task accomplished, albeit too late.

If the SAS observers had wondered at how confidently Kim Bok had marched from the gully and along the track to the apex, and then across the pangi field into the camp, they probably would not have been surprised to learn that it was because the Paymaster General knew the camp well. In fact, the great leader had commissioned the guerrilla fighter to lay the whole thing out. It had been Kim that had made all the compass bearings that determined the present shape of the camp. He had also designed and plotted the course of the aqueduct. And it had been he that had explored a small cave in the cliff face, discovering that it extended deep into the bowels of Gunong Chini to exit the mountain into the Chini Lake basin miles to the north. And because of that heaven-sent escape route Kim had recognised the rock shelf for its tactical importance in a successful withdrawal under fire.

The terrorists had since enlarged the cave entrance and turned the main cavern into living quarters for the Central Military Committee and off duty personnel of the 10th Regiment. The cavern that was over 100 yards in diameter with a ceiling of between six to ten feet in places also accommodated an armoury, a cooking and eating area, a store and an equipment repair shop.

The gold was destined for the armoury where it would be melted down into smaller lumps that would only leave the camp in loads that could be man-packed. The animals now became surplus to requirement and were earmarked for food; handed over to the chief cook they would be stabled in various sub-caverns to await slaughter.

There were now 266 men camped within the perimeter of the jungle fortress but not all of them slept in the cave. Half of them roughed it outside so as to be on standby alert for a possible attack. Every two days they swapped over giving everyone a fare share of the responsibilities and affording all some form of rest. Work parties for pruning the foliage around the pangi field, patrols, and aqueduct repair details were drawn from those men residing in the cave at the time.

The men whose duty it was to man the camp defences lived in bashas that had been erected immediately behind the inner ring of slit trenches. Well-worn tracks led from the cave to these shelters and more cleared ways provided a safe route through the booby-trapped area to the outer gun emplacements.

The duty officer in charge of the standby force was billeted in a hut that had been constructed just outside of the cave entrance.

The camp was well stocked with rice and tinned food. Patrols trapped pigs, monkeys and birds and caught fish in the Mentiga River tributaries. Now and again luxuries such as rice wine and cigarettes were brought in by patrols that had pillaged some village or other.

Of the 266 souls occupying the CT camp, twenty were women. Of Fantail we know about, how the remaining nineteen ladies shared their feminine favours with the men can only be imagined.

Since arriving at Chalky's base camp Caesar had in the course of his duties as a brilliant field commander actually managed to reconnoitre, together with Mercury, the CT camp perimeter less the high ground above the rock shelf. In ordering Lofty to supervise the deployment of the marker balloons he was giving the sergeant major the opportunity to do the same. It was important that Lofty take a look around before the shit hit the fan because amongst his many and varied duties he was Caesar's second in command. Should anything happen to the Major, then Lofty would have to take over and command the squadron, and he would be at a distinct disadvantage if he were not familiar with the ground. In a situation as hairy as this close reconnaissance the radio had to be permanently manned and Lofty and Ball were carrying out that duty at present, their turn around the enemy camp would come later.

Although Caesar did not envisage his men having to advance beyond the rock shelf some of the balloons would have to be positioned half way between it and the spur line that was occupied by the waiting Australian troops. It was a ticklish task and one that would be right up Lofty's street because you wouldn't find a cooler customer in a dangerous situation. By traversing the treacherous piece of terrain, Lofty would be in a position to provide valuable topographical information that Caesar could pass on to the tough infantrymen from down under.

Lofty with Ball in tow, set off from the base camp at 07.30 hrs on the twenty-seventh with all of the headquarter patrol's compliment of marker balloons and an adequate supply of water gassing for the use of. He was, not that he needed to be, being guided to the apex by Fred. Although they were sharing the same base camp the two men had not actually spoken to each other since the drop. 'Last seen you dangling from a tree, didn't I?' smiled Lofty.

'Yeah, but I haven't been hanging about much since then,' replied Fred.

'He's learning,' Lofty whispered to Ball. The Australian advisor to the British Army winked at Fred and gave him the thumbs up sign, in Australian English and under the present circumstances that meant, 'You've made it mate.'

Upon arriving at the apex, or rather, a distance of 100 yards back from it where the balloons were to be sited they met the first balloonist from Fatigue's troop. He was standing by a piece of string that had been anchored to a convenient branch, he had already launched the balloon and was grinning from ear to ear like a lunatic. 'It must be the gas,' Lofty observed, 'Give him a tot of rum to make him better.'

'But he might blow up,' grinned Fred.

'Precisely,' concluded Lofty.

'Strewth!' was Ball's comment.

In a more conventional regiment a sergeant major might be

more than a little annoyed to find that a task he was meant to supervise had already been carried out. But this was the SAS and like a lot of other things within it, the rank structure was peculiar to say the least. It has already been said that volunteer NCOs relinquish their rank upon joining the regiment. They retain that rank in their parent unit to take up from where they left off on returning from a tour of duty with the SAS, indeed, some of the more fortunate of them find that they have been promoted during their absence.

Lofty, like Chalky, was a brilliant field soldier and quite at home in the most inhospitable of places. He thrived on danger and was an inspiration to all around him in a tight spot. His coolness and that wonderfully dry sense of humour endeared him to other soldiers who would try and follow his example. But try as he might he was a non-starter in barrack type soldiering and was the bane of many an RSM's life. Lofty just could not make it above the rank of Corporal in his own county regiment. He had dropped two ranks in order to enter the SAS and a world that was made for him. Absolutely suited to the SAS way of life he had excelled in every field and had soon shot up to the rank of warrant officer class two, with the appointment of squadron sergeant major. However, in the SAS that was not a substantive rank although he was paid the going rate for it. In theory when he returned to his parent regiment he would have to revert again, this time back down three ranks to corporal.

So it was no use Lofty getting his knickers in a twist with 'he of the grinning chops' because that individual was the equivalent to an RSM in his own unit, and a substantive one at that, but was only a mere trooper in the SAS. He was, as anyone could see, quite happy with his lot and contented to remain a trooper. On return to his unit he would automatically assume the duties of a warrant officer, class one. In reality he was one rank above Lofty but in the SAS five ranks below. In the regiment promotions are largely based on merit, and demotions on cock-ups. The men tended to follow leaders for their SAS ability rather than the badge of rank.

The happy balloonist was in fact a bomb disposal expert from Army Ordinance and was carrying five more balloons that were to be launched along the front of Fatigue's aspect. Nicknamed Kamikaze he was more than willing to inflate all the balloons himself allowing Lofty to creep away periodically to observe the pangi field. When at last the sixth balloon was up and over Fatigue's patch, Kamikaze had a quick word with Lofty. 'I'm off to give Blaster a hand, he might need defusing after laying all those charges.' Then still grinning like a loony and seemingly none the worse after six successive gassings he disappeared into the jungle.

Another six balloons later, they reached the end of Crunch's aspect and the cleared area at the southern end of the rock shelf. Lamps and Cannibal led Lofty and Ball across the strip and into the jungle beyond, then they left the two headquarters men to their own devices.

With Lofty leading the way and plotting their progress they slowly climbed half way up the side of the spur before turning left, or north. Ball had to suffer the indignity of inflating and sending aloft the balloons praying to high heaven that his fellow countrymen above him would not venture down and witness his demise. *I'd never live it down,* he thought peering at Lofty through the clouds of gaseous vapour. *If I cough they'll bloody well shoot me, if they see me I'll die of shame, no matter which way I look at it I'm a gonner.* Lofty who could well imagine what was going on in Ball's mind, just smiled.

Ball put up four balloons in all and then thankfully the most difficult part of the mission was over. Although the Aussies above had been warned about the SAS movements below, the slightest mistake on Lofty or Ball's part such as displaced rocks tumbling down onto the rock shelf alerting the CTs would surely initiate a full-scale shooting match with Lofty and Ball caught in the middle. Far from holding Ball in ridicule, the tough Aussie troops would be more likely to take their hats off to both soldiers, the ribald insults would come later in some beer bar or other and deep down Ball knew all that really. The two men slowly descended to the northern end of the rock shelf and were met by Feather and Pole who then escorted them across the strip to Chalky's bailiwick.

Chalky, one of the most trusted men in the regiment had already launched his six balloons and Lofty did not question his judgement. Instead, he went into a huddle and produced a sketch map of a fissure that he had located about half way along and well above the rock shelf that led straight up towards the spur. 'It's almost like a track,' he explained, 'a fit man would make easy going of it, a fleeing man would fly up the bloody thing. Make a note of it up here,' he pointed at his temple, 'I'll get Caesar to inform the Diggers and Crunch's boys.'

It must be pointed out that the Gurkha Rifles are quite capable of blowing a clearing in the jungle for themselves, in fact, there is not much that a Gurkha battalion cannot do. But in this instance the Gurkha formation following the gold train, and therefore the closest, was a rifle company that did not carry explosives. The Gurkha assault pioneer platoon were well to the rear and even with the best will in the world would not be able to move up into the forward area in time to blow the clearing. The use of helicopters to transport them to the scene was out of the question because of the noise, both from the aircraft and the construction of a landing site that might well require the use of explosives. Back to square one and the SAS who always carried the means to blow things, or men, to kingdom come.

The entire supply of plastic explosives carried by the squadron had been stockpiled in Fatigue's base camp, delivered unto him by the other two troops. Fatigue, together with Blaster's patrol and Kamikaze carted the whole lot off to rendezvous with the Gurkha mortar platoon commander. That able individual had already sited the spot where he wished the clearing to be blown, 1,500 yards south of the CT camp it was designated as the mortar base plate position. There was no shortage of manpower because the Gurkha lieutenant had brought his entire platoon with him.

Under Blaster's supervision with Kamikaze acting as an advisor, the men got stuck into the job of preparing the trees for demolition and making up the charges.

First they carefully selected the trees that would bring many others down with them when they were blown. Having made the choice, two wedge-shaped pieces were cut out of the trunks of each of them, a large cut on the side that tree was to fall and a smaller one about two feet above it but on the opposite side of the trunk.

Plastic explosives had then to be moulded into the cuts, two thirds into the large one and the remaining third into the smaller cut. The total amount of plastic needed was dependent on the thickness of the tree in question. Both Blaster and Kamikaze had formulas for that indelibly imprinted on their brain boxes. The theory behind the wedge-shaped charges was that the two forces generated by the explosion would act against each other in a cutting action with the larger, lower charge kicking the trunk inwards therefore causing the top half of the tree to fall outwards in the required direction; the weaker charge being restricted to cutting the trunk only.

Gun cotton primers with detonators were pushed into the plastic and the whole taped to the trees. Instantaneous fuses that had been crimped into every detonator were then linked up to miles more of the washing line-like fuse to form a huge ring main. When the charge was initiated the whole shebang would go up in one enormous explosion. Smaller trees could be cut using just the powerful instantaneous fuse, again there was a formula but Blaster saw to all that.

The Gurkhas pitched in and worked like Trojans, keeping the noise down to a minimum was bloody hard work indeed but by 15.00 hrs the job was completed.

It was hoped that as a result of all the hard work a clearing would emerge from the confusion of the explosion extending fifty yards in all directions thereby enabling the Gurkhas to bed in their mortars with adequate muzzle clearance for the bombs to commence the flight to the target.

Fatigue and Kamikaze took their leave together with the Gurkhas; Blaster and his patrol remained behind to blow the clearing.

★

Fiona drove out to Simon's bungalow knowing that it would be for the last time. Although she loathed and despised the man now Fiona could still remember the carefree and delightful times that she had enjoyed with him in the past. She had resolved to take those memories with her into his bed this very afternoon in an attempt to make her ordeal bearable and to add realism to her deception.

Petherington had personally spoken to her about the task ahead. 'The attack,' he had confided, 'is to take place on the twenty-eighth, I want those rafts on the river the same day. So my dear you are to tell Belchard that the bogus gold shipment will be moving on the twenty-ninth, that will be enough to get them going. As the twenty-eighth is tomorrow the Tongs will have to know tonight.' He had paused to look at her kindly. 'Look here,' he had continued, 'let me assure you that Jeremy's position in the service is secure, there are to be no repercussions. Don't blow it my dear girl, give it all you've got, but don't blow it?' She was well aware that the Tong men would be rafting to their deaths and shuddered as she thought of how callous it all was. But the Field Marshal's words had given her strength and she would give Simon Belchard what he wanted in a way that she had never done before. *If he lives through all this,* she had thought at the time, *he'll spend the rest of his days craving for equal sexual satisfaction.*

Fiona arrived at the bungalow just before two in the afternoon to find that Simon was about to take a shower. Dressed only in a sarong he started to apologise but she hushed him up by placing a finger to his lips. Then as if she was performing in a strip-joint Fiona undressed slowly, tantalising him so that he became fully aroused and his sarong fell away to expose him in all his glory. A horrid and loathsome creature he might be but he did have a beautiful body, and as Fiona had often done before she grabbed him by his manhood and pulled him into the shower. They made love standing up with the tepid water cascading down their heaving, cavorting bodies. Then still wet and entwined the couple progressed to Simon's bed where they copulated frenziedly again as if there was no tomorrow. Again and again they went at it, Fiona put everything she had into this final act. Her simulated orgasms were very vociferous and the biting and clawing was done with a vengeance, it was her that took him and not the other way around; he was too exhausted to take the dominant role expected of the male. And when he did explode in the final great orgasm of the afternoon, and the last ever with her, it was Fiona that was straddling him. Simon fell into a fitful sleep, twitching and muttering meaningless utterances; it was as of their roles had been reversed. When he did eventually wake up it was to find Fiona fully dressed in the kitchen making a pot of tea.

★

Tom Nobles arrived in Kampong Masjid Tanet at about six in the evening long after Simon had had bypassed Abdul to inform Mr Tan that the six gold laden sampans were to depart from Kampong Lubok Paku on the twenty-ninth. He drove first to the police station where he produced some identity before requesting Abdul's address. At that moment the man himself put in an appearance and Tom explained that he was just passing through the area, inventing some cock and bull story to justify his reason for doing so. 'I was going to pop around to your home to see you and then I thought we'd go for a drink?' Abdul appeared to be undecided and a little uneasy but after listening to some suitably flattering comments from Tom concerning the efficient way the village police force was run, he mellowed and led the special branch man to his house. An hour later they were sat comfortably in Abdul's favourite watering hole.

Although Tom did not actually spot any of Mr Tan's watchers he felt their presence emanating from the shadows. They, like he had required in the case of Abdul meeting Belchard, only wanted proof of contact; now they had it. Tom departed from Kampong Masjid Tanet that night never to return, he felt no qualms about having condemned Abdul to death at the hands of the Tongs.

★

Dennis knew that things must be coming to a head in the Chini Mountain area that was not too many miles away from his location. He was not surprised, therefore, when Shu Ling woke him up from a snooze at five in the evening to inform him of the news. 'Kuantan say that boats move on twenty-ninth.'

'In that case,' announced Dennis after a suitable pause, 'we'll have to occupy the ambush position tomorrow, get the okay from your people.'

'Already done,' Shu Ling assured Dennis.

'Good, Get the men ready to move just after first light, I'll decide on the actual time of departure then.'

The Tong camp was by now a well-established affair with good communication tracks linking all the key areas. One of these led from the safety boat to Shu Ling's basha and was marked by a waist high vine guideline. Shu Ling felt his way along it in the dark to pass on the news. Dennis smiled when he heard the subdued buzz of excitement coming from the camp. Alone once more he fortified himself with a swig of arrack and wondered how Clancy was going to inform him of the precise time of the attack. By leaking out to the Tong thugs that the gold would be on the move on the twenty-ninth, Petherington was telling Dennis that the shindig was planned for the twenty-eighth. But there must be an H-Hour, and a time that Dennis should offer up the Tong sacrifice.

At 20.00 hrs the same evening Clancy's troop sergeant, four SBS Commandos and the 'one too many Malay policeman' that was now a proud bodyguard arrived by an assault boat at a point directly opposite the Tong Camp. From there the boat was paddled across the river to the sandbank from which the six men went on listening watch in an attempt to pinpoint the rafters by sound. It was the minder that picked up the clue, the others acknowledged the noise but only the Malay recognised it for what it was, it was the creaking, scraping sound of a boat's hull grinding against the roots of a mangrove tree as the vessel moved gently in the flow. *It's the bloody safety boat,* thought the sergeant, *and in it hopefully we'll find that eccentric bastard Dennis the bloody menace.*

He tapped his minder on the shoulder and in the dark found his hand and shook it firmly. The rain had stopped and the moon was breaking through the clouds providing some intermittent light. The policeman slipped over the side of the assault boat and placed his Malay kris between his teeth. The sergeant took it off him and replaced it with his own commando fighting knife, and then he gave the thumbs up sign to the little man and tapped him on the head. The sergeant had just enough time to see the glint of pride in his eyes before a cloud blocked out all.

Dennis was contemplating whether or not to consume

anymore arrack when he felt something touch his elbow that was resting on the gunwale of the boat. He froze in horror at the thought of have having the DTs at a time like this but slowly drew his pistol just the same. He tensed as he felt pressure being applied to his arm by a human hand but before he could react a voice whispered, 'From Mr Nancy sir.' Dennis found the hand and took the small package that was being offered to him by his visitor from the deep. And then the man had gone as silently as he had arrived.

The message read:

H-Hour is planned for 10.30 hrs tomorrow. Kindly have your victims in position by that time. The springing of the trap is the signal for the attack to begin. Good luck!

Chapter Sixteen

It would not be true to say that Petherington's office had been refurbished but changed in appearance it certainly had. Gone had the personal trappings of the great man together with his mementos of bygone campaigns. The wall clock was still there keeping company with a portrait of the Queen and the wall map of the CT camp. His desk had been shoved into one corner but the rest of the furniture removed. Occupying the centre of the room atop of some trestle tables was a huge cloth model of the camp made to perfection showing every detail found by Caesar's SAS Squadron. As an inset, in one corner had been included the section of the Sungei Pahang where the SBS ambush was sited. On the Field Marshal's desk was a selection of small models that would be used in conjunction with various stages of the impending attack. In one corner rested an extended snooker cue that had been borrowed from the sergeant's mess, it was far too long for Crazy Harry to use in his swirling dervishes act.

Into this command post walked two men, the Field Marshal and Crazy Harry Blunt. Neither of them had slept a wink and both were grey-faced with apprehension. It was not a time for frivolity because Petherington had committed thousands of men to this action, some of them would be killed and of that there was no question.

They both jumped as the telephone rang; Harry answered it and listened for a while before quietly putting down the receiver. 'That was Tom Nobles, sir.'

'And?'

'They've found Sergeant Abdul Hassan's body, he's been murdered and it was a pretty messy affair by all accounts.'

'Well that's what they wanted,' replied Petherington stone-faced. 'Let's hope that this little lot goes the same way,' he concluded, pointing at the inset. Harry looked at the clock. 'Nearly first light, Dennis should be stirring his stumps by now.'

'Yes,' agreed the Field Marshal, 'time to make a move.' He picked up a model raft and placed it on the river at the point where the SBS had reported the Tong camp to be. Then like Zeus and his son Hercules looking down from Mount Olympus the two soldiers looked pensively at the model.

Dennis awoke feeling like death warmed up but soon revived himself with an early morning livener. After the nocturnal visit of Clancy's sea serpent of the night before he had really hung one on. Supplies of the hard stuff were low but the fact that he would no longer be obliged to share his booze with Shu Ling seemed to justify his impromptu piss-up. Now with real blood flowing through his veins instead of that useless red stuff he got down to the job of leading his Chinese charges to the slaughter; actually, it might be more truthful to say that he ordered Shu Ling to do it for him.

At 07.30 hrs the Tong men had struck camp and all gear was stowed away aboard their respective rafts. Shu Ling gathered everyone together for a last-minute confirmation question session by Dennis, after which he wished them luck and ordered them to proceed.

One hour later they launched the rafts and headed east at about three knots. It now being 08.30 hrs, Dennis reckoned that the condemned Tong thugs should complete the voyage of death by 10.30 hrs, the precise time requested by the Field Marshal.

At 10.00 hrs the rafts passed Kampong Jempol and turned south for the ambush position, fifteen minutes later Dennis began to drop slowly behind.

Back at his office Zeus moved the raft up to Clancy's ambush position. He looked at Harry, then the clock and said, 'May Acis the river god be with you Dennis old chum.'

'Amen to that,' added Hercules and meant it.

In the grey mist of the first light of day Fred grabbed his slacks from the branch that they had been hanging on all night and put them on, cringing in anticipation of the freezing, wet material touching his skin. So as not to prolong the agony he smoothed the cold garment against his limbs, kneading the material into his crutch and the backs of his legs. This short, sharp shock to his system worked to a certain extent but he was still shuddering as he removed his jungle boots from their stakes and donned them too, first having vigorously shaken them and clad his feet in soaking wet socks. The ordeal of putting on his bush jacket surpassed that of his slacks and left him with chattering teeth that threatened to amputate his tongue. It took all of fifteen minutes for his body to warm up the clothing, but by then Fred had brewed up in his newly fashioned bamboo trough and was fortifying himself with a good old cup of char.

The attack, Fred knew, was planned for as near as possible to 10.30 hrs and was dependent on the springing of the SBS ambush. In other words, thousands of soldiers and dozens of airmen were being made to hang about for that cranky Dennis the bloody menace. Not that Fred was complaining about the late start, he well understood the reason for it and he never had gone along with the pundits that advocated the time honoured dawn attack where everyone knew when you were coming and even took to standing-to in order to greet you.

The actual ground attack was to be preceded by an air strike involving bombers as well as fighters. Should that occur before the SBS lads sprung their ambush they could kiss the Tong rafters goodbye thus adding another cock-up to the annuls of military history. The Tong men would be frightened off not only by the noise of the explosions but by the sound of aircraft manoeuvring overhead. In regard to the CTs they would not be able to hear the sound of small arms fire coming from the river, especially with the high ground of Gunong Chini being between them and the action.

Caesar had ordered the squadron to be packed and ready to move by 08.30 hrs, giving them plenty of time to prepare for battle. They were to leave their heavy Bergen rucksacks in hides and fight light carrying as much ammunition as possible.

Fred was reorganising the contents of his Bergen when he came across a cloth wallet affair that contained a small mirror. He removed the shiny, square shaped object that could fit into the palm of his hand from the wallet, it had a quarter-inch hole in the middle and on catching sight of it Fred smiled. Most people who upon looking in a mirror would be somewhat annoyed at their beautiful image being obscured by a bloody great hole. But one was not supposed to look into this mirror, no, it was the hole that should be used. What, look at nothing? is a question that springs to mind. Well yes, is the answer to that one because the correct name for the ancient and nifty bit of army issue kit is mirrors metal heliograph for the use of, and the hole in the middle is a sight. In the bygone days of the hill stations of India, the Northwest Frontier and other inhospitable dumps of note, reflecting the sun's rays from a mirror heliograph aiming the thing using the hole was a method of signalling. Thousands of them were made and issued to signallers, but unfortunately there were not thousands of soldiers that could read, let alone spell. Mirrors metal heliograph were practised with and misused to such an extent that the Khyber Pass resembled a sea of reflections that the eagle-eyed hill tribesmen fired at with great glee and accuracy. In more modern times the thousands of mirrors made and then withdrawn lay surplus to requirement in many an ordnance store located in hot and steamy climes. Until, that is, some bright spark came up with the idea of issuing every soldier involved in jungle warfare with a shaving mirror. So out of mothballs came the mirrors metal heliograph for the use of to give the soldier another bit of kit that he could lose. But this time the hole was used to hang the mirror up, like on the end of a twig or the point of a bayonet.

Fred was not bothered by the hole as he admired his facial growth in the mirror, he had sported a moustache for some time now but beards were taboo in the army. However, SAS soldiers engaged in deep penetration patrols in the jungle were not required to shave and most men took advantage of the privilege. In his present self-preening mood Fred thought, *In another month I'll look like that bloke on the Players Cigarette packets.*

What Fred was in fact doing by keeping his mind amused was conjuring up ways of combating the butterflies, to keep at bay the terrible nervous tension that was threatening his very sanity. Danger is a constant companion of a soldier on active service. In places like the Kenyan bush, the riot torn streets of Aden, the

Paphos mountain forests of Cyprus and the Malayan jungle, you can expect to come under fire at anytime and contacts such as the one at the Bukit Chermingat tree are a reality of life. But going into an attack was different and he likened the forthcoming battle to the Suez drop where he knew damned well that he was jumping straight into a fight. He knew that within a couple of hours he was going to have to stand up and be counted, it was a sobering thought, this cold-blooded advance through enemy fire.

A soft voice brought Fred back out of his reverie. 'That bloody beard has sparked off a serious mannerism, you can't stop stroking the damned thing and it's driving the rest of us nuts.' Chalky was right; of course, a man with a repetitive habit was bad news in a four-man patrol living in almost complete silence for three months at a time.

Bob grinned at Fred and said, 'We used to have four men in the Squadron who couldn't stop picking their noses so Caesar put them all in the same patrol.'

'Yeah,' butted in Worm, 'they didn't get much patrolling done because they were too busy swapping snot!' Fred left his beard alone, put his mirror heliograph away and finished packing.

They were ready to go. From the base camp Pole's patrol would proceed to and assault the north end of the rock shelf backed up by Caesar's patrol.

Jimbo was responsible for leading the Gurkhas to and across the pangi field on the north aspect. Once there the Gurkhas would take the outer defences and use them to provide flanking covering fires for the main assault troops.

Chalky's patrol was to take out the two machine gun positions at the apex. Once the enemy gunners had been killed, there were to be no prisoners, the guns were to be turned against the two immediate enemy weapon pits to the right and left of the apex.

Patrol Commanders throughout the squadron went over their plans one more time making sure that everyone knew their task backwards. Then at 10.00 hrs they all moved as close to their objectives as they dared and took whatever cover they could in preparation for the impending air strike.

At 09.00 the military aircraft took off from two separate airfields, the bombers from Butterworth in Northwest Malaya near the island of Penang, and the fighter-bombers from Singapore.

The bombers flew eastwards over the mountains of Perak, Kelantan and Trengannu and then out over the sparkling waters of the South China Sea using Kuala Trengannu as their first check point. They turned southwards keeping well off the coast to a point over the island of Palau Tioman where they circled like great birds of prey. The Australian airmen bided their time by flinging insults to and fro through the intercom whilst they awaited the order to attack.

The fighter-bombers too headed for Palau Tioman where they kept station at 12,000 feet, 2,000 feet above the bombers; there the British pilots were soon swapping ribald comments with their Australian counterparts. The combined force of five Lincoln bombers and four Venom fighter-bombers were assembled.

The Field Marshal and Crazy Harry had been joined by the Air Marshal, various Staff Officers and representatives of all the units taking part in the attack including the Commanding Officer of the SAS regiment. The Admiral was not present he being lodged with the Police Commissioner in Kuantan.

Zeus accepted the model aeroplane that was being offered to him by Hercules and placed it over the island of Palau Tioman.

Prior to backing off from the four rafts Dennis had kept pretty close, herding them and not allowing the rear raft to loose touch with the others. As a result the doomed expedition was proceeding in a compact formation contained within a distance of 200 yards. 'That's the best I can do Clancy old boy,' muttered Dennis to himself knowing full well that 200 yards was a hell of a long stretch for an ambush to cover.

They were approaching a right-left kink in the river and the rafts disappeared from view for a couple of minutes but once Dennis had negotiated the bends with the safety boat he could see them dimly silhouetted against a solid green wall of jungle that lay ahead of the rafts. He looked down at his map, the jungle background signified a V-shaped left-hand bend in the river where it almost doubled back on itself, it was less than a mile away. With Dennis and his safety boat now a good 400 yards behind the rear raft the leading one must just about be entering the killing ground. It was time for him to bow out of this venture for the time being so he nudged his boat into the overhanging jungle vegetation on the right bank of the river to await all hell to break loose.

The river at the killing ground was about 150 yards wide but the northern, or left-hand listening post could not see any further upriver than fifty yards because of the thick jungle growth along the home bank. The same restriction of view applied to every man deployed in the ambush along that stretch of the river.

However, one of the tasks given to the Boat Extraction Force other than delivering mail to Dennis was to observe the river from the sharp bend. From it they had no difficulty spotting the leading raft as it lumbered into the last straight, the last one for them that is anyway. When all four rafts were visible and the troop sergeant had observed that Dennis was taking cover, he informed Clancy over the radio.

Clancy in turn warned the listening post who should in fact have been alerting him. But within ten minutes the listening post got their own back when they were able to inform Clancy, 'Leading raft passing now!'

Other than that message Clancy had not heard a word spoken or a sound made by his men. But the message was coming down the line like some ghostly telepathic warning, a strumming of the sixth sense that caused fingertips to tingle, feet to itch and shivers to run down spines. It tuned the nervous system to hyper-alert and made men want to scream out for release. It made them afraid but proud too, eager to acquit themselves well. And like the Gurkha commanders had done along the Mersing-Kluang road; Clancy prayed that his men would hold firm until he saw fit to spring the ambush.

The first raft passed Clancy who was located in the exact centre of the ambush and at a range of seventy-five yards it was more or less in the middle of the river. In a situation where the tension was so great that men find it difficult to breathe and one can almost hear thoughts, Clancy tried hard to concentrate on doing just that, think. It had occurred to him that the Tong men on the rafts were not talking, perhaps they too were thinking it was about time that they put into the side to mount the ambush planned by Dennis. But something else was bothering the Tong men, the second raft was passing now and the crew was looking back with worried expressions on their faces. Clancy's heart missed a beat as he realised that the crooks were looking for signs of Dennis. Would the penny drop, he thought with throbbing temples, would they smell a rat and abort? It took all of Clancy's will power not to open the ambush there and then before the Tong villains leapt overboard in panic, but the outwardly cool SBS man did not do so. In the event the third raft closed up on the second and that was enough for Clancy, he squeezed the trigger of his rifle and with a single shot sprung the ambush.

The SBS commando aligned the sights of his rifle on the chest area of the right-hand man aboard the leading raft. *Something is spooking the bastards*, he thought as he took up the slack on his trigger. The rafters were shipping the long poles and swapping them for weapons and were looking decidedly worried. *Any second now*, thought the Marine, *the buggers have twigged that they've been sold down the river!* Then came the expected report of a single shot being fired, Clancy had opened the ambush and the commando fired. But the man he was aiming at suddenly knelt down and the shot destined for his chest hit him in the temple, the high velocity .303-inch bullet blew his brains out into the river beyond the raft. All along the line similar scenes were enacted as men with pent-up tension inside them exploded into action and claimed their right as warriors to scream out battle cries and so vent their overloaded systems. It was all over in the very first fusillade but the commandos and field force men continued to pour volley after volley into the blood soaked ranks of the vanquished. The rifles picked off the Tong men like targets in a coconut shy; the snub-nosed Lanchester sub-machine gun bullets tore flesh and limbs from the bodies and the powerful Bren guns ripped the rafts asunder into so much flotsam and consigned shredded Tong equipment to the deep. The enemy, if they could be called that, did not fire a single shot during the thirty-second devastating action that put paid to twenty of the worst criminals in the world; there would be no paperwork for Claude Rysdale's administrators.

There were no bodies to check or search and no weapons to capture and destroy; the mighty Pahang River had claimed all. And as the ambush party withdrew towards the boat extraction force the bubbling turbulence and dark red colouring of the water told of another battle being fought over the Tong remains by the reptiles beneath the surface.

Upon meeting up with his troop sergeant, Clancy enquired, 'Did you send the code word?'

'Yes, they acknowledged my message of "Thorn" sir.'

'Good, aren't you supposed to be extracting us or something?'

'Now, now sir, don't let a little success go to your head!'

The twenty assault boats were well underway and heading towards Kampong Lubok Paku when it suddenly dawned on Clancy that Dennis had not put in an appearance. He was about to turn back to mount a search when some sixth sense stopped him. *Perhaps he's got a hidden agenda?* he thought with a grin, *Good luck you old rascal.*

Zeus picked up the raft and threw it into a waste paper basket.

'Gentlemen,' said Petherington, 'the thorn has been removed from our side.' Hercules pointed at the model plane with the snooker cue. Zeus picked it up and moved it to the CT camp. 'Now we'll stick one into the CTs side!' He looked at the Air Marshal. 'May Vulcan the God of Fire go with your chaps today.'

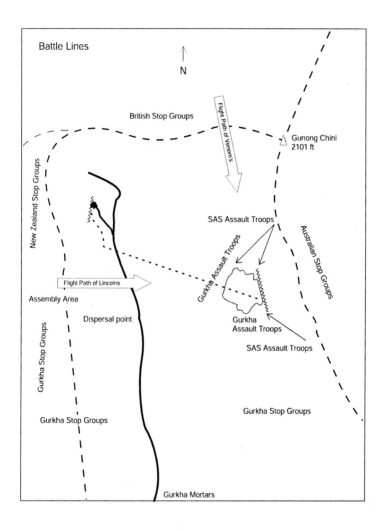

Battle Lines

N

British Stop Groups

Flight Path of Venom's

Gunong Chini
2101 ft

New Zealand Stop Groups

Australian Stop Groups

SAS Assault Troops

Gurkha Assault Troops

Flight Path of Lincolns

Assembly Area

Dispersal point

Gurkha
Assault Troops

SAS Assault Troops

Gurkha Stop Groups

Gurkha Stop Groups

Gurkha Stop Groups

Gurkha Mortars

On receipt of the code word 'Thorn' the five Lincoln bombers each carrying fourteen 1,000 lb bombs headed west-northwest for their first identification point, Bukit Chermingat. Before crossing the coastline they tested the aircraft armament, the air gunners took great delight in firing their .50-inch calibre machine guns and 20mm cannon. The enemy did not have an air force and the threat of fighter resistance was zero but they tested the weapons as a matter of procedure anyway. Bukit Chermingat loomed up and the diamond formation of bombers turned towards the second point, Bukit Bertangga. By the time that the Lincoln's had reached it, the pilots had brought their aircraft down to 4,000 feet and changed formation into line astern. This was because the target area was so small that only a single bomber at a time could safely drop its load of bombs without inflicting casualties on friendly forces. Even then because the SAS men were so close to the target the Air Marshal had decreed that each bomber would make two runs dropping seven bombs each time.

The five bombers now headed north-east directly towards the target area flying at 3,000 feet putting them 1,000 feet above Gunong Chini. They roared above the first spur and out over the depression following in the path of the gold train and Fatigue's troop before them. The healthy throb of the four Merlin engines took the leading aircraft ever closer to the target, and then from a range of three miles the pilot spotted the circle of bright orange marker balloons. 'Will you look at that!' he exclaimed over the intercom with admiration, 'you've got to hand it to those Pommy SAS bastards, they'd make good pathfinders!' He began his descent to 2,000 feet; the peak of Gunong Chini was 2,101 feet. 'Runt!' he commanded his bomb-aimer, a rather small man, 'Bomb doors open, get ready!'

As bombing raids go this one was a comparatively low-level affair, not on the same spectacular scale as the famous Dambuster operation. But given the nature of the terrain with the buffeting, bone-shaking thermals rising up from the jungle below to toss the huge bomber about like a leaf in the wind, it was a bloody hairy experience indeed. Levelling out, the pilot flew the plane steadily on his first run with the mountain peak 100 feet above him and to his left. The aircraft was now 50 feet above the tree line as it passed over the spur occupied by the Kiwi and Gurkha troops; the bomb-aimer pressed the tit and declared, 'Bombs away!'

The crew held on for dear life as the pilot banked the aircraft into a tight turn to the right and just managed to clear the treetops of the next spur. As the Lincoln flew in a circle to rejoin the queue the Aussies below prayed that their countrymen had got it right. But they need not have feared because as they hugged the ground the seven 1,000 lb bombs dropped within the circle of orange balloons and down onto the target 250 feet below.

The noise of the aircraft alone was frightening enough especially as those affected on the ground could not see up through the trees at the cause. But seven 1,000 lb bombs impacting the target area with an almighty ear-shattering explosion must have dealt a devastating blow to the CT's morale, courage and resolve, and that is in addition to any damage caused or casualties inflicted. But there was no respite because within seconds the second Lincoln released its stick of death-dealing bombs, and so it went on until the first aircraft commenced its second run.

The British soldiers on the Gunong Chini ridgeline winced at the thought of being down in the valley with the SAS men. Kiwis wondered about the mad fools, the Gurkhas admired their guts and the Aussies thought to buy them a schooner or two if they ever met up with the crazy bastards.

On his second run the pilot noticed that half the balloons were missing but smoke was rising up through the trees, and where some of them had been blown down and had taken others with them great swathes had been cut out of the jungle canopy thus making the bomb-aimer's task easier. Runt pressed the tit again. 'Bombs away!' came the cry, and the Lincoln too was away with only inches to spare.

The Lincolns were finished and they reformed into a diamond formation and headed back to Butterworth, the crews jubilant in the knowledge that they had accomplished their mission successfully.

One thousand five hundred yards south-east of the CT camp Blaster lit the fuse that would detonate the plastic explosive ring main. The Gurkha mortarmen had long since retired to the comparative safety of the spur line to the west of and above the gully leaving only Blaster and his three mates at the site. Blaster had waited for the first bombs to explode before initiating the charge and by the time that the second stick had arrived to shatter the nerves the safety fuse had set off the detonator that had ignited the primer, which in turn exploded the plastic charges attached to the trees. This sequence of events was, of course, instantaneous and resulted in one huge bang that was drowned out by the much louder detonations of high explosives falling from the bellies of the deadly flying machines. Blaster's show was less spectacular than the one being put up by the Air force boys but his charges cut cleanly, and out of the initial chaos of splintering timber, lethal flying debris and falling forest giants emerged a neat round hole in the jungle. A clearing that would enable the 3-inch mortar bombs to speed unimpeded into the high angle trajectory that would allow them to plummet down on the target over one thousand yards away. The Gurkha mortar platoon were now familiar with the route down from the spur to their new base plate position, but the explosions that include a couple of wayward 1,000 lb bombs had completely changed the appearance of the ground immediately surrounding the clearing; guides would still be needed. So, with ringing ears and the sound of Merlin engines receding into the distance, the SAS soldiers began to pick out an easy route through the blast damaged and obstacle littered terrain prepared to endure the second onslaught from the sky.

The four De-Havilland Venom FB 4 jet-fighter bombers circling high above the formation of Lincolns received the code word at the same time. The jets flew north to approach the target from the opposite direction to that of the piston engine bombers. They would adopt a different attitude too, for they were going to dive-bomb the CT camp. It was to be a quick and accurate sortie of two runs that would cover the movement of the Gurkha mortarmen into their base plate position and the initial stages of the SAS assault on the rock shelf and the apex gun positions. The Venoms did not hug the coastline but headed due north to take a long and circuitous route in order to give the bombers time to do their business with the heavy stuff. When on the same parallel of latitude as Kuantan they banked in a great half circle this time nearing the coast and losing height. At Kuala Pahang the Venoms turned right and flew low over the river and followed its course, then listening in to the chatter of the bomber pilots they got their cue to go in for the kill.

At Kampong Kinchur they climbed steeply and banked left keeping the peak of Gunong Chini on their left, then it was into the attack and the four jets followed each other in a screaming dive over the British-held Gunong Chini ridgeline down towards the target that was now clearly marked by smoke the balloons having been destroyed or released to the heavens. The first Venom delivered its stick of one 500 lb bomb accompanied by a long burst from both canon and machine guns. Then it pulled out of the dive to wing its way south, escaping out over the wetlands of the Mentiga River basin, left again and around Gunong Chini it flew climbing once more before hurtling down like an arrow of death on its second run. For ten short minutes the jungle reverberated to the 'crump-crump' of exploding bombs, the chatter of machine guns, the distinctive ripping sound of rapid cannon fire and the terrifying scream and roar of jet engines. Then silence, they too had gone now. The Air force lads had done their stuff and bloody well at that, but the real fight for the ground had yet to commence.

Zeus removed the model aeroplane; he did not consign it to the waste paper basket but swapped it with Hercules for three other toys. He placed a mortar on the base plate position, on each end of the rock shelf he positioned a miniature bust, to the north Mars, to the south Minerva. 'May your gods go with your men,' Petherington said to the SAS boss.

★

With the arrival of the gold train at the CT camp even the normally stern-faced individuals who comprised the Central Military Committee could not refrain from smiling with relief and elation. The rekindling of hope generated a feeling of pride and created an atmosphere of euphoria that spread through the camp like a tonic; a new lease of life had been delivered unto them. Even Kim Bok who of late had begun to liken himself to the prophet of doom was caught up in the fever of excitement and thinking that there was safety in numbers he completely relaxed his guard. When all the gold and other items that included a plentiful supply of rice wine had been unloaded from the faithful pack animals the Committee were unanimous in their decision that the occasion should be marked by a celebration. This they did with a vengeance and as the drink took its toll the CTs gradually moved into the cave affording the same privilege to the now revered elephants and mules too. This uncharacteristic lapse of discipline and tactical procedure was ironically instrumental in temporarily saving hundreds of lives; because when the bombers arrived to do their destructive work most of the CTs were inside the cave fast asleep.

The Lincoln bombers had wreaked havoc with the camp defences and the terrific din and the urgency of the situation had the effect of sobering everyone up instantly. When the terrorists had thought that the bombing raid was over they sprang into action knowing that a ground attack was imminent. First to rush out of the cave carrying an assortment of Bren light machine guns and Browning medium machine guns complete with tripods for the sustained fire role were the men who should already have been outside on standby. As they emerged out of the gloomy cave they were confronted by a scene of utter chaos, the carefully constructed aqueduct and pond had vanished; sunlight penetrated the jungle canopy through huge holes that had been torn out of it. The sun's rays highlighted the smoke and fumes from the high explosives, as well as the dust from shattered timber and the air was permeated with the acrid stench of it all. Not all of the terrorists were lucky enough to be under cover and everywhere lay the dead and wounded like rag dolls, adding the smell of spilt blood and voided body waste to the unpleasant atmosphere. The men struggled to make up for lost time finding it difficult to negotiate the once well prepared paths that were now littered with fallen trees and other debris. Along the way and despite their haste they could not help but notice that many booby traps had been sprung and great gaps had been blown in the cheese cutting wire. Many of the outer trenches had been turned into craters and the blast from these impact areas had flattened the waist high cover over the pangi field exposing the bamboo stakes and in some cases demolishing them. The men knew that they were pushed for time and began desperately to assemble the guns and tripods.

Meanwhile leaving the cave in their wake was the second line of defence who raced to man the inner circle of slit trenches, tumbling into what was left of them prepared to sell their lives dearly.

But before the thin line of terrorists that were to defend the rock shelf could get their act together and with the outer defences not yet ready to repel any form of attack, the CTs received another shock that appeared to come out of nowhere.

The first 500 lb bomb penetrated right through the tree canopy to the ground landing in the pangi field close to the apex. The explosion blew the sharpened stakes in all directions turning them into lethal shrapnel that hissed and zipped through the foliage. Cannon shells exploded on impact, most of them aloft in the upper branches and tree trunks created yet more missiles to lash exposed flesh. Machine gun bullets peppered the jungle canopy and the ones that got through buzzed and ricocheted like disturbed, angry hornets. The pilots could not see the target that lay 250 feet below the trees, but more frightening was the fact that although the CTs could hear the banshee scream of the jets they were unable to spot them. It was phantom-like, very disconcerting and nerve-racking to say the least. Of the eight bombs dropped three detonated high in the forks of trees severing enormous branches from mother trunks that then hung suspended by vines ready to come crashing down to the ground at the convenience of mother nature. Two bombs grazed the cliff face, one exploding against a bolder in the vicinity of Lofty's fissure opening it up, the other landed slap bang onto the rock shelf destroying the central part that partially blocked the cave entrance. Then it was over and the dazed, almost shell-shocked or bomb-happy guerrillas, looked about them fearfully. But encouraged by the brilliant leadership of

Kim Bok the heavily laden machine gun teams broke out of the cave intent on occupying the rock shelf.

It was at that point that the carefully planned manoeuvre that would allow the Central Military Committee to escape under sustained machine gun fire fell apart; because the first man to ascend a scaling ladder came crashing back to earth with his throat cut. In the same second a burst of light automatic gunfire came from the direction of the apex, then after a short pause, the rat-tat-tat of a heavier .30-inch Browning machine gun firing sustained bursts could be heard. *Ah,* thought Kim Bok, *that's one of ours firing back.* But he was wrong, it was a CT weapon all right but an SAS soldier was firing it. Then came a sound that was enough to send a shiver down the spines of troops the world over, it was the unmistakable hollow 'thonk' of a mortar being fired. Thirty seconds later the deadly 3-inch bombs began to rain down on the terrorists scattering shrapnel from high explosive and sending burning smoke cascading down through the trees from white phosphorus ammunition. And all the while bitter hand-to-hand fighting was taking place for the possession of the rock shelf. Inside the cave the men of the Central Military Committee had guessed that this was the end and were getting ready to move out prepared even to leave the gold behind. Kim whispered something to Fantail then went out to join in the battle, there was much fighting to be done before he would give up the ghost; the British would remember this battle for a long time.

The Gurkha Mortar Platoon Commander did not believe in letting the grass grow under his feet and judged it prudent to make a move from the spur to the base plate position about half way through the Venom sortie. So by the time that Blaster and his patrol had extracted themselves from the ring of tangled fallen trees and made a reasonable path through them the guides met up with those who were to be guided, thus saving valuable time.

The 3-inch mortar consisted of four main components, the barrel, the tripod, the base plate and the sight. The first three named weighing roughly 56 lbs each. There were six mortars in all and in addition to them the platoon had to hump enough ammunition for them to get started. Riflemen would bring more ammunition to the base plate position on their way to their assault start lines. Before the Venoms had completed their devastating trouncing of the area the plucky little Gurkhas had got their mortars into action not quite sure whose side the bloody planes were on. Apart from the smoke above the target the Venoms were firing blind and a lot of the stuff that they were spewing forth was getting uncomfortably close to the Gurkhas and their SAS friends. Nevertheless in no time at all the six mortars were bedded in and the platoon commenced their barrage of high explosive and phosphorus bombs.

Their task there completed, the SAS men left the Gurkhas to it and disappeared into the jungle to seek out and guide in the platoons that were to move into the right half of Fatigue's aspect.

Gurkha riflemen in fighting order without packs now poured over the spur line through the assembly area and down the slope to the dispersal point in the gully. There wincing from the brain-numbing detonations of the mortar bombs they picked up their SAS guides and proceeded to their respective start lines.

Blaster was to lead in a company HQ and two platoons to the south-west aspect. Others were taken to Crunch's south-east aspect to act as a right flank support unit and a similar force was picked up by Jimbo's patrol and led to the left flank located in Chalky's north aspect. As the last mortar bombs exploded, the Gurkhas were now too close for any more to be fired with safety, small arms fire could be heard coming from the apex. It was in fact Chalky's patrol taking out the two gun positions there. And through the clatter of the bitter struggle the poised Gurkha riflemen could hear the shouts and screams of dying men in the area of rock shelf.

Caesar leading his headquarters' patrol and that of Pole's prepared to move immediately after the first bombing run. It had taken only two sticks of seven bombs each for him to get the feeling of accuracy in the raid and that had given him the assurance needed to order the advance. The crux of the matter was that it was imperative for him to get his force as close to the objective as was possible before the fighter-bombers went in. So with the shrapnel of the last stick of 1,000 lb bombs still zipping through the jungle ahead Caesar and his men were on the move.

His strategy was entirely in keeping with the typical SAS tactical way of thinking, in the confusion of the second venomous air attack he would actually take the rock shelf before the enemy could get up onto it themselves, thereby forcing them to assault it and not the other way around. It was a daring, dangerous plan but bloody simple.

The eight men slipped through the jungle whilst the Venoms pounded the CT camp with high explosives, machine gun and cannon fire, the ground shook, trees fell and men screamed out in agony. The SAS men reached the northern cleared strip at the start of the fighter-bombers second and final run. With hearts in mouths and every nerve ending stretched to the limit they braved the wave of lethal destruction and crossed the clearing reaching the base of the rock shelf just as the last 500 lb bomb impacted, it seemed, onto the very objective. Pole's patrol had led the way across the cleared strip so they were in position to spearhead the assault. They hugged the ground for dear life gearing themselves for the task.

Caesar and his men could hear the sounds of frantic activity from within the camp perimeter and the pitiful cries of the wounded. *Let's hope that they don't get up onto that bloody shelf before we do,* prayed Caesar. Then Chalky's friend Allah came to the rescue for at that precise moment the first 3-inch mortar bombs plummeted down from the heavens and all hell was let loose once again.

Mortars are an area weapon and the bombs indiscriminate in their selection of victims and Caesar feared for the lives of him and his men; it caused him to pause for a moment. But that ice-cold individual Lofty had crawled forward to whisper in his commander's ear. As the bombs rained down with satanic fury he said, 'The Gurkhas are not always like this sir, they're nice chaps really. But there's an old saying, shells or bombs never fall in the same hole twice. So we'd be just as well off up there as we are down here.' He pointed up at the rock shelf.

'I suppose that's your way of saying get you're bloody finger out?'

Lofty just grinned. Caesar gave the signal for Pole to get going.

Pole in turn nodded to Feather. To access the objective he had first to climb up the cliff face for about fourteen feet before easing himself onto the rock shelf. The cliff at that point was not exactly perpendicular and had adequate hand and foot holds and posed no problem to men of the SAS ilk. But the circumstances under which Feather was working did, because his initial task was to establish whether or not the CTs were occupying the bloody ledge. If it were in enemy hands he was to climb back down again and a 'Plan B' would be effected. To actually climb up and observe over the edge of the rock shelf without being detected required a high degree of skill and courage. Should any CTs be up there, Feather would be only two feet away from any gunner manning the nearest weapon, and as that particular machine gun was sited at rock shelf floor level the two men would be face to face. But to Feather's relief and no doubt everyone else's too the objective was clear, clear that is of enemy soldiers.

The rock shelf that Feather had reconnoitred a few days ago bore little resemblance to the one that appeared before his eyes now; he did not, however, have time to ponder over the changes because things were beginning to happen that required his immediate attention. The top rung of a ladder appeared at eye level and he guessed that the CTs were about to scale the ledge and occupy the position. Feather signalled down to Pole indicating that he and the others should get up onto the shelf bloody quickly because the time for stealth was over and the shit was about to hit the fan.

Feather leapt forward as a head appeared at the top of the ladder, with one swipe of his parang he severed the man's carotid artery sending the fellow toppling out of sight. Then twisting the rungs of the ladder sideways he flung that to one side as well. Because Lamps, Cannibal and other SAS soldiers were working out of sight at the other end of the objective nobody dared risk firing their weapons along the length of the rock shelf so cold steel was the order of the day in these very early stages. More ladders were being propped up against the shelf and soon the SAS men were engaged in bitter hand-to-hand fighting, kicking and slashing with knives and parangs in a bid to deny the CTs access to their own ground. Reinforced by Caesar's patrol they kept the enemy at bay and attempts to gain access by way of scaling ladders were aborted. But the intrepid foe took to firing up at the rock shelf forcing the SAS men to lie flat along its length. Encouraged by this the CTs once again tried to use the ladders but the SAS men firing sideways from the rock shelf floor shot any terrorist that was foolish enough to poke his head over the edge. This ploy worked and a stand-off prevailed.

Taking advantage of the opportune lull, Caesar sent Mercury and Ball south along the ledge to make contact with Lamps and Cannibal. But when the two men returned it was to bring him some bad news, the rock shelf had been breached by one of the bombs and now there was a bloody great gap in it.

It was only a setback in as much as it effected the consolidating of the SAS defences and caused a slight hiccup in communications. But as luck would have it the breach was directly over the cave entrance and most of the rubble from the resulting rock fall did not afford the terrorist with a platform from which they could mount an assault because it did not form a slope against the cliff. Far from helping the CTs the boulders and rocks had partially blocked the cave entrance and was hindering their passage in and out of it. And, of course, down with the rubble had gone two gun platforms.

The 3-inch mortar platoon was firing at the enemy camp using bearing and ranges determined from maps and then applied to weapon sights. This was not unusual as mortars are seldom sited within sight of a target. The high angle trajectory characteristic of the weapon enabled commanders to site the mortars behind the crests of hills making detection by enemy observers difficult. Mortar fire control officers in forward positions acquired targets and corrected fire requested by other units, sending the relevant information back to the base plate position over the radio after having observed the fall of shots.

In this instance the corrections were being directed by two of the SAS guides that had led the Gurkhas up to Crunch's aspect. It was a difficult job because very few of the bombs actually made it to the ground to give the observers a fall of shot to work on. And when one did get through the SAS men could not spot the resulting ground burst because of the bloody trees. The two-man team was equipped with a radio each; one on the squadron net and the other tuned in to the Gurkha mortar platoon net. The procedure was that fire would only be corrected if the bombs started to fall above the heads of friendly forces, other SAS observers around the camp would send their corrections to the south-east aspect OP over the squadron net to be forwarded on to the Gurkha base plate position. As yet there had been no cause for alarm.

Access to the southern end of the rock shelf had been easier than the north because of a rock-strewn slope leading up to it. The defenders had made a half-hearted attempt to booby trap the approaches but it was quite obvious that they had not anticipated an infiltration of this kind.

Lamps and Cannibal were easily up and over the edge of the objective, knives at the ready. Almost immediately they heard the sound of Feather dispatching his adversary and the ladder falling to the ground. Then they were at it in a no holds barred, furious attempt to repel boarders from below, so to speak. Two men from the headquarters group should have reinforced the four-man patrol but the breach was preventing the link up. This left Lamps short on manpower; conversely, the other end of the rock shelf was overcrowded. To complicate matters Cannibal was down on his knees because he was unable to stand anymore due to deep shrapnel wounds in his left thigh. The two men who had followed Lamps and Cannibal onto the shelf had leap frogged forward to the breach and were desperately defending the ground so bravely taken. The CTs manning the inner defences now turned around and began firing up at the rock shelf over the heads of the machine gun crews that were milling about in confusion. Because the shelf was obscured by foliage, the CTs could not pick out clear targets so, luckily for the SAS raiders, the fire was not all that effective and most of the shots were going high. Lamps glanced at Cannibal who just happened to be facing his way and thought, *It's about time we got our bloody heads down.* He was surprised to see that the Fiji warrior was about to throw a knife, which he did straight towards him. It flashed past Lamps at bollock height to plunge right up to the hilt into the throat of a

CT that was creeping up the rock slope behind him.

Sneaky bastards, thought Lamps as he dropped his own knife to engage three more guerrillas with his Tommy Gun, the stubby .45 rounds making short work of them. Firing then broke out behind him and he suffered a moment of panic until he realised that the reports were coming from weapons being fired by his own side. Lamps adopted the lying position ready to defend the access point with his life. Cannibal crawled back to join him; the wounded soldier picked up Lamp's knife on the way and retrieved his own from the gaping throat wound of his victim.

The breach in the rock shelf now proved to be advantageous to the SAS defenders. This was because the new configuration of the damaged rock structure afforded the SAS men on the northern half the luxury of being able fire across the front of the southern half. The same tactical arc of fire was available to the men on the southern shelf; now both elements of the SAS assault party could put down a withering crossfire along the base of the cliff face thus discouraging any more attempts by the enemy to scale their way up onto what had now become to them an objective.

Mortar bombs continued to bombard the enemy position wreaking havoc amongst friend and foe alike. Lofty attracted Caesar's attention because there comes a time in a raid or battle when experienced soldiers know instinctively if they have won or lost. Caesar looked at his sergeant major. Lofty gave him the thumbs up sign; they had won.

When Caesar had interrupted Chalky's culinary demonstration to give him the task of taking out the apex gun positions he did not have in mind a gung-ho charge across the pangi infested field or a mad dash through the gap under heavy enemy machine gun fire. The Gurkhas were quite prepared to do both of those things and would have revelled in the task. But that was not the SAS way, no, a more subtle approach was needed here.

Chalky, Fred, Bob and Worm were only 200 yards short of the apex when the bombing raid had commenced and had closed up on it by the time that the last bomb had impacted the ground.

They had just adopted the lying position at the start of the gap when that had happened, the bomb in question exploded right in the middle of the pangi field turning the lethal bamboo stakes into shrapnel. Fred winced and cringed as one whizzed overhead so close that he felt the disturbed air of its passing, another embedded itself in a tree trunk only inches above Bob's head. The stakes collected foliage on their whirlwind passage that together with metal shrapnel scythed down the undergrowth; whilst from the branches above dripped blood, testimony to the fact that not only destructive humans were caught up in this devastating conflict.

Chalky knew that as soon as the terrorist thought that the air raid was over they would move helter-skelter towards the outer trenches hell-bent on setting up shop. With debris still dropping from the trees he rose from the ground and sprinted across the gap followed by Worm and covered by Fred and Bob. Safely over, they occupied the right-hand weapon pit and took up firing positions. Now it was the turn of the other two to run like hell for the left-hand pit and this they did in record time tumbling into it ready to do battle. In typical SAS style Chalky had not taken out the two gun positions, he had stolen them.

The four men could hear the gun crews approaching long before they appeared out of the jungle. In addition to the crashing of foliage as they negotiated their way through the bomb-blasted area the terrorists were shouting. Men under fire often do this to vent their feelings, bolster flagging resolves and give themselves the courage to move on into an attack or defend with tenacity ground that they have already taken. But the CTs did not have tenure of their own trenches, the SAS did and those devils stood ready, for they had the objective and were keen to take the weapons.

The first inkling that the terrorists had that something was awry came in a hail of Owen gun bullets fired at them by Chalky and Fred, followed very shortly after by rounds fired from Bob's rifle and Worm's carbine. An inkling was all that they got because both gun teams died in the first volley, dropping their arms and ammunition where they lay. The great impossible suicide attack on the apex was nearly over.

Now came the task of capturing the actual weapons and

setting them up for action before the enemy rushing to man the next two trenches each side of the apex could direct their fire onto the four SAS men. Although still within range of the Owen guns, Chalky decreed that the rifle and carbine were more suitable tools for the task of keeping the terrorists' heads down. And so it fell to Chalky and Fred to retrieve the two .303-inch Browning machine guns and the discarded belts of ammunition, whilst Bob and Worm engaged the enemy soldiers that were trying to occupy the adjacent gun pits.

Meanwhile the Venoms had arrived to join in the fray and the SAS men took their chances and hoped for once that the Air force were having an off-day. But they were not and Chalky lost an ear lobe and Fred received an emergency haircut from a wad of flying thorns that took his jungle hat from his head along with most of his tousled mop. 'That was a close shave,' remarked Bob with a laugh as Fred dived into the trench pulling in the Browning machine gun behind him. He mounted the gun on the tripod, loaded the weapon and opened fire. Satisfied that his mate had the gun firing all right, Bob ceased firing and applied a filthy sweat-stained camouflaged face veil to Fred's bleeding head as a temporary bandage. Their presence was being felt as the bullets tore up the ground around the enemy position. Chalky's gun joined in and the two weapons poured sustained fire into the terrorist ranks killing many of them and rendering the gun pits untenable. The taking out of the apex gun positions by the SAS had been accomplished in ten minutes flat.

The heavy chatter of the Browning machine guns being fired by the SAS men was a signal to the platoon commanders of both the right-flank platoon of Chalky's aspect and the left-flank platoon of Fatigue's. The mortars had stopped firing and Gurkha Riflemen were pouring small arms fire into the outer defences from across the pangi field.

The two platoons streamed through the gap in the pangi field to peel off right and left. They did not pause or falter in their stride; Gurkhas leapt over Chalky's weapon pit to go rushing at the next trench along, Kukris at the ready, their fellow riflemen who had been giving them covering fire prepared to make a move.

And so trench by trench they advanced, slaying the defenders until they had taken one hundred yards of ground. Then the platoon that had provided covering fire, themselves now being protected by a third platoon, hurried through a pre-cleared strip of the pangi field to take up from where the first platoon had left off. The Gurkhas took all three aspects in this fashion attacking from the side yard by yard, gone forever were the days of mindless frontal assaults through withering machine gun fire; the Gurkhas took no prisoners.

Having taken the perimeter the fierce warriors from Nepal turned their fire inwards to probe the jungle wall for unseen targets, and whilst doing so cut down the remaining cheese cutting wire and neutralised many booby traps.

The CTs manning the inner defences that were engaged in the stand-off with the SAS on the rock shelf were now required to turn their attention outwards once again, to face the threat posed by the bloodthirsty Gurkha Riflemen.

The SAS men on the rock shelf were safe enough providing that they kept their heads down. Because of the acute angle of the line of sight from the inner defences to the shelf, there was a triangular area between the edge of it and the cliff face known to the licentious soldiery as a safety space. Caesar and his men needed that space now because the expected fire from the Gurkhas dealing with the perimeter was coming in with a vengeance, however, the safety space had been reduced somewhat by the flatter trajectory caused by the increased range.

The twelve men hugged the rock shelf floor, watched their limited field of view and listened as the battle raged. The din was terrific with the sound of small arms fire, screams of pain and frantic words of command, defiance and blood-curdling battle cries echoing through the jungle. And now added to the bitter stench of high explosives, fumes and death came the unmistakable and sickening smell of cordite that began to manifest itself in evil grey clouds that enveloped all and permeated even the lungs.

The Gurkha Riflemen who had taken the two flanks turned their attention to the centre of the camp laying down a furious carpet of fire to cover the next move in the attack, the final assault. They could do this without hitting each other because of two reasons; the first was that the camp straddled a rise in the ground, a topographical fault that ensured that both flanking units when firing towards one another did so at an elevated angle. The second was distance; it was unlikely that rifle or machine gun bullets would travel hundreds of yards through the jungle without being stopped by a tree.

Under the cover of this blanket of hot lead, more Gurkhas soldiers braved the crossing of the pangi field, these men were relatively fresh and raring to go as they lined up for the assault.

At a given signal, the flanking fire switched to concentrate on the rock shelf giving the assault troops some leeway with safety. With a great cheer and screaming battle cries that put the fear of god in the foe the splendid fighting machine that is the Gurkha soldier moved relentlessly forward into the attack.

'May Allah protect me,' screamed Fred in genuine fear. Lofty winked at him and grinned.

The attackers worked not in the old extended line of bygone campaigns, but in pairs, one man firing his rifle whilst his buddy did the business of moving and killing, swapping over in tactical bounds. On they advanced taking out one enemy group after the other all along the line, it was nothing but methodical butchery and the Gurkhas were not getting it all their own way.

The guerrillas fought furiously and with great courage and not without some fanaticism. With scant regard for personal safety they were brave and daring.

One individual who had run out of ammunition got out of his trench and charged at the advancing Gurkhas waving an empty ammunition box above his head as a weapon, only to be bayoneted to death for his bravery.

Another actually made a bayonet charge with an empty rifle that had no bayonet fixed to it; he fell to the ground riddled with .303-inch bullets from a Bren gun being fired from the hip by a Gurkha soldier.

Men became as animals as the bitter hand-to-hand struggle continued, soldiers lunged and parried with bayonets and Kukris; defenders fought back with knives, rocks, broken weapons and anything else to hand. The covering fire had ceased and gunfire from both sides was now almost non-existent as control was lost and men became involved in private duels, reacting to crisis of the moment in a ferocious battle for survival; it was combat in its truest form. The adversaries screamed, cried, laughed maniacally and sweated blood and tears. Then came silence as the battle came, as they often do, to a sudden end. And when the smoke had cleared, the dust had settled and men could once more comprehend things, they found that not one Communist Terrorist was left alive in the camp.

But it was not a time to relax or celebrate. Men who were ready to drop with exhaustion were galvanised back into action by shots that that were being fired from somewhere above the rock shelf. SAS men who had effectively been pinned down by both sides fired up at the cliff face but to no avail. And Gurkha Riflemen peppered the air above Caesar's position with the same negative result.

'That was a message,' said Lofty coolly to Caesar, 'It means they're not finished.'

Whilst Caesar's men had been forced to keep their heads down because of the intense small arms fire of the advancing Gurkhas; four staff members of the Central Military Committee chose not to escape via the cave and chanced their luck by attempting to get out over the mountain instead of through it. They managed to break out of the south-east corner of the camp but one of them was killed whilst crossing the southern cleared strip. The three survivors ascended the side of the spur angling over to their left to find the fissure that had been opened up considerably by a bomb blast. This had loosened many climbing holds that broke free to clatter down upon the rock shelf. In the main the SAS men positioned there put it down to natural causes, but Lofty was not so sure.

Half way up when the cliff gradient became as a steep slope the bandits paused for a rest. One of them fired his ancient Japanese rifle in bravado at nothing in particular, the other two followed suit until returning fire from below zipped and snarled through the foliage and the fools saw the error of their ways. *Better not advertise our presence,* thought their leader rather belatedly.

They continued to climb, their passage through the jungle

getting easier by the minute, but the damage had been done. Because of Lofty's information regarding the fissure and the stupidity of the CTs in firing their weapons unnecessarily, the waiting Aussies were ready for them. As the leader approached the broad main track that served the spur he found himself confronted by a huge giant of a man armed with a rifle and bayonet who looked wild eyed and ready to consign the terrorist to his grave, but he did not open fire.

The Australian infantrymen manning the stop positions on the spur line east of the enemy camp had lived through the bombing raid glad of the fact that they were not down in the valley at the time. But at the same time they were peeved that they were not taking part in the main attack. After the noise of the battle had died down and they were waiting patiently to pick off any would-be escapees the men of Shovel's platoon were alerted by the sound of shots coming from directly below their position. More shots followed but it was obvious that friendly forces down in captured enemy camp were firing them.

Shovel, who since the death of the boy had graduated from being the Number One on the Bren gun by being promoted to Lance Corporal and appointed as the NCO in charge of the Bren gun group, heard the terrorist approaching his area of responsibility. Being denied the use of his trusty light machine gun he was now armed with a rifle and bayonet, the latter being fixed ready for action. Because of the convex shape of the ground at that particular point he rose first up onto his elbow and then adopted the kneeling position in order to get a better view of the approaching foe; he brought the rifle up into the aim and pointed it at a terrorist who slowly emerged from the jungle background; two others were visible behind him.

Afterwards Shovel could not explain why he did not open fire immediately. 'Perhaps it was because they didn't either?' he was often heard to say. Whatever the reason, Shovel held his fire and as the enemy seemed in no hurry to engage either, he saw a hangman's noose in his mind's eye and decided to take the sods prisoner so that they could swing for the boy's death. The fact that the terrorist responsible for that murder was already dead did not count in Shovel's book.

Shovel was a big man and a brave one too, he was taciturn, normally fair-minded, honest but an utter rogue with it; but this action proved him to be naïve as well. He motioned with his rifle, indicating that the terrorists should advance right up onto the track and this they did seeming to be in a compliant mood and resigned to captivity. Shovel was just about to order them to drop their weapons in his best Malay when their leader drew his pistol and fired a shot at the Australian hitting him in the right shoulder. Shovel did not go down, this man who could have flattened all three terrorists with his jaw bone saw red and it was not from his own blood. He lunged at the CT in a classic bayonet fighting thrust. 'In out, on guard,' he screamed pulling out the bloody spike-shaped blade known as a Pig Sticker, butt stroking the man to the ground and making ready to engage another foe. He took a pace forward and executed a second perfect thrust and followed it up by hitting his adversary under the nose with the stock of his rifle, down went the stricken terrorist and Shovel stomped on his windpipe. The third guerrilla had started to run down the spur but before he could take more than a few steps, and other Aussie infantrymen could react by shooting him, Shovel threw his rifle like a spear that landed bayonet first in the middle of the bandit's back. The butt being heavier than the muzzle fell to the ground and arrested the man's progress and held him hooked by the point of the bayonet for a second or two with arms akimbo as if in supplication, then man and weapon toppled to the ground.

Shovel recovered his rifle, the man was dead as was the second terrorist that he had engaged, but the leader and the man who had shot him was still alive and moaning with pain. Shovel picked up the wounded man's pistol, held it to his head and blew his brains out. 'That one's for the boy,' he said aloud.

By then the platoon sergeant had arrived on the scene. 'Need any help Shovel?' he asked with a grin.

'No Sarge, but I could do with something for this shoulder, the bloody mosquitoes around here are getting bigger!'

'No sweat mate, I'll get the MO to send up a crate of lager!'

'Good on you Sarge,' replied Shovel and passed out.

For all intents and purposes the attack was over, the battle won;

and the British had delivered a blow to the terrorists that they would never recover from.

The guerrillas had acquitted themselves well but had paid the ultimate price. A body count was in progress but it would never be known exactly how many men had defended the camp.

Bodies were heaped up in front of the rock shelf portraying a graphic picture of that particular phase of the battle. An assault on the cave itself had been planned but in the initial stages of its execution, no resistance was met and it was found to be empty of any human inhabitants. But glorying in the comfortable residence and basking in absolute luxury were six elephants and eleven mules; of the mahouts and muleteers there was no sign.

When the body counts had been concluded it was revealed that the attackers had killed 237 terrorists with the loss of eight Gurkha soldiers and two SAS men killed; and 23 Gurkhas, 3 SAS men and an Australian infantrymen wounded.

Inspecting the enemy dead time and time again, Caesar could not identify either Kim Bok or Fantail. He called on the Gurkhas who had followed the gold train for assistance; they had got to know the terrorists well during the long march from Mersing. The Gurkhas were adamant that Kim Bok and Fantail were not amongst the dead.

Later when Caesar had imparted this news, to his Sergeant Major the latter queried, 'I thought there were twelve mules in the gold train?' The two men looked at each other for a minute then dashed into the cave to where the gold bullion was stacked up. A quick count established that there were only 272 gold bars. 'That's sixteen ingots missing,' observed Caesar aloud.

'And one mule,' added Lofty, 'that adds up to only one thing,' he suggested looking into the cavernous depths of the cave...

Chapter Seventeen

Before the wildlife creatures that had been lucky enough to escape from the bomb-stricken area could return to reclaim their territory the peace was shattered once more, this time by the thunderous, throbbing clatter of helicopter rotor blades slicing the air. A flight of Whirlwinds arrived first and out of the doors of those old workhorses were thrown ropes, down which a troop of Gurkha field engineers shinned to be met by the Gurkha mortar platoon commander in the centre of the mortar base plate position. Lowered down on more ropes came explosives and heavy cutting equipment that included chain saws. The helicopters flew off and the jungle reverberated to the sound of buzz saws and explosions as the Gurkhas began to convert the mortar base plate position into a helicopter landing site; there would be no peace for the animal kingdom this day. By 15.00 hrs the small clearing blown by Blaster had been developed into a stable landing point with an angled approach large enough to take one Sycamore helicopter. A succession of these nifty little machines landed bringing with them much needed supplies for the jungle weary troops, and taking away the dead and wounded.

As Lofty and the Gurkha medical orderly who had treated Cannibal's wound helped that man to board the last chopper, the big Fijian said with a grin, 'I didn't really mind being patched up by a bloody wog but you might have found one from my own tribe!' Although Chalky and Fred were technically classed as wounded, albeit of the walking kind, the Gurkha Medical Officer was heard to remark with tongue in cheek, 'Well now you skiving pair of sods, I can't justify putting you down as fit for eff all so off you go back to your fighting.'

Rain stopped play as it usually does in the jungle and no more helicopter missions were flown after 16.00 hrs. The dead bodies that remained were heaped up in an area between the inner and outer trenches well away from the Gurkha soldiers who now occupied them. The Mortar platoon and engineer troop were tasked with the job of defending the newly built LP; on the morrow they would extend it to accommodate two Whirlwinds or Sycamores. It was to be a busy day for the choppers that had to bring in specialist equipment for the SAS troops, fly out the rest of the dead bodies and begin to ferry hundreds of Gurkha Riflemen to various road heads.

Also at 16.00 hrs came the anticipated order for Caesar to mount a follow up; the squadron was to pursue the fleeing Central Military Committee, Kim Bok, Fantail and the missing gold bars. The Field Marshal had dismissed out of hand any notion of trying to guess the whereabouts of the cave's exit point from the mountain, as he had stated in the signal, 'It would be worse than trying to find a needle in a haystack. Follow them out,' had been his directive to Caesar, 'put those bloody hounds of yours to work!' Caesar could have given chase post haste but even the SAS cannot see in the dark and any torches that they did have were totally inadequate for the job, in any case, his men needed at least a few hours of rest.

The Gurkha Rifle battalion commanding officer had ordered the SAS squadron into the cave for the night for just that reason. He had never worked with the regiment before and was impressed. These men had found the enemy's camp and had lived near and moved around it for a week without being detected, and the information that they had passed back was invaluable. All that should have been good enough but they had been asked to do more and had produced the goods, killing eight CTs at the apex in addition to capturing two machine guns that they had then used against the enemy. They had inflicted twenty-three casualties on the enemy at the rock shelf, all dead, and had calmly blown a clearing for his mortar platoon whilst being bombed by their own side, what a bunch! Now they were being asked to continue with the chase when all others would be pulling out to the comparative comfort of regimental base locations. The Lieutenant Colonel looked over to where the SAS men had billeted themselves around the gold bars. Even now just hours after a hell of a fight they were busy plotting away on their maps and expounding upon theories as to where the bandits would lead them to next.

★

Kim Bok had fought his heart out with the best of them. He had witnessed the absconding of the four-committee staff members, and as brave as he was, it came home to him then that the situation was hopeless. With a heavy heart he withdrew to the cave leaving behind his comrades to fight on to the last man.

Inside the cave he found Fantail, the mahouts and muleteers but no Central Military Committee. 'They've gone,' Fantail informed him before he could ask.

'Did you manage to do that job?' enquired a now very dejected Paymaster General.

'Yes,' she answered pointing at a fully laden mule, it was Ulu and his jealous handler, 'and we'd better be off too or we'll be dead meat!' Fantail had found two lamps and she handed one of them to Kim. He took a last look around the cave lit by the glowing embers of the armoury fire and some hurricane lamps positioned here and there, then led the way to a passage at the eastern end of the great cavern. Hearing a frustrated exclamation behind him Kim glanced over his shoulder to see the mahouts and muleteers following behind Ulu but without their charges. 'Oh let them come,' he said in answer to Fantail's unspoken question.

★

Caesar had summoned forth into his august presence a short stocky individual who looked more like a professor than an SAS soldier, but then, he was a communications technician out of the signals corps. The man went under the name of Swede, not because his head was shaped like that particular vegetable or that he came from Sweden but because he hailed from a place called Priddy down in deepest Somerset. When in some of his more vacant moods his name was often preceded by, Thick.

'Swede,' greeted Caesar, 'I have called you over to pick your brains.'

'Christ!' spluttered Lofty, 'It must be harvest time!'

'What about?' enquired a puzzled looking Swede.

427

'One of your hobbies,' replied Caesar.

'Oh,' murmured Swede wondering what chess and butterfly collecting had to do with the current situation in South East Asia.

'Or perhaps I should say sport,' Caesar corrected himself reading Swede's mind, 'I distinctly recall reading in your confidential records that you're a pothole or cave freak?'

'Ah yes,' said Swede seeing the light, 'where I come from it's more of an occupational hazard really, I spent most of my childhood falling down mine shafts. "Where's that lad of mine got to?" my father used to say. My mother always told him not to worry. "He's only under the Mendips somewhere my dear, he'll be home in a fortnight or so," would be her comforting words.'

Whilst the rest of the squadron who had gathered round to listen pissed themselves laughing, Caesar could only manage to respond with, 'Well that's nice to know!'

Lofty could not resist butting in with, 'A bloody Troglodyte, I might have known that they lived in caves down there!'

Caesar coughed and steered the conversation back on course, 'Being a sapper and miner myself I thought we'd pool our knowledge in order to get us through this infernal mountain, the rest of it can't possibly be as large as this great reception hall.'

'Cavern sir,' corrected the undisputed expert on holes both vertical and horizontal.

'Cavern it is,' conceded Caesar congratulating himself on obtaining Swede's co-operation without seemingly losing face. And so the two men with a very attentive audience plunged into the intricacies and mysteries of caving, finally concluding their deliberations on the subject of suitable lighting for the forthcoming underground enterprise. 'Oh, what we need are Nife Cells.'

'What cells?' asked Lofty.

'Nife Cells,' confirmed Swede, 'they're also known as Edison Cells or Oldham Cells, you know, they're long lasting batteries that power miners' lamps and there's none better to be found.' Caesar added the item to the long list he had compiled. 'But,' added Swede with a grin, 'I don't think we'll need most of the stuff that I've mentioned.' The great cave explorer studied his map.

Caesar coughed and looked peevishly at his pencil. 'Now he tells me,' he complained.

'Because,' continued Swede with an air of superiority, 'I think that we have a straight forward march ahead of us through reasonably sized passages and caverns; this is where I think it'll lead us to.' He rattled off a map reference. He then proceeded to give the whole squadron a lecture on geology to explain his reasoning that left everyone completely baffled but bloody impressed. And he, one must not forget, was only a humble trooper.

It will never be known for certain if the non-availability of suitable lighting equipment to Caesar and his men that day was a blessing in disguise, what is certain is the fact that it influenced his decision not to carry out an immediate follow up. Had he in fact embarked on such an action the squadron would have run slap bang into the enemy column that consisted of five members of the Central Military Committee, Kim Bok, Fantail, Ulu the mule and the entire entourage of animal handlers. Another indisputable fact was that no pursuing force could have proceeded through the echoing confines of the cave system without making a hell of a clatter, and even with the dimmest of illumination they would have been seen coming. The enemy who had long since arrived at the end of the cave would be static and on the defensive, giving them the tactical advantage. Without a shadow of doubt the SAS squadron would have suffered serious casualties.

Kim Bok and his party caught up with the Central Military Committee members at midnight having taken over twelve hours to complete the journey from one end of the cave to the other. Progress had been slow due to the mahouts and muleteers trailing back along the passages trying to follow the faint glimmer of Fantail's lamp ahead. For safety they had resorted to holding hands in order to keep in contact and in this daisy chain fashion they stumbled along until so pitiful had become their plight that Fantail dropped to the rear of the column to give them light and reassurance; much to the disgust of Ulu, and the elation of his handler.

The same problem that had prevented Caesar from

committing his squadron to the chase was now affecting the fleeing enemy force, lack of light. Only in this instance it was the absence of sunlight that was causing the delay, for even with the brightest of torches and the best will in the world passage through the jungle during the hours of darkness was well nigh impossible. The terrorists were trapped at their end of the cave by the pitch black of the night.

If the mahouts and muleteers, who were not by nature soldiers, had been less then happy with the nightmarish experience of cave walking they were terrified out of their wits by the nocturnal creatures that inhabited the huge cave entrance, the bats. There were millions of them flying and diving about in agitation, screeching outrageously in protest for all it was worth.

The bats did not bother the guerrilla fighters because over the years they had learned to live with them in the caves that honeycombed the high mountain regions of the Malaya-Thailand border country.

At first light on the day after the attack the Gurkha engineers continued with the task of improving the helicopter LP and the fully refreshed SAS men prepared themselves for the task ahead.

The Gurkhas had commandeered the CT cooking area and regimental cooks had brewed gallons of tea strong enough to stain a man's innards. Lofty being as a wise old owl went the rounds of his men to warn them not to cook a breakfast. At precisely 09.00 hrs the whole squadron knew why.

As if by some strange telepathic medium the Gurkhas downed tools and converged on the cookhouse to collect their main meal of the day, a huge helping of curry and rice. The Gurkha Quartermaster had included the SAS soldiers in his ration roll and they were invited to tuck in. Fred who thought that he was god's given authority on all things curried wished fervently that his old pal Abercrombie were present to taste the Gurkha version of the spicy dish. It was red hot and pure nectar and Fred was sold on it for life. 'Not bad,' said Lofty to Caesar, 'but there's something missing.' Caesar raised an eyebrow. 'Those bloody bombs have frightened away all the leeches!'

'Never, oh my goodness,' laughed the Major.

The first chopper landed at 10.00 hrs bringing in all the caving equipment requested by Caesar the night before, a miracle of administration when one thinks about it. The miners' lamps, of which there were twenty, had been cadged off an engineer tunnelling troop who were burrowing into the Batu Caves district of Kuala Lumpur to construct an underground workshop. Most of the other stuff had been flown up to the capital from Singapore by fixed wing aircraft and then transferred to the helicopters. It included rope ladders, protective clothing, abseiling gear, digging tools, climbing equipment and miles of rope. The Ordnance Depot in Singapore had done the SAS men proud but in the event the squadron took only the lamps and climbing gear with them. The choppers also brought in rations, ammunition and those great morale boosters, cigarettes plus some army issue rum. And so fortified with the explosive properties of a fine Gurkha curry and a tot of the dark brown, 100% proof spirit, the SAS lads said farewell to the Nepalese warriors and disappeared into the bowels of Gunong Chini.

The order of march through the cave was Fatigue's troop leading with Caesar's HQ close on his heels. Chalky's mob came next with Crunch's troop bringing up the rear. The lamps were worn on hard hats with a battery pack fitted on the waist belt; they were issued to the first and last man in each patrol.

Distributed in this fashion with ten yards between patrols Swede had declared that no one patrol could possibly lose contact with another. In accordance with good SAS humour tempered with the rumour that he could see in the dark, Lamps led the way out of the cavern into the first passage that ran at a fairly constant level for 1,000 yards in an easterly direction. Compass needles were erratic in the underground environment and each patrol was required to record bearings and distance, the latter being determined by the number of paces marched. Periodically Caesar planned to average out the findings to plot the squadron's progress through the cave. Had the passage or gallery continued to lead them along on the present course for an equal distance it would have taken them to the other side of the main spur spilling them out into the open within the hour.

It would have been a relief to all concerned but it was not to

431

be because, as predicted by the man from Priddy, the gallery developed into another cavern. Smaller than the previous one, it was still big enough to accommodate the entire squadron who gazed around in amazement at the timber and stone defensive positions constructed therein. Unable to dig in through the rock floor the CTs had resorted to building protective walls around themselves creating a system of circular shaped structures that were known to desert warfare veterans as sangers. It was, supposed Caesar, to be a last ditch delaying position that luckily for him and his squadron was unmanned.

It had been Swede's guess that the cave would eventually follow along a path beneath the main spur line towards the central mass of the mountain, he was correct because after a short search Lamps and he discovered another gallery leading off in that very direction.

The long crocodile of bobbing lamps continued on its laborious way meandering generally in a north-westerly direction. The heavily laden men were cursing under their breaths at the slow stop-and-start nature of the march; packs are so much dead weight under those circumstances. Five hundred paces into the new passage and the ceiling became lower and the walls began closing in but the going was so far free of major obstacles. Before they had gone another 500 paces the cave sloped down at a slight angle, the air was dry but the SAS soldiers were sweating profusely. Swede had warned them of the perils of exposure and the consequent threat of hypothermia. But at that moment in time the lads were undecided as to whether they were experiencing some local phenomena, the result of so many bodies being in a confined space or that the devil was stoking up the fires of hell.

Two miles into the mountain the squadron suffered a near fatality. The ground had taken a steep turn downwards for twenty-five feet before levelling out again, at that point the passage was about five feet wide and seven feet high. All went well for another 200 paces when from up front came a muffled exclamation followed by the sound of mad scrambling, falling rocks and creaking timber. Lamps the intrepid sniper, of whom it was said could shoot off a canary's knackers at 1,000 yards in a howling blizzard at night, had done the impossible. He had failed to notice a wooden structure lying in his path and had stubbed his toe on the offending obstacle, that action tripped him up and he went flying flat on his face. (Nobody actually believed the canary story by the way; whoever heard of a canary going out in a blizzard let alone at night, it must have been an owl!) Spreadeagled across what appeared to be a trestle table with his arms dangling over each side of it, Lamps was suddenly alarmed by the fact that his groping fingers were in contact with nothing other than bloody thin air. He was lying flat out on a flimsy wooden bridge that spanned some sort of shaft or pitch of indeterminate depth. To his dying day Lamps would never be able to remember how he got off the bridge to end up on the other side of the pitch. But he did and together with Swede ensured that the well-constructed crossing was safe enough to take the weight of the rest of the squadron. Lofty came forward to lend some stability to the situation and organised several of the miners' lamps to be placed on each side of the obstacle rather like airstrip landing lights. It took an hour to get the squadron across the pitch in some sort of tactical, soldierly like manner befitting a unit of their calibre. Lofty's ability to instil calmness into a situation came to the fore and the SAS flair for taking everything in their stride did the rest. The crossing complete and the lamps redistributed, the crocodile continued on its way. Weeks later in the NAAFI beer bar the lads would say, 'If it hadn't have been for bloody Blind Pew tripping up we wouldn't have known the damned hole was there.'

Three miles into the mountain, Caesar was thinking, *we must be well nigh under the peak of the bloody thing!* He was checking his latest calculations when the signal came back down the line that Lamps had broken out of the gallery into an enormous cavern. It was much lower in many places but extended a lot further than the one at the start point. When Caesar arrived to take a look he knew instinctively that they would have to search very hard to find the way out. He would really need Swede's expertise on this one but going by the look on that individual's face, the bloke was there but not in, so to speak. The Mendip man was completely enraptured by the wondrous sights being thrown back at him from out of the darkness by his lamp. Caesar let him have his moment and followed him as he explored the extent of the cavern. In many places around the sides where the floor rose up towards the roof to create chambers, grottoes decorated with stalagmites and stalactites presented a stunning spectacle. Dripping water had formed these two icicle-shaped formations that when joined together formed beautifully moulded pillars. Here and there where water had dripped for years into shallow rock pools were to be found cave pearls. These almost perfectly round objects had started life as a grain of sand or suchlike that had been kept in constant rotation by the dripping water increasing in size by the addition of concentric layers of calcite depositions. Not such a pretty sight were several irregular heaps of fallen boulders that were, according to Swede, known as ruckles; he suggested that a possible way out may lie behind each one. When Caesar considered that he once more had Swede's undivided attention, a plan was formulated and the entire squadron went to work on investigating the many ruckles. Most of them led into likely galleries where work had to stop because the passageways were blocked by fallen rocks and other debris. Caesar pondered over the possibility that perhaps one of these chokes, as they were named, may have been the result of a deliberate attempt by the CTs to secure their rear and so prevent him from following them. A daunting thought but one he did not have to suffer for long because good news came in from Chalky's patrol. When that evil personage approached him from out of the gloom he was grinning from ear to ear. 'He's done it again!' he said.

'Who, Allah?' joked Caesar.

'No, Fred, he's gone and found the bloody way out would you believe?' Nobody could think of anything to say for a couple of seconds. 'Well, he is a personal friend of Allah's after all!' Lofty reminded them all, 'Allah told me so himself!' Another slight pause followed.

'How can you be so sure?' enquired Caesar in a more serious vein directing the question at Chalky. 'Here's all the proof that you should need,' answered the old soldier handing Caesar a lump of mule dung.

Caesar ordered that the men take a thirty-minute break to give them the chance to brew up. The light thrown up by twenty-heximine fuel tablets burning merrily away on the Tommy cookers highlighted the men's faces in a peculiar reddish hue. The flickering flames gave the scene a ghoulish atmosphere in which human features seemed to be caught up in a dance macabre. 'It's the laterite in the rock,' explained Swede to the small group sitting in the immediate vicinity of Caesar, 'the mountain is loaded with the stuff near the surface.'

'Not far to go then,' said Ball hopefully from the shadows.

'About two thousand yards,' reckoned Lofty peering at some calculations with a pencil torch, 'if the Trog has got his sums right.'

'You'll see,' said Swede not in the least bit offended by his new name, 'but it'll get more difficult from here on in.'

'I want you to go up front with Chalky's lot,' commanded Caesar of the cave man, 'they'll take the lead for this last leg. You should get on well with Fred, you both coming from the same hole in a manner of speaking!' Lofty, for once, could find nothing suitable to add to that.

And so it came to pass that the two Somerset men, one from Weston-on-the-Mud and the other from Priddy, led the triumphant SAS squadron out of the mountain and back into the green wilderness. But as prophesied by Mendip Man the going did indeed get rough in places, straight forward enough, but difficult because of the very narrow passages. On several occasions Fred had found stiff, brown hairs and skin stuck to the cave wall, proof that the mule was finding it a tight squeeze; for that is what such places are called. At 16.00 hrs with only thirty minutes of daylight remaining, Fred came to the end of the last gallery and the squadron entered the bat cavern; they had made it. And from that point on whenever the squadron encountered even the smallest of cavities in the ground, they sent for Swede.

In the short time available to him, Fred had cast about the cave entrance and was able to determine that the CTs had split up into three groups. But the light was fading; there would be time enough in the morning to work out which group was which.

Meanwhile Lofty had been regarding the now silent, sleeping

bats with culinary interest. 'Oh my god,' murmured a horrified Caesar recognising the look on his sergeant major's face, 'not curried bats?'

On catching up with the Central Military Committee group Kim Bok was furious to discover that they had completely given up the ghost. Not even the fact that he had managed to bring out sixteen gold bars could rekindle the patriotic fervour that had once been so vibrant within them. It would seem that without the presence of the Great Leader at the helm the cause had become as a sinking ship. But this once powerful group of men did drum up enough interest to comment on something that they considered to be a major problem, and that was the presence of the mahouts and muleteers. To a man the Committee were of the opinion that the 'hangers on' should be shot. The poor, hapless wretches were on the brink of death when Kim Bok came to the rescue with a sound argument. 'If,' he explained, 'you are going to split up this force and scatter for the Thailand border then a few more sets of track can only serve to confuse the enemy. If the troops that are bound to follow us are from the SAS they will be operating in small numbers and we can reduce their effectiveness by thinning them out on the ground even further. Let's use these people to plant false spoor and so outfox the hunters.'

Reluctantly the five Committee members saw the sense in the old guerrilla fighter's logic and conceded the point; and so the animal handlers lived to serve their purpose. An hour later came the parting of the ways and the Central Military Committee departed to make good their escape whilst Kim Bok and the others attempted to lead the enemy trackers away from the scent. The sixteen gold bars were appropriately left in the Paymaster General's charge. That person now divided the animal handlers into two separate groups, the mahouts were to be dispatched in one direction, the muleteers less Ulu's handler in another. Both groups would be travelling along well-established jungle tracks that led to main Kampong's that were situated on the banks of the Sungei Pahang. Kim Bok knew the area well; shortly, armed with detailed sketch maps that he had given them, the two columns of the faithful would set off never to see Kim Bok, Fantail, Ulu and the lone muleteer again. Kim Bok looked around the cave that he had discovered so many years ago and knew that it was for the last time, sadly he led the way off the mountain with a fortune in gold but nowhere safe to go in order to spend it.

The cave entrance, or in this case exit, was split in two by a mammoth cleft in the mountainside that had created a V-shaped formation with a wide ledge on either side of it. The ground fell away steeply from the feature for 100 feet then became undulating and rugged in the extreme. Both ledges followed the contours of the mountain for a short while before well-worn access paths guided travellers to and from the fissure that had once spewed forth molten lava. 'No wonder it was so bloody hot in there!' had exclaimed Ball when Mendip Man had imparted that little gem to him.

Fred had found three sets of tracks leading away from the cave, none of which were difficult to follow. Only one trail led out of the left-hand ledge there being five sets of imprints all identified as hockey boots, the consensus of opinion was that the Central Military Committee had made these tracks. The rest had departed by way of the right-hand ledge in one long column to start with then had split, one group that included the mule descending straight down the mountain in a northerly direction. They were shod in an assortment of hockey boots and other forms of footwear, from this Fred deduced that they must be Kim Bok, Fantail and the muleteers. The third group had continued to follow the contour along a lesser used track and the signs indicated that the men were barefooted and therefore must be the Indian mahouts of which there should be six. But it was impossible for Fred to determine the number because of the faint nature of the signs. Caesar did some plotting on his map and then summoned his three troop commanders, it was time to split up his squadron again.

He tapped his map with a pencil and looked directly at Fatigue. 'Take your troop and follow the Central Military Committee. I think they'll make for Kampong Lubok Paku, cross the river there and head for Maran. Then it'll be all points north for the border. Chase them, catch them up and put paid to the bastards!' He paused to look at Crunch. 'Leave one patrol with me and get after the mahouts, by the look of it they've been sent towards the Mentiga River and Kampong Batu Balic?'

'Oh, not that place again!' grumbled Crunch good-naturedly.

'Chalky!' barked Caesar, 'I believe you have something to say to me?'

'Yes I have,' answered Chalky wondering where his boss had learned to read people's minds, 'I think the remaining column will split up if your theory is correct.' He was alluding to the fact that Caesar had guessed that the CTs would try and give them the run around.

'Go on,' prompted Caesar seeing that Chalky had not finished.

The old soldier coughed. 'I took the liberty of sending out a patrol at first light to have a look around.'

'Oh, I suppose your going to tell me that Allah said it was okay to do so, are you?' Any further discussion on the matter was curtailed by the demonic chattering of Mercury's Morse key as he acknowledged an incoming signal.

'If I may be so bold,' he said sarcastically. 'That was from Jimbo, I'll read it out to you. "Track split – Three plus mule heading due north – Eleven turned east for Chini Lake." Here, this is the position,' said Mercury handing Caesar a scribbled map reference.

The Major studied his map again. 'Right,' he said to Chalky, 'Kim Bok is yours. Send Jimbo after the muleteers just in case they're up to something. 'I'. He announced by way of passing, with Crunch's little lot, am going to force march to Bintang so I can be in a central position when any of you make a breakthrough. Good luck to you all.'

Kim Bok led the way down the steep slope off the ledge and by the sound of falling rocks behind him he knew that Ulu had dug his heels in and was sliding most of the way. He thought of turning back to help but dismissed the idea as being too dangerous given Fantail's close proximity to the animal, hell hath no fury to match a jealous mule. One thousand yards north of the fissure he said goodbye to the muleteers, they were to head east for Chini Lake and follow the shoreline to the tributary that fed the lake from the Sungei Pahang. Kim had opted not to take that route because it was filthy country and the going would be hard. Better for the muleteers to lure some of the enemy into the low-lying wetlands to wallow helplessly in the mosquito infested hellhole. Kim and his party continued northward towards a huge bend in the Sungei Pahang to the east of and just beyond Kampong Bintang. Ulu, that stout-hearted fellow who rarely balked at a challenge voiced his displeasure when they passed through the same ponds of quicksand that Chalky had encountered on his way up the mountain. The place had an evil atmosphere and they were all glad to see the back of it, including Ulu who soon settled down to his normal old cheerful self.

The trail was not difficult to follow even after the split where the muleteers had taken off eastwards to be dogged by Jimbo and his patrol. The mule was easy to track and it seemed that the two terrorists were not proceeding with their customary caution and skill. *Was this a ploy to lull him into a false sense of security*, thought Fred, *were they planning to hit him with pockets of resistance when they thought that his guard was down?* Fred now began to picture the enemy not as fleeing away from him in panic but as turning at bay to engage the patrol with delaying actions as and when they thought fit. His eyes lost their cool calculating look and became furtive and shifty, the scout found himself freezing in mid stride at the slightest sound and shadows took on a menacing, threatening aspect. Trees developed limbs and knots became as eyes watching his every move waiting for the first mistake. Fred was peering into a clump of bamboo sure that he could see a man's features concealed within the dark green gloom. On the point of reacting violently to this threat he was brought up short by a hand touching his arm and a voice whispering into his ear. 'It's an old trick lad,' said Chalky, 'that's what they want you to think. But just remember this, in this volcanic hellhole they'll be finding it bloody hard going and are bound to leave plenty of sign.' Chalky stopped the patrol for ten minutes to give his scout time to get over his momentary lapse of concentration. Fred was grateful for this and wondered if there was anything that the old campaigner did not know. Chalky did not replace Fred as point man but ordered him to continue as scout with the remark. 'Into the breach my boy, and don't let them get to you!'

And so Fred once more picked up the trail and with it his self-confidence. For the rest of that day he did not falter in his task and tracked with such skill and professionalism that it amazed even Chalky.

On the second day the patrol negotiated the mud ponds and then they were out of the lava-scarred terrain of the Gunong Chini foothills. The jungle became more lush and the ground softer and much easier on the feet. On they laboured yard by yard and Fred noticed that as the animals had done before them, the enemy group had bypassed Kampong Bintang but much further east, about half way between the village and the feeder tributary of the lake.

By 10.00 hrs on the third day the SAS patrol had successfully tracked Kim Bok's party to the southern extremity of a huge 'U' bend in the Sungei Pahang. And naturally, because the terrorists had apparently taken to the water, they lost the trail.

Despite his fancy title of Paymaster General and the pen pushing style of life that it suggested, Kim Bok was a tough, hard man, a vicious fighter in a tight spot he was renowned for his bravery. But he had his softer side too and could be kind, loving and considerate. Such a mood possessed him now as he looked out over the vast expanse of flowing water that was the Sungei Pahang. The river was speeding by at his feet from left to right, faster than normal because the tight bend was forcing the muddy water to accelerate around his side of the curved bank. Entry into it would not be a problem, as Kim had located a wildlife watering hole and bathing point with shallow sloping bank. Both he and Fantail were strong swimmers and there were plenty of places where their feet would touch the sandy bottom. But sadly Kim did not fancy the chances of the mule that was loaded down with the gold. He thought of building a raft on which to float the ingots across the river to give the mule a chance, but dismissed the idea immediately because it would take too long. Splitting the gold down into smaller loads was another option that flitted through his mind but that too was discarded; the gold as far as he was concerned anyway, had lost its value and purpose. Besides, he knew damned well that he could not take the stuff to the place where he was going. Literally chancing his arm, Kim moved close to Ulu and the muleteer and spoke to the man softly pointing at the river as he did so. 'You may not make it across there,' he said, 'so I'm giving you the chance to clear out.'

'But what about the gold?' asked the bewildered muleteer.

'It's yours. Take it, dump the stuff or do what you will with it.' The muleteer just stared at Kim with tears in his eyes. Fantail smiled and Ulu snorted in disgust at the close proximity of Kim. 'But remember this,' added Kim, 'once people get to know what you've got they'll kill for it. In your shoes I'd take one bar and dump the rest. That alone will be enough to keep you in wine woman and mule fodder for life.' Kim Bok solemnly shook hands with the now-millionaire mule man and then walked towards the water's edge. Fantail attempted to say goodbye to Ulu who bared his teeth as Kim dragged her back, then they both took to the river and soon their bobbing heads disappeared from view.

The current sped and spun them out of the bend into a long straight where they were able to break free of the turbulence to join the smooth central flow. The couple hitched a lift on a massive branch complete with foliage that was drifting majestically along; Kim knew that sooner or later it would snag on overhanging trees affording them access to the river bank with plenty of hand holds to assist them. But for the moment he was content with letting the log take him and his beloved Fantail as far as possible downriver; the further they went the longer it would take for the SAS to pick up their trail again, and that was something that they would surely do.

At first it seemed to Chalky that the four sets of prints, three made by humans and one by a mule had led straight into the waters of the Sungei Pahang, but he was wrong. Fred tapped him on the shoulder. 'Take a look at this,' he whispered, 'something odd went on here.' Fred was pointing at some tracks leading away from the messy edge of the watering hole, a human imprint preceding that of a mule's.

'So they've split up again?' observed Chalky.

'But they haven't,' said Fred, 'I've followed these tracks for twenty yards, the bloody things stop, turn round and head back to enter the river; come and have a look.' He led Chalky around the edge of the semi circular bank and sure enough there was the double set of tracks again leading directly to the water's edge and into the river.

Chalky looked thoroughly pissed off and prophesied, 'Well there's one thing for sure, if this lot have crossed as two separate groups at different times then it's doubtful that they'll land in the same place. We'll be looking for two landing points on the other side, but,' he added, 'if that poor bloody animal was weighed down with gold he may not have made it at all.' Chalky declared that they would achieve sod all by mooning about on the south bank of the river, so cross to the northern side they must but in a controlled, tactical military fashion. That was not a simple task given the nature of their heavy equipment, all of which should end up on the other side of the river with the soldier. He gave the order for the patrol to prepare for a river crossing.

Kim Bok and Fantail had gone before the muleteer could collect his thoughts still not able to comprehend his good fortune. Dazed and bewildered he led Ulu along the riverbank towards he knew not where. After only a few paces he stopped, it was no good, the simple soul was used to serving others and he needed a master. 'Come on good fellow,' he commanded turning Ulu around in his tracks, 'let's go and find them, perhaps we can share the lovely female's favours now that I'm a rich man?'

The SAS patrol had been busy getting ready to cross the obstacle that was the mighty Pahang River. First each man had laid his poncho out on the ground having sealed the hole in the middle that was meant for the head to make it watertight. Light foliage was then gathered and placed onto the poncho. Equipment had to be laid on top of this springy mat; everything went in, packs, belt webbing and even boots. More foliage was packed on top of and around the kit and the poncho folded over and rolled tight. The now tubular looking ends were tied to seal the canvas bundle, and then folded inwards and secured together. Tying a toggle rope around the whole finished off this masterpiece of floatation. The foliage around the kit created an air pocket and when consigned to the water the bundles floated with lively buoyancy. The patrol would cross in pairs, each one covering the other. They were all strong swimmers and Chalky had calculated that they should all land 350 yards downriver from the starting point.

The mule liked water, it was nice to drink and he loved the cool feeling of it on his flanks when it was raining. He did not even mind paddling through small streams of it but he was not very happy with the brown gurgling mass that was flowing past him rapidly now. He could tell by the bad vibes that were emanating from the Upright One that he was alarmed at the prospect of crossing the raging waterway too. But the only Upright One that he loved, except for the female who had gone now, stroked him and talked softly into his ears and the mule was reassured and allowed himself to be coaxed to the water's edge. Gently the kind and thoughtful upright beast that cared for him so much led the mule into the water, and before he took the plunge he thought fleetingly if he would ever see the female again. He remembered how the possessive male had dragged her into the water. Ah yes; the wise mule knew jealousy when he saw it.

Deeper they went and the mule found it to be quite pleasant. *This isn't so bad,* he thought as he easily moved his legs and kept his head above water. The Upright One kept pulling at his bridle so that they both made good progress across the giant stream as well as down it but after a while the mule found it hard going; it was the load on his back, he was not coping well with the gold. Only the fact that his hooves touched the bottom here and there gave him the encouragement to keep trying, the opposite bank was very close now but they seemed to be drifting faster and he could not work out how he was going to get out of the water.

A shout told him that the Upright One was in trouble. The mule's eyes were only just above the water and he could see the horrified expression on the kindly beast's face, his head disappeared for a second and the hands released the bridle. As if some powerful bond had been broken the mule felt suddenly alone in the world and with that terrible mental wrench came the realisation of how much the Upright One had meant to him. But for a moment hope returned as the head reappeared, the beast coughing and spluttering in a desperate attempt to breathe and stay afloat, and then he was gone again and the hopes were cruelly dashed. The mule felt something akin to the rough bark of an old tree grind against his legs and he wondered what kind of monster of the deep was lurking beneath the surface, he also knew that whatever it was had drawn blood and he could smell it on the now red, discoloured water. A flurry of violent movement in front of him sent more blood to the surface and the Upright One appeared once more with the precious life giving red liquid spraying from his mouth. And as he surged away from the mule faster than a man can swim, taken by some underwater predator that gradually dragged the Upright One down into the depths; the mule knew that he would never see his friend again.

With the distraction and the heartbreaking feeling of grief the mule had lost his way and was now in deep trouble. He thought of praying but could not bring himself to stoop to the primitive ways of the Upright Ones and summoned one last great effort to reach the riverbank. An effort he knew to be in vain as his mouth filled with water and his nostrils sank below the waterline.

As if in a dream and resigned to his death the mule felt strong arms grab hold of his neck and once more he saw the green leaves of his beloved ulu. The arms, those of a strange Upright One, first kept his nose above the water and then dragged him into the shallows where the weight on his back was removed. There he stood belly in the water shivering and shaking with exhaustion whilst snorting violently like no good mannered mule should do.

The Upright One was a kindly creature and nursed the mule back to full strength and then went foraging in the ulu for food. The mule balked at partaking of this strange fare at first, but the beast radiated an aura of authority and firmly encouraged him to eat. The food was succulent and surprisingly tasteful to the mule who instinctively knew that he did not need a lot of it. Darkness fell and the mule was glad of the long night's rest that lay ahead of him; by morning he was sure he would be fully recovered.

He watched as the strange creature drank some evil smelling liquid from a light coloured container before he went to sleep.

Could this kindly beast be advanced enough to be embraced by the more intelligent animal kingdom, he thought, but immediately discarded the notion because he knew in his heart that the Upright One was member of the herd that sported smoking sticks that belched fire and they were a very destructive race. *No,* he reflected, *it will be some time yet. But there's no harm in being friendly, I'll do his bidding tomorrow.*

Had the patrol been part of a larger formation a strong swimmer would have been sent across the river with some rope that would have provided the men with a safety line making their task somewhat easier. But the long lengths of climbing rope that they had carried through the cave had been dumped there and all four of the patrol's toggle ropes joined together would only have given them eighty feet; the river at the point of crossing was at least 100 yards wide.

Chalky elected to go first and together with Worm launched their flotation bundles, quickly followed them into the water and then struck out for the far bank but soon disappeared from the field of view of both Fred and Bob whose task it was to cover them.

Although the two men could not see the swimmers they did not take to the river, they waited for a realistic period of time in which they figured that their mates had made it across. As no shots had been fired they assumed that everything was okay, had there been shots Fred and Bob would not have been able to do much about it whilst splashing around in the river. On the point of suggesting that it was time to go Fred was alerted by the sound of a demented gentleman of the trees howling with great gusto.

'That's Worm,' said Bob with a grin, 'I guess he's telling us to get a bloody move on.' So good was this imitation that it was accepted as genuine by hundreds of tree dwellers who joined in and suddenly the jungle was alive with impromptu chatter, but as Worm did not encourage a lengthy discussion the noise soon returned to normal.

But before it did Fred was afloat pushing his bundle before him, both his weapon and himself were attached to it by a length of cord, the Owen gun lying flat across the top of the kit. The bundle was not meant to be an aid to swimming, it was merely a means of getting one's kit across the river and to keep it dry, but try telling that to a soldier in the middle of a crocodile infested waterway. The very fact that it was there gave the men a feeling of stability; Fred was not just grabbing at something that floated.

He swam like hell to propel himself out of the fast stream and it was a good fifty yards downriver before he felt an easing of the current tugging at his slacks. The bundle had been hard to control during that trip through the turbulence and had it not been attached to him the bloody thing would have bobbed off on its own, Owen gun and all! Fred held onto it lightly and kicked strongly with his legs for all his might, the bundle was so buoyant that firm holds made it completely unmanageable and time spent on bringing it back under control was time wasted. But all went well and he soon found himself pushing through the overhanging foliage of the far bank and suddenly there was a helping hand in the form of Worm. Chalky was there too to assist Bob out of the water and then the four men undid their bundles, donned their boots and kit in readiness for the chase.

Chalky first dispatched Fred on a scouting mission to establish if the enemy had landed at a point anywhere upriver from them, this was highly unlikely given the fitness and expertise of the SAS men but the possibility had to be checked out. There was a fairly good track running along the riverbank that afforded jungle travellers with a convenient way of sorts and this one linked Kampong Lubok Paku with Kampong Kinchur. After an hour Fred returned to inform Chalky that, 'If they landed anywhere down that way they must have taken to the bloody trees since.' Chalky accepted Fred's judgement and because it was fast coming to the end of the day he ordered the patrol to make camp.

Before settling down for the night Chalky confided with the others. 'I've a feeling in my bones that this is going to be a long haul. Our mission is to kill Kim Bok and his woman. If they've split from the gold then we'll have to let it go. But those two are animals and can live like them. We're going to run out of rations before long and under the present circumstances we can kiss any airdrops goodbye. Get a good night's rest, you'll need it.'

The floating branch did not take Kim and Fantail as far as he had wished it to. After they had negotiated the long straight, the branch had encountered a sharp right-hand bend where the river opened up from being 100 yards wide to almost half a mile. That would have been fine but for a series of sandbanks that effectively spit the river in two. As Sod's Law would have it the couple were swept down the left-hand channel and their convenient platform was forced into the side eventually coming to rest tangled up in the overhanging vegetation. Reluctantly the two terrorists scrambled ashore hardly out of the bend.

They headed east along a good track making for a junction of the Sungei Pahang and a smaller river named the Sungei Lengkor. On coming ashore Kim had studied his map and he reckoned that by following its course they would reach the Maran Road. Kim Bok's sixth sense must have been on the wane because he did not feel the presence of the unseen watcher as they walked by him. Kim and Fantail just about made it to the junction before last light; too exhausted to even build a shelter they collapsed in a huddle together to endure the long night.

The next morning after a handful of rice that had been cooked back at the camp days previously, and a drink of water, pre-cooked rice being the staple diet of most guerrillas, they continued the journey. Kim made a great play at making sign and crossed the Lengkor marching 500 yards before breaking track. Then the couple retraced their steps ten yards into the thicker growth alongside the riverbank track until they once more reached the Lengkor. They did not cross back over it but headed north along the opposite bank taking great pains to leave only the slightest sign of their passing. Kim wanted the enemy to follow him, but at a price.

Fred found the spoor of the mule first and what he thought were tracks made by the muleteer. It was obvious that the spot had not only been the exit point from the river but an overnight camp as well. Just as obvious to the scout was the fact that the mule had a human companion and if it were the muleteer Fred would eat all the patrol's crap and not even bother to curry it first. After careful scrutiny of the ground he noticed that the man had actually gone into the water alone and come back onto the riverbank with the mule. Fred summoned Chalky and explained his findings. Together they studied the sign leading off along the track and came to the same conclusion, which Chalky voiced, 'Well I'll be damned, the mule made it with the gold after all but his handler didn't.' For it was pretty plain to see by the deep imprints left by the animal that it was heavily laden. But try as they might they could not identify the spoor of the human so skilled was he at making light of himself.

'Christ,' said Bob, 'It'll be just like tracking Feather, he that walks on air.'

Chalky put away his map that he had been scowling at for five minutes then he regarded the patrol with a knowing look. 'I bet you all a year's issue of rum ration that if we had the time to look back there somewhere,' he challenged pointing back towards Kampong Lubok Paku, 'we'd find a safety boat that has run out of fuel.' He did not have to mention a name.

One and a half hours and fifteen hundred yards later they came across the passenger-carrying branch and found the exit point from the river of Kim Bok and Fantail. Fred's assessment of both sets of tracks put them a whole day ahead of patrol. Another hour at patrol pace brought them to the junction of the Pahang and Lengkor rivers. And it was there that Chalky showed his worth as a first class leader and jungle fighter.

The first thing he did once he had inspected the mess of tracks at the Lengkor crossing point was sit down with his map and compass and do some sums with a thoughtful look on his face. With a grunt of satisfaction he summoned the others around him for a powwow. Waving a hand in the general direction of the enemies' apparent line of advance eastwards he said, 'About two miles the other side of this smaller river lies the village of Kampong Kinchur, off where we've been told, the *Sea Pearl* is anchored. I'll accept that our nameless Yorkshire Lord together with his new-found mule with its load of gold ingots is heading for that haven, that makes complete sense.' He paused to point at the tracks of Kim Bok and Fantail.

'But you don't think that those two bastards are going that way at all, right?' butted in Fred taking his life into his own hands.

'Right,' conceded Chalky with a pained expression on his face. Fred took the hint and shut his gob whilst Chalky continued. 'Unless our friend Kim Bok has a death wish I don't think that he has any intentions of going anywhere near Kampong Kinchur. He knows quite well that the place is bad news for his kind and he will avoid it like the plague. He is not being lured there by his lost gold because the bloody mule carrying it is behind him.' Chalky looked at Fred. 'I'll bet you my last tin of corned-dog that if I sent you over there,' he indicated a point about twenty yards up the Sungei Lengkor on its opposite bank, 'you'll find Kim Bok's tracks heading north. Remember that Caesar said that they'd give us the run around in order to let the Central Military Committee escape into Thailand, and that's exactly what he's doing here.' He nodded this time inviting a response.

'So,' guessed Bob, 'we're supposed to go chasing off towards the east to waste time whilst he's already making tracks north?'

'Tracks,' answered Chalky with a grin, 'is the operative word because we're meant to find them sooner or later, the latter being the general idea.' He added, 'But, he's made his first mistake by being too obvious, he's shown me his hand and I'll make him pay for it.' So by sitting down and working at the problem for fifteen minutes instead of barging ahead towards Kampong Kinchur on a wild goose chase Chalky had saved the patrol many hours of tracking and reduced the CTs' lead by at least half a day.

Although classified as a river the Lengkor was only about ten yards wide at the junction and four feet deep in the middle. Chalky sent Fred and Bob across the river first with the task of picking up Kim Bok's tracks and this they did in a matter of minutes proving the old campaigner's theory to be correct. The patrol managed to cover a thousand yards before the rain came, not at 16.30 hrs as was normal but earlier by an hour, the monsoon was making itself felt.

Whilst the rain thundered down onto their poncho shelters the men had ample time to cook a meal and study their own maps. The Sungei Lengkor would lead them north; the river itself flowed south to run into the Sungei Pahang having started out in life as tributaries originating from the Tapis, Lerek and Serudom mountains well to the north the Maran Road. The river actually passed under the road that lay sixteen miles to the north of their present position, or about twenty-eight thousand yards. That translated into a four-day slog taking into consideration the loss of one hour per day due to the monsoon, and nobody but complete idiots would march through that lot. But according to Chalky another three days could be added for the embuggerance factor he felt sure that Kim Bok would impose on the chase. 'He'll go straight through major obstacles, the sod will create diversions, backtrack, go off on a limb and generally muck us about. But I'll tell you this lads, he made one mistake at the Lengkor and he'll make another one, and when he does, it'll put us right up his arse and then we'll bloody well have him.'

Kim Bok did indeed put the SAS patrol through their paces, always leaving a sign but making the four men work for their pay. But the terrorist was unaware that he had lost some ground and was losing even more by the day because he was having to work hard at his task. That was slowing him down, in fact, he was turning the tables around on himself because all the SAS men had to do was keep calm and keep going; and that was something they were very good at.

The patrol ran out of army issue food on the fourth day and was required to live off the land. Chalky decreed that they go on a fish and vegetation diet for the chase. They could not really trap animals because by the time that some poor unfortunate creature had fallen for their dastardly tricks the SAS men would be long gone from the vicinity and the fare would be wasted. 'Fish traps are the answer,' he'd advised. 'Set them at night and eat well in the morning.' Accordingly on the first night of returning to mother nature they all set to work making the traps out of vines and sapling strips. Constructed like long narrow baskets with a funnel-shaped entrance at one end, the fish could swim into it with ease but could not get out again. Anchored to the river bottom at night the traps invariable contained fish by the morning. The traps only had to be made once because the intrepid SAS survivors carried them away with them, spare fish and all. The *Ikan*, the Malay word for fish, were delicious and

Fred still had some curry powder left to spice them up with. The fish alone would have been sufficient but Chalky Bob and Worm took Fred in hand and in the short time available between making camp each evening and last light they introduced him to various life-sustaining plants. The foursome ate well and Fred wondered why the bloody hell they bothered to carry ration packs in the first place. But as Chalky knew well that it would, the novelty would soon wear off and youthful exuberance waned in the face of time and lack of proper vitamins. Luckily for them all they still had a plentiful supply of water sterilising tablets and the dreaded Paludrine tablets. The former to ward off a hellish disease caught from rats' piss in the water called Lepto, short for Christ knows what. And the latter to suppress the symptoms of malaria, it did not stop a man from contracting the disease but allowed him to carry out his duties as a soldier unimpeded. If the symptoms did materialise the answer was simple; the culprit could not have taken his bloody pill and would have to suffer the indignity of a trial by court martial. That is in addition to enduring years of painful relapses and maybe death! Oh, what joy to be in the service of the Queen!

Six days later and far in excess of everyone's estimate they reached the Maran road on 13 October, a full fifteen days after the attack. The enemy spoor took them east at first along the side of the road so as to miss an area of swampland then gradually the tracks angled north again this time to follow another river named the Sungei Lepar. Beyond the river lay a mountain called Gunong Serudom and Chalky knew in his bones that Kim Bok and Fantail, like elephants making their mysterious trips to some unknown graveyard, had chosen this god forsaken hole for their last resting place.

Kim Bok was having a nightmare in which he was being captured by the SAS troops that he knew to be pursuing him. Panic ridden, for his plan was to go out fighting, he strove for control and with his heart pounding like a trip hammer and with sweat pouring from every gland he forced his eyes open to face reality and then nearly died of shock. For standing above him and pointing a rifle at his head was a man. 'No', he screamed in frustration, 'This can't be true, please let it be a dream!'

'You should be more careful,' said a voice in Cantonese, 'the filthy British might be about. I and my two friends are from the 10th Regiment and we are at your service.' Kim Bok could only stare open mouthed up at the fellow terrorist with astonishment and relief. Now focused to the situation he could see two more men openly admiring Fantail, but they knew better than to overstep the mark for they had recognised the woman whose reputation had preceded her.

The newcomers had heard about the disaster on Gunong Chini and were fleeing north for the high border country, the entire guerrilla army now being thoroughly demoralised and in a state of panic. They were carrying provisions and gladly offered to share them with Kim and Fantail, an offer the exhausted and hungry couple thankfully accepted. Of the earlier offer of services Kim Bok requested but one thing involving about four days of their time. 'I want you to lay a second trail and then fight a short delaying action. Fire at the enemy and then break off and continue with your journey north, that's all I want.'

The three men agreed and Kim gathered them about his map, 'See this point here where the Lepar splits into two channels for a mile, well I want to split them up too, make them follow both routes to thin them out on the ground and confuse them so that when I do confront them myself, it'll be on my own terms.' Kim Bok went into details whilst Fantail prepared him some food, his first meal in days. By the time he had fortified himself with the feast and was feeling comfortable with his plans it was past eleven in the morning, the enthusiasm generated by the opportune arrival of his very helpful guests had completely captivated his mind and he had unwittingly lost half a day. It was a mistake on his part, a mistake that was to prove fatal.

There was no track alongside the Sungei Lepar; the trail Fred was following passed through thick, lush undergrowth well nourished by the plentiful supply of water. The trees were mainly about 100 feet high and some sunlight penetrated the canopy encouraging a vigorous secondary growth. Water vines abounded like snakes twisting around tree trunks and entwining themselves through a tangled pattern of branches, palms and ferns were prolific and fungus adorned the dark green moss-covered lower limbs of the trees and rocky outcrops by the riverside. Thick clumps of bamboo formed natural, impenetrable barriers. There were no flowering plants in evidence; it was a dark, dank and oppressive world of russet and various shades of green. There was a feeling of expectancy in the air and Fred sensed a slight change in the tempo of wildlife sounds as if a conductor was preparing his orchestra for a closing crescendo.

He came upon the spot where Kim Bok and Fantail had stopped for the night just after noon. The timing was right if they were, as Chalky had surmised, to be half a day behind the pair of terrorists. But to Fred's amazement he discovered three more sets of prints that had been made by someone approaching Kim Bok's camp from the west coming up out of the river leaving plenty of wet sign. Even more alarming to the young scout was the fact that where the terrorists had flattened leaves as they had vacated the campsite, some were just beginning to spring back into shape. The indisputable evidence facing Fred was that the five terrorists had only just left the camp; the patrol had caught up with them.

Chalky surveyed the campsite with a look of elation and whispered to Fred, 'It's time to consult Allah again,' then he took out his map and sat down to study it in the very same place that the enemy had done only minutes previously. 'It is time,' he announced solemnly, 'to bring this chase to a close and I intend for it to happen here,' he emphasised pointing at a spot on his map. It was a fork in the river that started 1,500 yards ahead of them and extended northwards for over a mile before joining up again. 'First of all,' he continued, 'I haven't a clue as to who these other three men might be but I'm assuming they're CTs that just happened to bump into our two friends. And that Kim Bok has recruited their help in order to confuse and maybe get rid of a few of us.' Fred, Bob and Worm listened intently with eager anticipation. 'There are two things that Kim Bok will be unaware of. One, he will not know what our fighting strength is. Two, he'll be ignorant of the fact that we latched on to his ploy back at the junction resulting in him losing half a day's advantage over us. And as a result of meeting up with these reinforcements he has conceded another five hours or more putting us right up their arses. It is my considered opinion that he'll split his force at the fork, and I am meant to divide my formation in order to keep tabs on both groups.'

'It's to be at the fork then?' guessed Worm.

'Right on lad, before the bastards can split up. I think they'll slow right down now and play it cool to lure us into a trap.'

'But you're not going along with that, of course?' joked Bob.

'No son, I intend to bypass the sods, overtake them and put paid to the bastards by ambushing the fork.'

'Oh! That's all right then,' commented Fred with more than a hint of sarcasm, 'everyone knows we do that sort of thing as a matter course. Why are we in such a damned hurry all of a sudden?'

'Because I'm fed up with eating bloody fish,' explained Chalky with a deadpan expression, 'with them out of the way we'll be able to trap some pig!'

'Yeah,' added Bob, 'you need red meat for the vitamins.'

'It'll save your bacon, Fred,' advised Worm with a grin. Fred conceded that he was acting like a prat by holding up his hands. Chalky plunged into the intricacies of his tactical masterpiece and an hour later the patrol was ready and spoiling for a fight.

At 13.30 hrs with two good hours of patrolling left in the day they departed from Kim Bok's overnight camp, crossed the Lepar and struck out north on the opposite bank to the terrorist. Silently they forged ahead intent on being in front of the enemy by last light.

Chalky had got it right except for one thing, had he in fact continued to follow the enemy tracks it would soon have become obvious that far from slowing down their pace, the CTs had increased speed to the point of being negligent and had left sign of their passage that would have been clear to even a novice in the art of tracking.

Five hundred yards short of the fork both the SAS patrol and the CTs were forced to take shelter from the torrential rain that was being blown in by the monsoon. At that time the CTs were one hour ahead of the SAS soldiers and still on the right bank of the river.

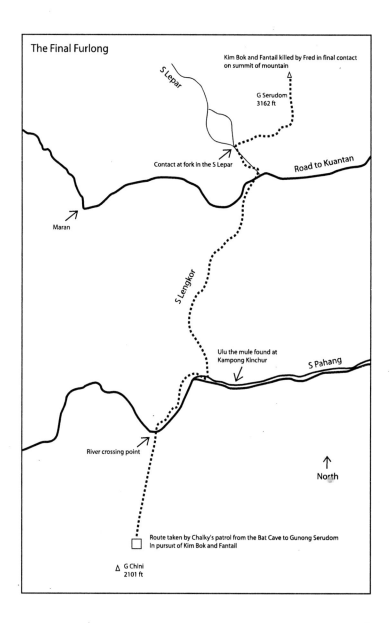

The Final Furlong

S Lepar

Kim Bok and Fantail killed by Fred in final contact
on summit of mountain

G Serudom
3162 ft

Contact at fork in the S Lepar

Road to Kuantan

Maran

S Lengkor

Ulu the mule found at
Kampong Kinchur

S Pahang

River crossing point

North

Route taken by Chalky's patrol from the Bat Cave to Gunong Serudom
in pursuit of Kim Bok and Fantail

G Chini
2101 ft

The bandits did not build shelters but huddled together under some attap leaves for the night. The next morning at the crack of dawn they were up and away making haste for the fork in the river. There, they intended to rest for a while before splitting the trail and so put into effect their plan to force the pursuing enemy troops into deploying their men in reduced numbers. At ten in the morning they arrived at the fork in the Sungei Lepar.

The SAS patrol did make a proper camp and slept in comparative comfort because of it. The next morning thinking that they were ahead of the terrorists the SAS men did not make haste, nevertheless they were on the move before 08.00 hrs.

Something is not quite right, thought Fred. He could not put his finger on it but he was getting the bloody jitters so strong was the feeling. Instincts were developing within his being that in future years he would learn never to doubt, but those legendary days had yet to come and he was but a mere learner. He had slowed down the pace to such an extent that Chalky came up front to investigate and as he looked into the weary but wary eyes of the youngster the urgency reflected by them communicated itself to the veteran and set the alarm bells ringing. Chalky whispered into Fred's ear, 'I'm with you all the way son, perhaps I've got it wrong. I must learn not to put my trust in that bloke Allah so much. It may be us that's walking into a trap!'

'Could be,' Fred answered, impressed that Chalky could concede to a younger man's hunches. 'But they'll have no idea that we're the other side of the river.' Chalky indicated that Fred should lead the patrol to the riverbank, 'Don't lose sight of that bloody water from now on,' he emphasised, 'follow it for 100 yards and then stop whilst I have a rethink.'

Fred liked fish but having eaten nothing else but the white meat for bloody days now he was getting sick of the stuff. He glanced at Chalky who was studying his map again; he would, Fred guessed, soon order him to re-find the enemy tracks for the old soldier was convinced that he had made a mistake and the enemy might still be ahead of the patrol. Fred looked back down at the slow flowing water of the Lepar and noticed a bubble floating by. It brought his mind back to the subject of food and fish in particular. *A bloody Ikan probably made that bubble, must be a shoal down there,* he thought as two more bubbles passed before his tired eyes. Fred had noticed of late that he was suffering a lot from cramp and dizzy spells were becoming quite common. 'It must be the change from red meat to white,' he muttered to himself as a long line of bubbles came into his field of view. He stiffened and thought, *that's no bloody fish.* The bubbles in question each reflected the colours of a rainbow and were accompanied by long line of white froth; what Fred was looking at was soapsuds. He frantically signalled with his hands to attract Chalky's attention. The patrol commander looked long and hard at the bubbles and then grinned, and a very evil grin it was too.

The terrorists were enjoying their rest at the fork where the width of the river was a good eight feet and only three feet deep, the water was clear and looked inviting in the morning heat. Although they had roughed it the night before the visitors were still well provisioned, one of them was sorting out the contents of his pack when Fantail, who had been watching him, almost squealed in delight as she spotted a bar of soap. The man threw it to her and in a flash she had stripped off and was scrubbing herself furiously in the river. Kim Bok looked on in astonishment as the three men joined his lover in the water taking it in turns to use the soap. He declined to take a bath and it was obvious by the expression on his face that he was disgusted with this total breakdown in tactical security. The situation was getting out of hand so Kim signalled to Fantail that the party was over and that she should get her shapely arse out of there. His look broached no argument and she complied immediately but the others lingered on for a moment.

Fred was once more on the move, stealthily stalking his way forward through the thick growth clogging the riverbank. The bubbles kept coming and gradually as they increased in volume he picked up the smell from the scented soap. Then came the sound of splashing water as the bandits ahead cleansed their murdering hides. And then he saw them, one gorgeous looking female and three men, all starkers as the day that they had been born. Fred

457

stopped and gave the thumbs down sign to Chalky. Bob moved up to a position on Fred's left and Chalky and Worm crossed to the other side of the river. Now in extended line they advanced. In the closing seconds before he opened fire Fred noticed that the woman was not in sight.

Kim Bok helped Fantail up out of the water and even in his agitated state he could not help but feel excited at the sight of her naked body, *Soon we will be alone,* he was thinking when all hell broke loose. His senses reeled as the ear shattering reports of rifles and sub-machine guns broke the silence and brought instant death to the three men still in the river. Bullets tore at their flesh and smashed bones until only bloody remains were left on the surface to float away and this time the bubbles were red.

Fred opened fire first with a long burst of a complete magazine from the hip. The 9mm rounds impacted the left-hand man at knee height cutting his legs from under him. They caught the second man across the waist as the weapon jumped up and to the right, the last of the twenty-eight bullets landed in the chest and right shoulder of the third CT as the Owen gun finished its cycle of movement. He quickly changed magazines and continued to engage the enemy with aimed bursts of three to four rounds moving from target to target. As he did so he could see ammunition from the other weapons doing deadly damage adding to the carnage. Then silence as the patrol ceased firing as one; Kim Bok's diversionary tactic had been thwarted in a thirty-second confrontation. It could hardly be described as a fight or battle as no shots were exchanged, with their weapons still on the riverbank the CTs had not stood a chance. There was no immediate sign of Kim Bok or Fantail but her clothes were missing from the heap that lay next to the piled weapons. Fred could not help but smile at the thought of the naked dame fleeing though jungle; Talk about going back to mother nature.

The patrol quickly reorganised and prepared for an immediate follow up. 'This is it,' Chalky informed them, 'we'll do the job slowly and methodically. Kim Bok knows as do I, that it is only a matter of time now. The end is in sight and the outcome inevitable.'

The patrol hid the captured enemy weapons; they did not have to check the bodies as nobody could have lived through the hail of fire put down by them. The follow up could not begin until it had been established which fork Kim Bok had taken, if indeed he was using the river line at all. 'It'll not be easy,' warned Chalky as the patrol fanned out to search the area beyond the fork. Worm was the man who discovered the new trail. 'You're not the only two who can bloody track,' he said, then handed Chalky a sweat-soaked head band that he had found; a form of headdress that they knew was much favoured by Fantail.

Kim Bok had picked up Fantail's clothing on the run as he dragged her away from the terrible slaughter at the fork. He knew that Fantail could not proceed far in her state of undress without incurring serious flesh injuries from the many varieties of sharp leaves and thorns. Knowing that the British would have to cast about in order to find their sign, he paused long enough for Fantail to put her on her slacks and a bush jacket, the sum total of her wardrobe. It was five minutes later that Fantail realised that she was minus a headband. Although Kim wanted the soldiers to follow him he was hoping to gain a little time so that he could choose the place where this fight would end. Accordingly the couple went to great lengths to cover their tracks, not completely but making sure that the pursuing SAS men would have to work bloody hard at detecting their spoor.

And bloody hard work it proved to be too. By the time that the wind heralded the oncoming downpour, now arriving even earlier at three in the afternoon, the patrol had progressed a mere 500 yards, it was time to call it a day.

The next day was much of the same thing, when whoever was scouting had reached the end of their tether, a sign would materialise as if by magic to bring them back on course; Kim was playing with the SAS men and bloody good at the game he was too. By midday they had reached the other end of the fork and the tracks continued along the right bank of the Lepar. Then in the late afternoon the patrol hit a tributary that fed into the river from the right. Chalky studied his map as the rain began to fall, 'Serudom!' he announced, 'As I bloody told you he would, he's heading for Gunong Serudom; and that's where he's going to die.'

459

On the third day after the contact at 13.00 hrs Kim Bok made his destination even plainer to the SAS men. The tracks left the tributary and took a route up a steep-sided spur and by the end of the day the SAS patrol had been lured onto the main spur line that led all the way up to the 3,436 feet high summit. They camped on the spur and with the rain that night came thunder and lightning that despite the thick tree canopy lit up the jungle floor and highlighted the gaunt faces of the hunters.

'Allah,' said Chalky to his men, 'has sent me a warning. Some of us are undoubtedly going to get hurt in the not too distant future.' Nobody thought fit to contradict him or make any funny remarks for the man was deadly serious. 'Let me remind you,' he continued, 'of a great military tactic known as an "Advance to Contact". This is when a large formation of troops are told to advance into an area known to be occupied by the enemy but no one knows quite where they are? So the way to find out is for the poor bloody infantry to march forward until they come under effective fire, that is to say, someone gets hit and ends up screaming on the deck with a gut full of lead. Hey presto! The enemy have been found, a cold blooded affair but it works.'

'And where's this leading us to?' asked Fred, but like the others, he had an idea of what Chalky was trying to say. 'Kim Bok has chosen his last resting place, and that is if you haven't already guessed, at the top of this bloody great mountain. I have consulted with Allah in the form of my map and quite soon this nice little spur turns into a razor-back nightmare with almost perpendicular sides. Kim Bok can't get off it and once we follow him up there neither can we, unless we come down again and he knows that we won't do that. There are no clever tactics involved here, we advance until he is ready to make contact and he could choose to do that in more than one place picking us off one by one. Lads, we go up tomorrow and by the end of the day it will be over one way or another.'

Kim Bok and Fantail had camped on a false crest 100 feet below the summit of Gunong Serudom. From there they would commence their last stand on the morrow. They had built a shelter under an outcrop of rock and comfortable within its confines and knowing that they were safe from intrusion they made love for the last time. Not a hurried last moment affair, but a long night of passion full of fond memories with no thoughts for their future fate. Not even the tough SAS men would have denied them those final treasured moments.

At the first light Kim left Fantail at their love nest and moved towards the crest where he took up a firing position.

Chalky had decided that they would carry their packs for the first thousand yards up to a point where the spur really got steep and reached the 2,000-feet contour where they would dump the Bergens; up to there, he had reckoned that they would not encounter any resistance. There was no need to appoint a scout for the purpose of tracking the enemy, only as a point man for everyone knew where they were going. How far they would get and whether or not they would return was another question.

The patrol dumped the packs at noon having climbed steadily all morning without incident. They could not hide them because the spur was too narrow and had there been no trees the terrain each side of the spur would have been terrifying to look at and even strong-willed men would have wilted and become dizzy. But what the eyes cannot see... goes the saying, and the SAS men coped with the situation well.

After a brief rest they were ready to take on the final task, the killing of Kim Bok and Fantail. There was not going to be a long stint at leading scout for anyone, the patrol was to advance in a leap-frogging fashion in bounds of twenty yards; a game of chance, a kind of Russian roulette that promoted a remark from Bob. 'I take it that your friend Allah dreamed that one up?'

'But of course,' defended Chalky.

'Who else?' grinned Fred. And so stripped down to fighting order the four men advanced to contact the foe.

The going was steep and much ground was lost on the slippery spur, one pace forward and two backwards, so to speak. At two thirty the light had faded to such an extent that it seem darkness was about to fall. The hot humid afternoon had changed suddenly and it became cold and the trees rustled as the monsoon blew its evil song through the jungle, and the roaring of the approaching rain could be heard above the excited screeching and howling of the primates high in their lofty domain. The winged ones sang in the rain as the daily deluge commenced to soak everything and everyone in the dank and evergreen hell.

Kim Bok did not hear the soldier coming but saw his face as the man appeared just above the crest line. He fired a single shot from his ancient Japanese rifle and then started to run back towards Fantail. So exhilarating was the feeling that he was at long last facing his destiny that it took four or five paces for him to comprehend that he had been shot in the left side.

Worm felt a stinging sensation in his left hand and at the same moment saw a man running away from him. He aimed his carbine with his right arm only because the sting in his left one was a bullet. He had the satisfaction of seeing Kim Bok stumble as a round hit him somewhere in the lower torso, and then he dived to the ground as Chalky jumped over him to take up the chase.

Fantail knew that Kim had been hit but he did not stop, the plan was for him to withdraw through her position to take up another one to her rear whilst she engaged the next enemy soldier to appear. She gave Kim a fleeting glance as he went past then looked back to her front to see a man charging towards her. Surprised at the speed in which the SAS men were responding she was caught off guard and fired in haste, the man spun around in mid stride and fell to the ground. Fantail got the hell out of there and followed quickly after Kim.

Chalky hardly heard the light crack of Worm's carbine but the thump of the rifle report that had preceded it was very clear indeed. He had barely time to notice if Worm had been hit as he leapt over him before he received a terrible blow to his right shoulder. The world seemed to spin around and then he found himself flat on his back staring up at the jungle canopy. Bob flew past him like hell on legs bound for the rock outcrop pouring a magazine of 9mm bullets after the fleeing woman.

Worm came up to Chalky and helped him to his feet whilst

Fred took over from Bob, he too firing his Owen gun up the slope for effect. The time for silence was over now that battle had been joined. 'Keep the bloody momentum going,' shouted Chalky surprised at the sound of his own voice, 'this wound is bugger all, get after them!' Bob started up the last hundred feet of the mountain for this was still his bound and collected a bullet in his leg for his trouble; the shot had been fired by Kim Bok from his second position.

Now it was Fred's turn and he fired a burst at Kim Bok's back before moving after him. The rain was torrential now and the vegetation was thinning out making the effect of the downpour almost immediate. It drowned out noise so Fred had no audible clue as to whether he had hit the target or not, but of one thing he was sure, the buggers were not firing back anymore. Fifty feet to go and he guessed that the two terrorists had fallen back to the summit for a last stand. Fred had not been relieved of his bound and reckoned that their wounds were slowing the others down. The rainwater was flowing down off the summit in torrents; thunder clapped and exploded; the flash and bang being simultaneous so near to the centre of this awesome natural phenomenon was he. His hands were bleeding with the effort of clawing his way up the ninety-degree gradient, fingernails had been torn off and his legs were shaking with the strain of maintaining the height gained. Twenty feet to go and he could see that the summit was bare. The sky was a dark green blanket matching the jungle carpet below it and the wind whipped the rain across the mountain top stinging the flesh like a sand blaster and all the while numbing the brain with its shrieking banshee chorus of doom.

They saw each other at same time, these two men, one old and the other so young. Perhaps it was youth that prevailed, but maybe Kim Bok was losing his touch because of his injuries, for both Bob and Fred had been successful earlier and the Paymaster General had sustained two more gunshot wounds. Whatever the cause Fred fired first in this duel that resembled a Wild West shoot-out. Kim did not in fact get a shot off and he crumbled to the ground like a broken doll riddled with 9mm Owen gun bullets. Then Fred was in trouble and a shot seemingly fired from beneath Kim Bok's body grazed his inner thigh just below his crotch narrowly missing his wedding tackle. Another round found the mark passing straight through his upper left arm luckily missing the bone. He felt no pain just a numbing blow that deadened all feeling in that arm. From behind Kim Bok's prone form rose a spectre from hell, her face seething with hatred and mouth frothing with blood that was bubbling from her lungs, was lit up by the now continuous flashes of lightning. Fred fired from the hip with his right hand, only the first rounds found the target because he could not control the weapon for more that a few seconds. Fantail, the murdering witch from Malacca, was blown back by the force of the burst and disappeared from view over the edge of the summit.

Fred found the strength to move forward and in the flickering, macabre storm-ridden light he found Fantail clinging to an exposed tree root, barely alive grasping onto life with disorientated and false hope.

Fantail knew that she was dying but not knowing that her beloved Kim was already dead she summoned up the courage to open her eyes for one last look at him, then she felt herself slipping.

Fred saw the hand holding onto the root losing its grip and involuntary grasped hold of Fantail's wrist with his good hand, for a moment the rain washed the blood from her face and she looked almost angelic.

She looked up at the male form above her not able to see clearly because of the blood that was obscuring her vision. 'Oh Kim my love,' she started to say, her heart full of joy. Then the mist cleared and she saw the face of the hated enemy. The grip on her wrist relaxed and for a moment they seemed to be shaking hands. Fantail died, denied in death a last glimpse of the man she loved so much.

Fred let go and watched as Fantail slipped down the muddy slope until she had been claimed by the jungle that she had lived in for so long; a wild grave for a wild woman. It was over.

Epilogue

Ulu the mule was found tethered to a tree outside of a Malay dwelling on the outskirts of Kampong Kinchur. Wrapped up at its feet was a bar of gold and a short letter. The finder was encouraged to enjoy the new-found wealth but under the pain of death was to ensure that the mule enjoyed a trouble free retirement.

The inhabitants of the Kampong Kinchur had grown used to seeing the pilot strutting around the decks of the *Sea Pearl* quite alone. But when the junk suddenly departed the day after the village had been thrown into a turmoil over the arrival of the wealthy mule, they could not but help notice that two men were on board the vessel.

The junk was taken to Pekan on the Pahang River where she was converted into a seafood restaurant and drinking place named the Oyster Bar. No one knows how the old pilot, now the captain, managed to finance the project.

The two Englishmen were enjoying a drink whilst sitting on stools at a circular beach bar in the Bahamas. Hearing a commotion coming from the direction of the plush hotel entrance they cast inquisitive eyes that way. Down the grand marble steps marched four burly servants carrying a sedan chair, two more men walked alongside of it fanning the reclining occupant. Following behind the sedan walked a dusky woman and two children. The servants helped the man out of the sedan to a table set for four and the whole party sat down. 'Good lord!' exclaimed one of the men. 'Who the devil is that odd chap?' asked the other of the barman. 'Oh! He owns the hotel. I've heard him called His Lordship, but everyone here both high and a low address him as just plain Dennis.'

The four wounded men of Chalky's patrol marched back down

the mountain and along the Sungei Lepar to the Maran Road, a Herculean feat of endurance by any standard. From there they were flown by helicopter to Kuala Lumpur where they received medical treatment.

The Central Military Committee made good their escape. The Communist Terrorists never did surrender.

Fred served on in Malaya until the closing stages of the emergency when his squadron was rushed off to Oman and another kind of warfare. But that is another story!

Rest now fellow warrior. Salutations from Pegasus and Bellerophon, may Mars and Minerva continue to favour you and our friend Allah to bless you.

Printed in the United Kingdom
by Lightning Source UK Ltd.
9552300001B